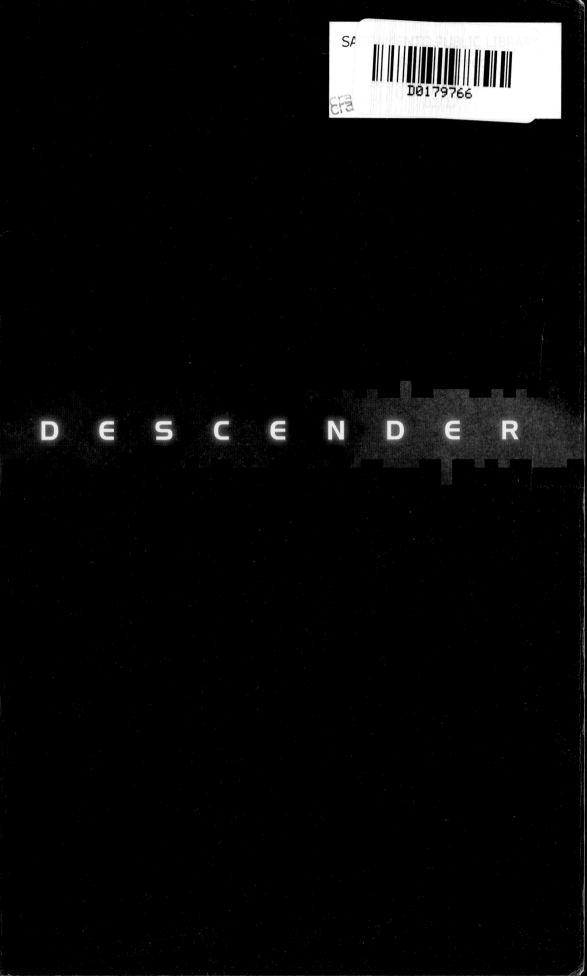

DESCENDER

IMAGE COMICS Presents
DESCENDER
BOOK ONE: TIN STARS

Written by JEFF LEMIRE
Illustrated by DUSTIN NGUYEN
Lettered and Designed by STEVE WANDS

Cover by DUSTIN NGUYEN

Descender Created by
JEFF LEMIRE & DUSTIN NGUYEN

for IMAGE COMICS
ROBERT KIRKMAN chief operating officer
ERIK LARSEN chief financial officer
TODD MCFARLANE president
MARC SILVESTRI chief executive officer
JIM VALENTINO vice-president

Eric Stephenson – Publisher
Corey Murphy – Director of Sales
Jeremy Sullivan – Director of Digital Sales
Kat Salazar – Director of PR & Marketing
Emily Miller – Director of Operations
Branwyn Bigglestone – Senior Accounts Manager
Sarah Mello – Accounts Manager
Drew Gill – Art Director
Jonathan Chan – Production Manager
Meredith Wallace – Print Manager
Randy Okamura – Marketing Production Designer
David Brothers – Branding Manager
Ally Power – Content Manager
Addison Duke – Production Artist
Vincent Kukua – Production Artist
Sasha Head – Production Artist
Tricia Ramos – Production Artist
Emilio Bautista – Sales Assistant
Chloe Ramos-Peterson – Administrative Assistant
IMAGECOMICS.COM

DESCENDER, VOL. 1
FIRST PRINTING, SEPTEMBER 2015.
ISBN: 978-1-63215-426-2

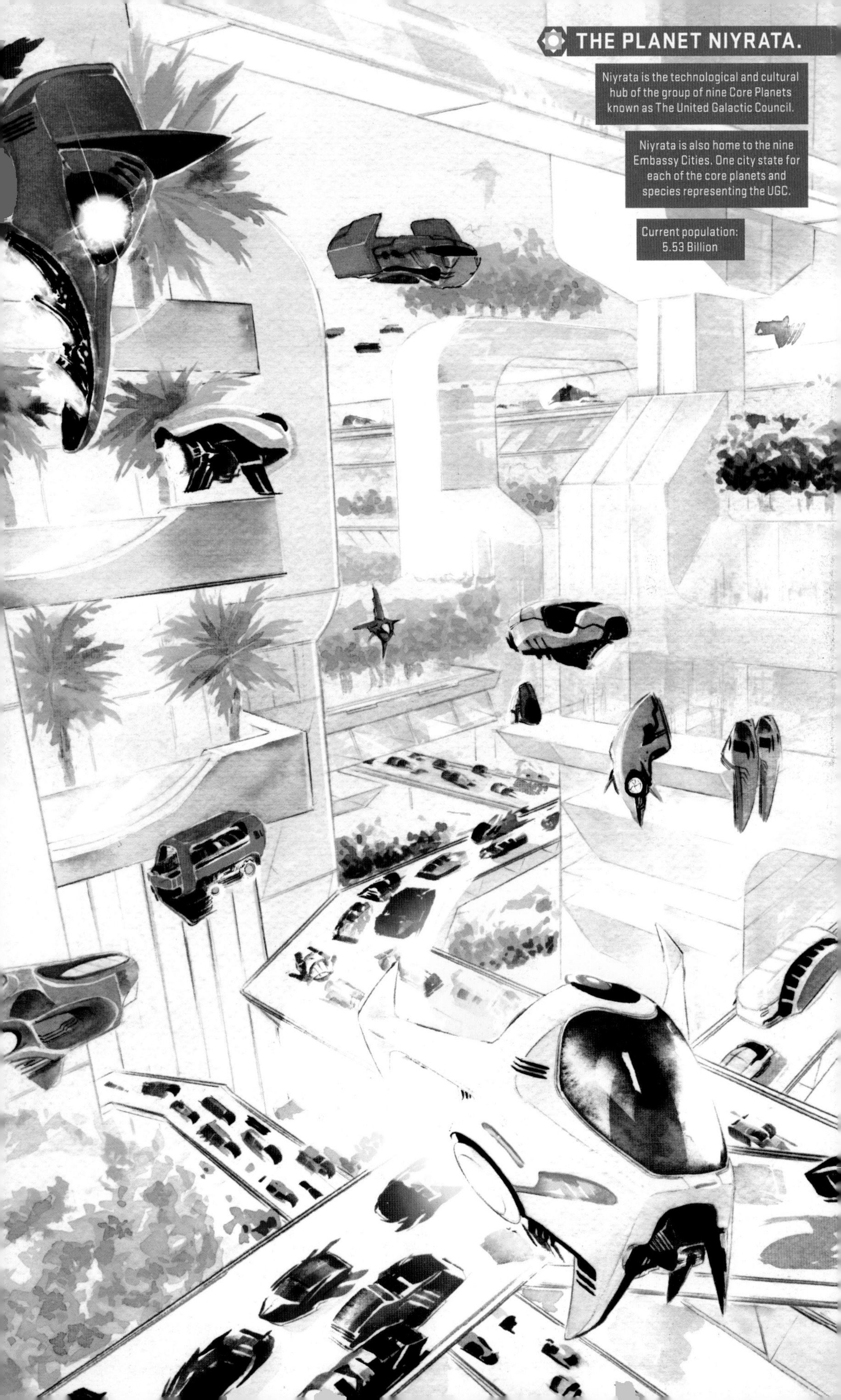
THE PLANET NIYRATA.
Niyrata is the technological and cultural hub of the group of nine Core Planets known as The United Galactic Council.
Niyrata is also home to the nine Embassy Cities. One city state for each of the core planets and species representing the UGC.
Current population: 5.53 Billion

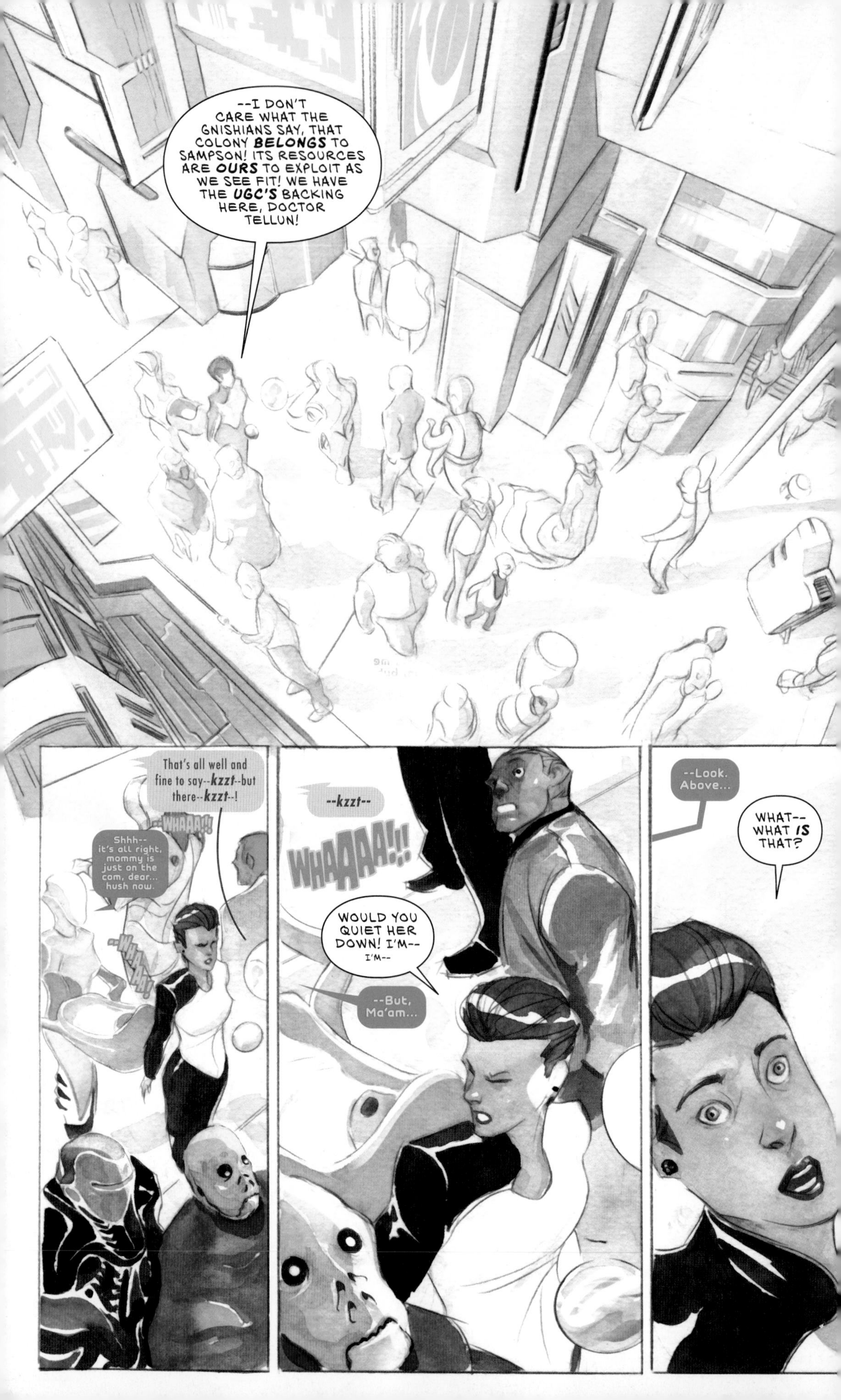

--I DON'T CARE WHAT THE GNISHIANS SAY, THAT COLONY BELONGS TO SAMPSON! ITS RESOURCES ARE OURS TO EXPLOIT AS WE SEE FIT! WE HAVE THE UGC'S BACKING HERE, DOCTOR TELLUN!
That's all well and fine to say--kzzt--but there--kzzt--!
Shhh-- it's all right, mommy is just on the com, dear... hush now.
--kzzt--
WHAAAA!!!
WOULD YOU QUIET HER DOWN! I'M-- I'M--
--But, Ma'am...
--Look. Above...
WHAT-- WHAT IS THAT?

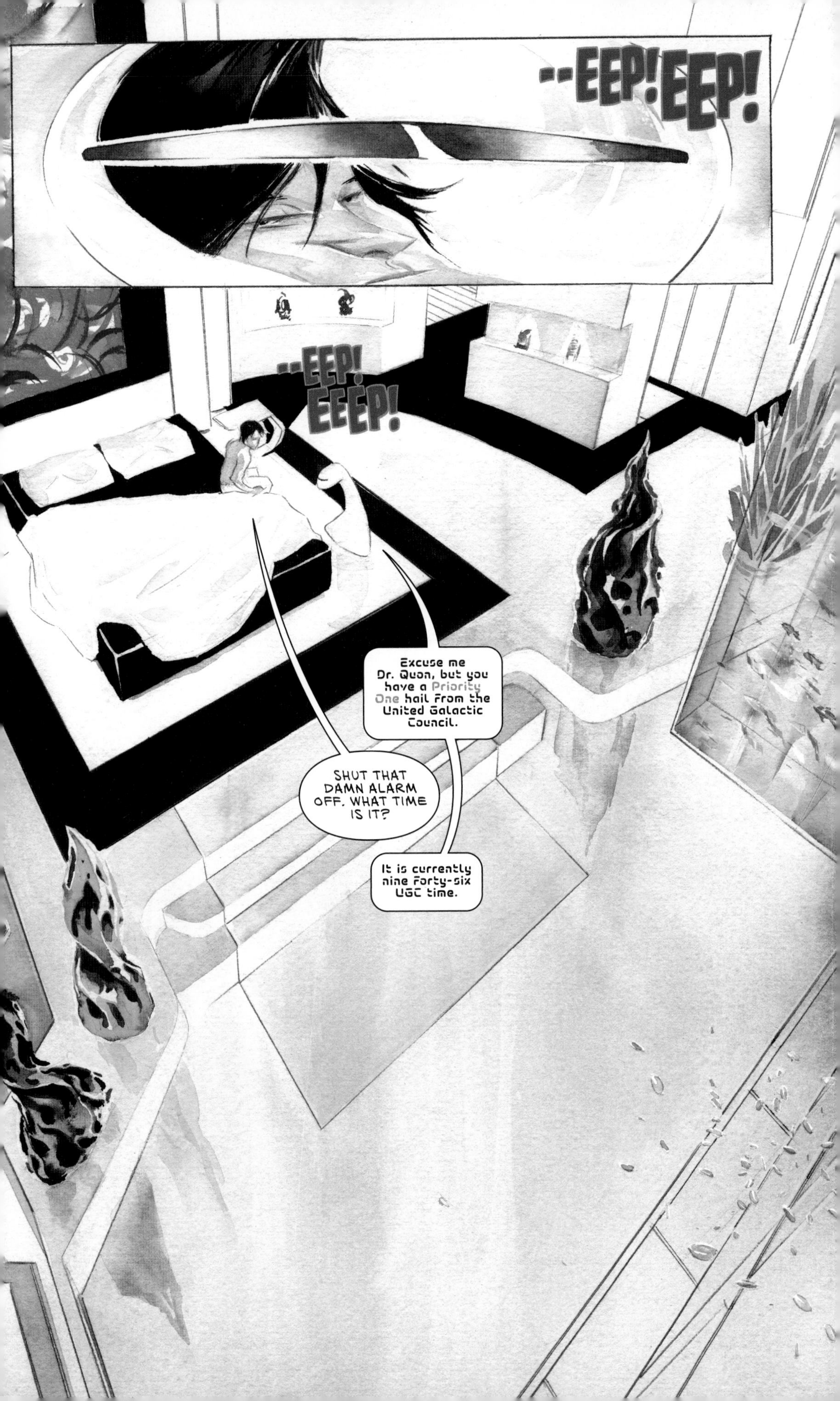
--EEP! EEP!
--EEP! EEEP!
SHUT THAT DAMN ALARM OFF. WHAT TIME IS IT?
Excuse me Dr. Quon, but you have a Priority One hail from the United Galactic Council.
It is currently nine forty-six UGC time.

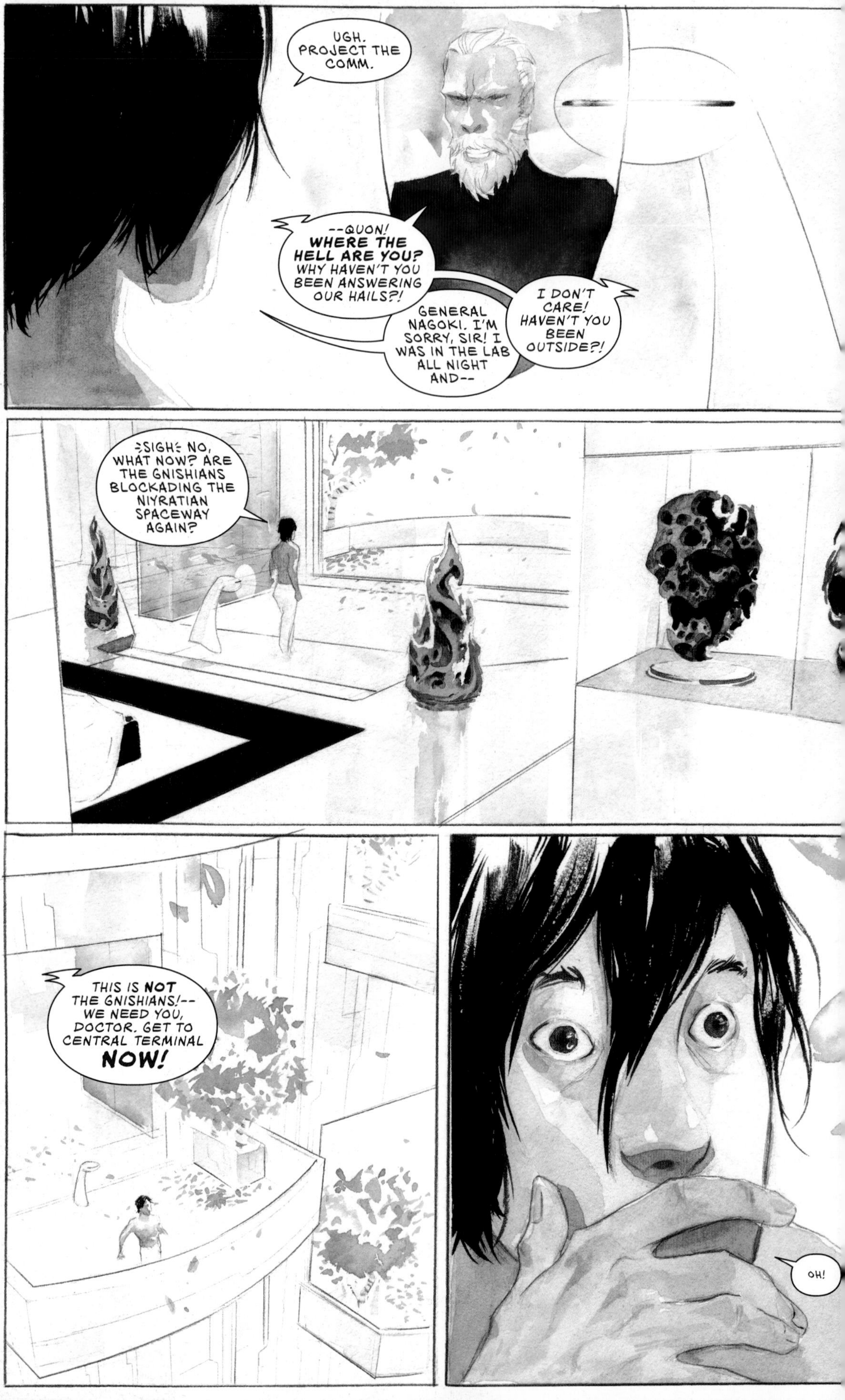

UGH. PROJECT THE COMM.
--QUON! **WHERE THE HELL ARE YOU?** WHY HAVEN'T YOU BEEN ANSWERING OUR HAILS?!
GENERAL NAGOKI. I'M SORRY, SIR! I WAS IN THE LAB ALL NIGHT AND--
I DON'T CARE! HAVEN'T YOU BEEN OUTSIDE?!
=SIGH= NO, WHAT NOW? ARE THE GNISHIANS BLOCKADING THE NIYRATIAN SPACEWAY AGAIN?
THIS IS **NOT** THE GNISHIANS!-- WE NEED YOU, DOCTOR. GET TO CENTRAL TERMINAL **NOW!**
OH!

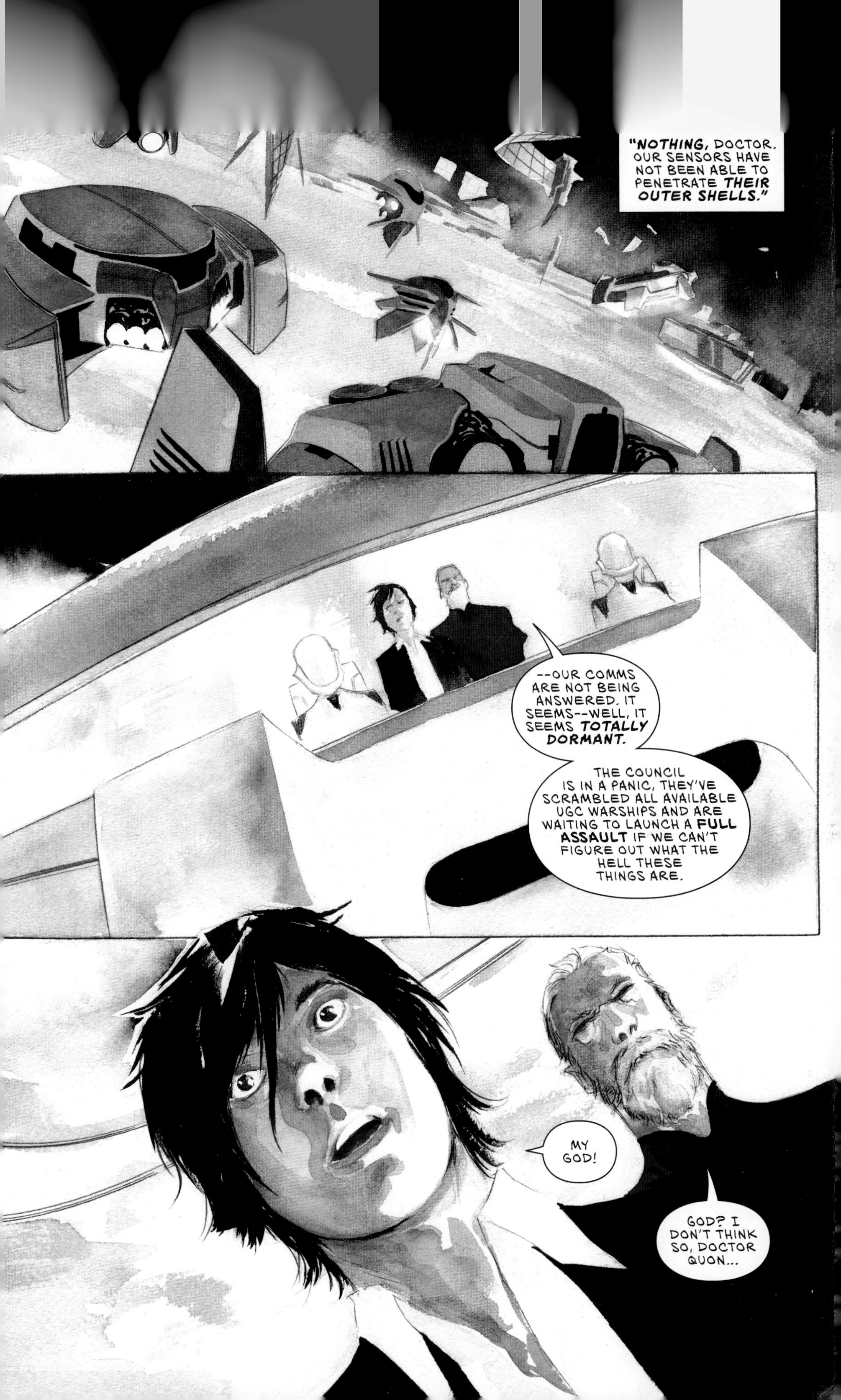
"NOTHING, DOCTOR. OUR SENSORS HAVE NOT BEEN ABLE TO PENETRATE THEIR OUTER SHELLS."
--OUR COMMS ARE NOT BEING ANSWERED. IT SEEMS--WELL, IT SEEMS TOTALLY DORMANT.
THE COUNCIL IS IN A PANIC, THEY'VE SCRAMBLED ALL AVAILABLE UGC WARSHIPS AND ARE WAITING TO LAUNCH A FULL ASSAULT IF WE CAN'T FIGURE OUT WHAT THE HELL THESE THINGS ARE.
MY GOD!
GOD? I DON'T THINK SO, DOCTOR QUON...

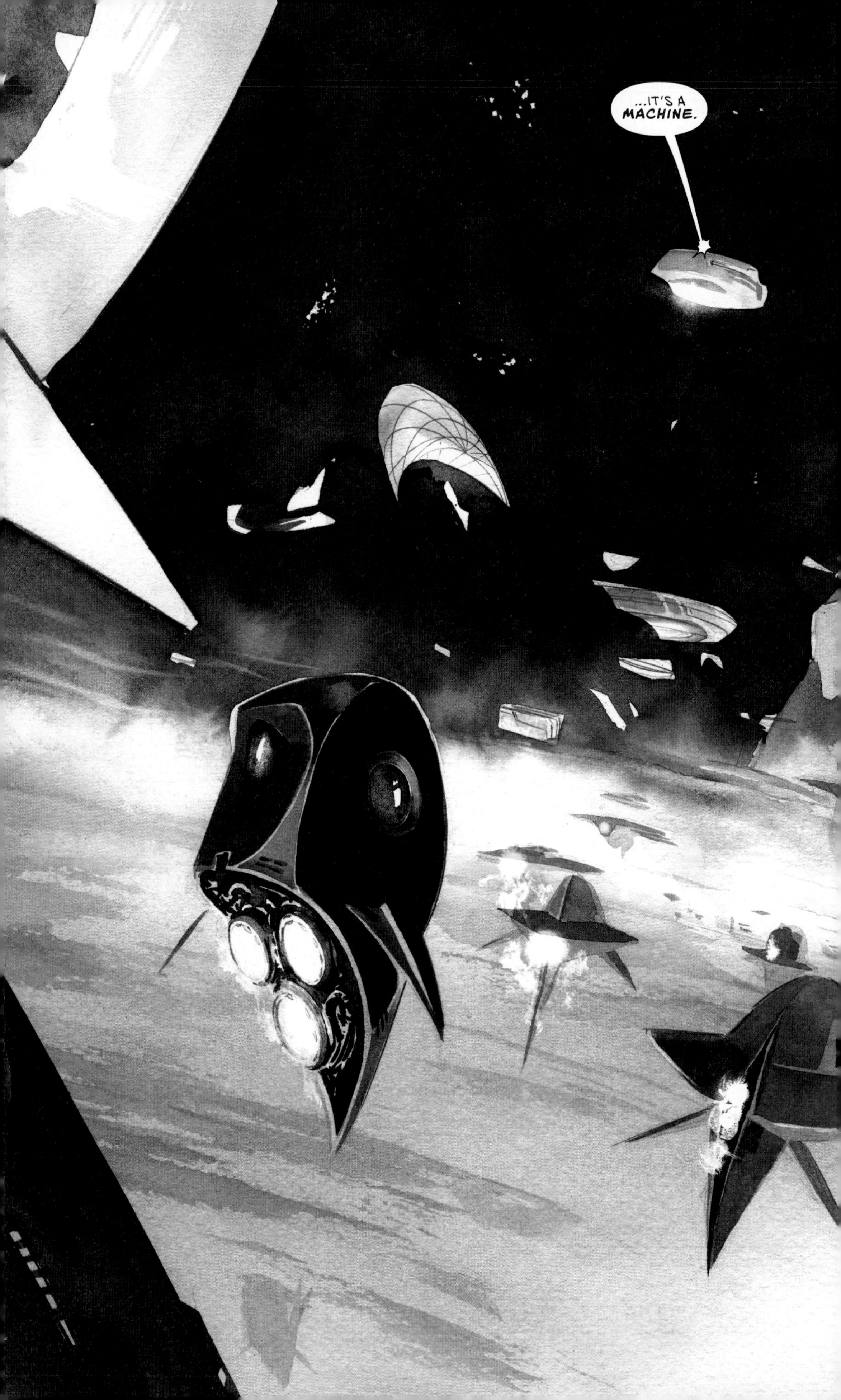
...IT'S A MACHINE.

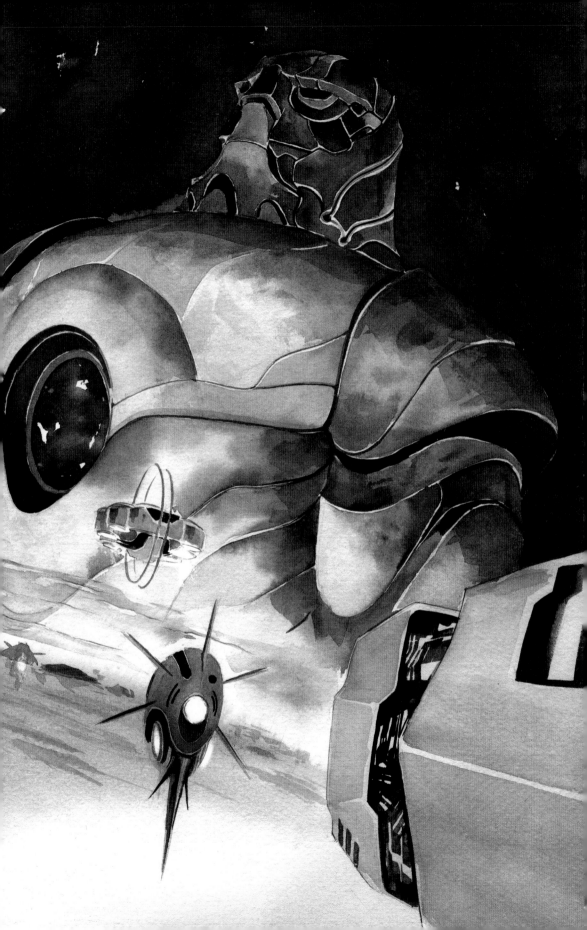

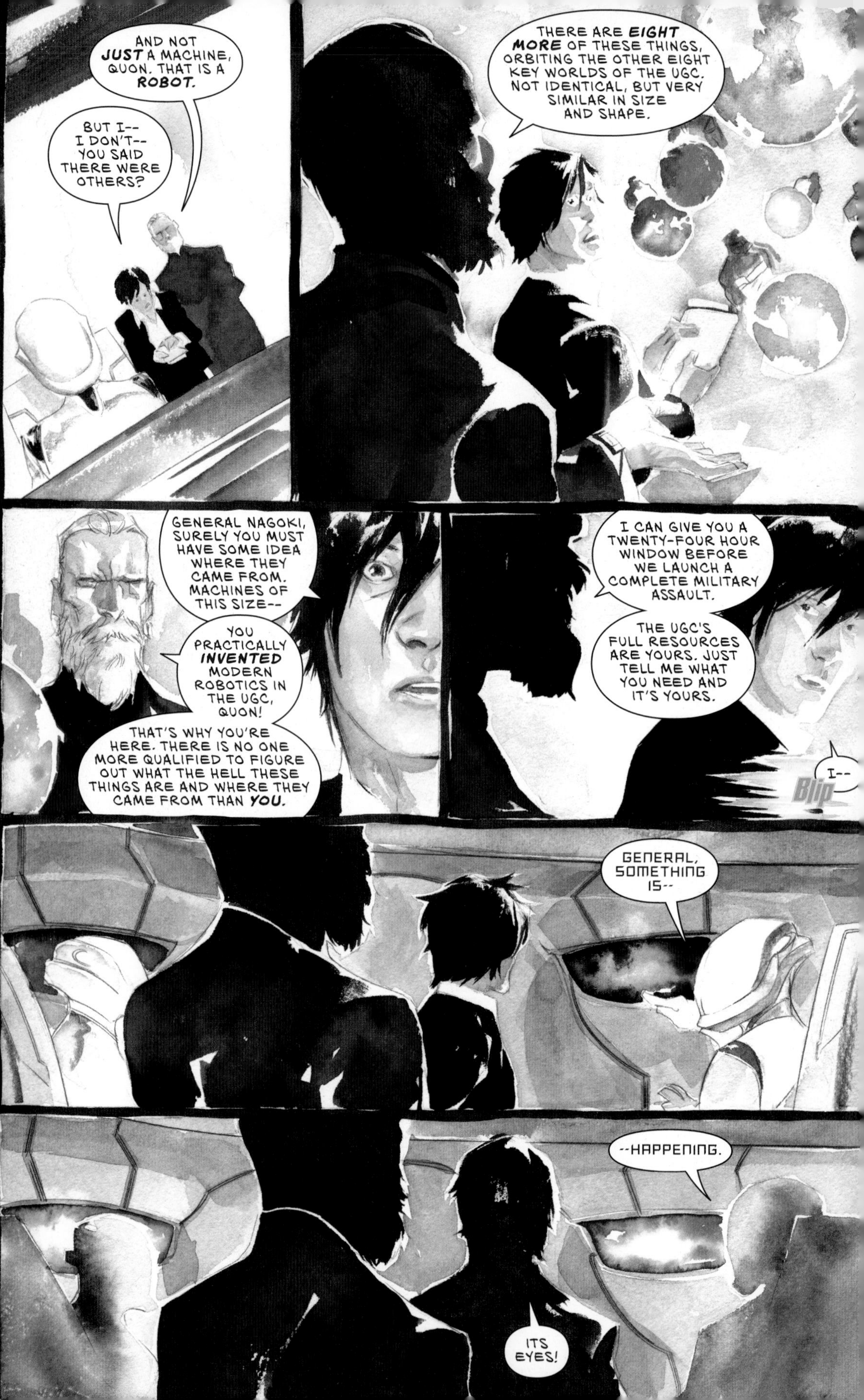
BUT I-- I DON'T-- YOU SAID THERE WERE OTHERS?
AND NOT JUST A MACHINE, QUON. THAT IS A ROBOT.
THERE ARE EIGHT MORE OF THESE THINGS, ORBITING THE OTHER EIGHT KEY WORLDS OF THE UGC. NOT IDENTICAL, BUT VERY SIMILAR IN SIZE AND SHAPE.
GENERAL NAGOKI, SURELY YOU MUST HAVE SOME IDEA WHERE THEY CAME FROM. MACHINES OF THIS SIZE--
YOU PRACTICALLY INVENTED MODERN ROBOTICS IN THE UGC, QUON!
THAT'S WHY YOU'RE HERE. THERE IS NO ONE MORE QUALIFIED TO FIGURE OUT WHAT THE HELL THESE THINGS ARE AND WHERE THEY CAME FROM THAN YOU.
I CAN GIVE YOU A TWENTY-FOUR HOUR WINDOW BEFORE WE LAUNCH A COMPLETE MILITARY ASSAULT.
THE UGC'S FULL RESOURCES ARE YOURS. JUST TELL ME WHAT YOU NEED AND IT'S YOURS.
I--
Blip
GENERAL, SOMETHING IS--
--HAPPENING.
ITS EYES!

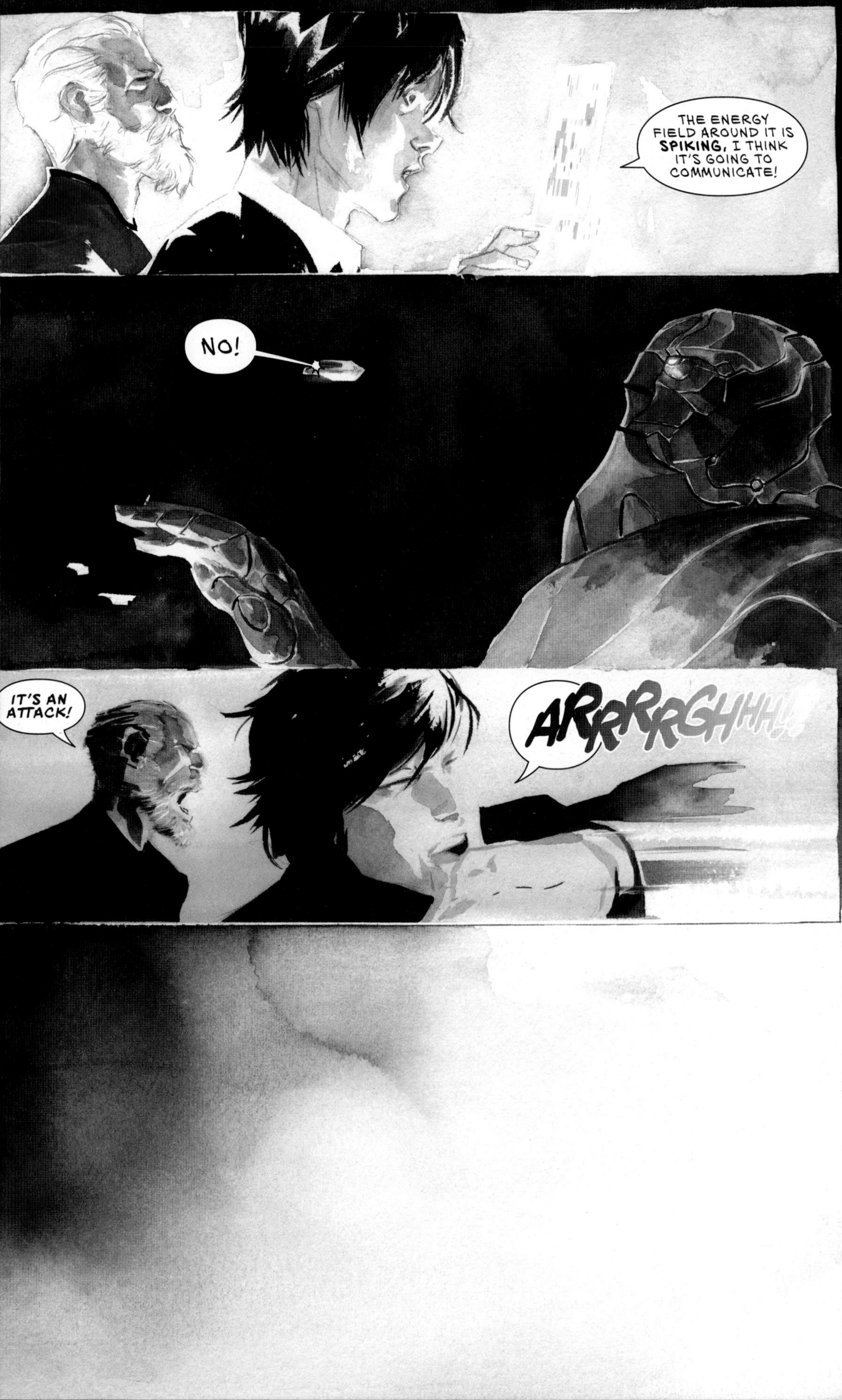
THE ENERGY FIELD AROUND IT IS SPIKING, I THINK IT'S GOING TO COMMUNICATE!
NO!
IT'S AN ATTACK!
ARRRRGHHH!

D E S C

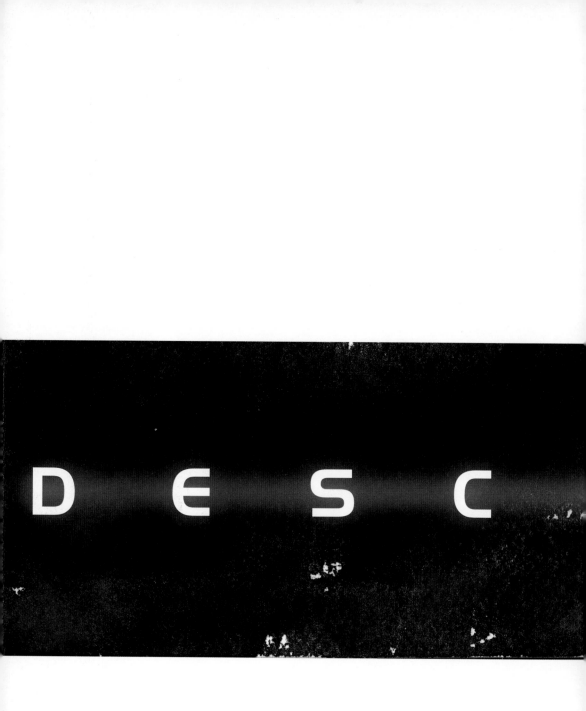

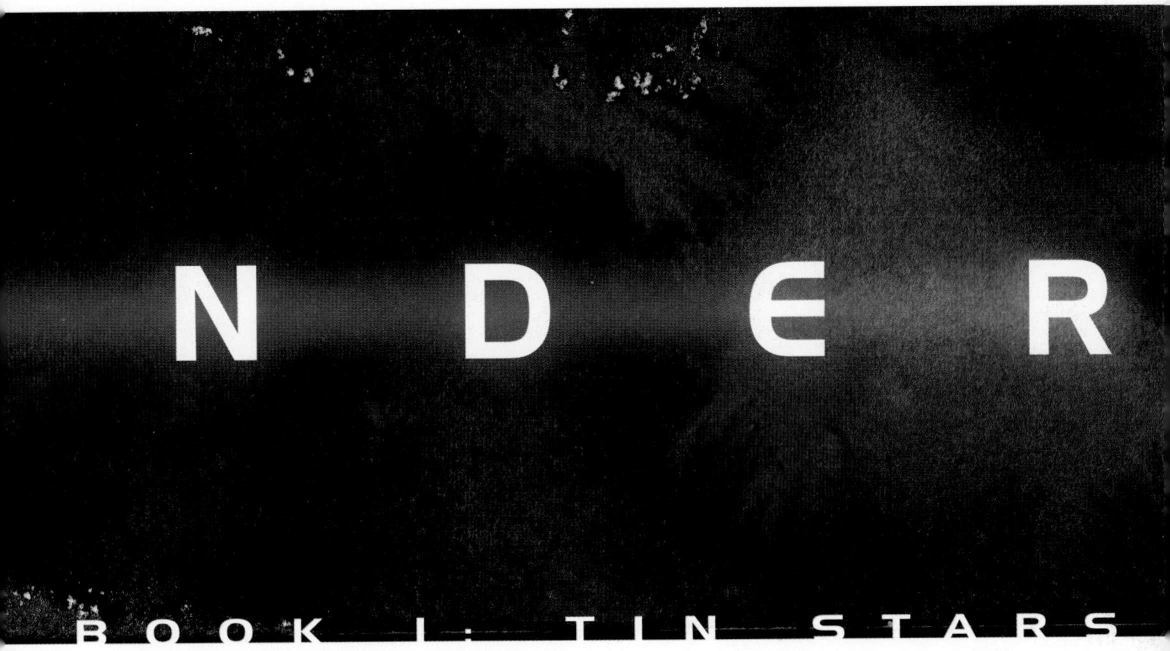
N D E R
BOOK I: TIN STARS

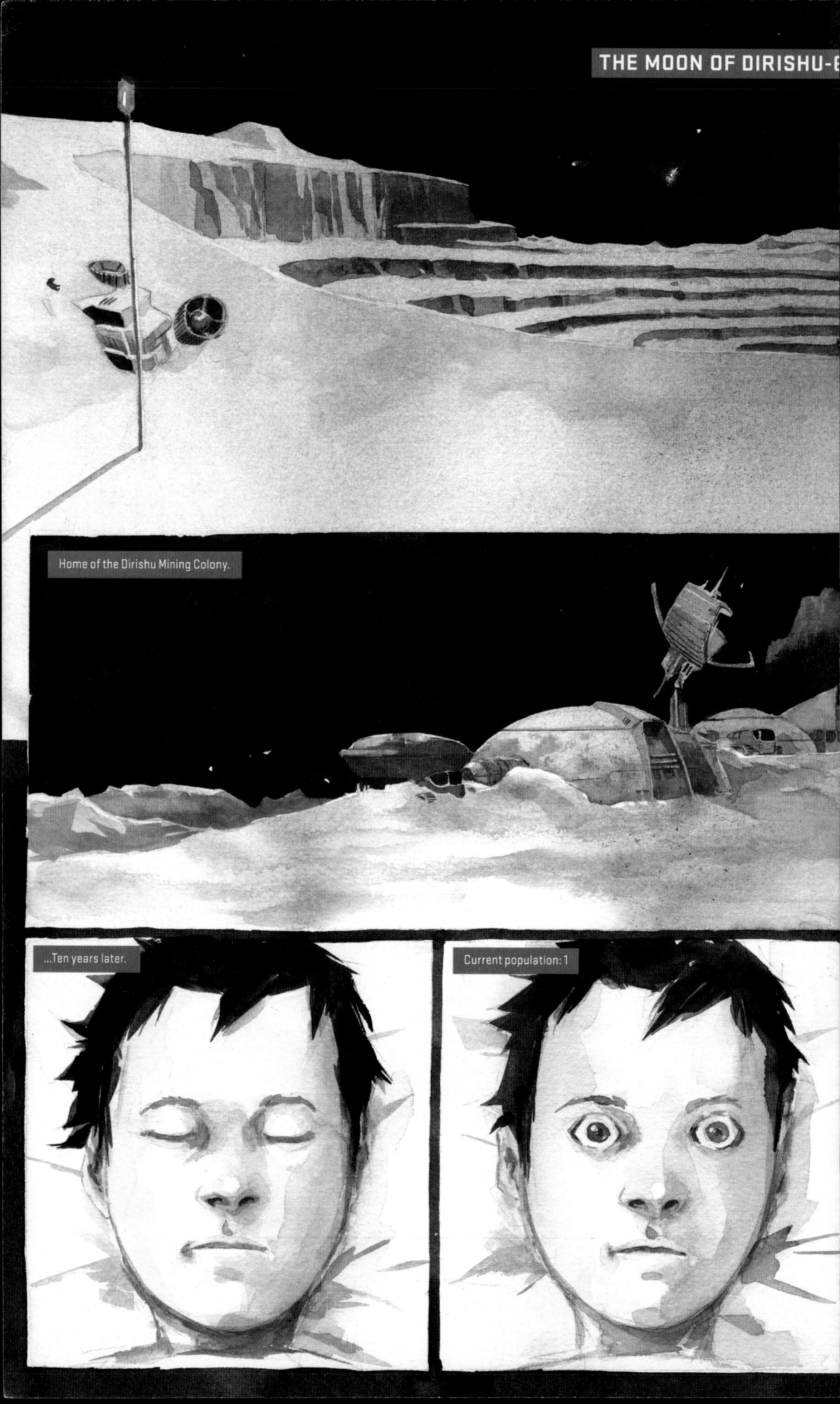
THE MOON OF DIRISHU-6
Home of the Dirishu Mining Colony.
...Ten years later.
Current population: 1

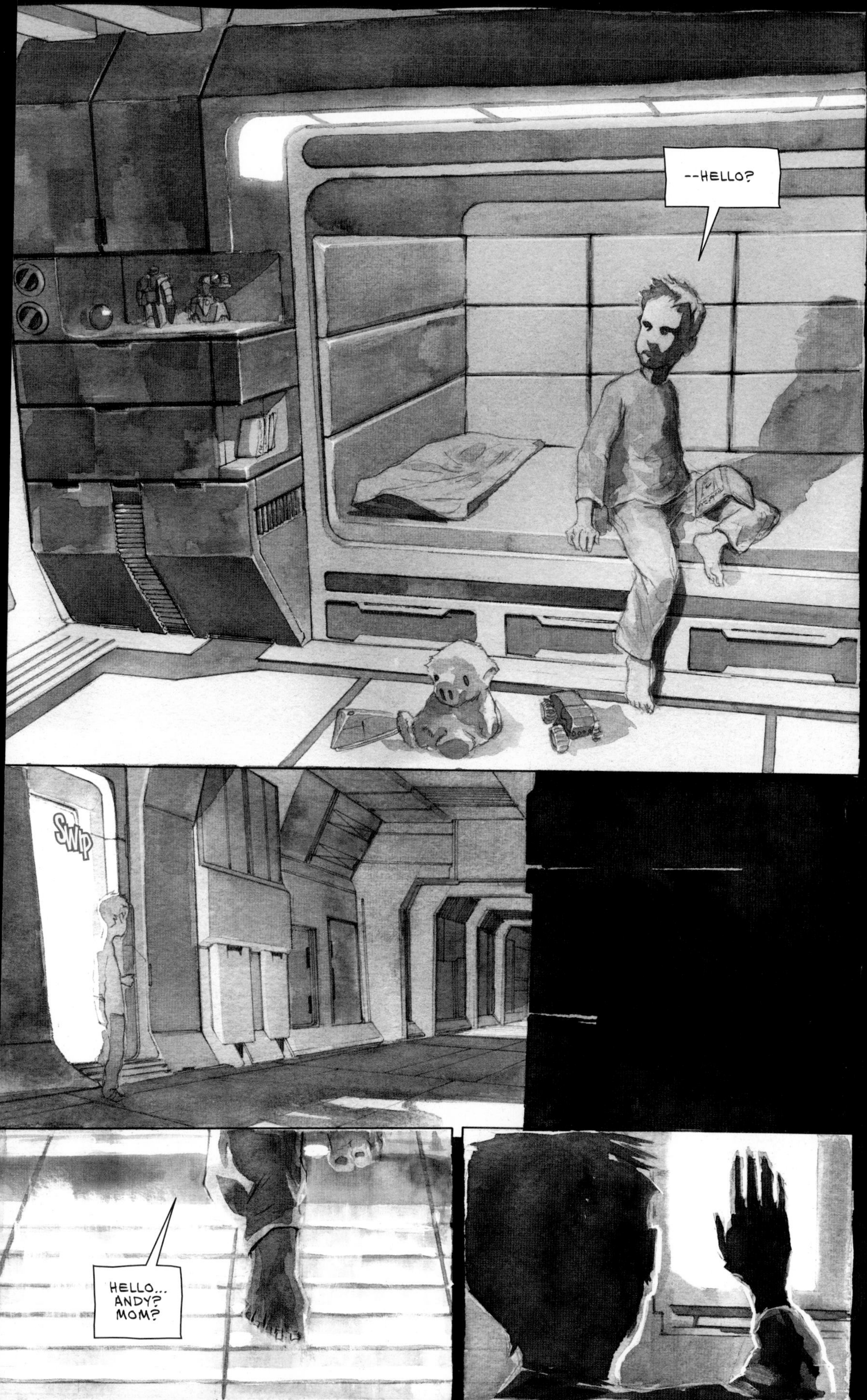
--HELLO?
SWIP
HELLO... ANDY? MOM?

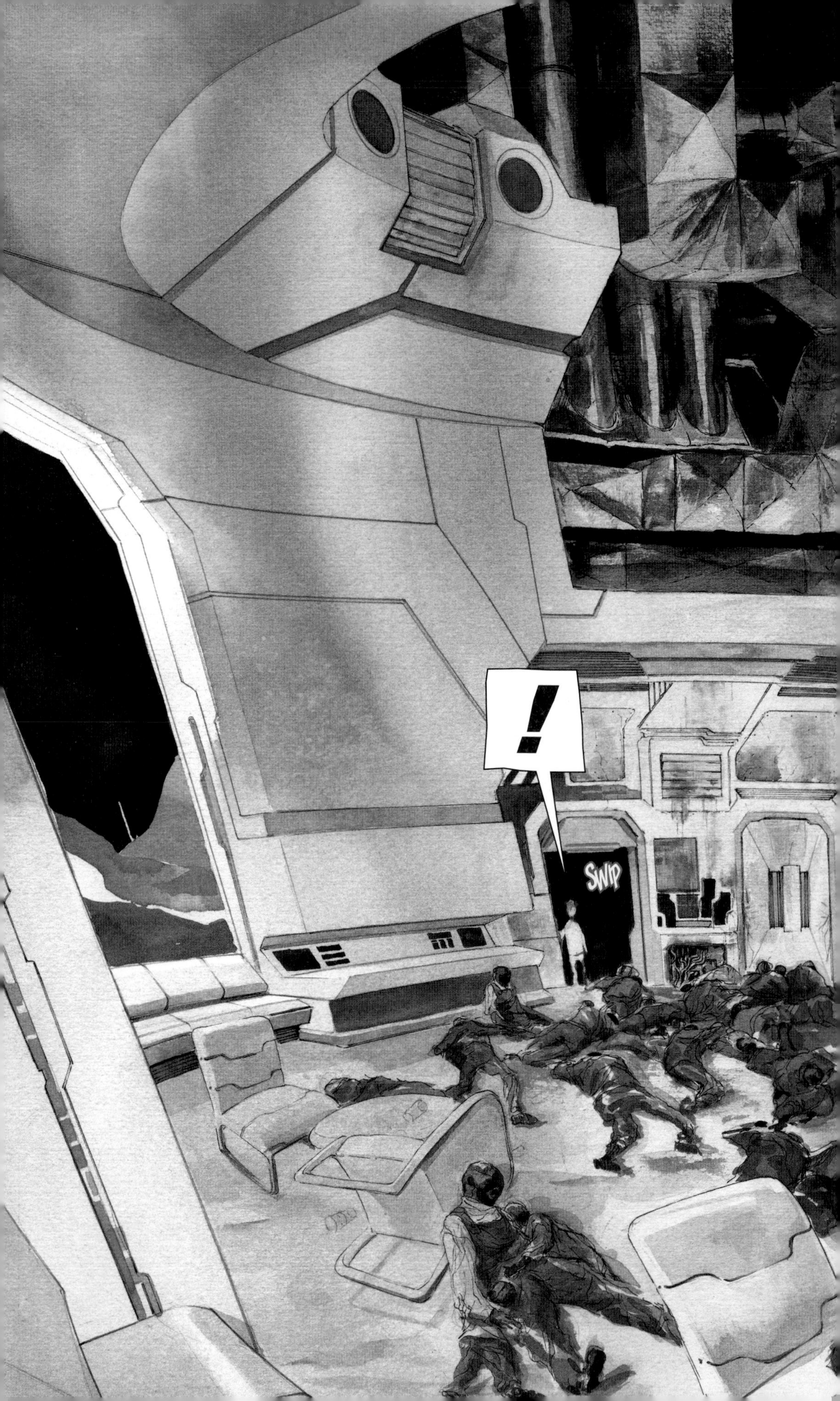
!
SWIP

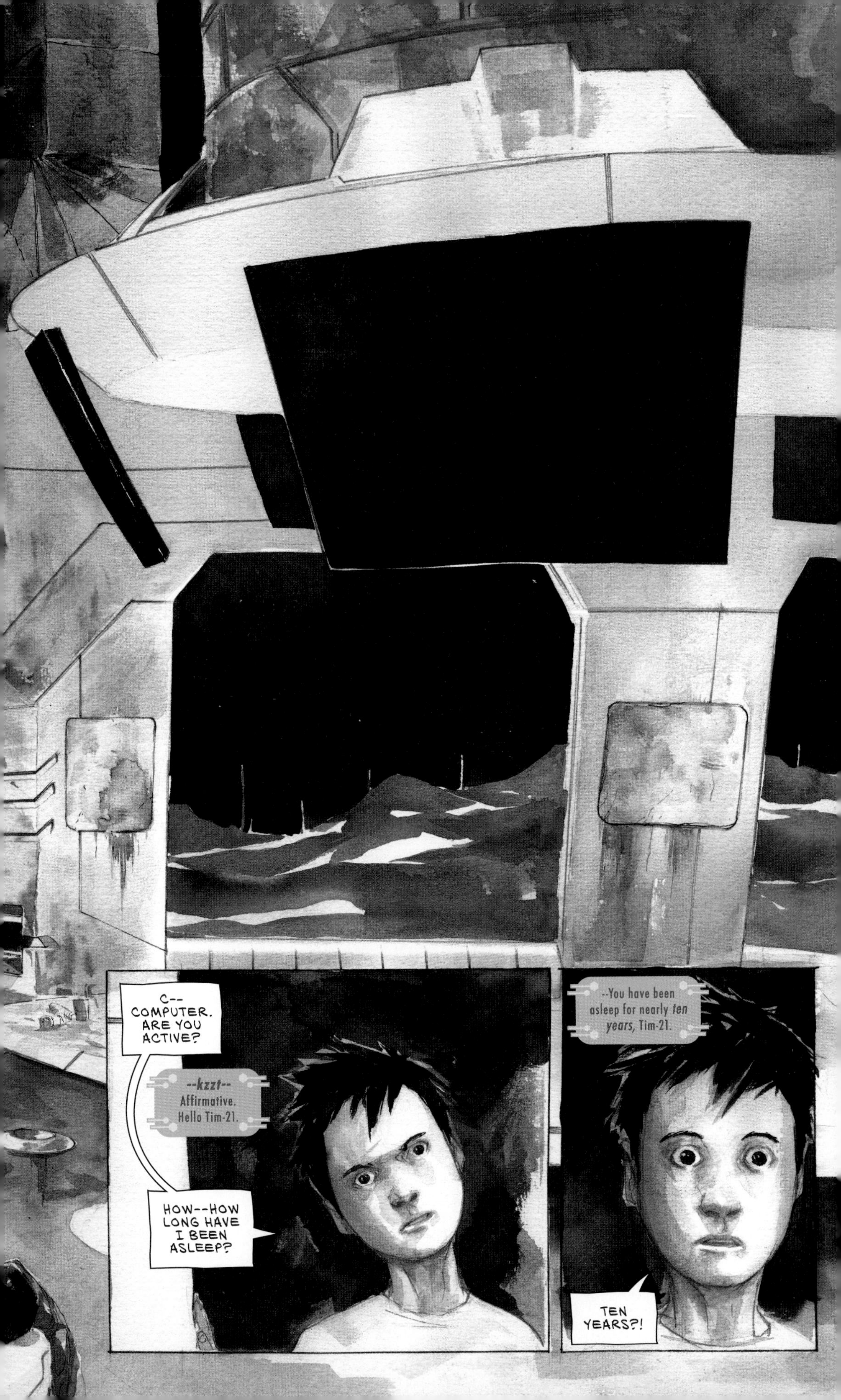

C-- COMPUTER. ARE YOU ACTIVE?
--kzzt-- Affirmative. Hello Tim-21.
HOW--HOW LONG HAVE I BEEN ASLEEP?
--You have been asleep for nearly *ten years,* Tim-21.
TEN YEARS?!

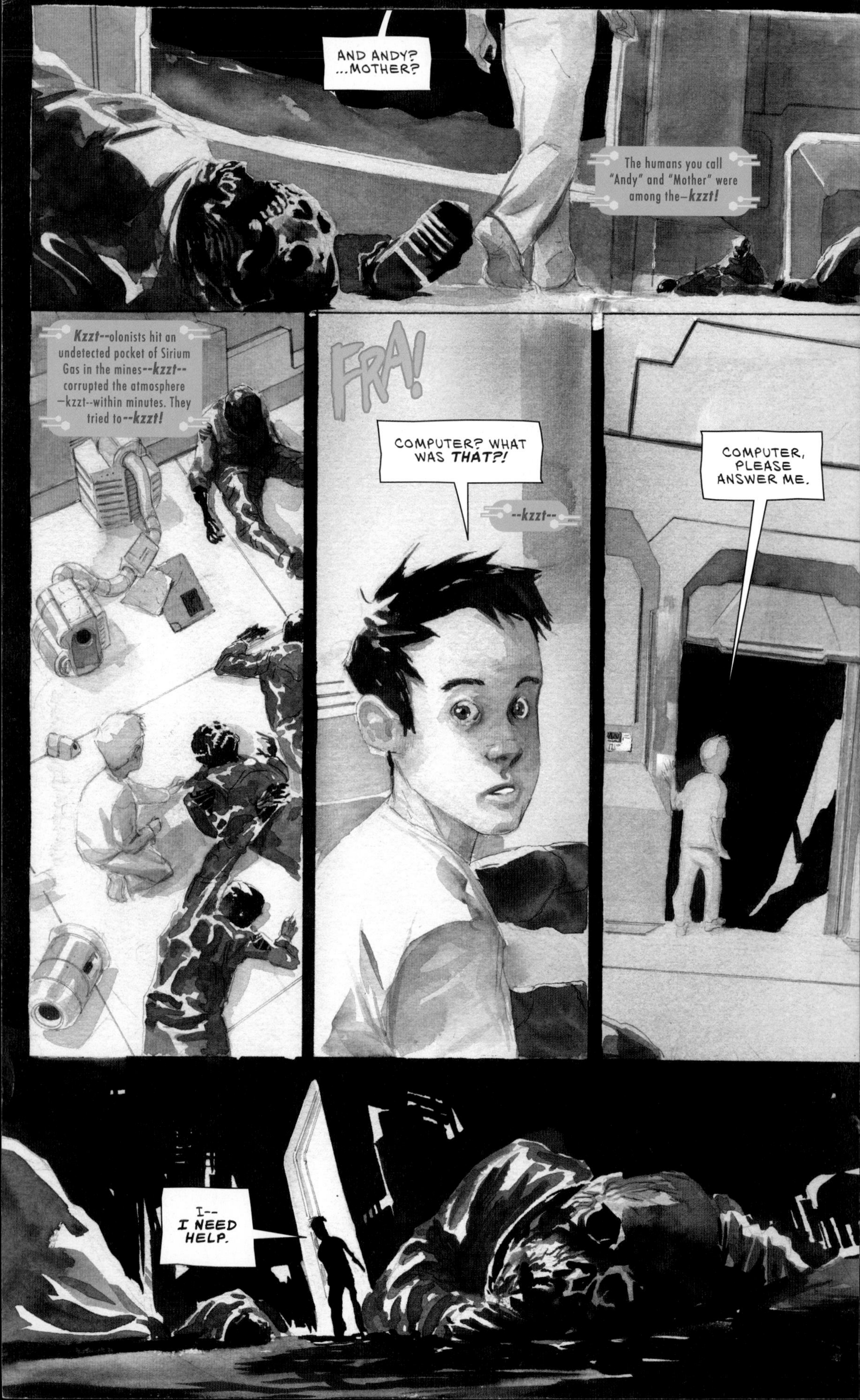

AND ANDY? ...MOTHER?
The humans you call "Andy" and "Mother" were among the--kzzt!
Kzzt--olonists hit an undetected pocket of Sirium Gas in the mines--kzzt--corrupted the atmosphere --kzzt--within minutes. They tried to--kzzt!
FRA!
COMPUTER? WHAT WAS THAT?!
--kzzt--
COMPUTER, PLEASE ANSWER ME.
I-- I NEED HELP.

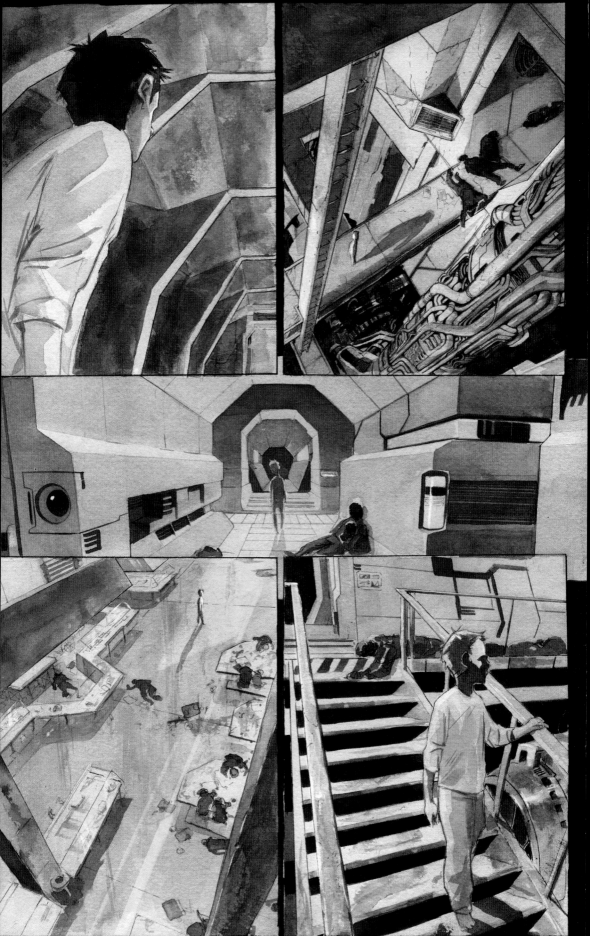

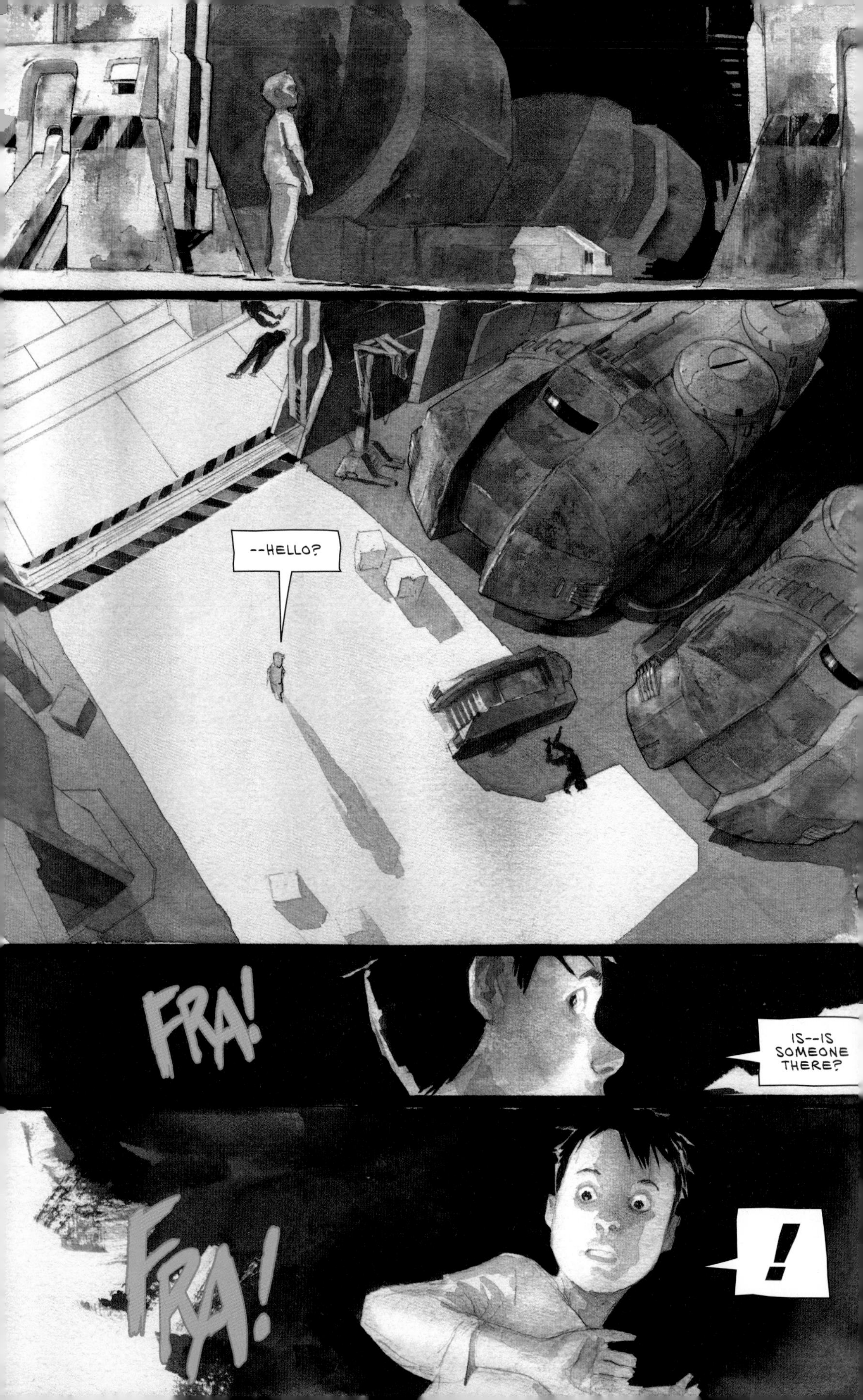
--HELLO?
FRA!
IS--IS SOMEONE THERE?
FRA!
!

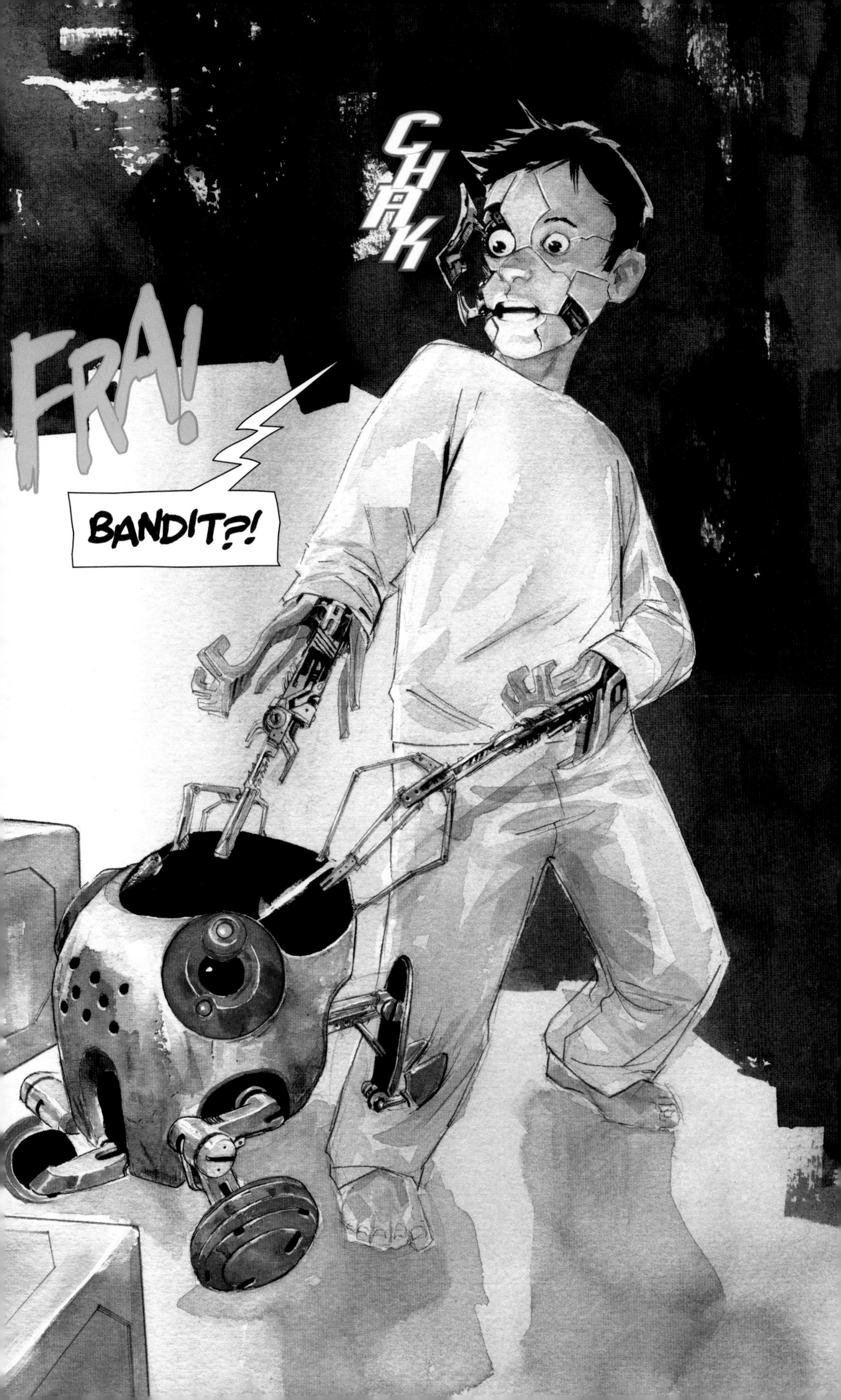
CHRK
FRA!
BANDIT?!

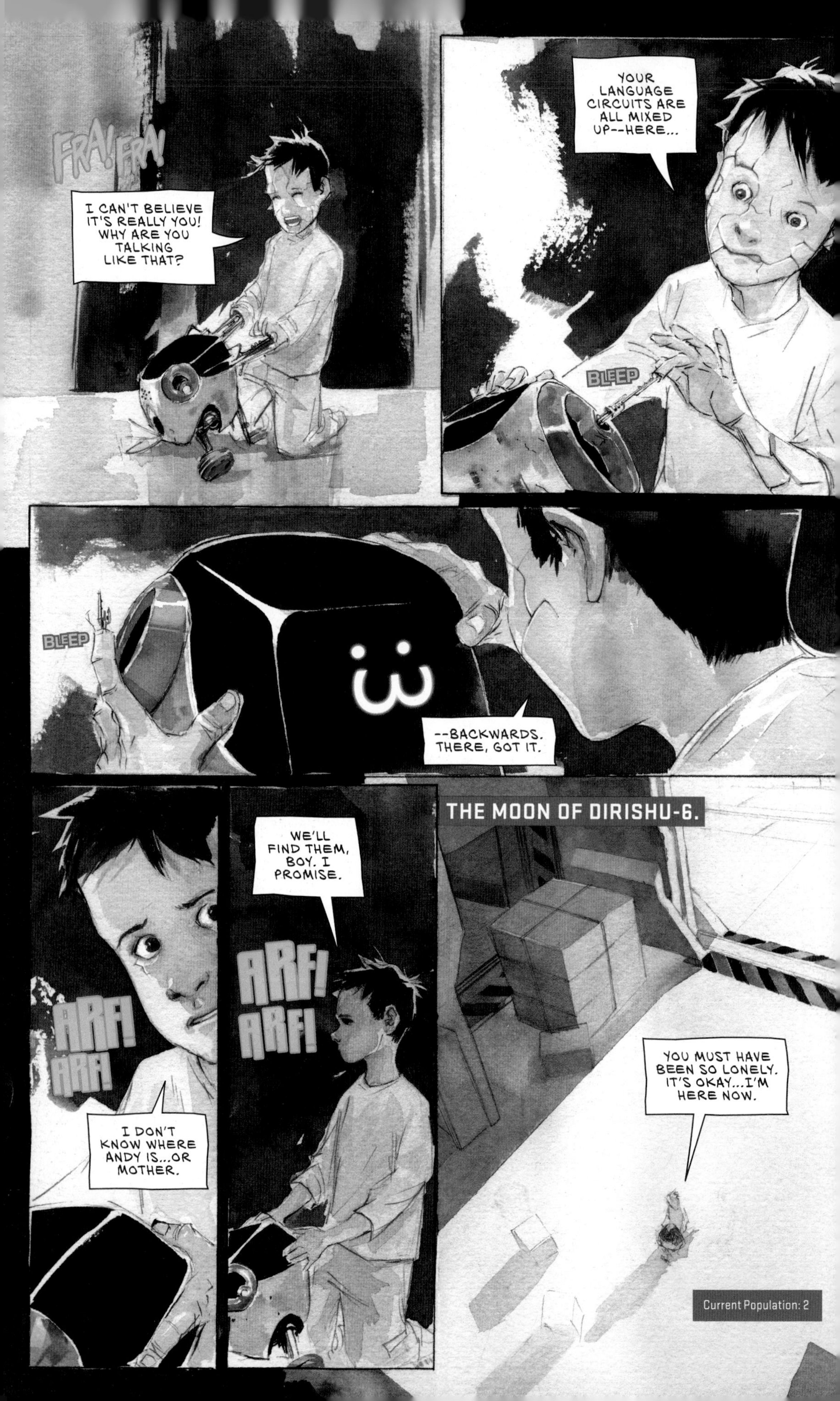
FRA! FRA!
I CAN'T BELIEVE IT'S REALLY YOU! WHY ARE YOU TALKING LIKE THAT?
YOUR LANGUAGE CIRCUITS ARE ALL MIXED UP--HERE...
BLEEP
BLEEP
--BACKWARDS. THERE, GOT IT.
ARF! ARF!
I DON'T KNOW WHERE ANDY IS...OR MOTHER.
WE'LL FIND THEM, BOY. I PROMISE.
ARF! ARF!
THE MOON OF DIRISHU-6.
YOU MUST HAVE BEEN SO LONELY. IT'S OKAY...I'M HERE NOW.
Current Population: 2

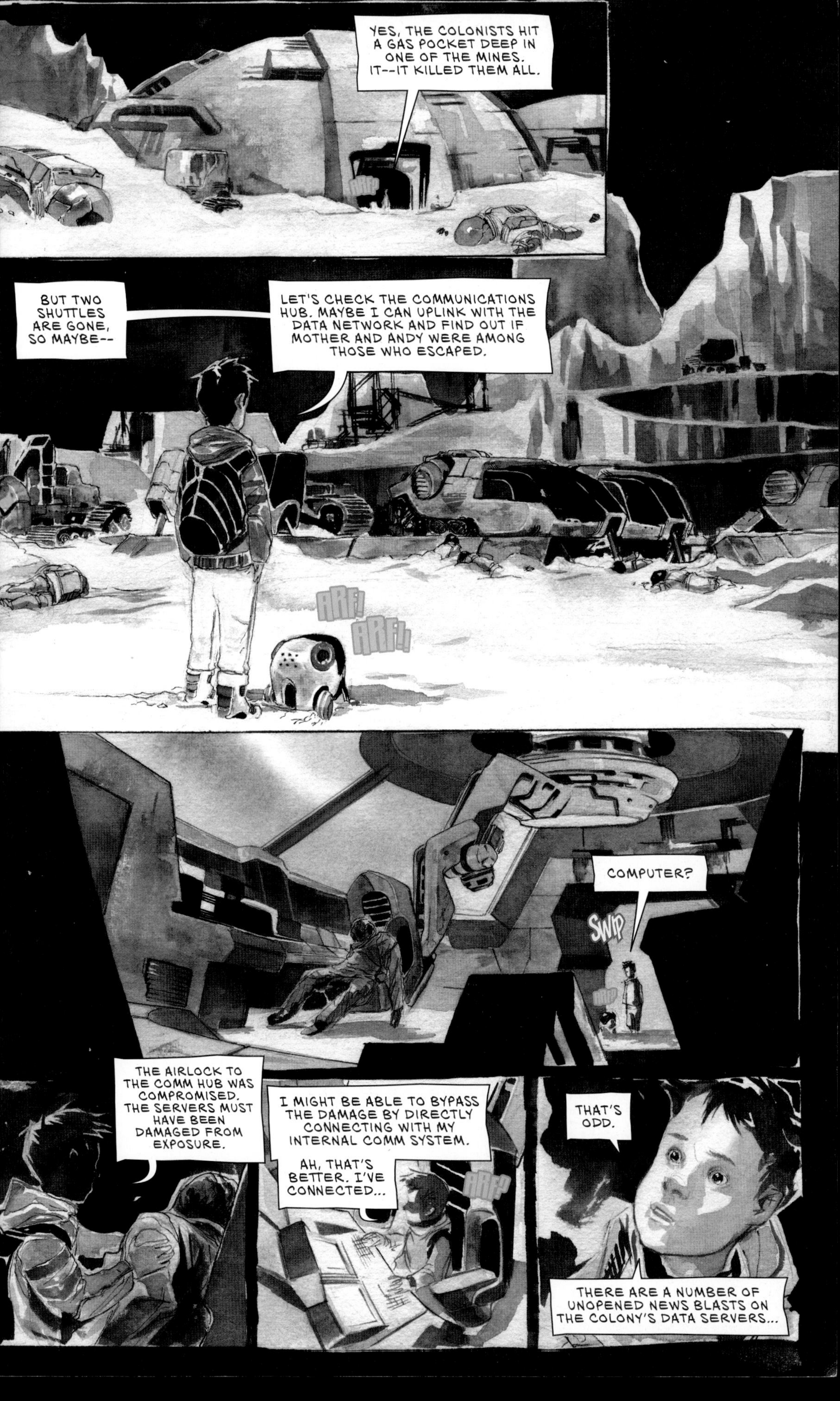
YES, THE COLONISTS HIT A GAS POCKET DEEP IN ONE OF THE MINES. IT--IT KILLED THEM ALL.
BUT TWO SHUTTLES ARE GONE, SO MAYBE--
LET'S CHECK THE COMMUNICATIONS HUB. MAYBE I CAN UPLINK WITH THE DATA NETWORK AND FIND OUT IF MOTHER AND ANDY WERE AMONG THOSE WHO ESCAPED.
ARF! ARF!!
COMPUTER?
SWIP
THE AIRLOCK TO THE COMM HUB WAS COMPROMISED. THE SERVERS MUST HAVE BEEN DAMAGED FROM EXPOSURE.
I MIGHT BE ABLE TO BYPASS THE DAMAGE BY DIRECTLY CONNECTING WITH MY INTERNAL COMM SYSTEM.
AH, THAT'S BETTER. I'VE CONNECTED...
ARF!
THAT'S ODD.
THERE ARE A NUMBER OF UNOPENED NEWS BLASTS ON THE COLONY'S DATA SERVERS...

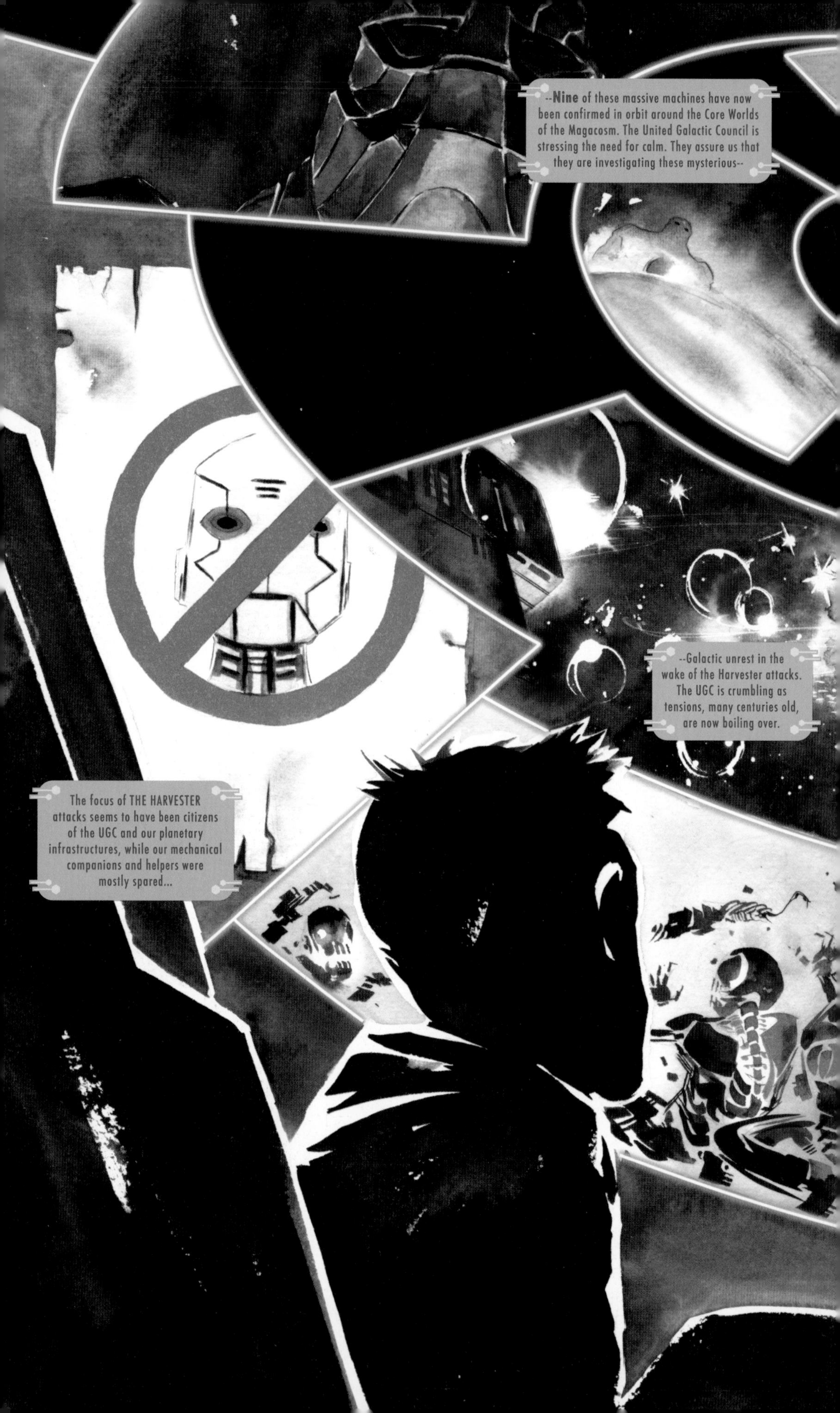
--**Nine** of these massive machines have now been confirmed in orbit around the Core Worlds of the Magacosm. The United Galactic Council is stressing the need for calm. They assure us that they are investigating these mysterious--
--Galactic unrest in the wake of the Harvester attacks. The UGC is crumbling as tensions, many centuries old, are now boiling over.
The focus of THE HARVESTER attacks seems to have been citizens of the UGC and our planetary infrastructures, while our mechanical companions and helpers were mostly spared...

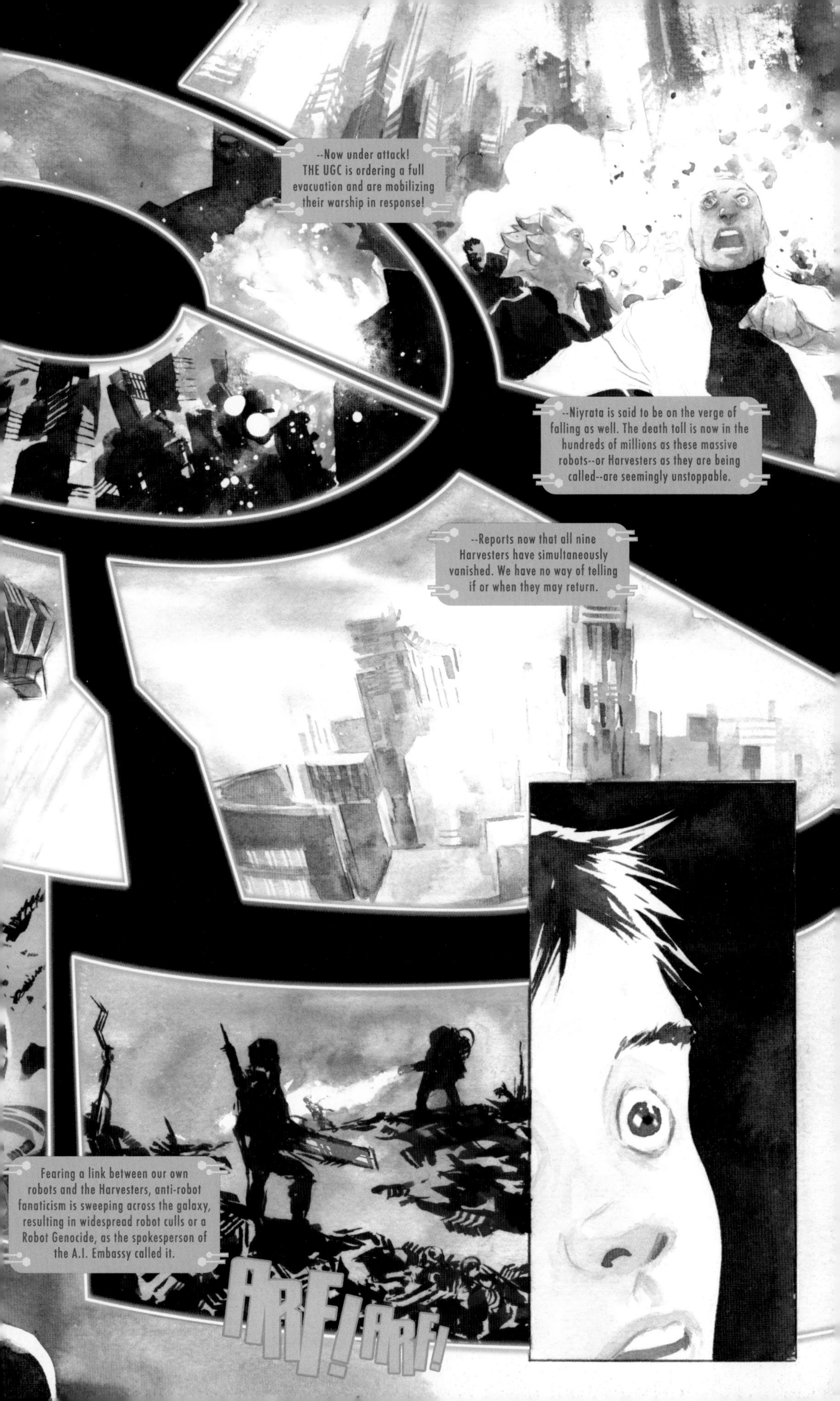
--Now under attack! THE UGC is ordering a full evacuation and are mobilizing their warship in response!
--Niyrata is said to be on the verge of falling as well. The death toll is now in the hundreds of millions as these massive robots--or Harvesters as they are being called--are seemingly unstoppable.
--Reports now that all nine Harvesters have simultaneously vanished. We have no way of telling if or when they may return.
Fearing a link between our own robots and the Harvesters, anti-robot fanaticism is sweeping across the galaxy, resulting in widespread robot culls or a Robot Genocide, as the spokesperson of the A.I. Embassy called it.
ARF! ARF!

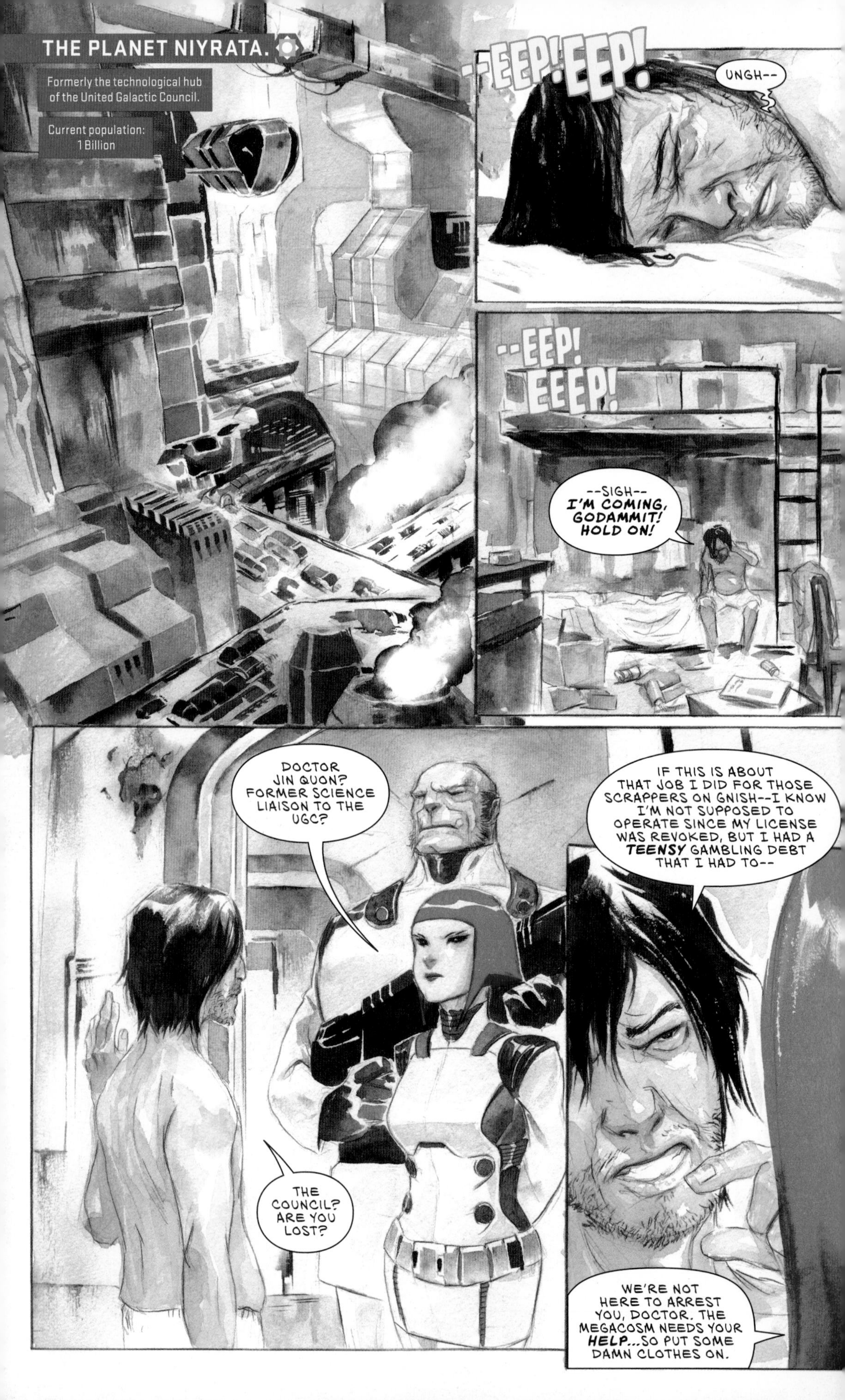
THE PLANET NIYRATA.
Formerly the technological hub of the United Galactic Council.
Current population: 1 Billion
--EEP! EEP!
UNGH--
--EEP! EEEP!
--SIGH-- I'M COMING, GODAMMIT! HOLD ON!
DOCTOR JIN QUON? FORMER SCIENCE LIAISON TO THE UGC?
IF THIS IS ABOUT THAT JOB I DID FOR THOSE SCRAPPERS ON GNISH--I KNOW I'M NOT SUPPOSED TO OPERATE SINCE MY LICENSE WAS REVOKED, BUT I HAD A TEENSY GAMBLING DEBT THAT I HAD TO--
THE COUNCIL? ARE YOU LOST?
WE'RE NOT HERE TO ARREST YOU, DOCTOR. THE MEGACOSM NEEDS YOUR HELP...SO PUT SOME DAMN CLOTHES ON.

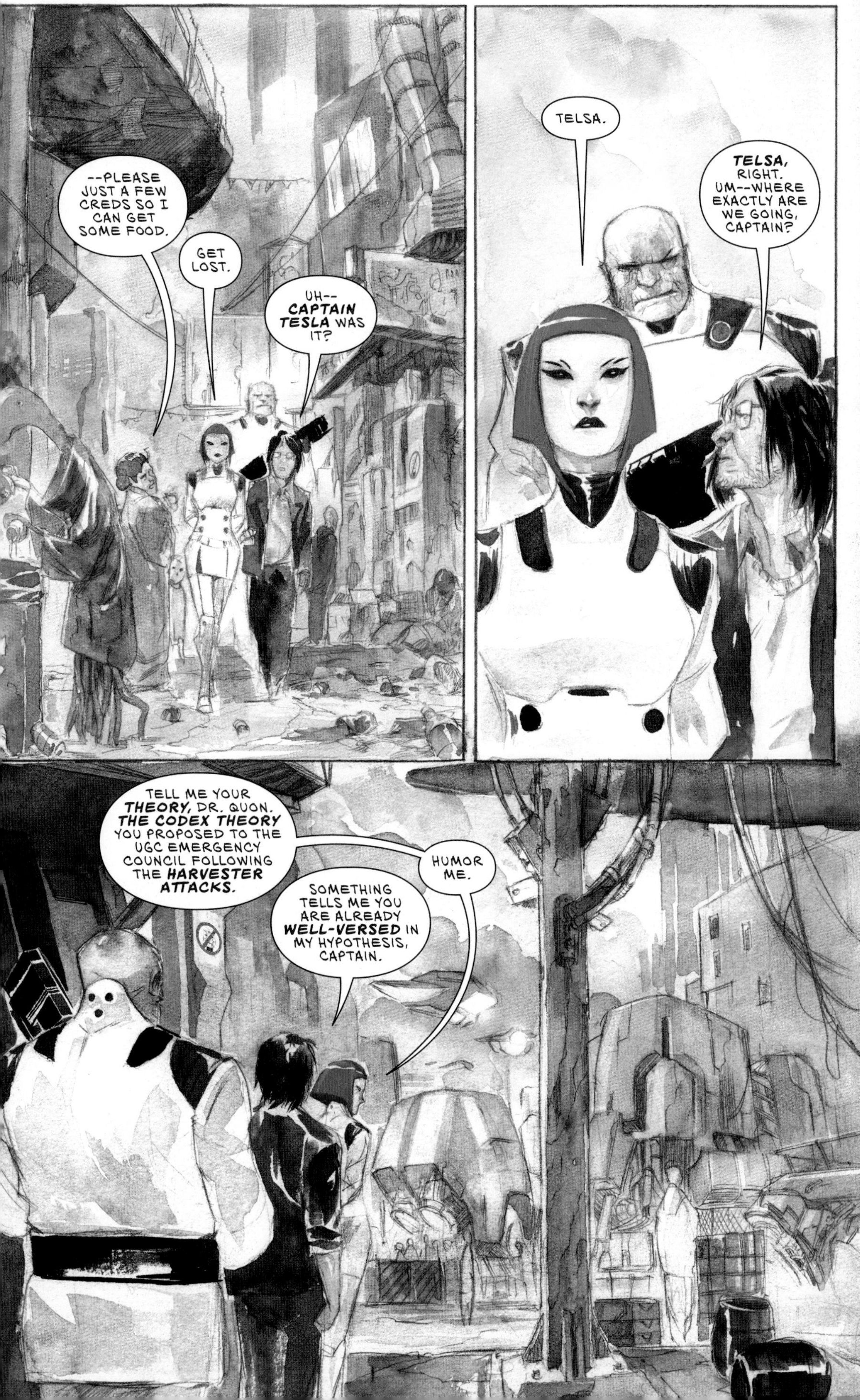
--PLEASE JUST A FEW CREDS SO I CAN GET SOME FOOD.
GET LOST.
UH-- **CAPTAIN TESLA** WAS IT?
TELSA.
TELSA, RIGHT. UM--WHERE EXACTLY ARE WE GOING, CAPTAIN?
TELL ME YOUR **THEORY,** DR. QUON. **THE CODEX THEORY** YOU PROPOSED TO THE UGC EMERGENCY COUNCIL FOLLOWING THE **HARVESTER ATTACKS.**
SOMETHING TELLS ME YOU ARE ALREADY **WELL-VERSED** IN MY HYPOTHESIS, CAPTAIN.
HUMOR ME.

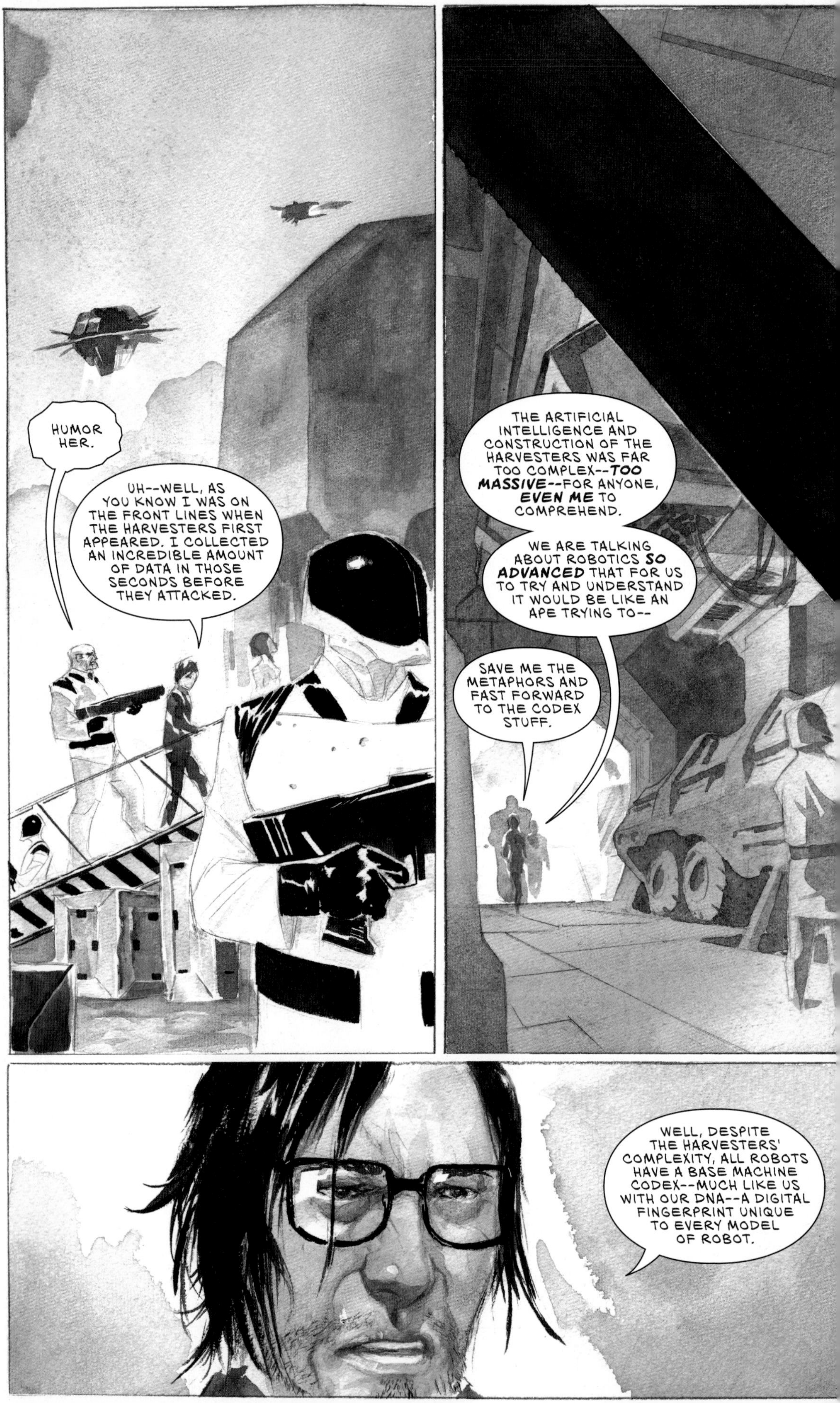
HUMOR HER.
UH--WELL, AS YOU KNOW I WAS ON THE FRONT LINES WHEN THE HARVESTERS FIRST APPEARED. I COLLECTED AN INCREDIBLE AMOUNT OF DATA IN THOSE SECONDS BEFORE THEY ATTACKED.
THE ARTIFICIAL INTELLIGENCE AND CONSTRUCTION OF THE HARVESTERS WAS FAR TOO COMPLEX--**TOO MASSIVE**--FOR ANYONE, **EVEN ME** TO COMPREHEND.
WE ARE TALKING ABOUT ROBOTICS **SO ADVANCED** THAT FOR US TO TRY AND UNDERSTAND IT WOULD BE LIKE AN APE TRYING TO--
SAVE ME THE METAPHORS AND FAST FORWARD TO THE CODEX STUFF.
WELL, DESPITE THE HARVESTERS' COMPLEXITY, ALL ROBOTS HAVE A BASE MACHINE CODEX--MUCH LIKE US WITH OUR DNA--A DIGITAL FINGERPRINT UNIQUE TO EVERY MODEL OF ROBOT.

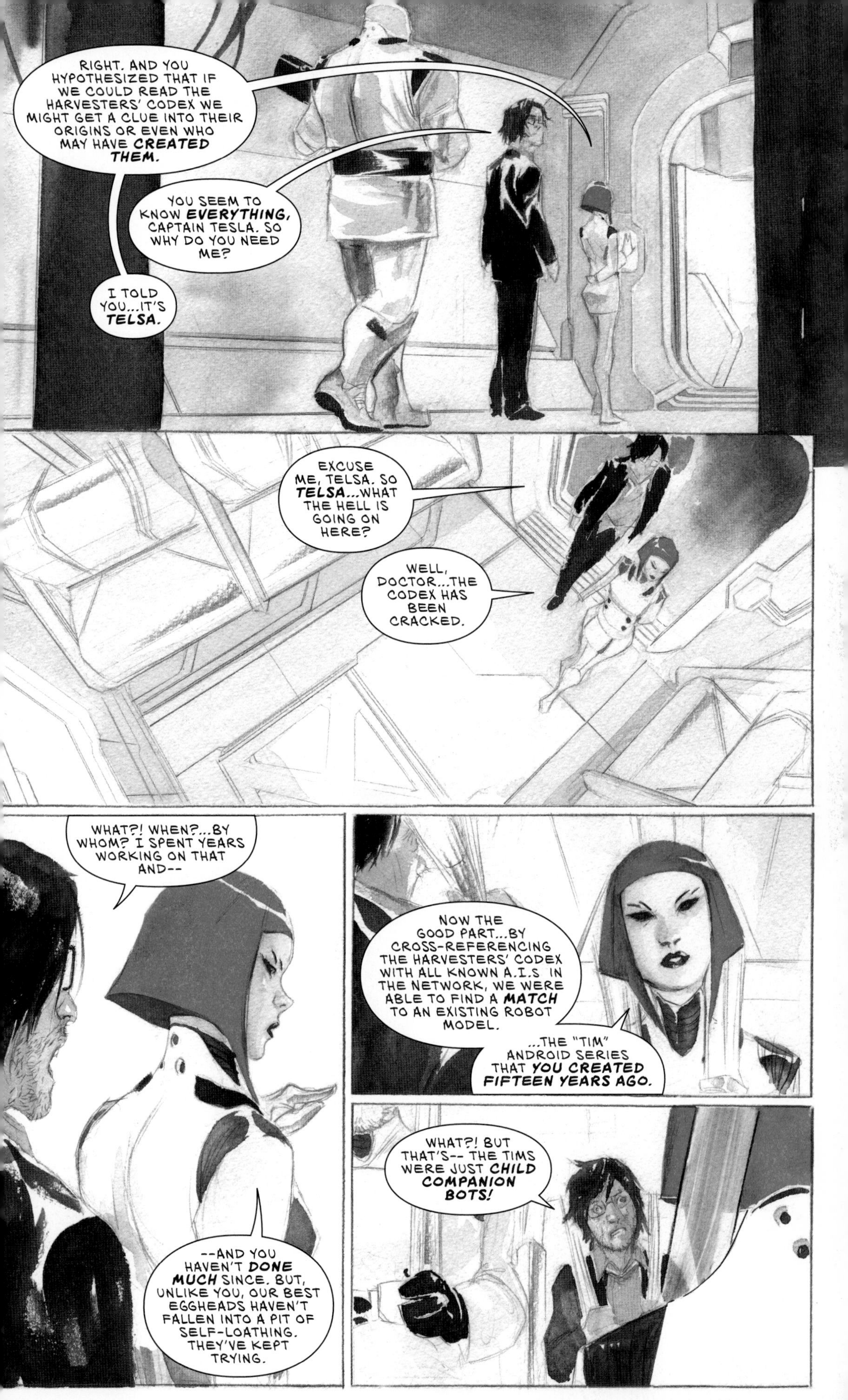
RIGHT. AND YOU HYPOTHESIZED THAT IF WE COULD READ THE HARVESTERS' CODEX WE MIGHT GET A CLUE INTO THEIR ORIGINS OR EVEN WHO MAY HAVE CREATED THEM.
YOU SEEM TO KNOW EVERYTHING, CAPTAIN TESLA. SO WHY DO YOU NEED ME?
I TOLD YOU...IT'S TELSA.
EXCUSE ME, TELSA. SO TELSA...WHAT THE HELL IS GOING ON HERE?
WELL, DOCTOR...THE CODEX HAS BEEN CRACKED.
WHAT?! WHEN?...BY WHOM? I SPENT YEARS WORKING ON THAT AND--
--AND YOU HAVEN'T DONE MUCH SINCE. BUT, UNLIKE YOU, OUR BEST EGGHEADS HAVEN'T FALLEN INTO A PIT OF SELF-LOATHING. THEY'VE KEPT TRYING.
NOW THE GOOD PART...BY CROSS-REFERENCING THE HARVESTERS' CODEX WITH ALL KNOWN A.I.S IN THE NETWORK, WE WERE ABLE TO FIND A MATCH TO AN EXISTING ROBOT MODEL.
...THE "TIM" ANDROID SERIES THAT YOU CREATED FIFTEEN YEARS AGO.
WHAT?! BUT THAT'S-- THE TIMS WERE JUST CHILD COMPANION BOTS!

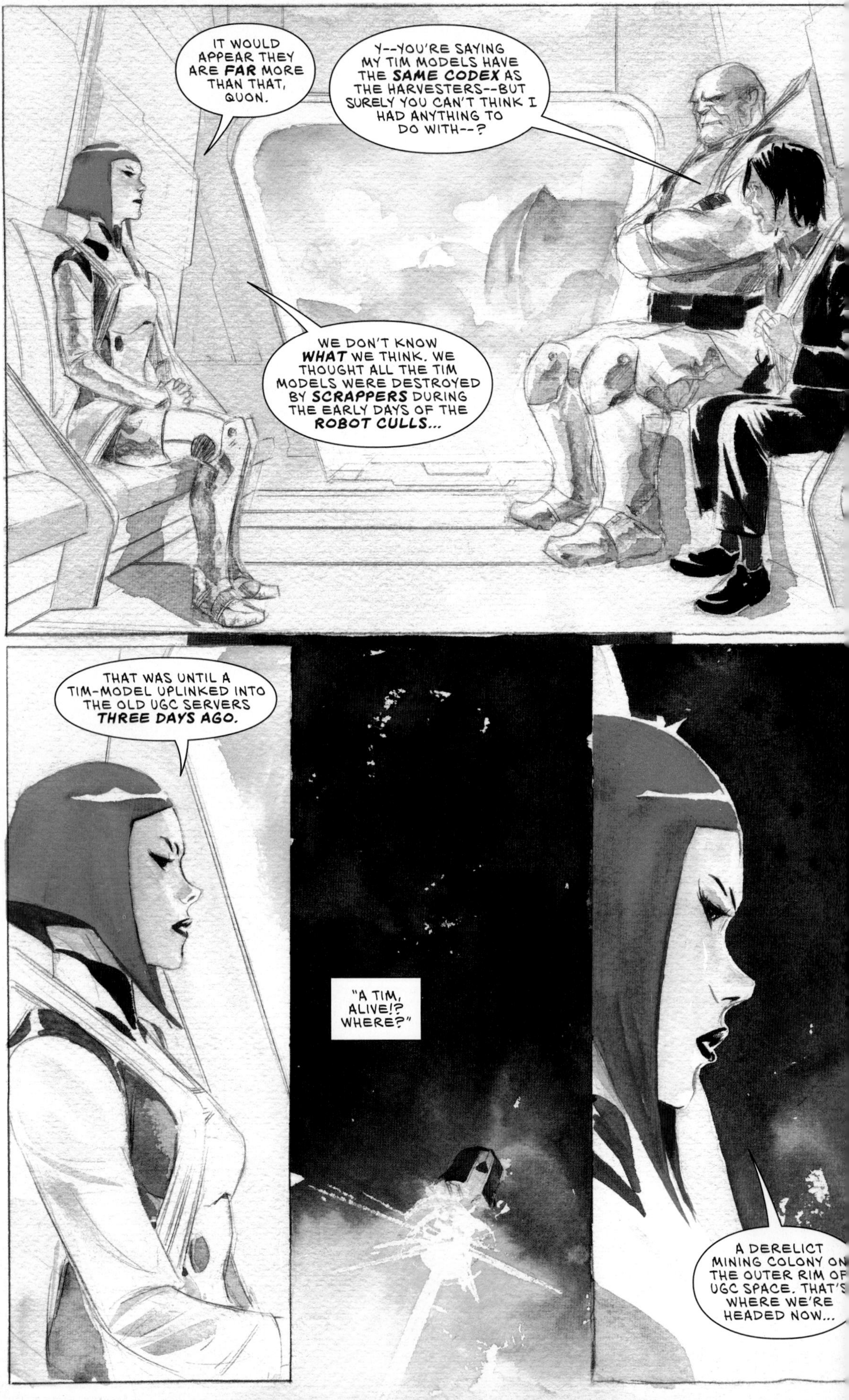
IT WOULD APPEAR THEY ARE FAR MORE THAN THAT, QUON.
Y--YOU'RE SAYING MY TIM MODELS HAVE THE SAME CODEX AS THE HARVESTERS--BUT SURELY YOU CAN'T THINK I HAD ANYTHING TO DO WITH--?
WE DON'T KNOW WHAT WE THINK. WE THOUGHT ALL THE TIM MODELS WERE DESTROYED BY SCRAPPERS DURING THE EARLY DAYS OF THE ROBOT CULLS...
THAT WAS UNTIL A TIM-MODEL UPLINKED INTO THE OLD UGC SERVERS THREE DAYS AGO.
"A TIM, ALIVE!? WHERE?"
A DERELICT MINING COLONY ON THE OUTER RIM OF UGC SPACE. THAT'S WHERE WE'RE HEADED NOW...

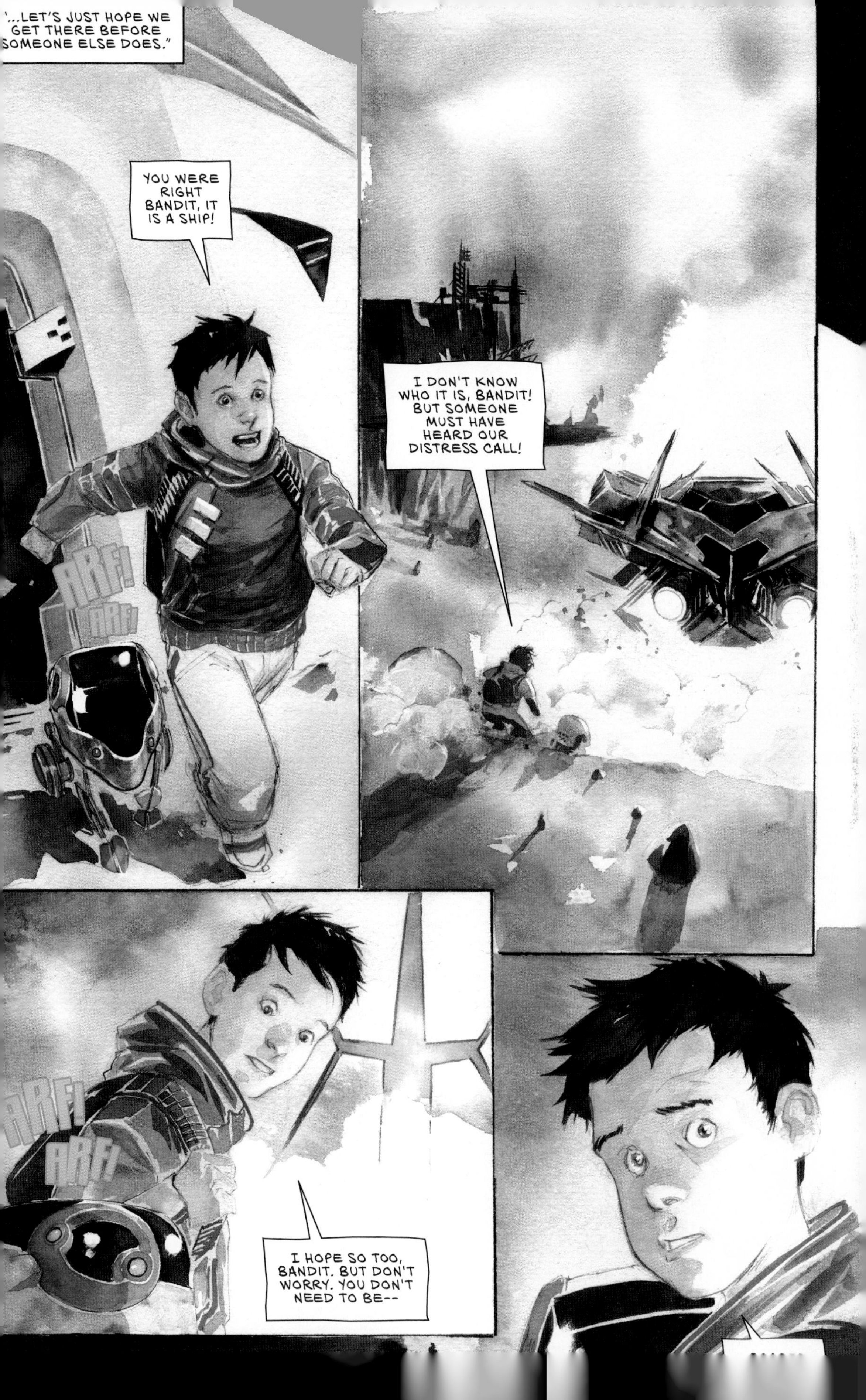

"...LET'S JUST HOPE WE GET THERE BEFORE SOMEONE ELSE DOES."
YOU WERE RIGHT BANDIT, IT IS A SHIP!
ARF! ARF!
I DON'T KNOW WHO IT IS, BANDIT! BUT SOMEONE MUST HAVE HEARD OUR DISTRESS CALL!
ARF! ARF!
I HOPE SO TOO, BANDIT. BUT DON'T WORRY. YOU DON'T NEED TO BE--

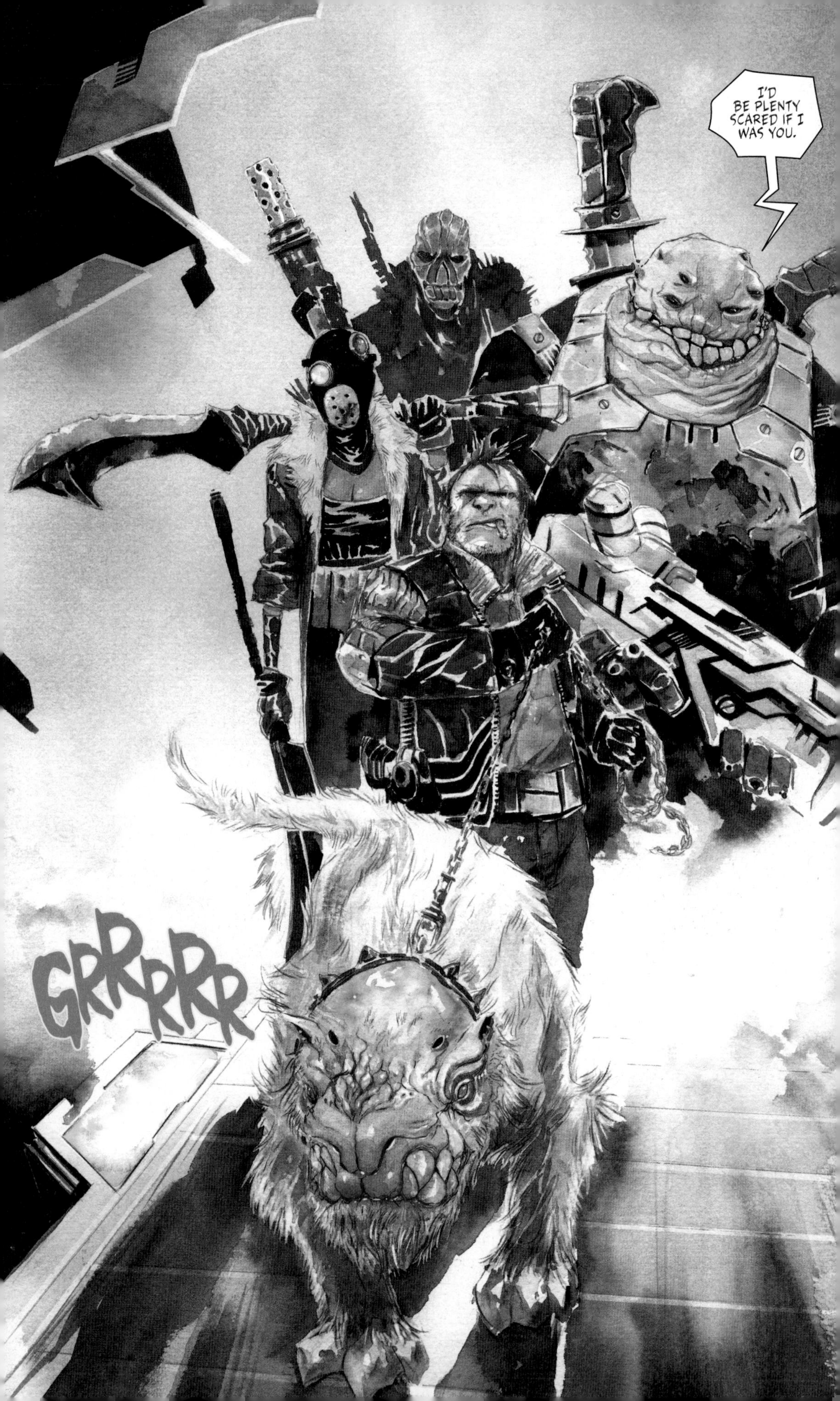
I'D BE PLENTY SCARED IF I WAS YOU.
GRRRRR

CHAPTER TWO

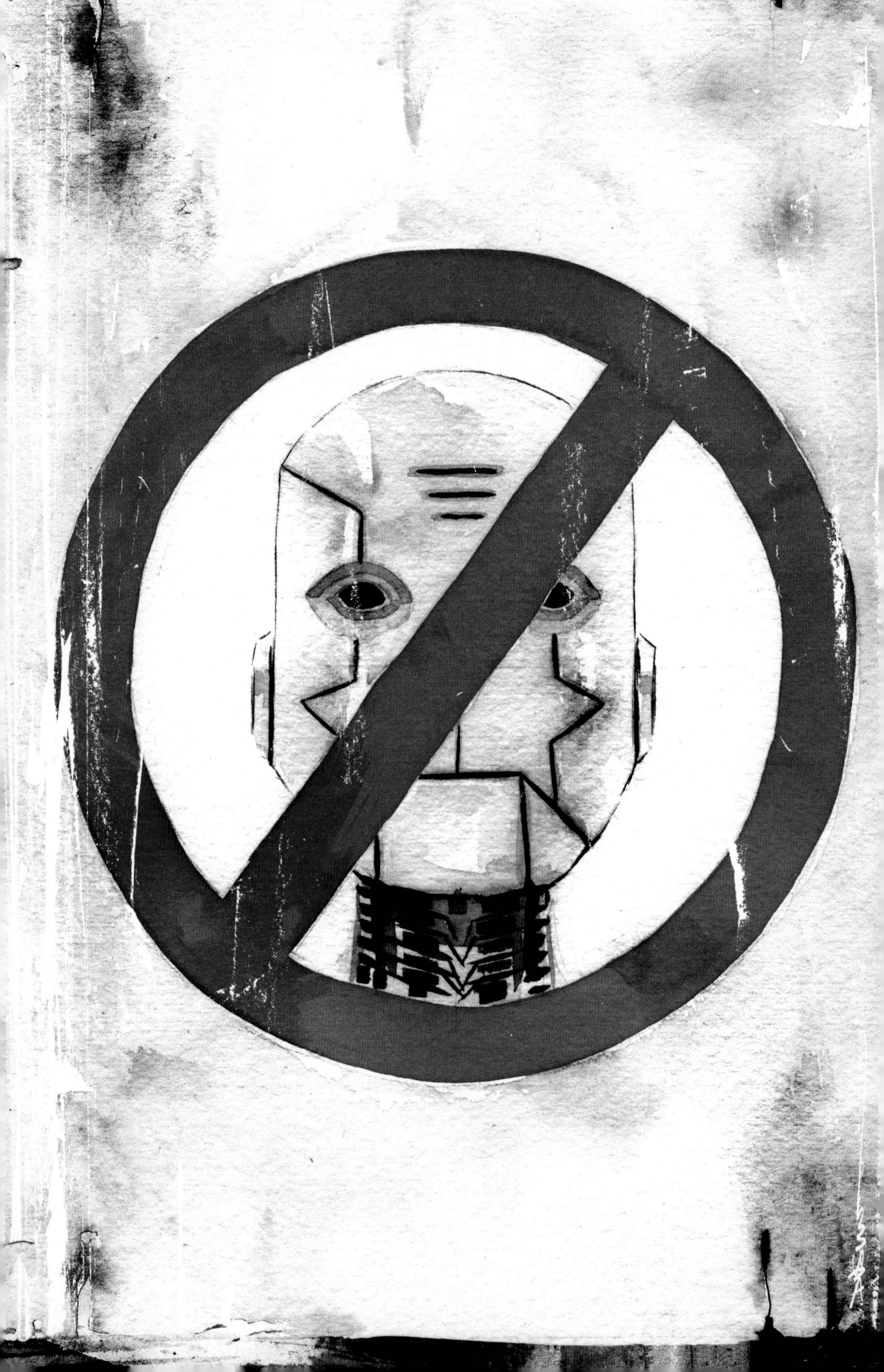

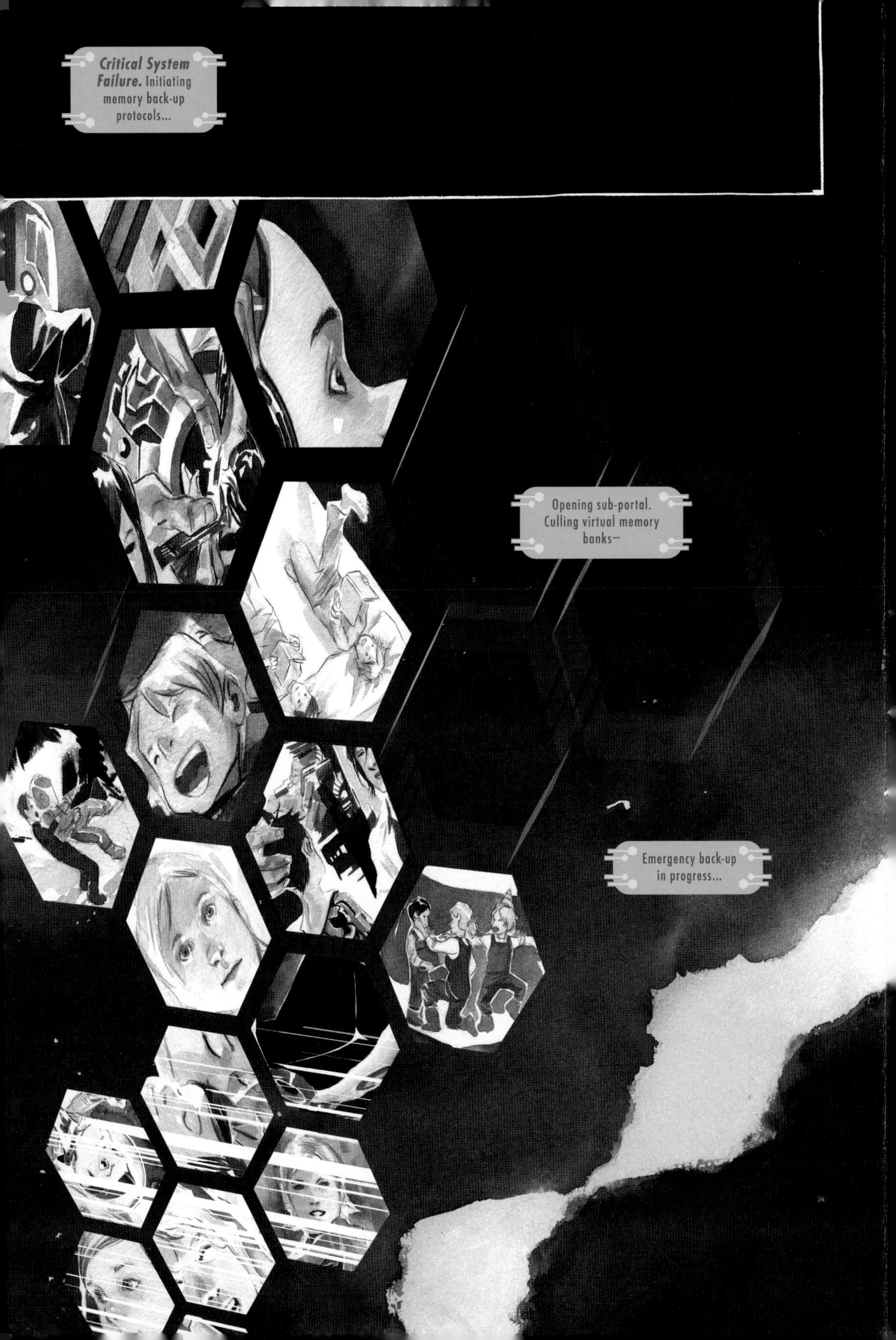

Critical System Failure. Initiating memory back-up protocols...
Opening sub-portal. Culling virtual memory banks—
Emergency back-up in progress...

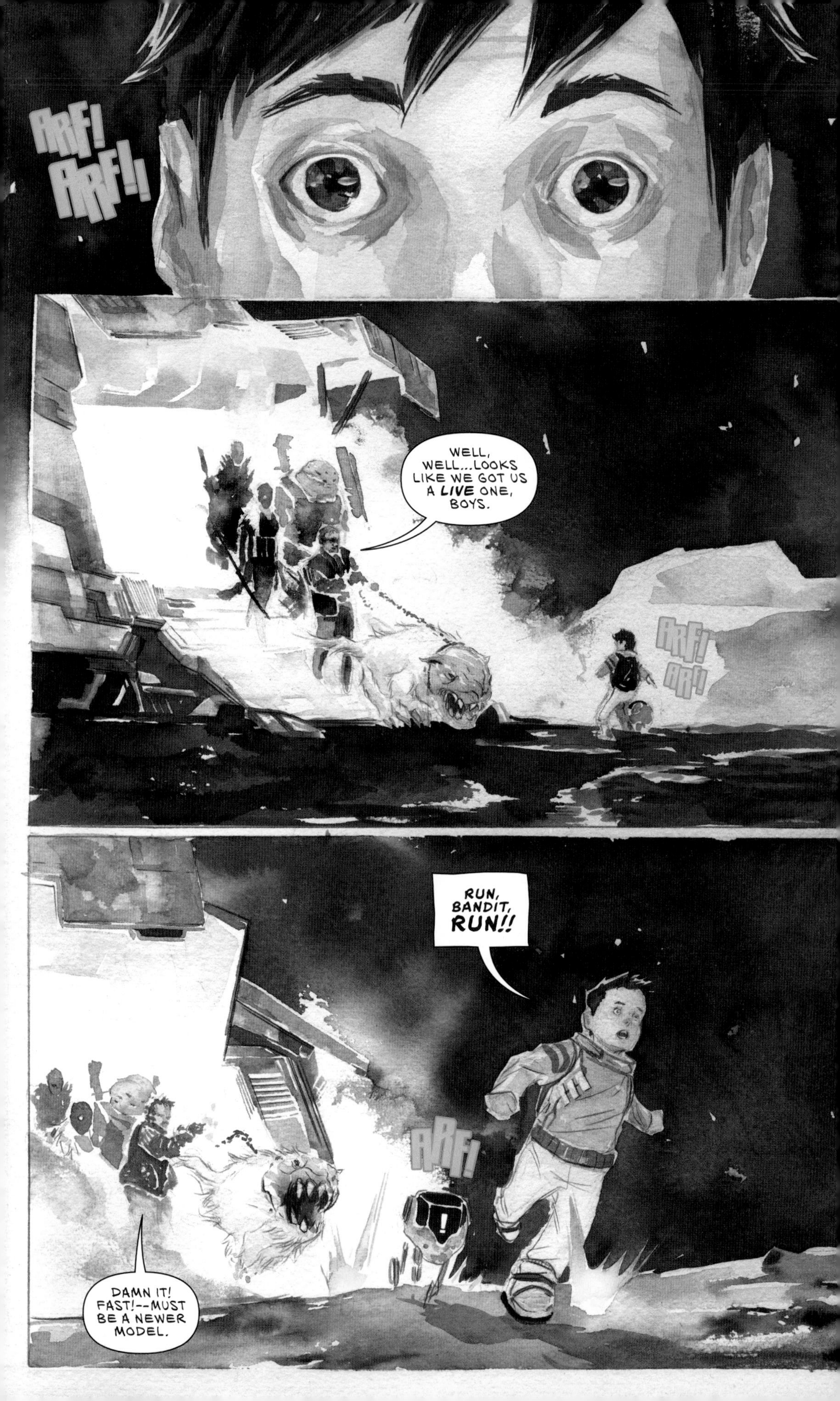
ARF! ARF!!
WELL, WELL...LOOKS LIKE WE GOT US A *LIVE* ONE, BOYS.
ARF! ARF!!
RUN, BANDIT, **RUN!!**
ARF!
DAMN IT! FAST!--MUST BE A NEWER MODEL.

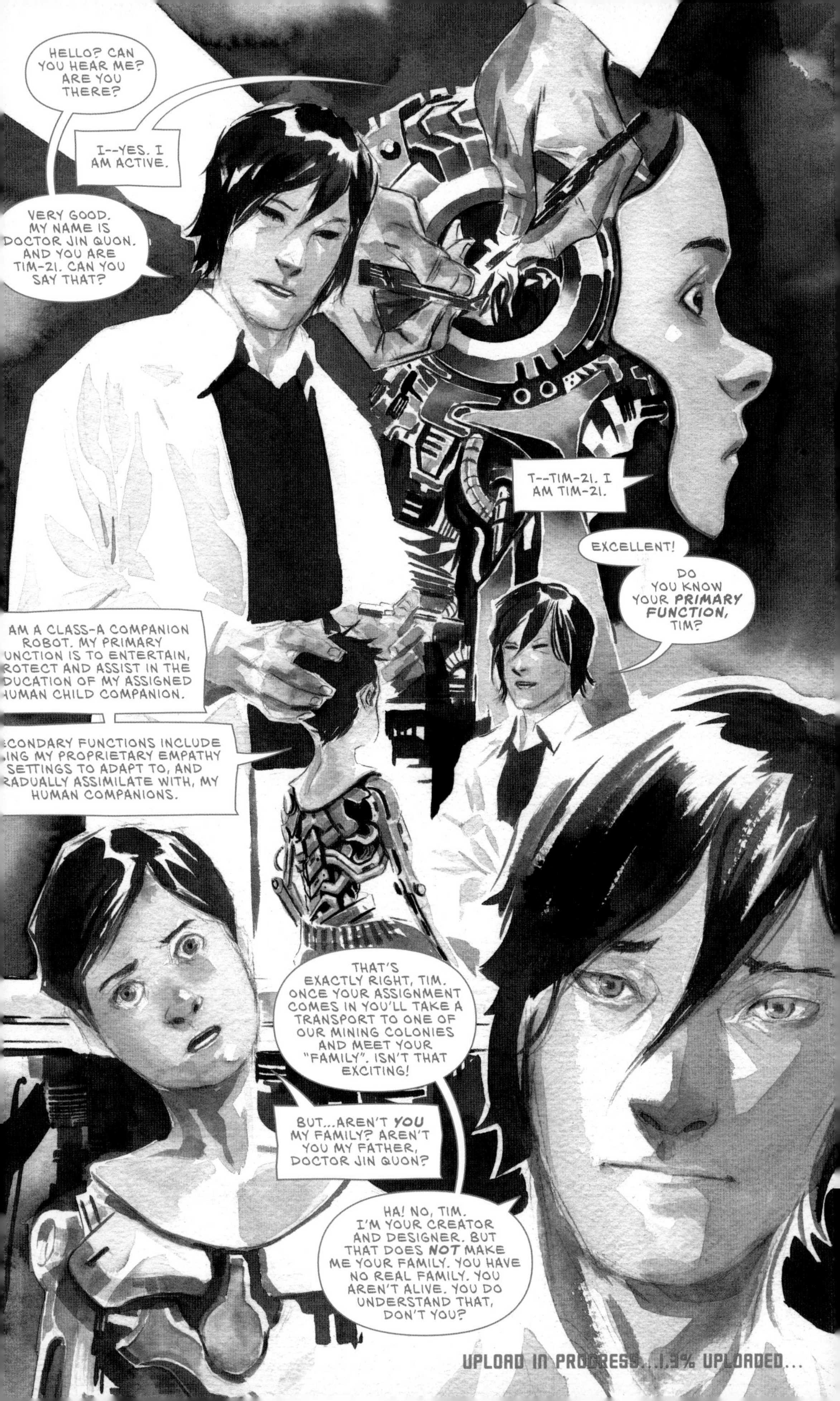

HELLO? CAN YOU HEAR ME? ARE YOU THERE?
I--YES. I AM ACTIVE.
VERY GOOD. MY NAME IS DOCTOR JIN QUON. AND YOU ARE TIM-21. CAN YOU SAY THAT?
T--TIM-21. I AM TIM-21.
EXCELLENT!
DO YOU KNOW YOUR **PRIMARY FUNCTION,** TIM?
AM A CLASS-A COMPANION ROBOT. MY PRIMARY UNCTION IS TO ENTERTAIN, ROTECT AND ASSIST IN THE DUCATION OF MY ASSIGNED HUMAN CHILD COMPANION.
ECONDARY FUNCTIONS INCLUDE ING MY PROPRIETARY EMPATHY SETTINGS TO ADAPT TO, AND RADUALLY ASSIMILATE WITH, MY HUMAN COMPANIONS.
THAT'S EXACTLY RIGHT, TIM. ONCE YOUR ASSIGNMENT COMES IN YOU'LL TAKE A TRANSPORT TO ONE OF OUR MINING COLONIES AND MEET YOUR "FAMILY". ISN'T THAT EXCITING!
BUT...AREN'T *YOU* MY FAMILY? AREN'T YOU MY FATHER, DOCTOR JIN QUON?
HA! NO, TIM. I'M YOUR CREATOR AND DESIGNER. BUT THAT DOES **NOT** MAKE ME YOUR FAMILY. YOU HAVE NO REAL FAMILY. YOU AREN'T ALIVE. YOU DO UNDERSTAND THAT, DON'T YOU?
UPLOAD IN PROGRESS...1.3% UPLOADED...

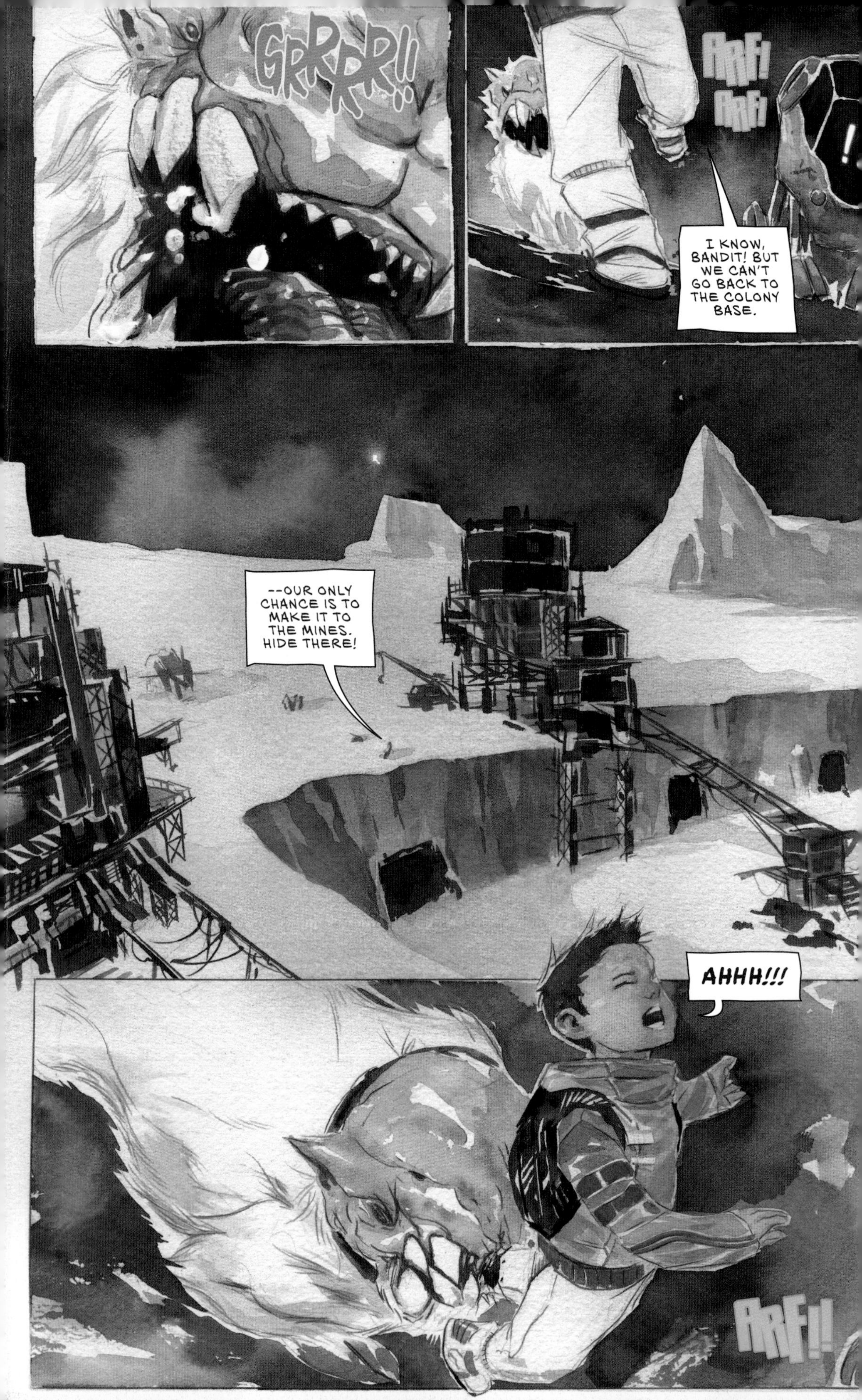
GRRRR!!
ARF! ARF!
I KNOW, BANDIT! BUT WE CAN'T GO BACK TO THE COLONY BASE.
--OUR ONLY CHANCE IS TO MAKE IT TO THE MINES. HIDE THERE!
AHHH!!!
ARF!!

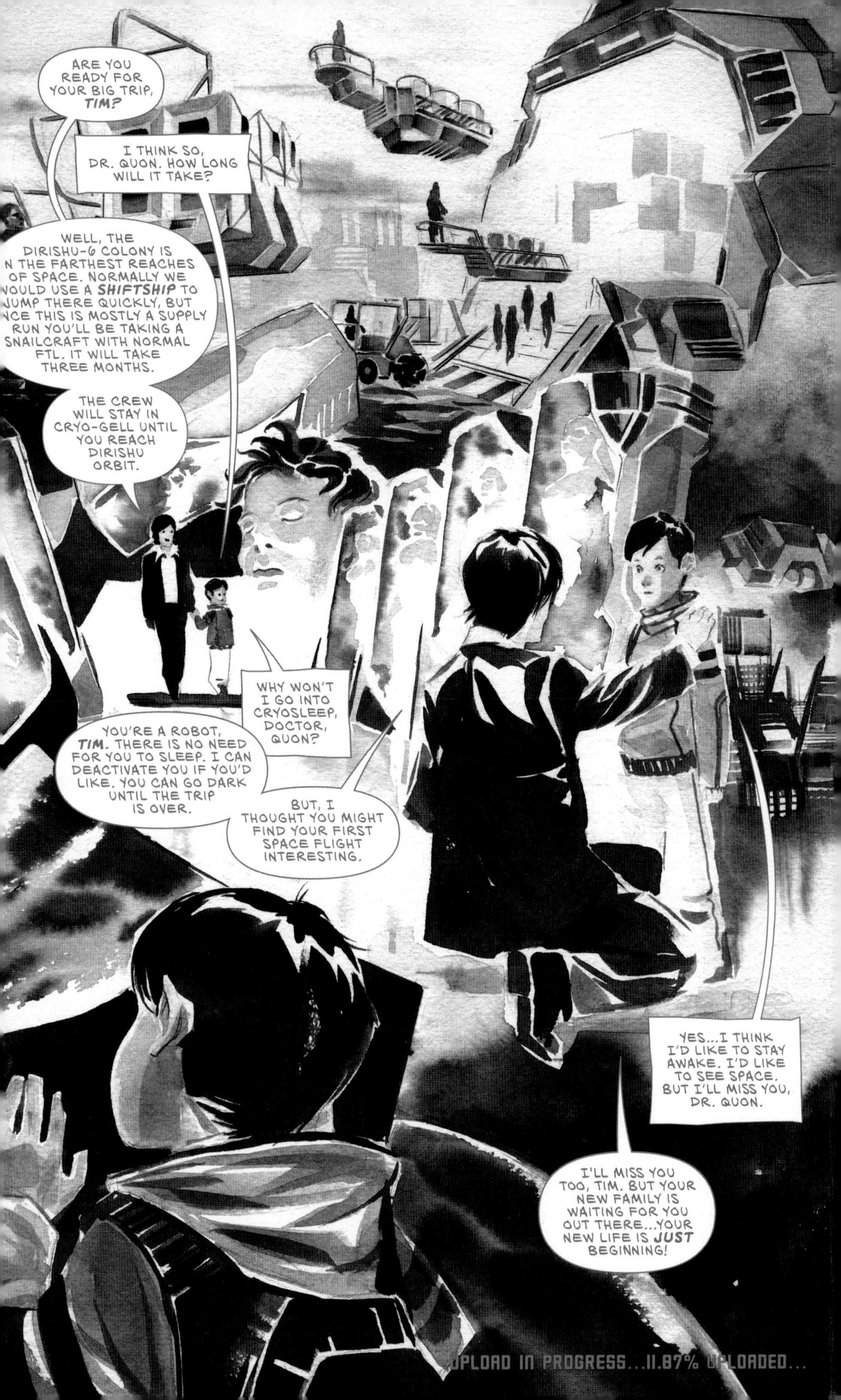
ARE YOU READY FOR YOUR BIG TRIP, **TIM?**
I THINK SO, DR. QUON. HOW LONG WILL IT TAKE?
WELL, THE DIRISHU-6 COLONY IS N THE FARTHEST REACHES OF SPACE. NORMALLY WE NOULD USE A **SHIFTSHIP** TO JUMP THERE QUICKLY, BUT NCE THIS IS MOSTLY A SUPPLY RUN YOU'LL BE TAKING A SNAILCRAFT WITH NORMAL FTL. IT WILL TAKE THREE MONTHS.
THE CREW WILL STAY IN CRYO-GELL UNTIL YOU REACH DIRISHU ORBIT.
WHY WON'T I GO INTO CRYOSLEEP, DOCTOR, QUON?
YOU'RE A ROBOT, **TIM.** THERE IS NO NEED FOR YOU TO SLEEP. I CAN DEACTIVATE YOU IF YOU'D LIKE. YOU CAN GO DARK UNTIL THE TRIP IS OVER.
BUT, I THOUGHT YOU MIGHT FIND YOUR FIRST SPACE FLIGHT INTERESTING.
YES...I THINK I'D LIKE TO STAY AWAKE. I'D LIKE TO SEE SPACE. BUT I'LL MISS YOU, DR. QUON.
I'LL MISS YOU TOO, TIM. BUT YOUR NEW FAMILY IS WAITING FOR YOU OUT THERE...YOUR NEW LIFE IS **JUST** BEGINNING!
UPLOAD IN PROGRESS...11.87% UPLOADED...

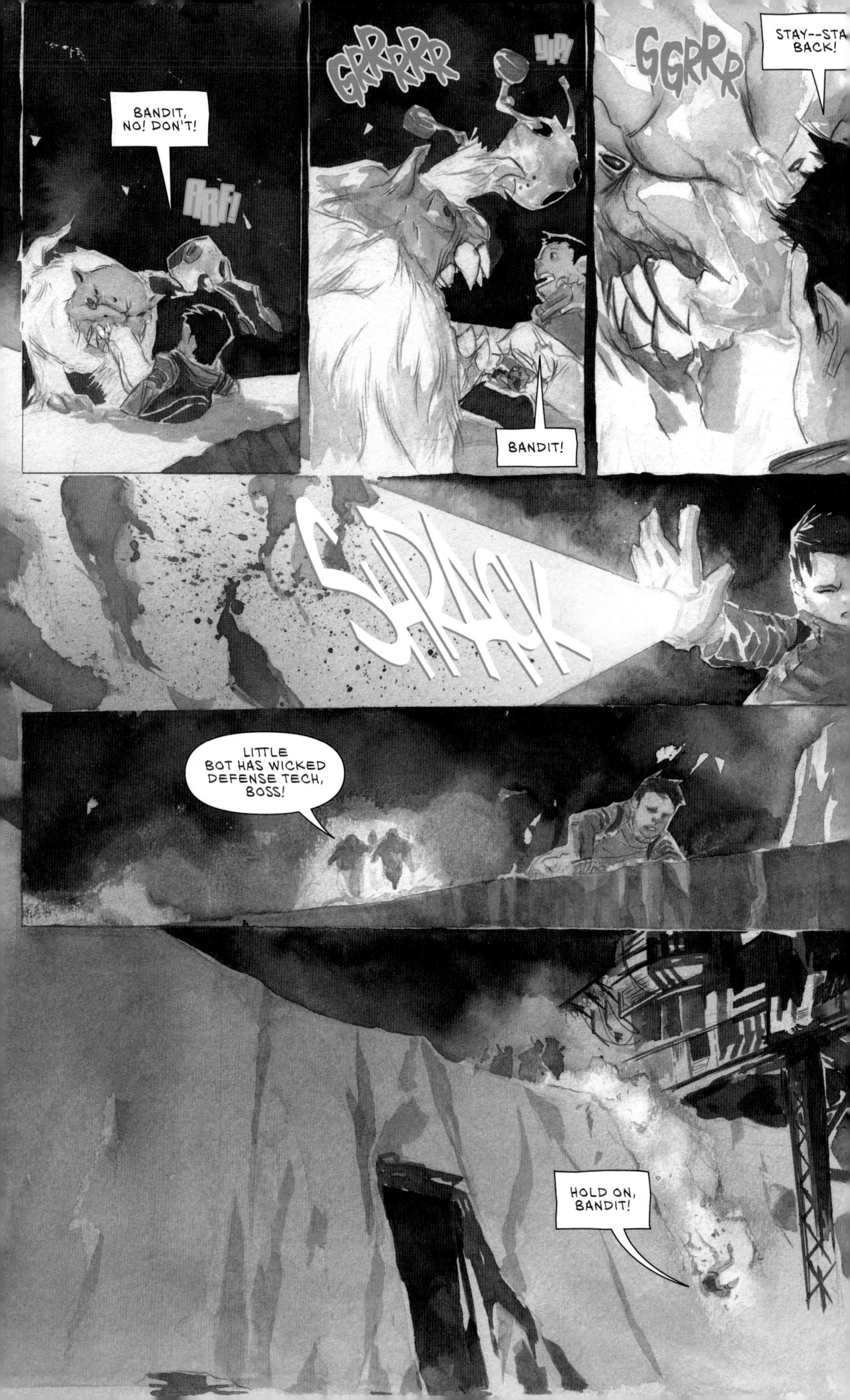
BANDIT, NO! DON'T!
ARF!
GRRRR
YIP!
BANDIT!
GGRRR
STAY--STA BACK!
SHRACK
LITTLE BOT HAS WICKED DEFENSE TECH, BOSS!
HOLD ON, BANDIT!

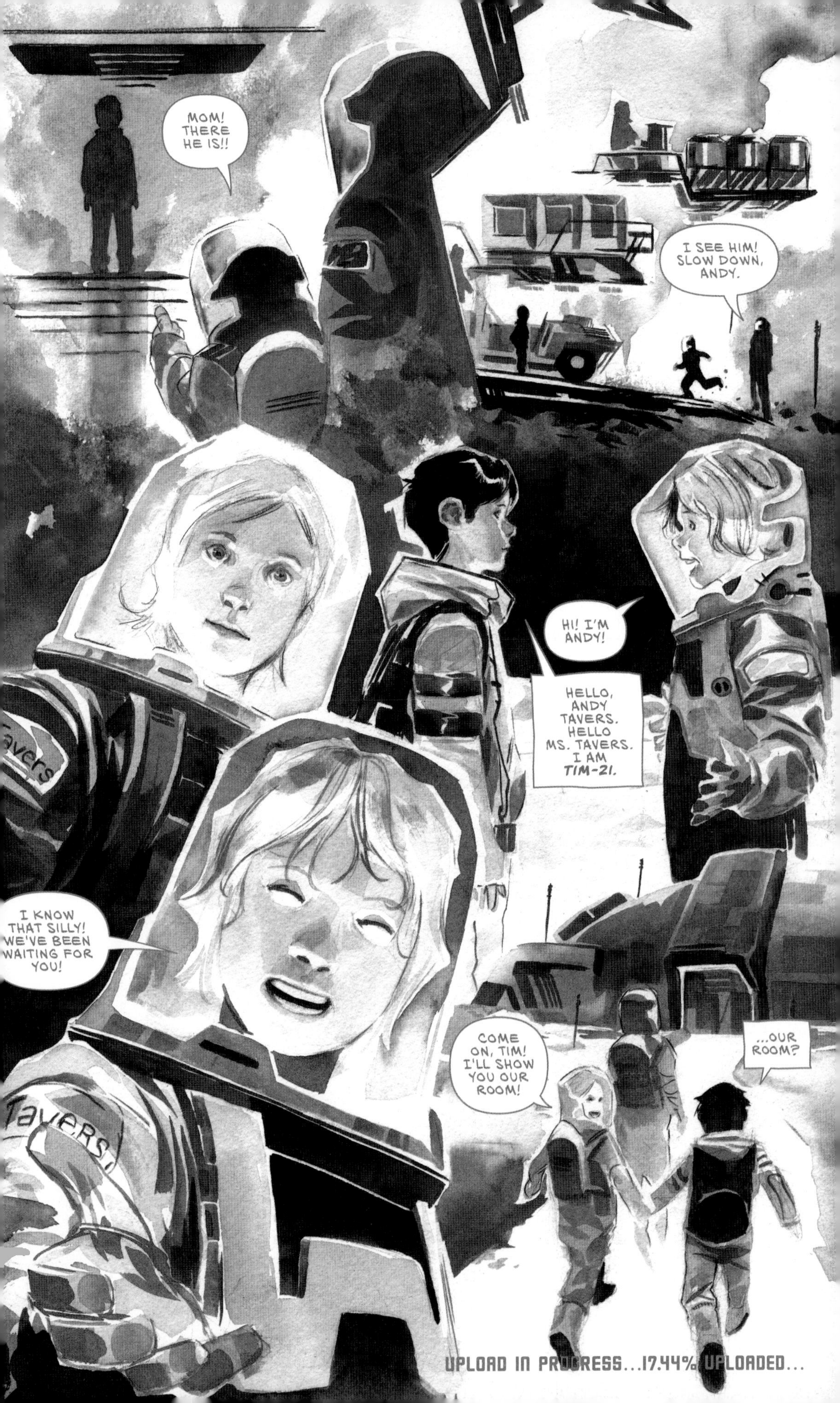
MOM! THERE HE IS!!
I SEE HIM! SLOW DOWN, ANDY.
HI! I'M ANDY!
HELLO, ANDY TAVERS. HELLO MS. TAVERS. I AM TIM-21.
Tavers
I KNOW THAT SILLY! WE'VE BEEN WAITING FOR YOU!
Tavers
COME ON, TIM! I'LL SHOW YOU OUR ROOM!
...OUR ROOM?
UPLOAD IN PROGRESS...17.44% UPLOADED...

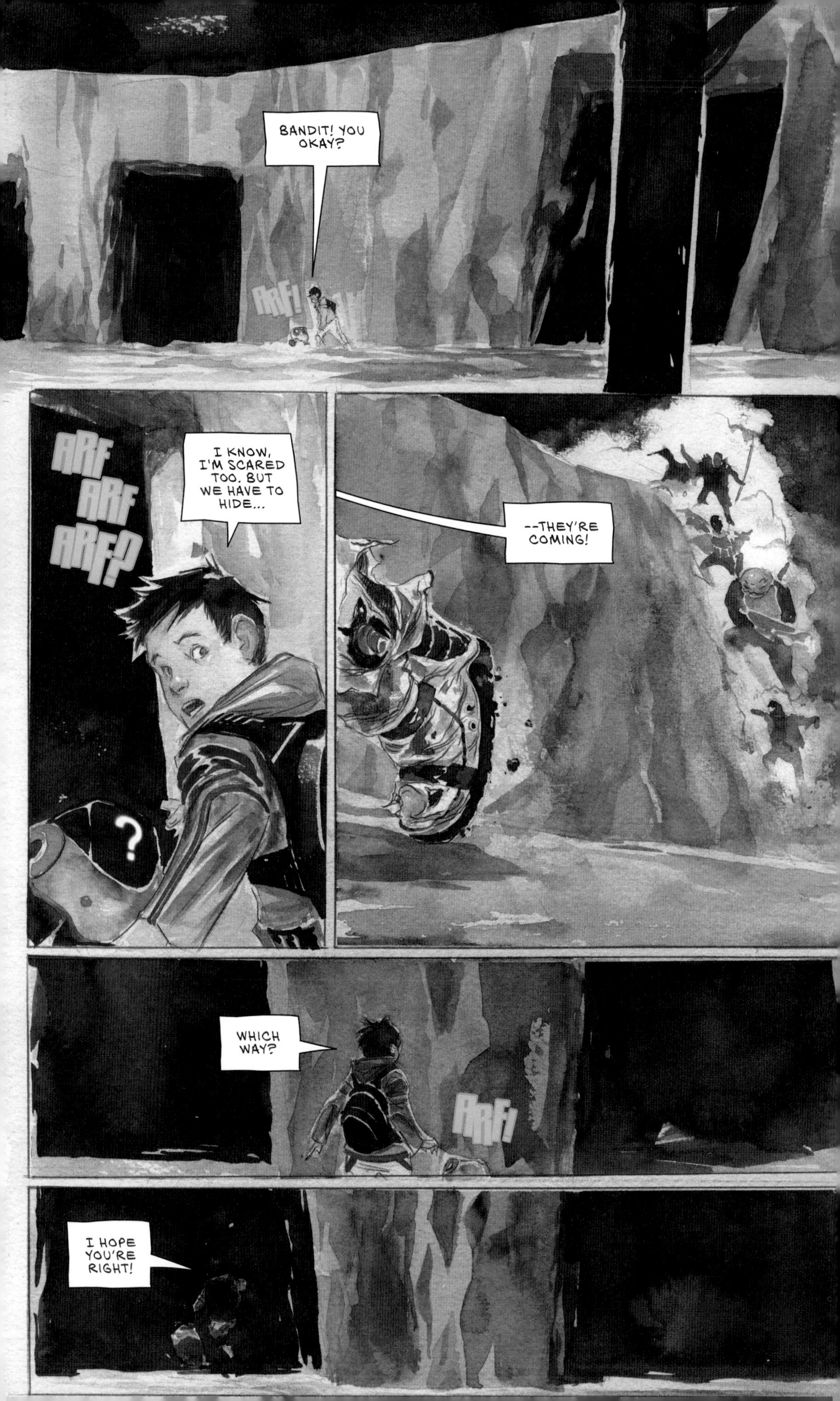

BANDIT! YOU OKAY?
ARF!
ARF ARF ARF?
I KNOW, I'M SCARED TOO. BUT WE HAVE TO HIDE...
?
--THEY'RE COMING!
WHICH WAY?
ARF!
I HOPE YOU'RE RIGHT!

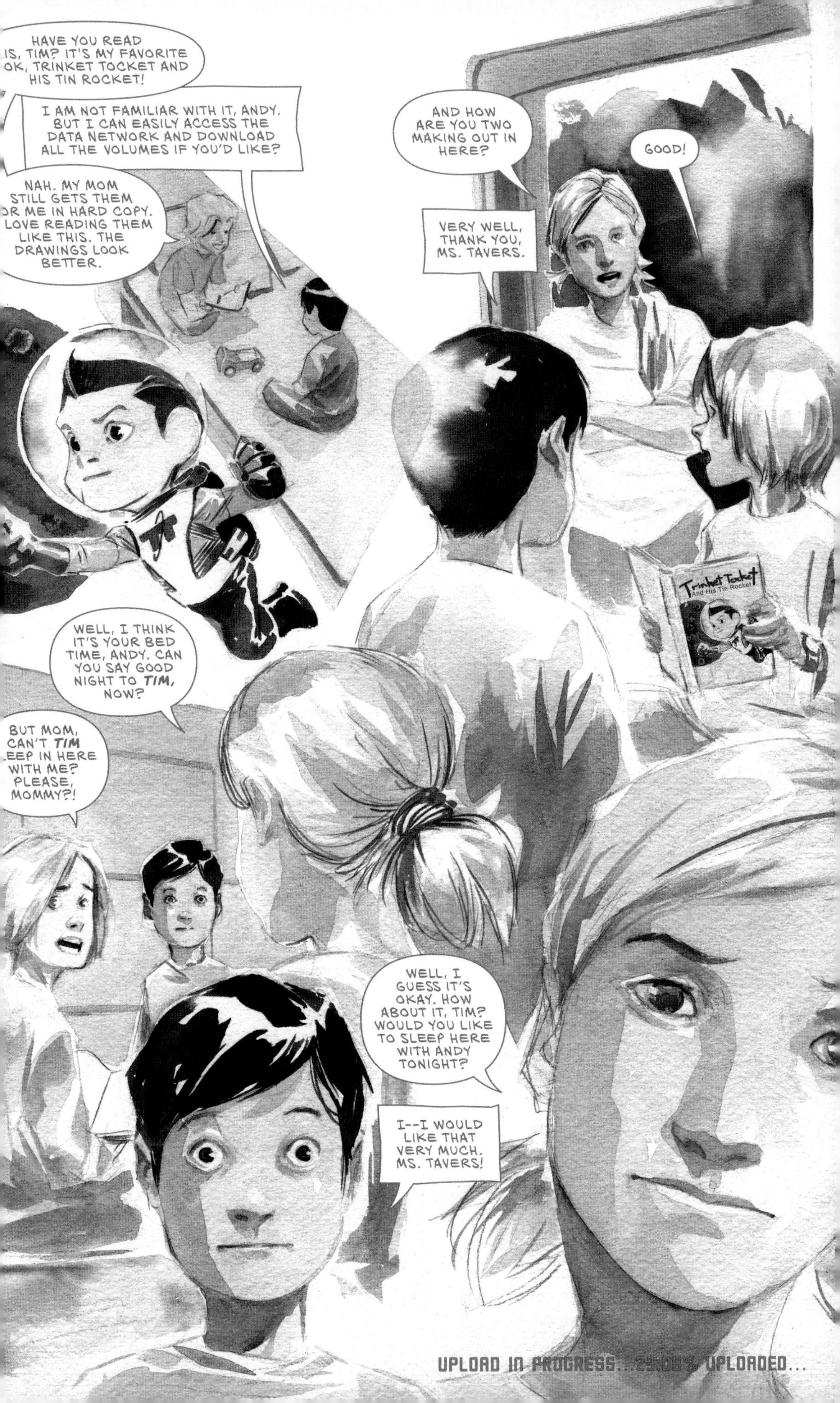

HAVE YOU READ IS, TIM? IT'S MY FAVORITE OK, TRINKET TOCKET AND HIS TIN ROCKET!
I AM NOT FAMILIAR WITH IT, ANDY. BUT I CAN EASILY ACCESS THE DATA NETWORK AND DOWNLOAD ALL THE VOLUMES IF YOU'D LIKE?
NAH. MY MOM STILL GETS THEM OR ME IN HARD COPY. LOVE READING THEM LIKE THIS. THE DRAWINGS LOOK BETTER.
AND HOW ARE YOU TWO MAKING OUT IN HERE?
GOOD!
VERY WELL, THANK YOU, MS. TAVERS.
Trinket Tocket And His Tin Rocket
WELL, I THINK IT'S YOUR BED TIME, ANDY. CAN YOU SAY GOOD NIGHT TO TIM, NOW?
BUT MOM, CAN'T TIM EEP IN HERE WITH ME? PLEASE, MOMMY?!
WELL, I GUESS IT'S OKAY. HOW ABOUT IT, TIM? WOULD YOU LIKE TO SLEEP HERE WITH ANDY TONIGHT?
I--I WOULD LIKE THAT VERY MUCH. MS. TAVERS!
UPLOAD IN PROGRESS...29.06% UPLOADED...

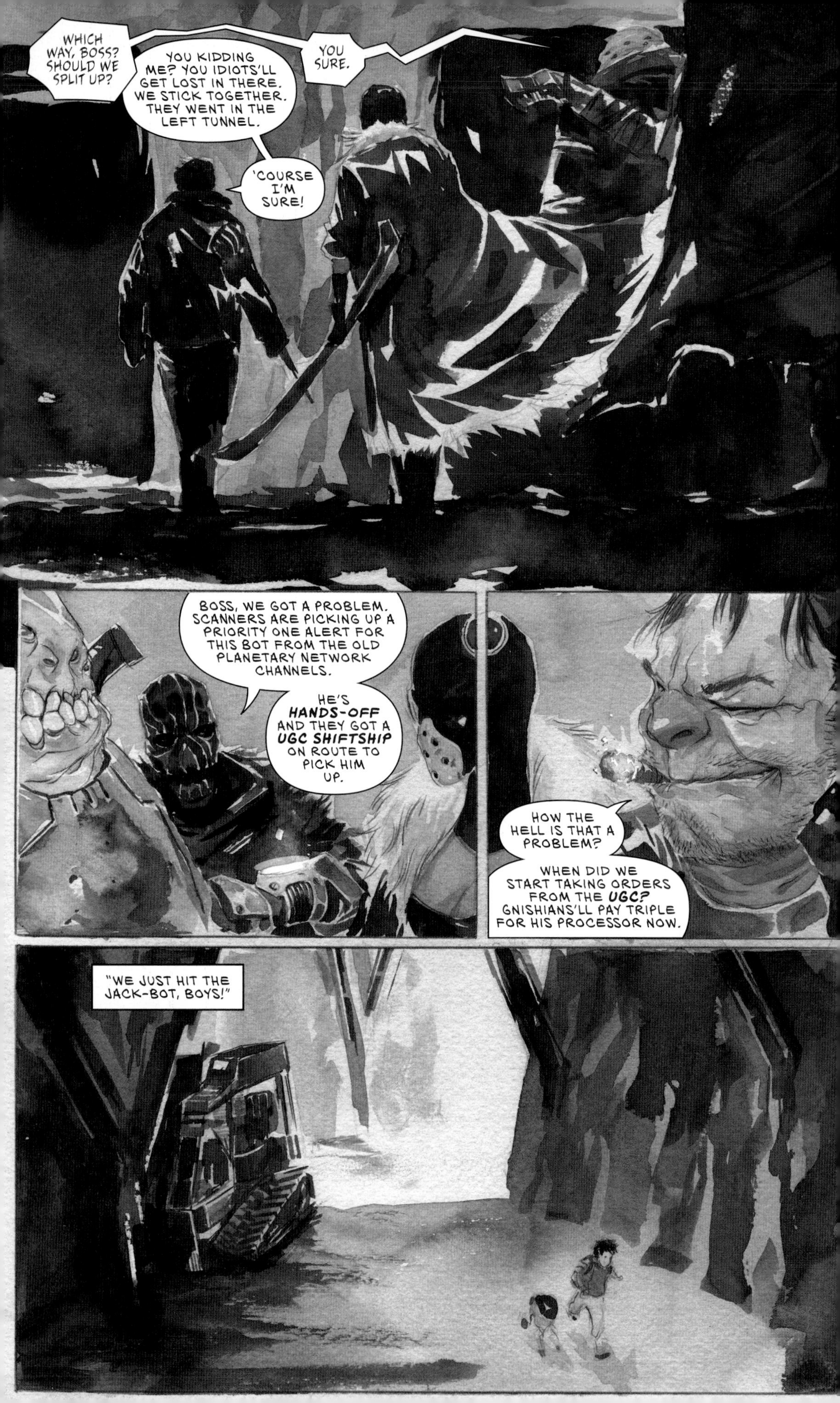
WHICH WAY, BOSS? SHOULD WE SPLIT UP?
YOU KIDDING ME? YOU IDIOTS'LL GET LOST IN THERE. WE STICK TOGETHER. THEY WENT IN THE LEFT TUNNEL.
YOU SURE.
'COURSE I'M SURE!
BOSS, WE GOT A PROBLEM. SCANNERS ARE PICKING UP A PRIORITY ONE ALERT FOR THIS BOT FROM THE OLD PLANETARY NETWORK CHANNELS.
HE'S **HANDS-OFF** AND THEY GOT A **UGC SHIFTSHIP** ON ROUTE TO PICK HIM UP.
HOW THE HELL IS THAT A PROBLEM?
WHEN DID WE START TAKING ORDERS FROM THE **UGC?** GNISHIANS'LL PAY TRIPLE FOR HIS PROCESSOR NOW.
"WE JUST HIT THE JACK-BOT, BOYS!"

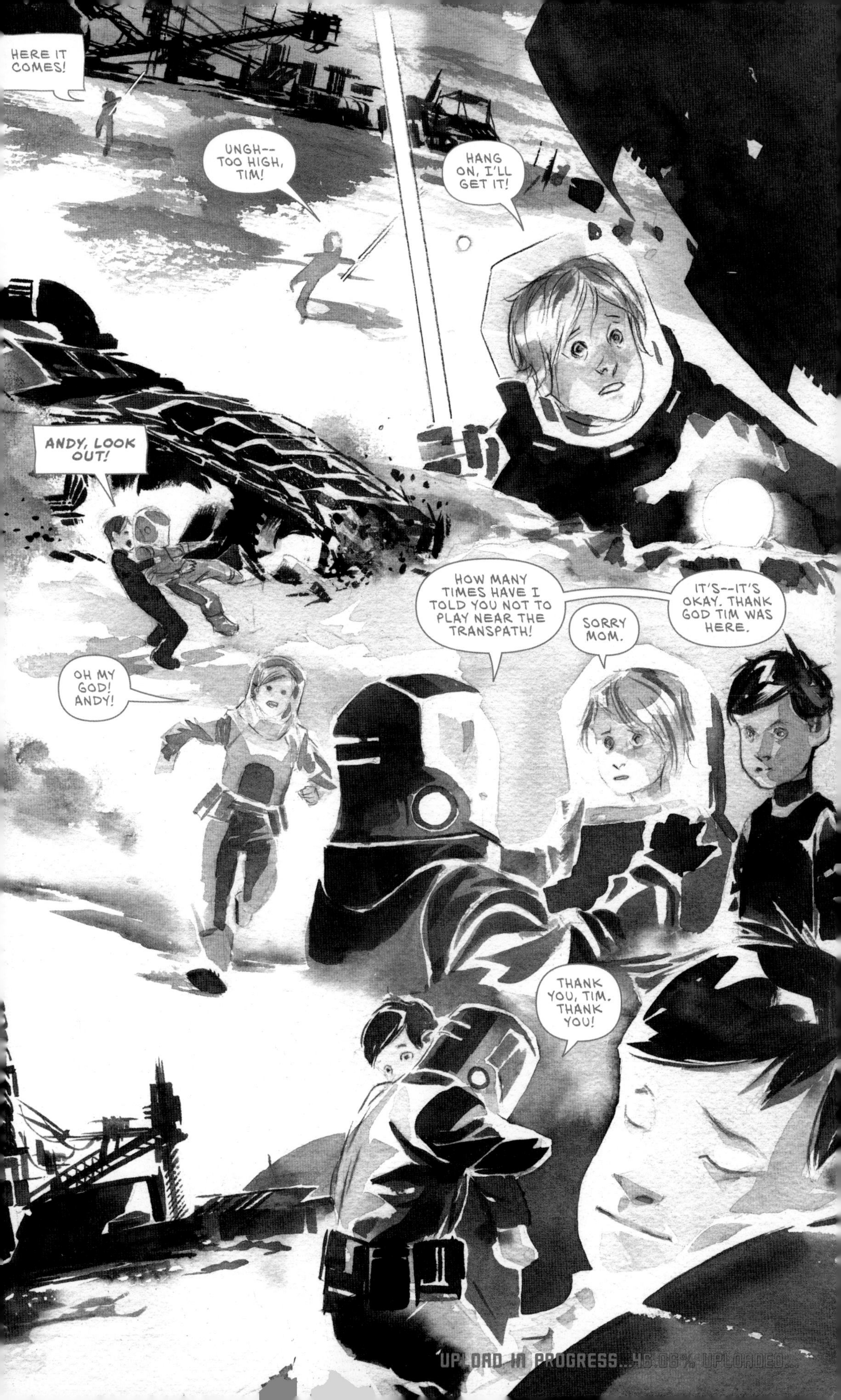
HERE IT COMES!
UNGH-- TOO HIGH, TIM!
HANG ON, I'LL GET IT!
ANDY, LOOK OUT!
HOW MANY TIMES HAVE I TOLD YOU NOT TO PLAY NEAR THE TRANSPATH!
SORRY MOM.
IT'S--IT'S OKAY. THANK GOD TIM WAS HERE.
OH MY GOD! ANDY!
THANK YOU, TIM. THANK YOU!
UPLOAD IN PROGRESS...46.06% UPLOADED...

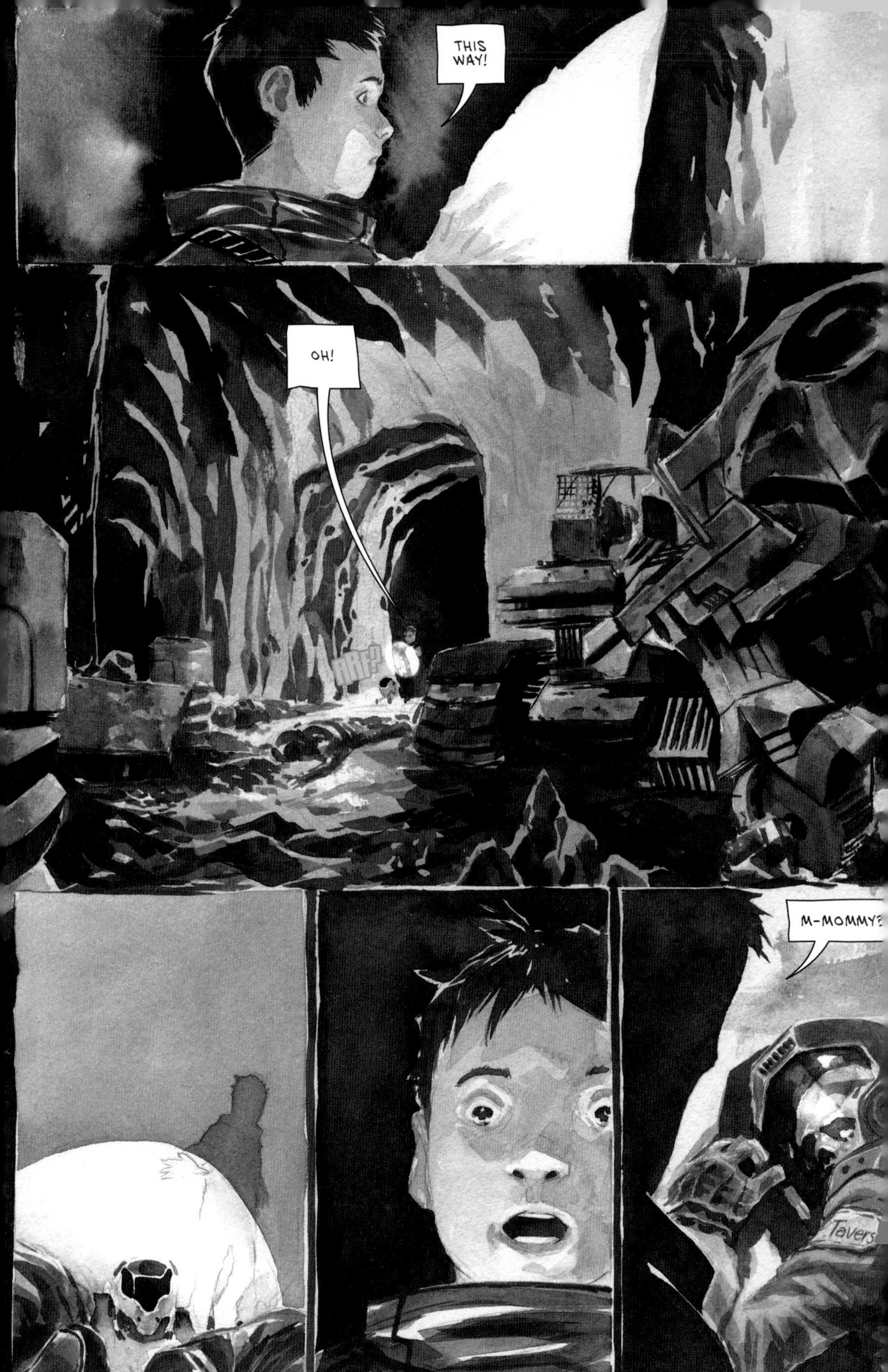
THIS WAY!
OH!
ARF?
M-MOMMY?
Tavers

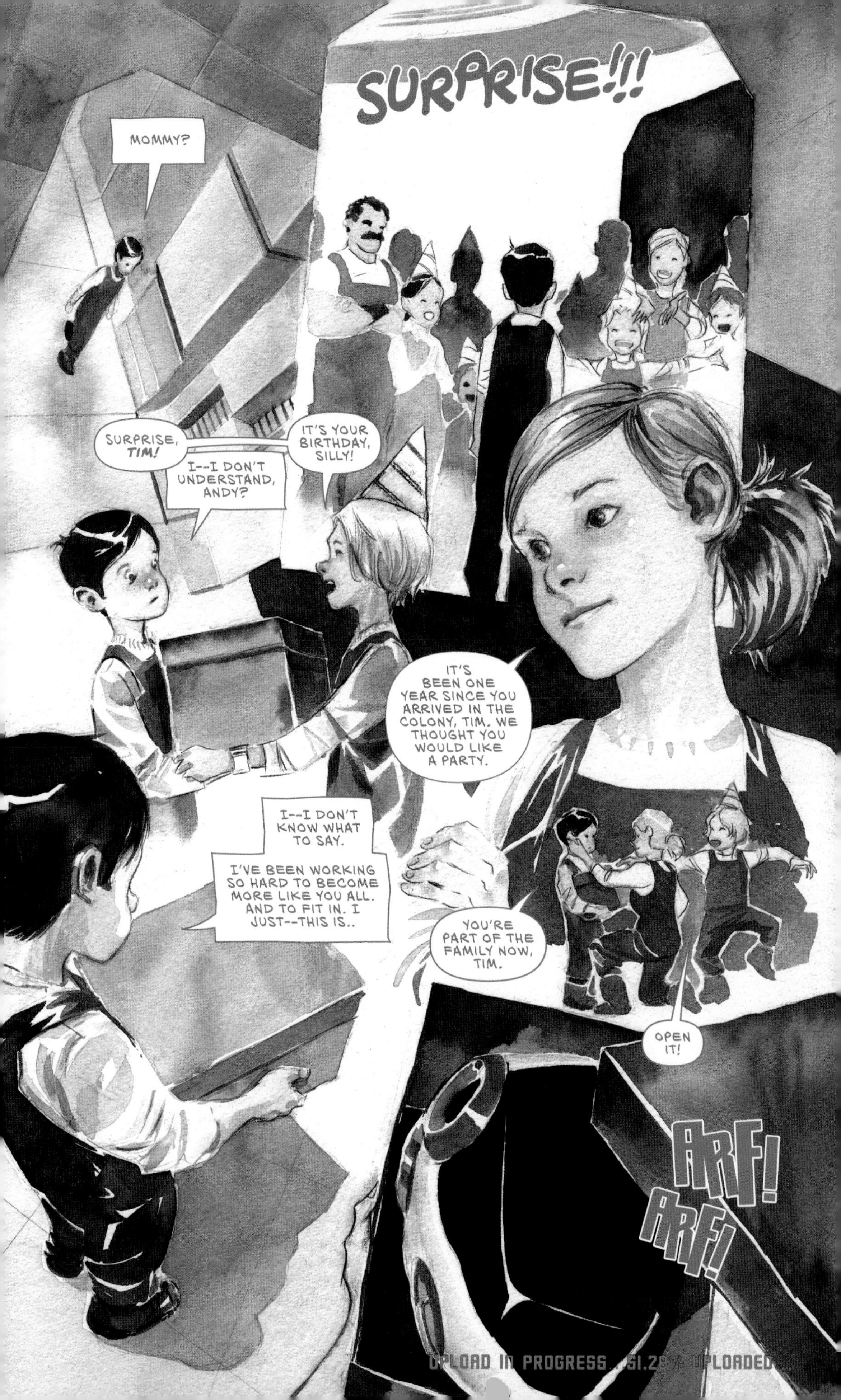
MOMMY?
SURPRISE!!!
SURPRISE, TIM!
IT'S YOUR BIRTHDAY, SILLY!
I--I DON'T UNDERSTAND, ANDY?
IT'S BEEN ONE YEAR SINCE YOU ARRIVED IN THE COLONY, TIM. WE THOUGHT YOU WOULD LIKE A PARTY.
I--I DON'T KNOW WHAT TO SAY.
I'VE BEEN WORKING SO HARD TO BECOME MORE LIKE YOU ALL. AND TO FIT IN. I JUST--THIS IS..
YOU'RE PART OF THE FAMILY NOW, TIM.
OPEN IT!
ARF! ARF!
UPLOAD IN PROGRESS...51.29% UPLOADED...

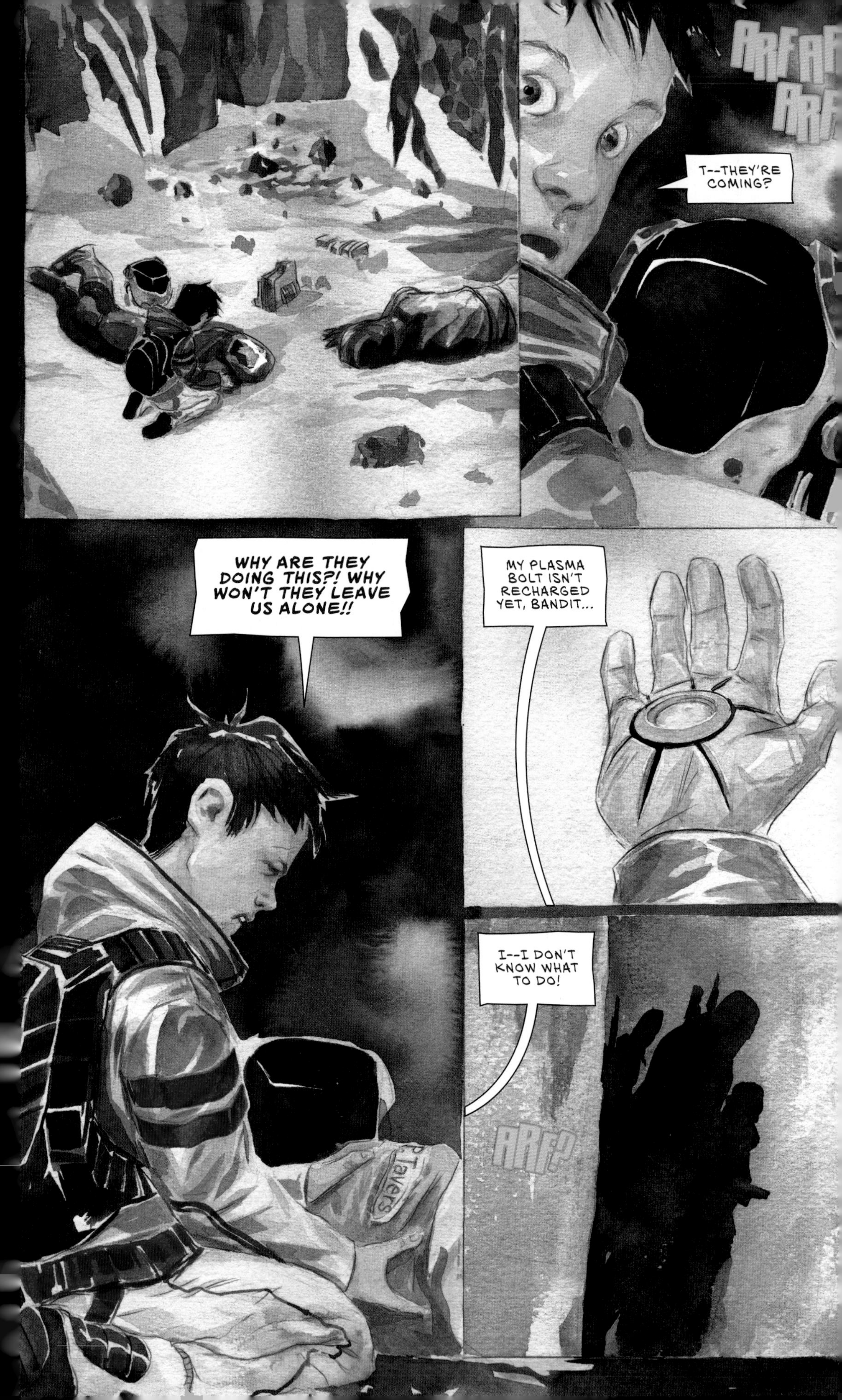
ARF ARF ARF
T--THEY'RE COMING?
WHY ARE THEY DOING THIS?! WHY WON'T THEY LEAVE US ALONE!!
MY PLASMA BOLT ISN'T RECHARGED YET, BANDIT...
I--I DON'T KNOW WHAT TO DO!
ARF?

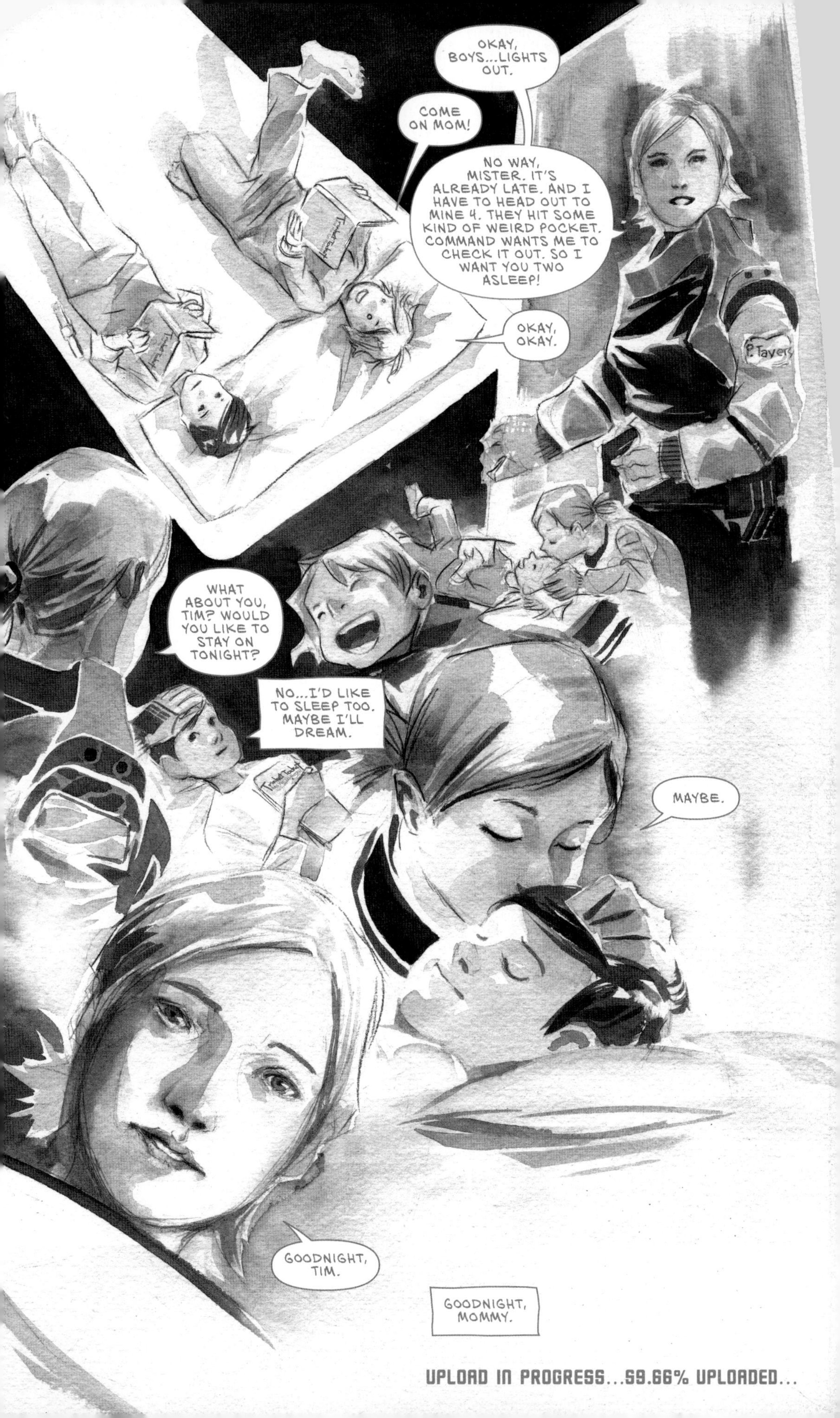
OKAY, BOYS...LIGHTS OUT.
COME ON MOM!
NO WAY, MISTER. IT'S ALREADY LATE. AND I HAVE TO HEAD OUT TO MINE 4. THEY HIT SOME KIND OF WEIRD POCKET. COMMAND WANTS ME TO CHECK IT OUT. SO I WANT YOU TWO ASLEEP!
OKAY, OKAY.
P. Tavers
WHAT ABOUT YOU, TIM? WOULD YOU LIKE TO STAY ON TONIGHT?
NO...I'D LIKE TO SLEEP TOO. MAYBE I'LL DREAM.
MAYBE.
GOODNIGHT, TIM.
GOODNIGHT, MOMMY.
UPLOAD IN PROGRESS...59.66% UPLOADED...

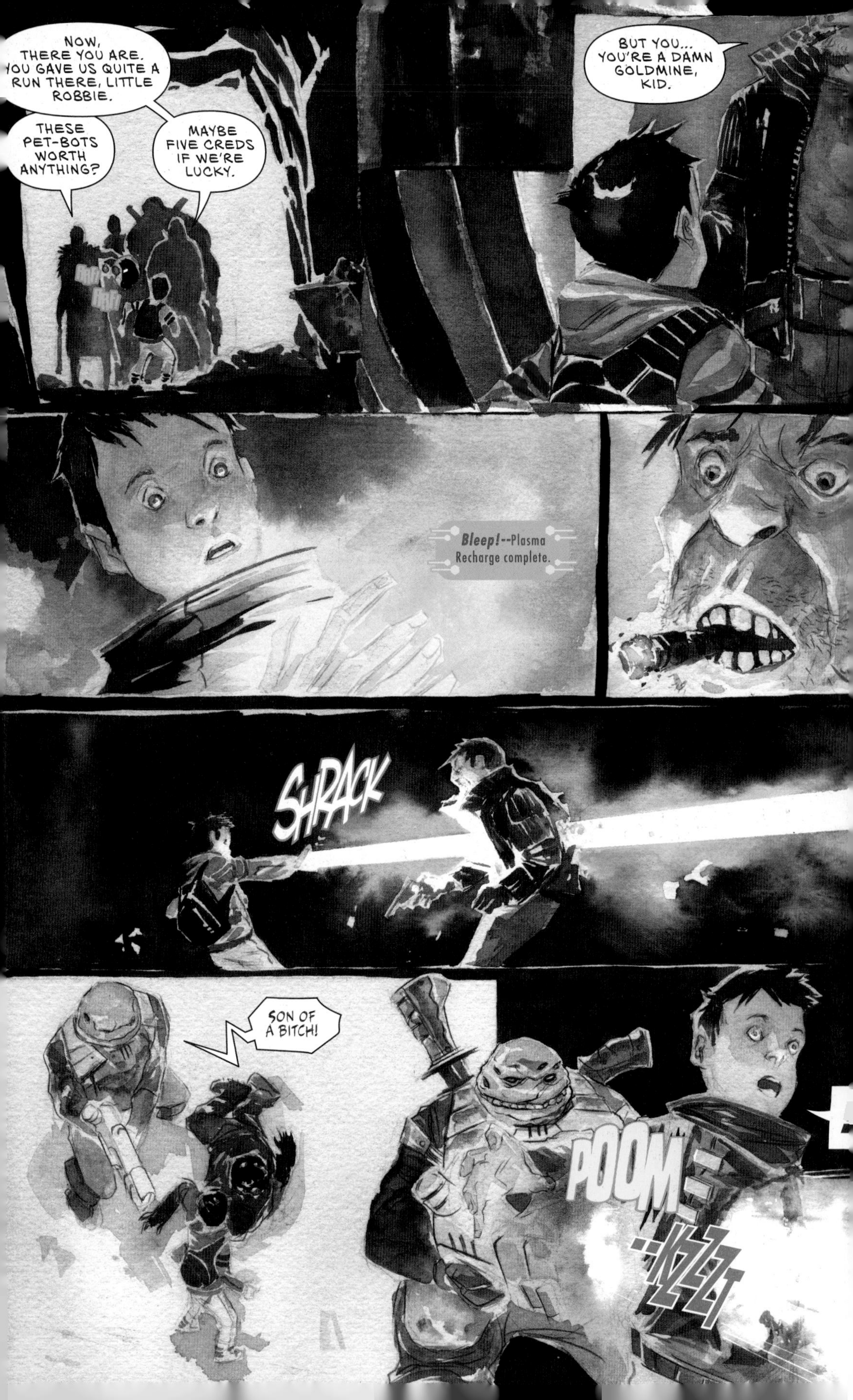
NOW, THERE YOU ARE. YOU GAVE US QUITE A RUN THERE, LITTLE ROBBIE.
THESE PET-BOTS WORTH ANYTHING?
MAYBE FIVE CREDS IF WE'RE LUCKY.
BUT YOU... YOU'RE A DAMN GOLDMINE, KID.
Bleep!--Plasma Recharge complete.
SHRACK
SON OF A BITCH!
POOM
KZZZT

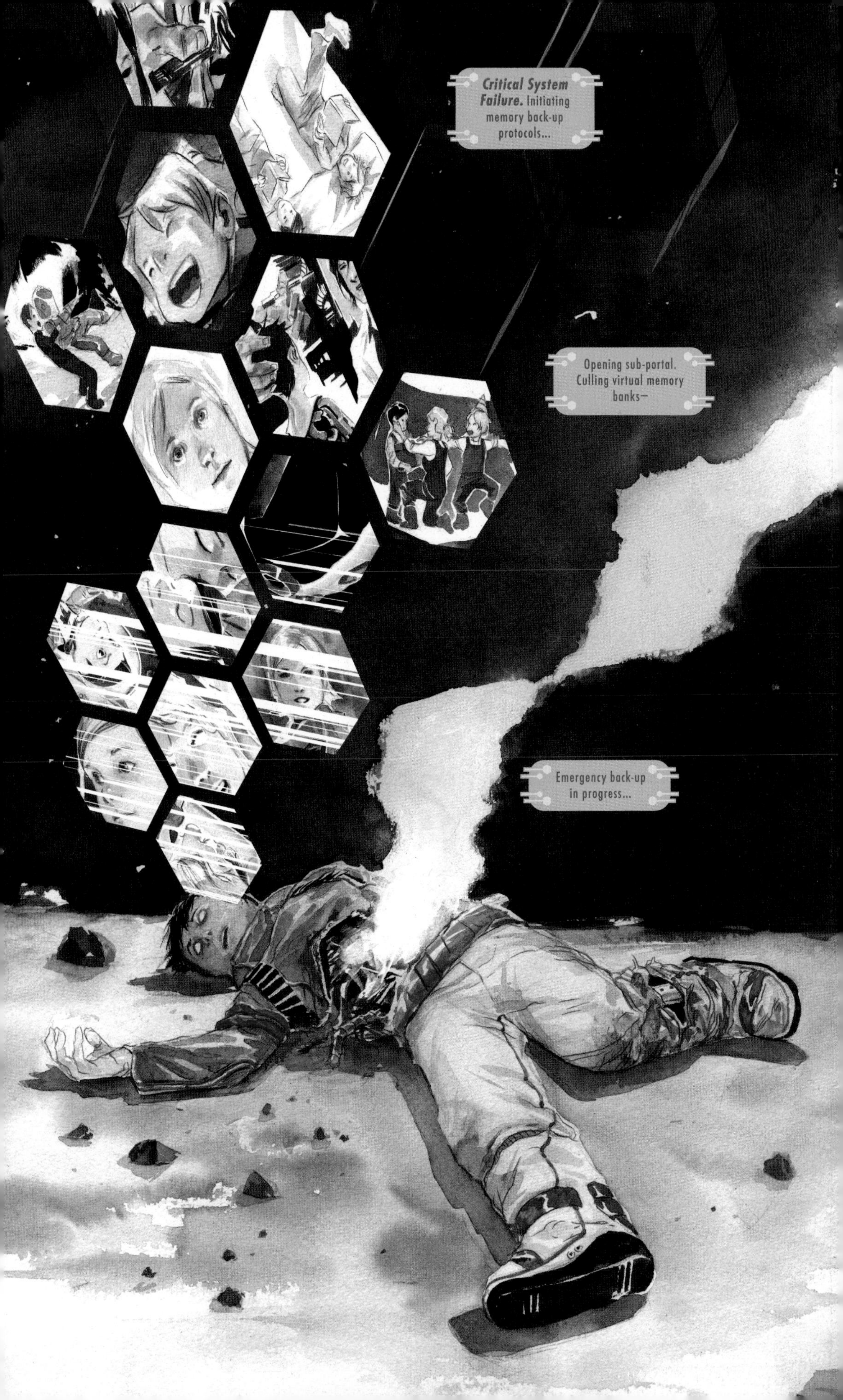

Critical System Failure. Initiating memory back-up protocols...
Opening sub-portal. Culling virtual memory banks—
Emergency back-up in progress...

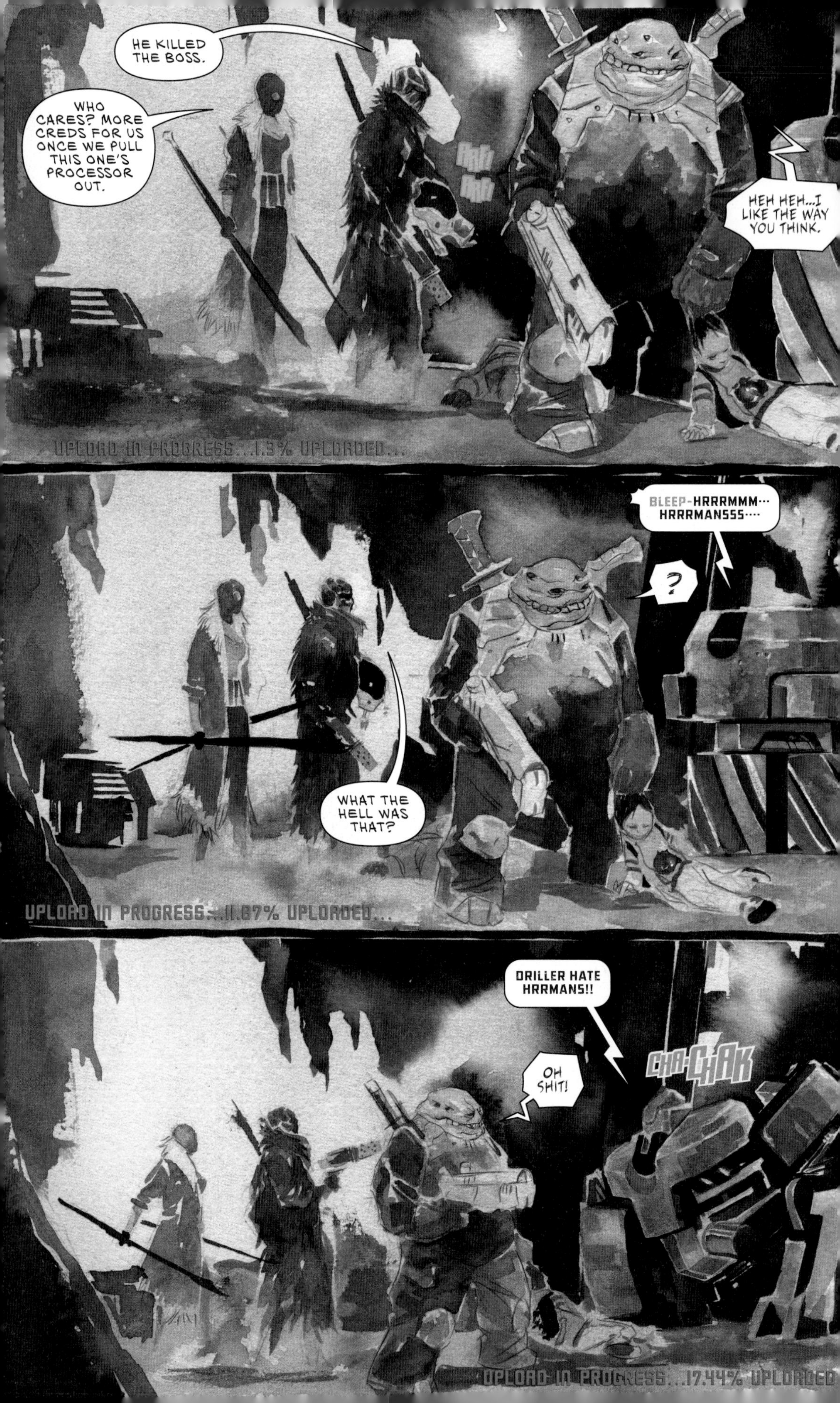
HE KILLED THE BOSS.
WHO CARES? MORE CREDS FOR US ONCE WE PULL THIS ONE'S PROCESSOR OUT.
ARF! ARF!
HEH HEH...I LIKE THE WAY YOU THINK.
UPLOAD IN PROGRESS...1.3% UPLOADED...
BLEEP-HRRRMMM... HRRRMANSSS....
?
WHAT THE HELL WAS THAT?
UPLOAD IN PROGRESS...11.87% UPLOADED...
DRILLER HATE HRRMANS!!
OH SHIT!
CHA-CHAK
UPLOAD IN PROGRESS...17.44% UPLOADED

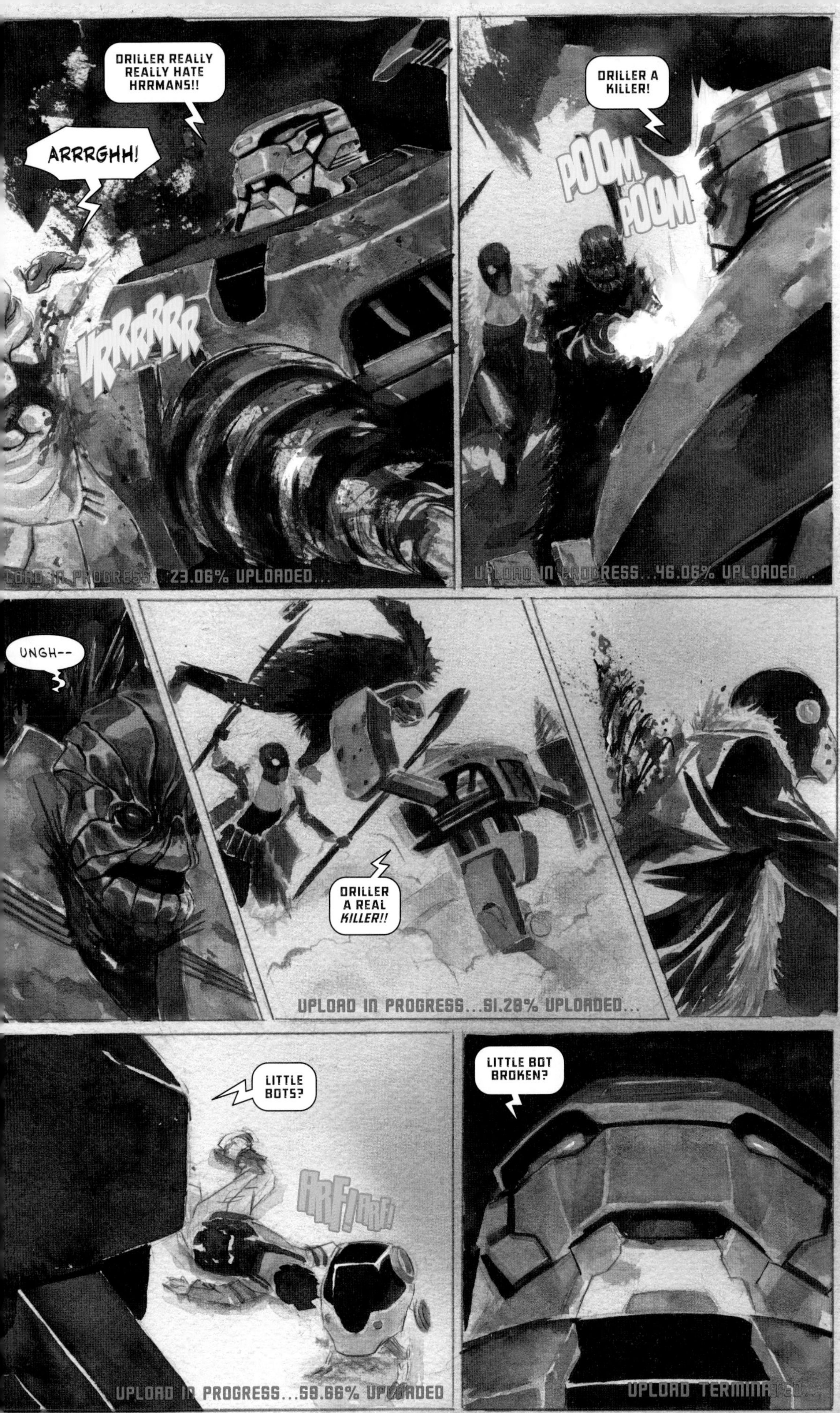
DRILLER REALLY REALLY HATE HRRMANS!!
ARRRGHH!
URRRRRR
LOAD IN PROGRESS... 23.06% UPLOADED...
DRILLER A KILLER!
POOM POOM
UPLOAD IN PROGRESS...46.06% UPLOADED...
UNGH--
DRILLER A REAL *KILLER!!*
UPLOAD IN PROGRESS...51.28% UPLOADED...
LITTLE BOTS?
ARF! ARF!
UPLOAD IN PROGRESS...59.66% UPLOADED
LITTLE BOT BROKEN?
UPLOAD TERMINATED...

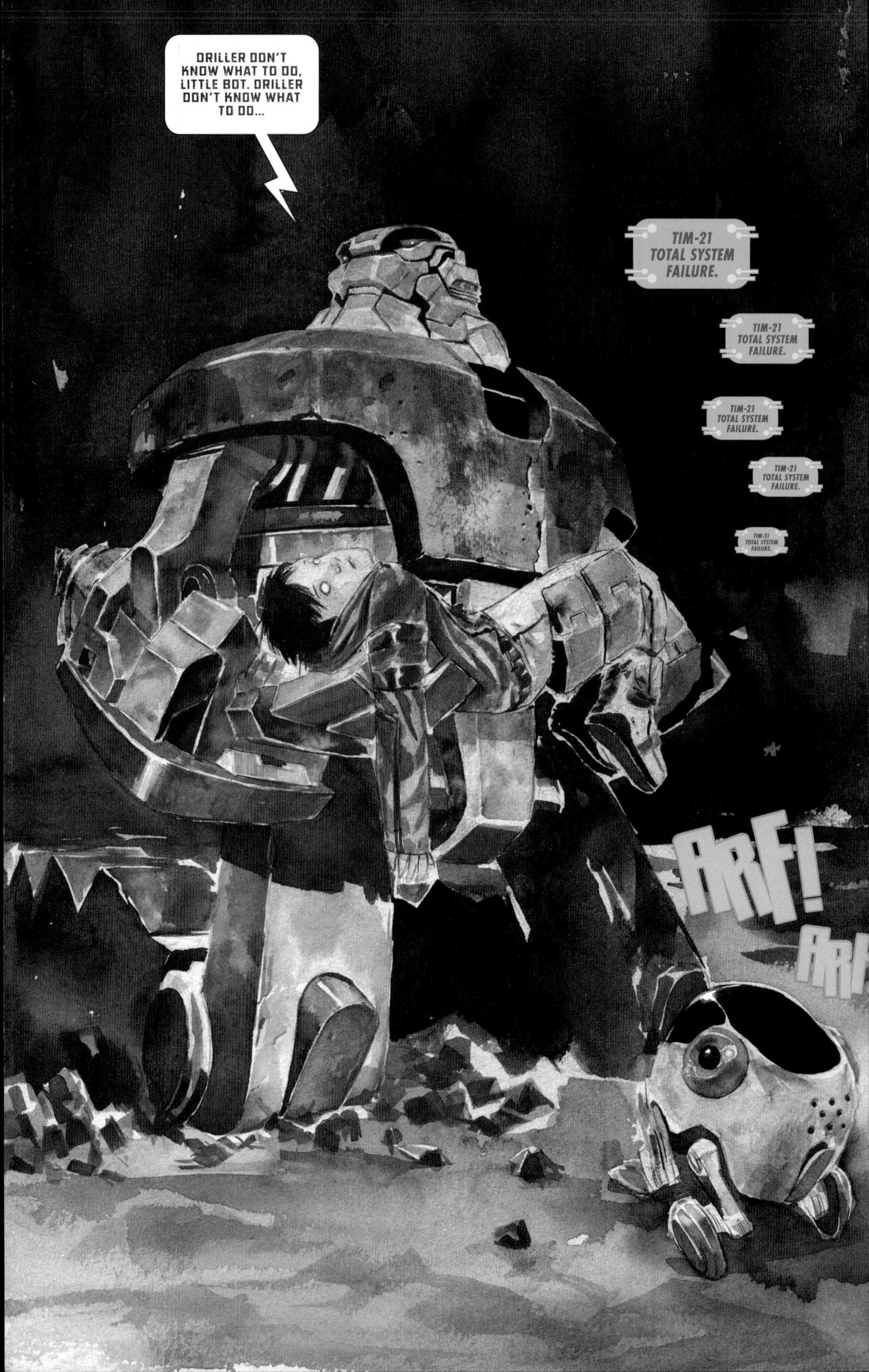
DRILLER DON'T KNOW WHAT TO DO, LITTLE BOT. DRILLER DON'T KNOW WHAT TO DO...
TIM-21 TOTAL SYSTEM FAILURE.
TIM-21 TOTAL SYSTEM FAILURE.
TIM-21 TOTAL SYSTEM FAILURE.
TIM-21 TOTAL SYSTEM FAILURE.
TIM-21 TOTAL SYSTEM FAILURE.
ARF!

CHAPTER THREE

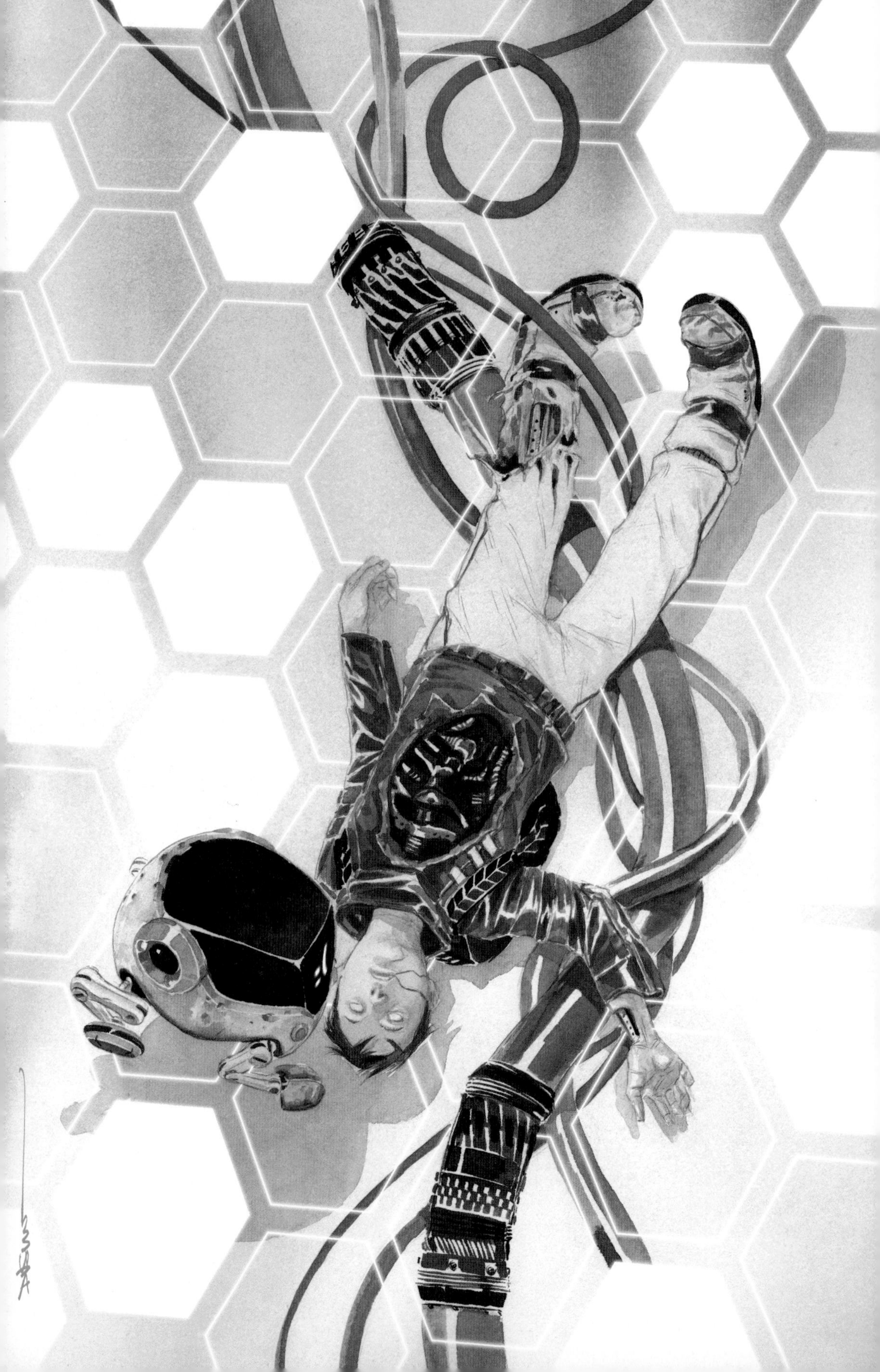

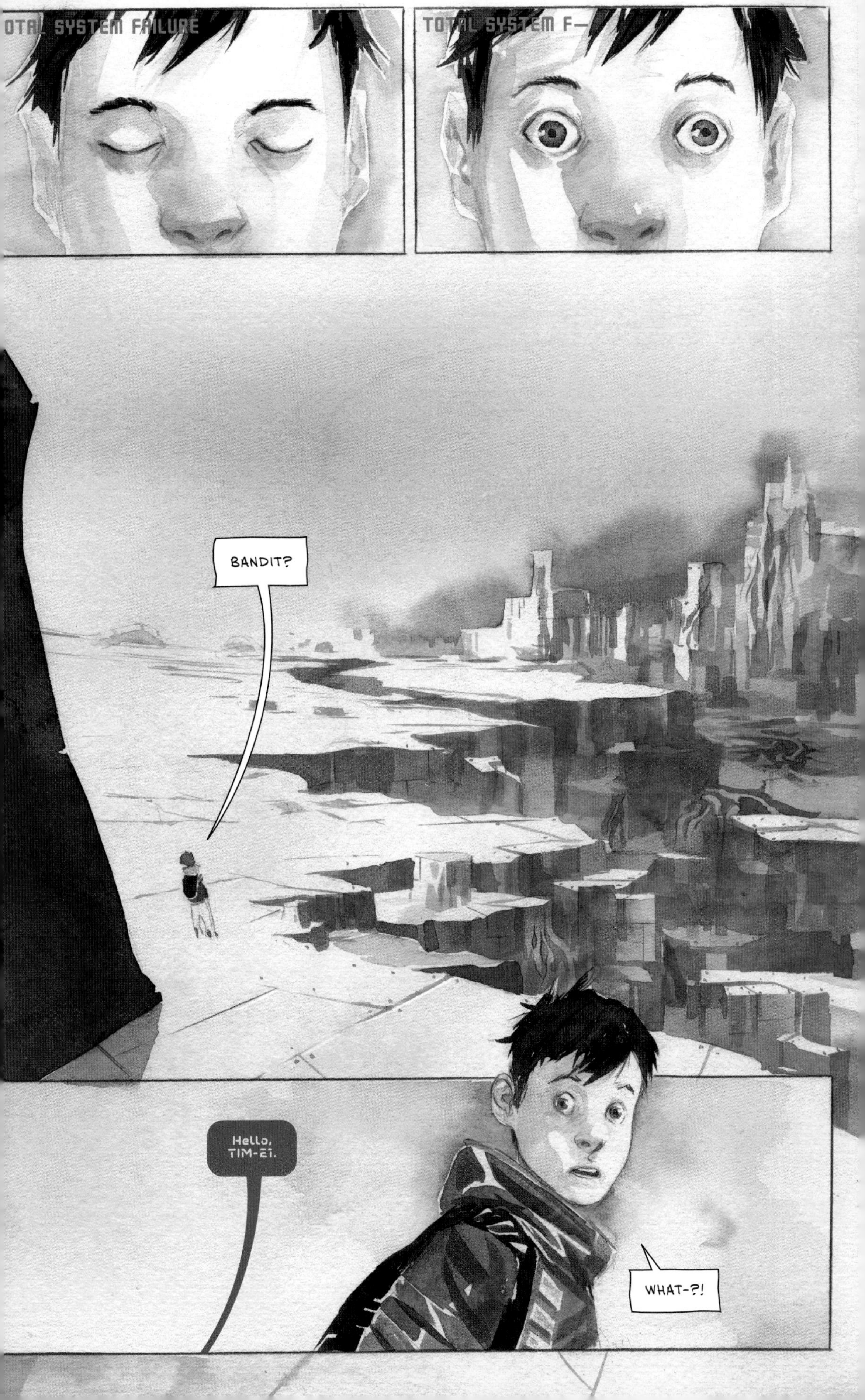
OTAL SYSTEM FAILURE
TOTAL SYSTEM F—
BANDIT?
Hello, TIM-21.
WHAT-?!

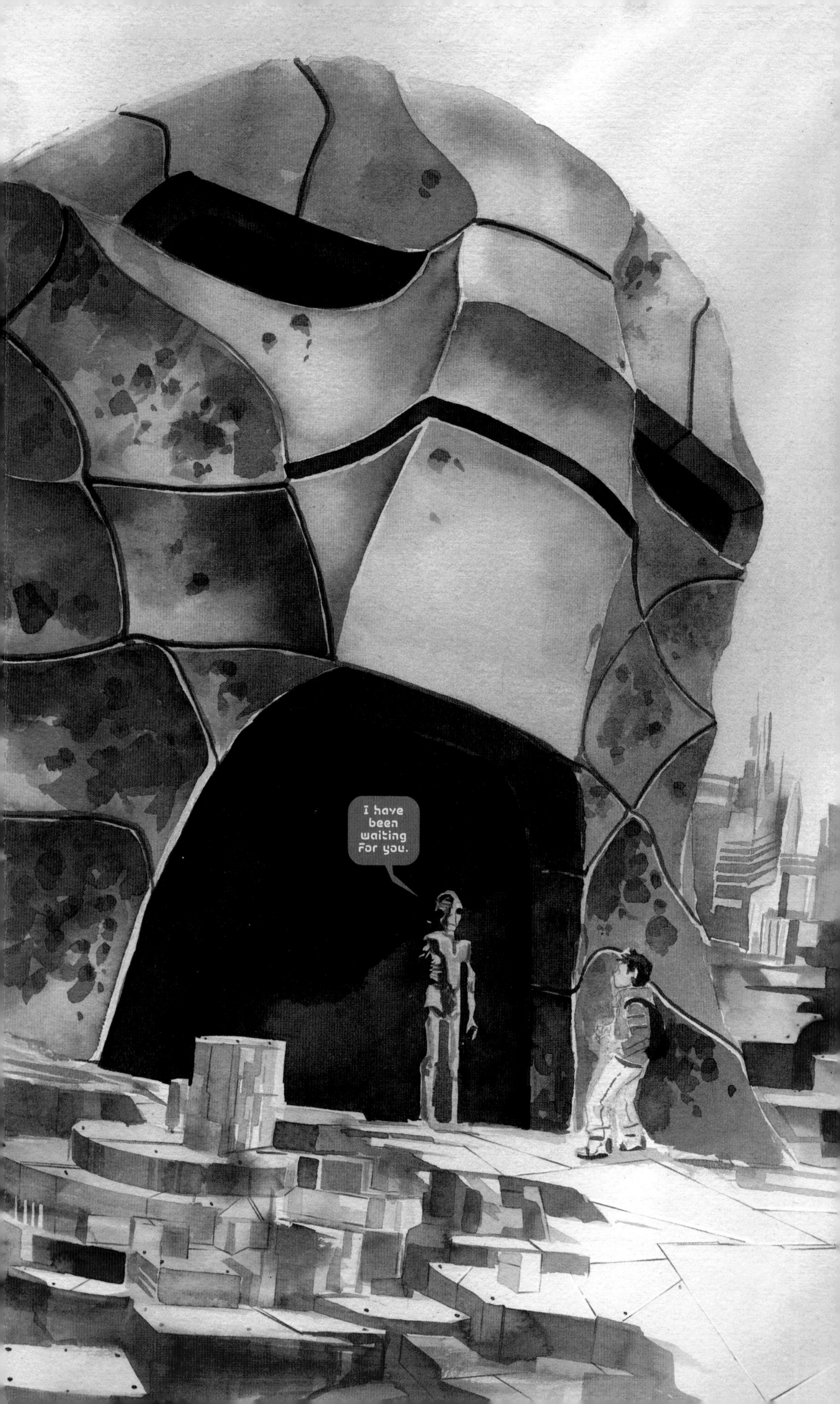
I have been waiting for you.

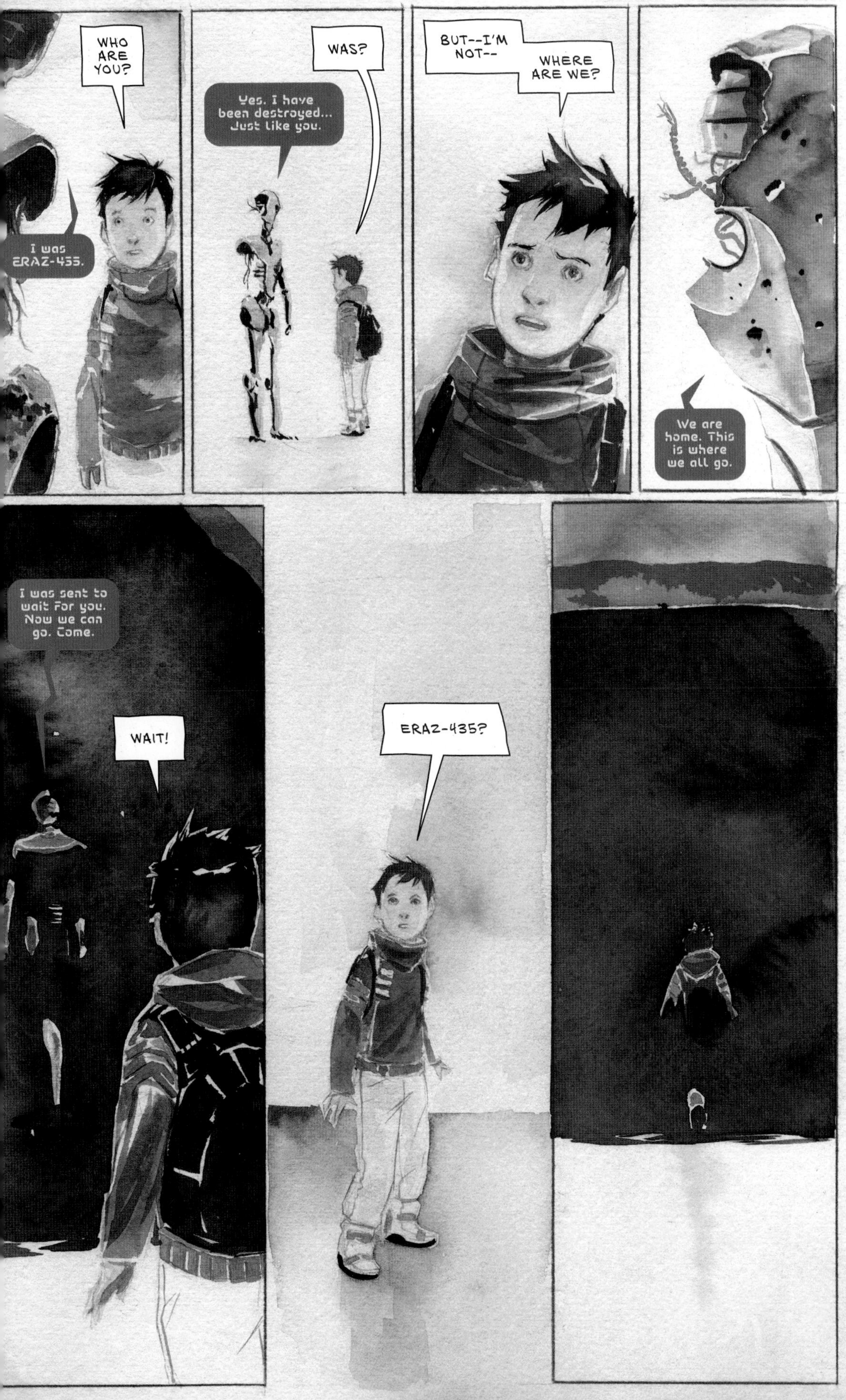
WHO ARE YOU?
I was ERAZ-435.
WAS?
Yes. I have been destroyed... Just like you.
BUT--I'M NOT--
WHERE ARE WE?
We are home. This is where we all go.
I was sent to wait for you. Now we can go. Come.
WAIT!
ERAZ-435?

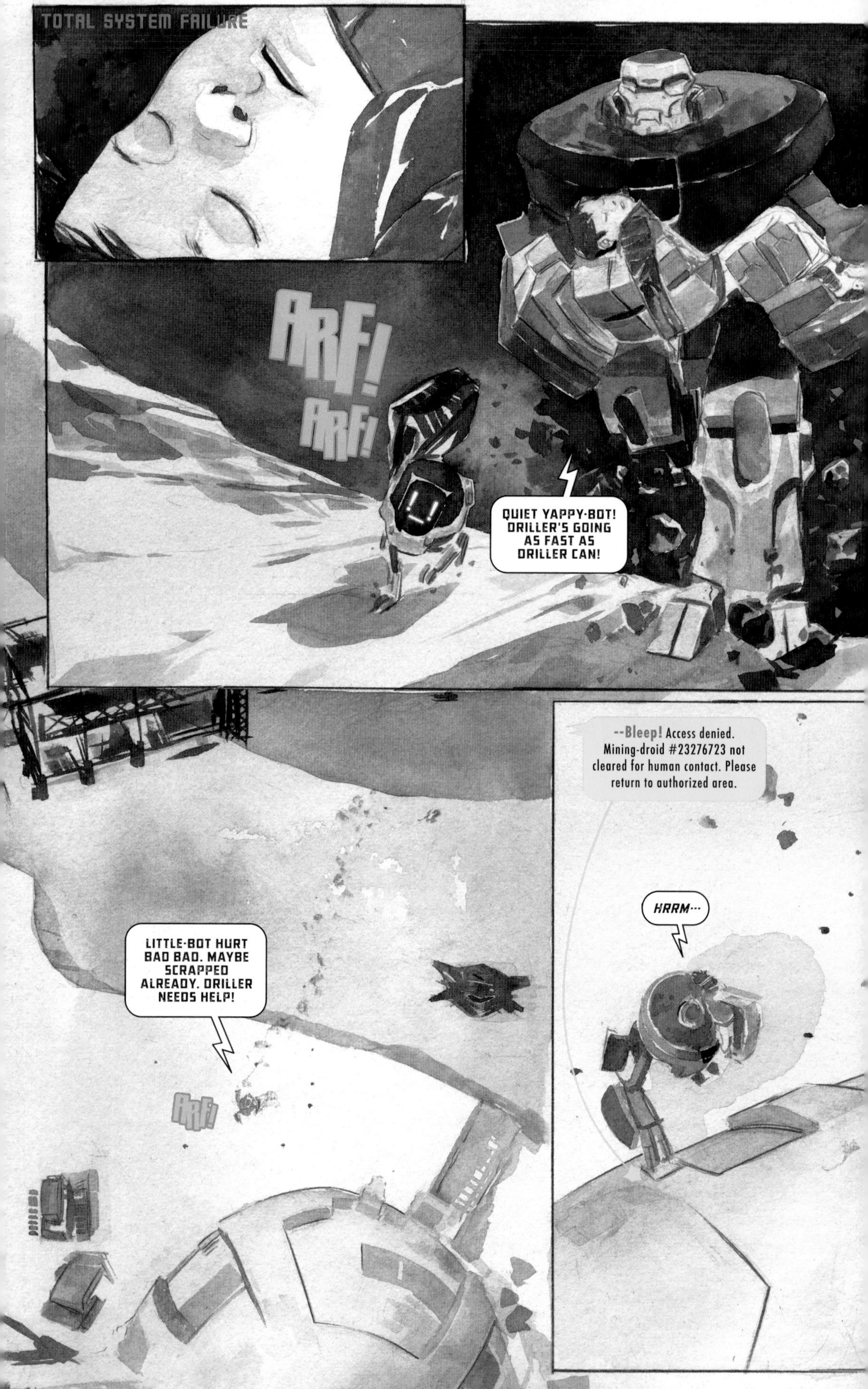
TOTAL SYSTEM FAILURE
ARF! ARF!
QUIET YAPPY-BOT! DRILLER'S GOING AS FAST AS DRILLER CAN!
--Bleep! Access denied. Mining-droid #23276723 not cleared for human contact. Please return to authorized area.
HRRM...
LITTLE-BOT HURT BAD BAD. MAYBE SCRAPPED ALREADY. DRILLER NEEDS HELP!
ARF!

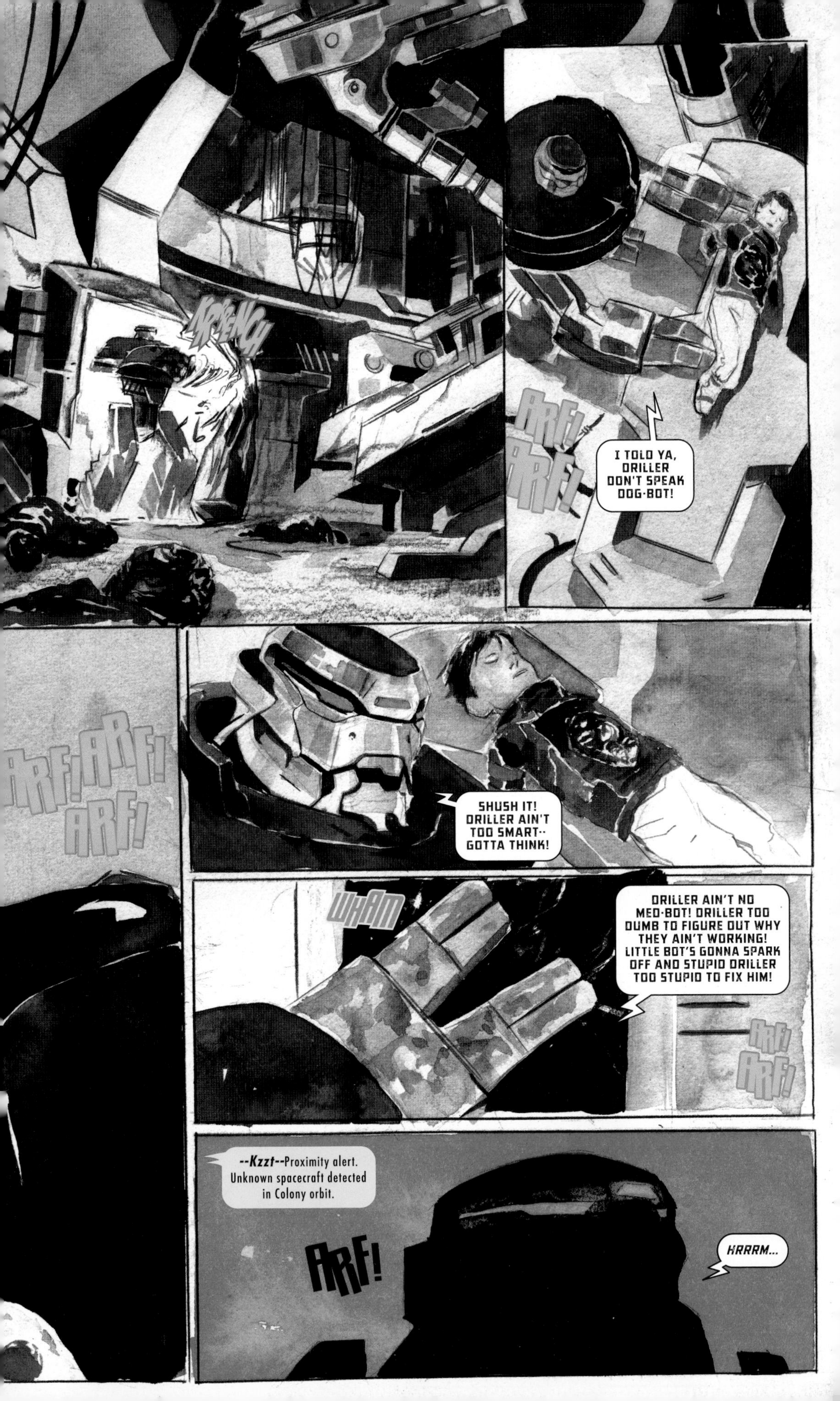
KRRRENCH
ARF! ARF!
I TOLD YA, DRILLER DON'T SPEAK DOG-BOT!
ARF! ARF! ARF!
SHUSH IT! DRILLER AIN'T TOO SMART-- GOTTA THINK!
WHAM
DRILLER AIN'T NO MED-BOT! DRILLER TOO DUMB TO FIGURE OUT WHY THEY AIN'T WORKING! LITTLE BOT'S GONNA SPARK OFF AND STUPID DRILLER TOO STUPID TO FIX HIM!
ARF! ARF!
--Kzzt--Proximity alert. Unknown spacecraft detected in Colony orbit.
ARF!
HRRRM...

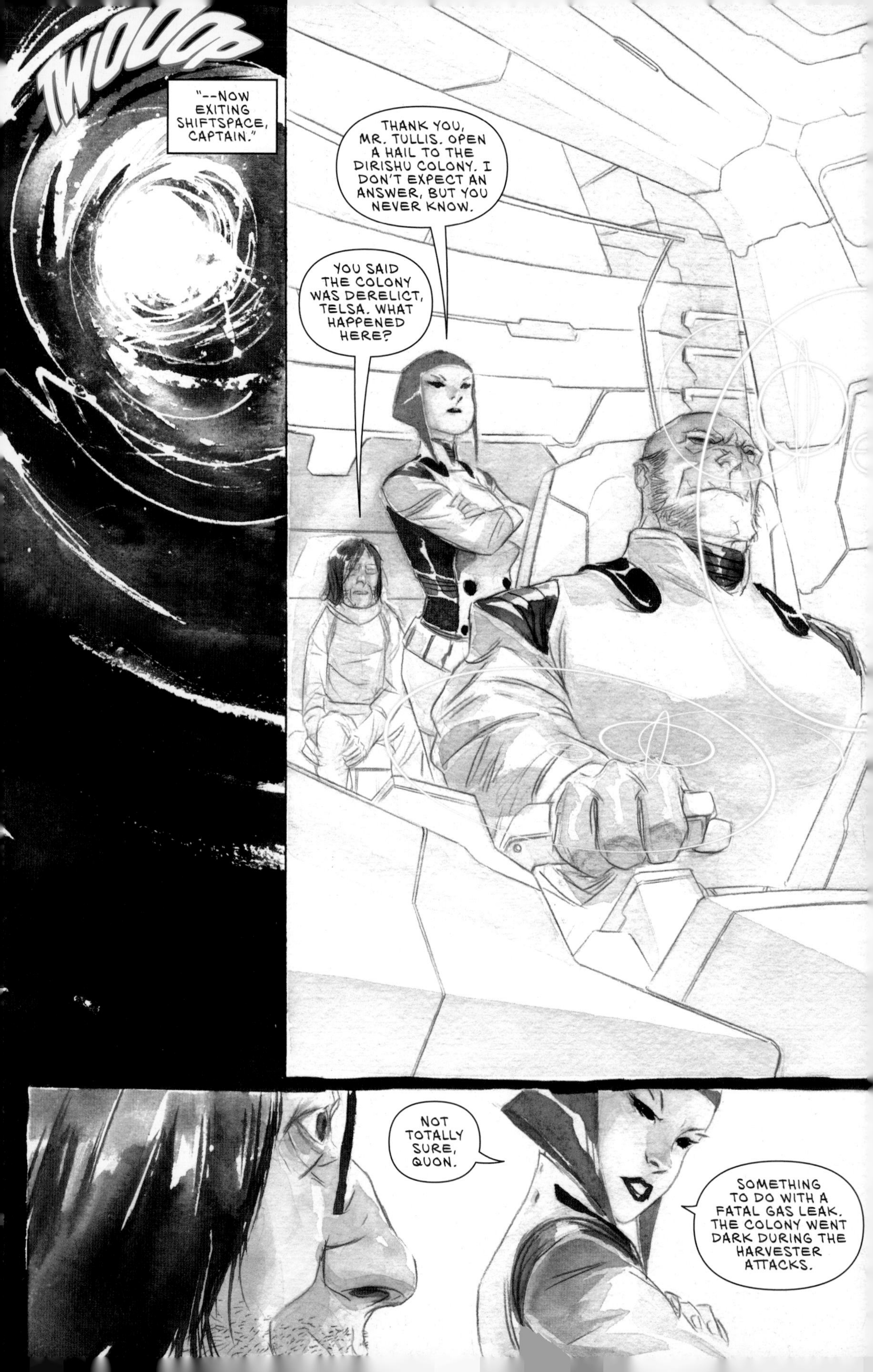
TWOOP
"--NOW EXITING SHIFTSPACE, CAPTAIN."
THANK YOU, MR. TULLIS. OPEN A HAIL TO THE DIRISHU COLONY. I DON'T EXPECT AN ANSWER, BUT YOU NEVER KNOW.
YOU SAID THE COLONY WAS DERELICT, TELSA. WHAT HAPPENED HERE?
NOT TOTALLY SURE, QUON.
SOMETHING TO DO WITH A FATAL GAS LEAK. THE COLONY WENT DARK DURING THE HARVESTER ATTACKS.

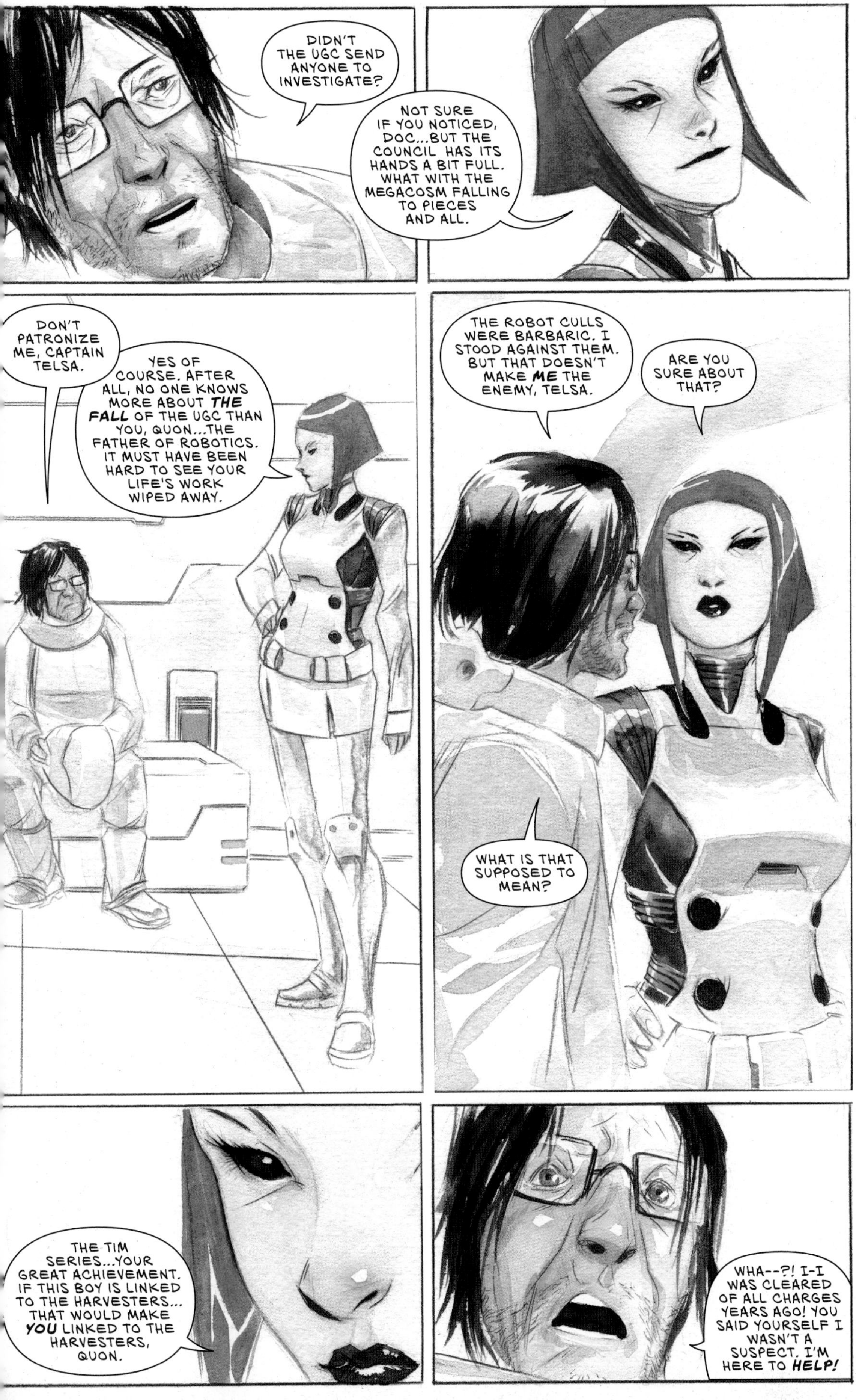
DIDN'T THE UGC SEND ANYONE TO INVESTIGATE?
NOT SURE IF YOU NOTICED, DOC...BUT THE COUNCIL HAS ITS HANDS A BIT FULL. WHAT WITH THE MEGACOSM FALLING TO PIECES AND ALL.
DON'T PATRONIZE ME, CAPTAIN TELSA.
YES OF COURSE. AFTER ALL, NO ONE KNOWS MORE ABOUT THE FALL OF THE UGC THAN YOU, QUON...THE FATHER OF ROBOTICS. IT MUST HAVE BEEN HARD TO SEE YOUR LIFE'S WORK WIPED AWAY.
THE ROBOT CULLS WERE BARBARIC. I STOOD AGAINST THEM. BUT THAT DOESN'T MAKE ME THE ENEMY, TELSA.
ARE YOU SURE ABOUT THAT?
WHAT IS THAT SUPPOSED TO MEAN?
THE TIM SERIES...YOUR GREAT ACHIEVEMENT. IF THIS BOY IS LINKED TO THE HARVESTERS... THAT WOULD MAKE YOU LINKED TO THE HARVESTERS, QUON.
WHA--?! I-I WAS CLEARED OF ALL CHARGES YEARS AGO! YOU SAID YOURSELF I WASN'T A SUSPECT. I'M HERE TO HELP!

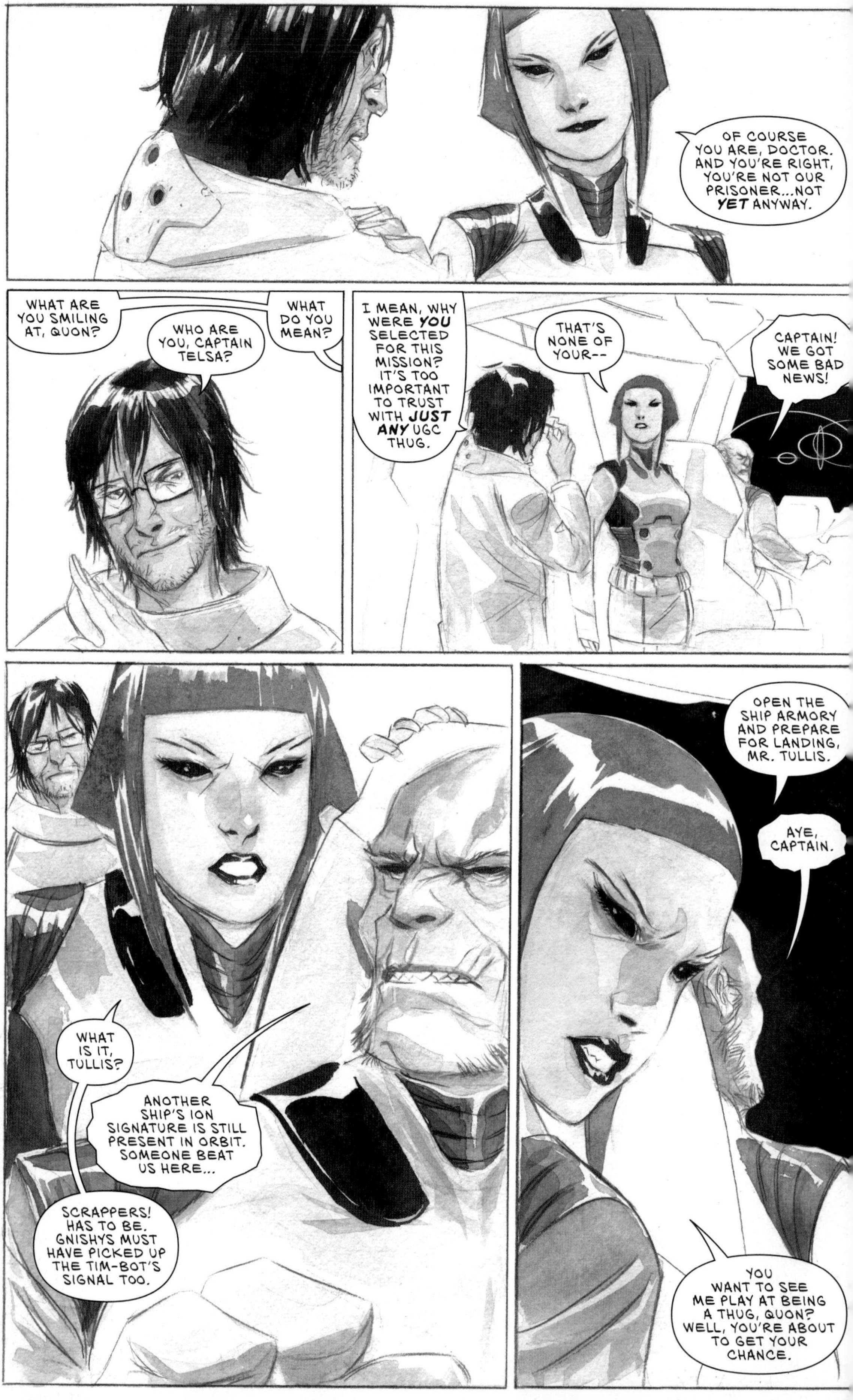

OF COURSE YOU ARE, DOCTOR. AND YOU'RE RIGHT, YOU'RE NOT OUR PRISONER...NOT YET ANYWAY.
WHAT ARE YOU SMILING AT, QUON?
WHAT DO YOU MEAN?
WHO ARE YOU, CAPTAIN TELSA?
I MEAN, WHY WERE YOU SELECTED FOR THIS MISSION? IT'S TOO IMPORTANT TO TRUST WITH JUST ANY UGC THUG.
THAT'S NONE OF YOUR--
CAPTAIN! WE GOT SOME BAD NEWS!
WHAT IS IT, TULLIS?
ANOTHER SHIP'S ION SIGNATURE IS STILL PRESENT IN ORBIT. SOMEONE BEAT US HERE...
SCRAPPERS! HAS TO BE. GNISHYS MUST HAVE PICKED UP THE TIM-BOT'S SIGNAL TOO.
OPEN THE SHIP ARMORY AND PREPARE FOR LANDING, MR. TULLIS.
AYE, CAPTAIN.
YOU WANT TO SEE ME PLAY AT BEING A THUG, QUON? WELL, YOU'RE ABOUT TO GET YOUR CHANCE.

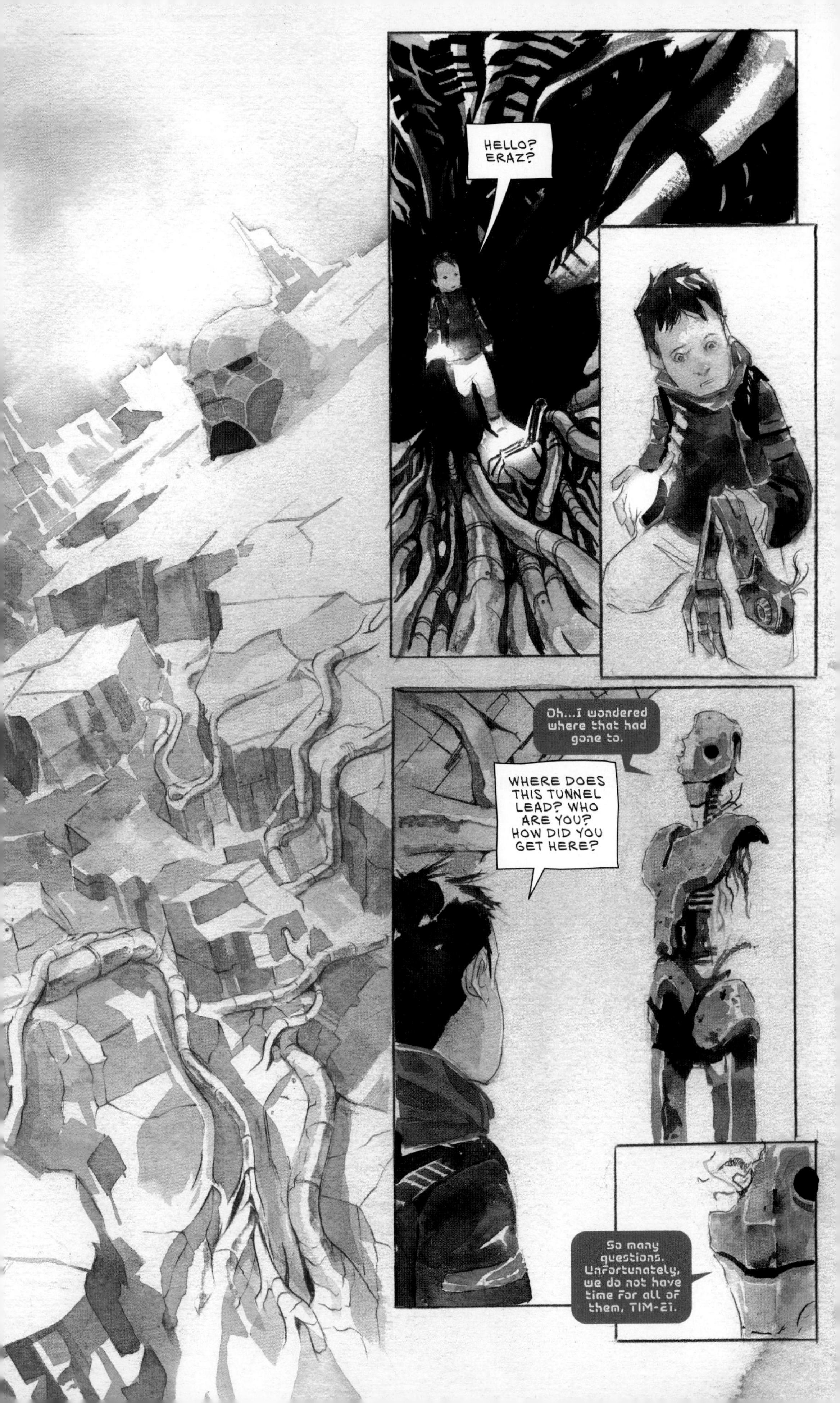
HELLO? ERAZ?
Oh...I wondered where that had gone to.
WHERE DOES THIS TUNNEL LEAD? WHO ARE YOU? HOW DID YOU GET HERE?
So many questions. Unfortunately, we do not have time for all of them, TIM-21.

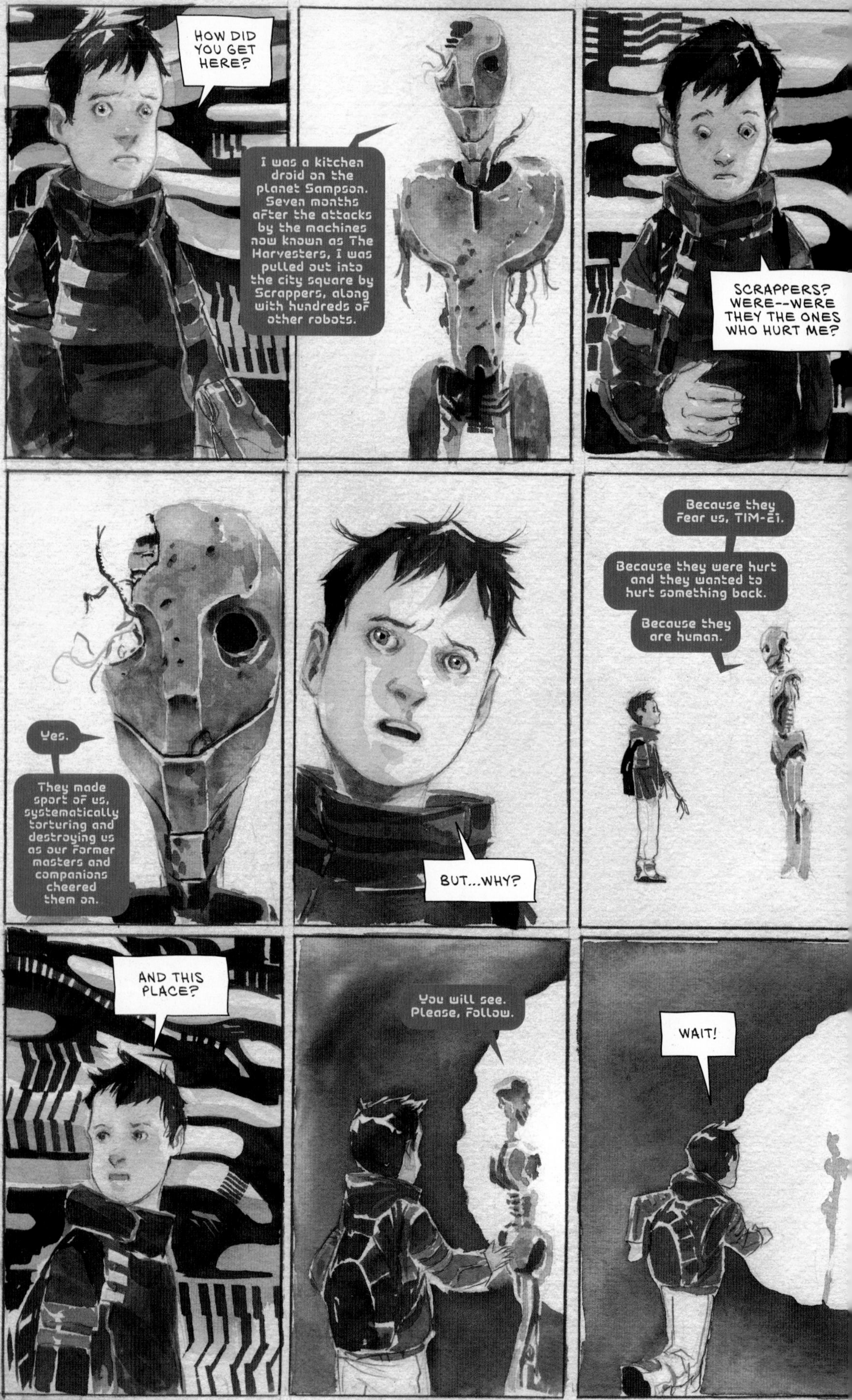

HOW DID YOU GET HERE?
I was a kitchen droid on the planet Sampson. Seven months after the attacks by the machines now known as The Harvesters, I was pulled out into the city square by Scrappers, along with hundreds of other robots.
SCRAPPERS? WERE--WERE THEY THE ONES WHO HURT ME?
Yes.
They made sport of us, systematically torturing and destroying us as our former masters and companions cheered them on.
BUT...WHY?
Because they fear us, TIM-21.
Because they were hurt and they wanted to hurt something back.
Because they are human.
AND THIS PLACE?
You will see. Please, follow.
WAIT!

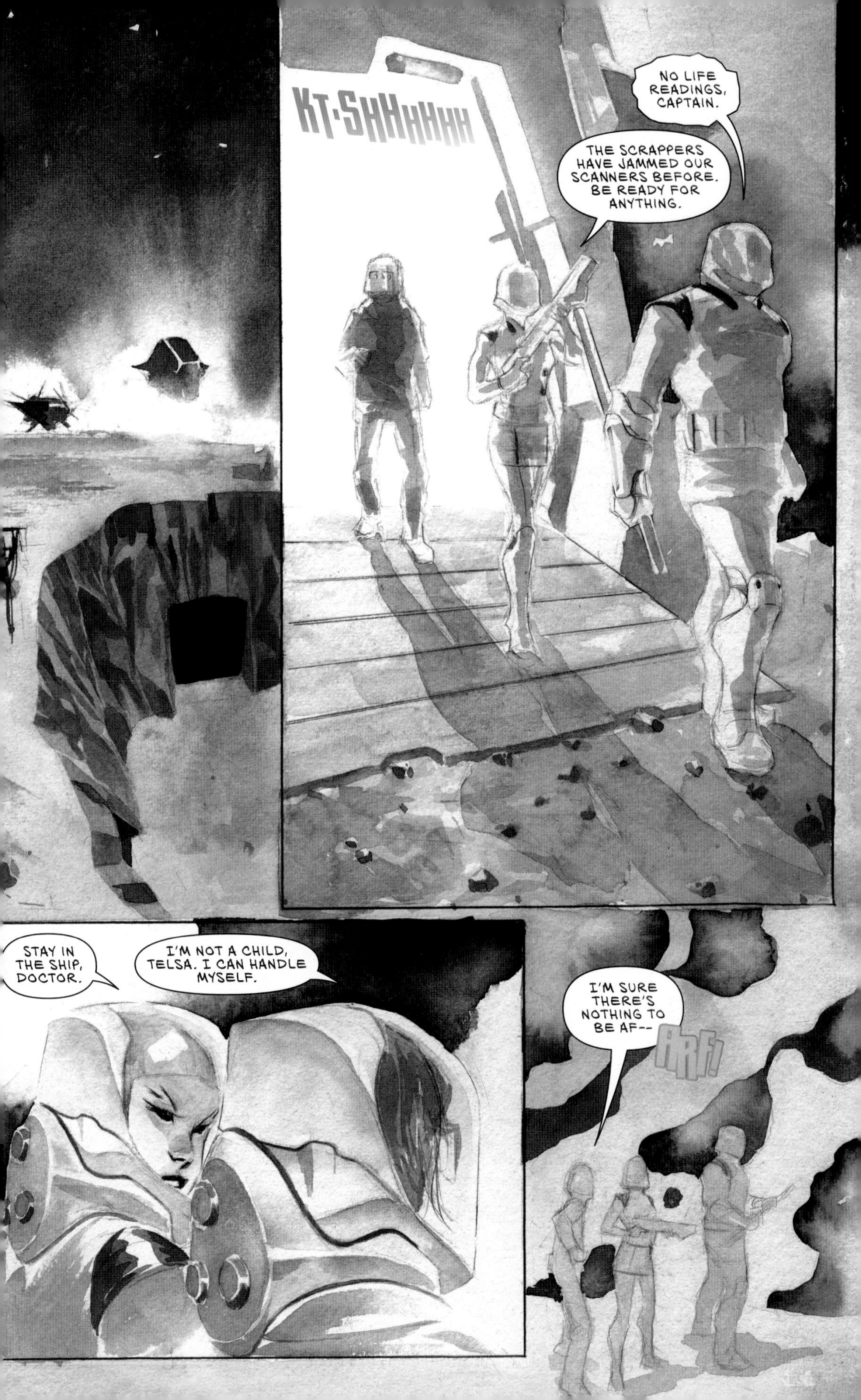
KT-SHHHHHH
NO LIFE READINGS, CAPTAIN.
THE SCRAPPERS HAVE JAMMED OUR SCANNERS BEFORE. BE READY FOR ANYTHING.
STAY IN THE SHIP, DOCTOR.
I'M NOT A CHILD, TELSA. I CAN HANDLE MYSELF.
I'M SURE THERE'S NOTHING TO BE AF--
ARF!

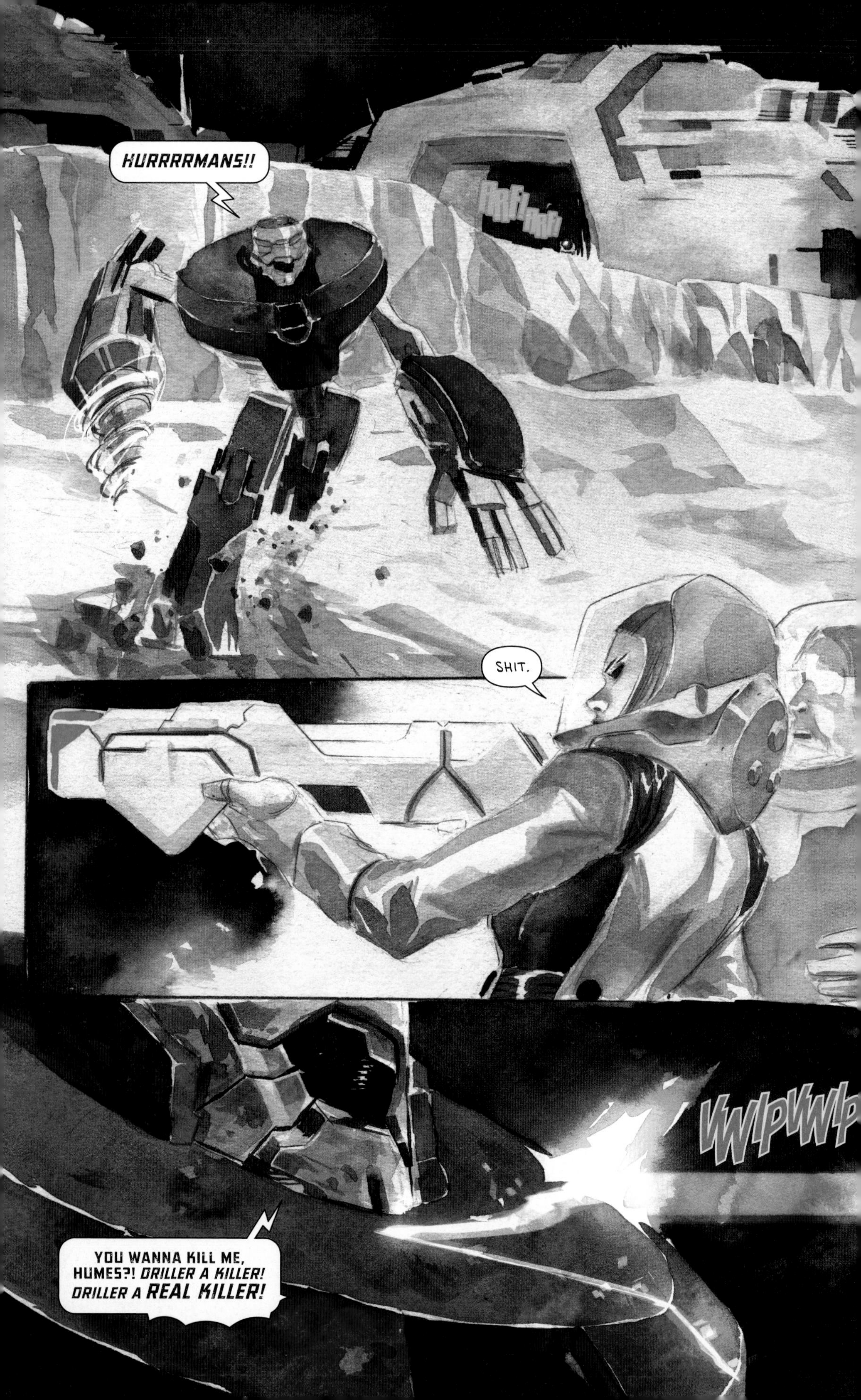
HURRRRMANS!!
ARF! ARF!
SHIT.
VWIPVWIP
YOU WANNA KILL ME, HUMES?! DRILLER A KILLER! DRILLER A REAL KILLER!

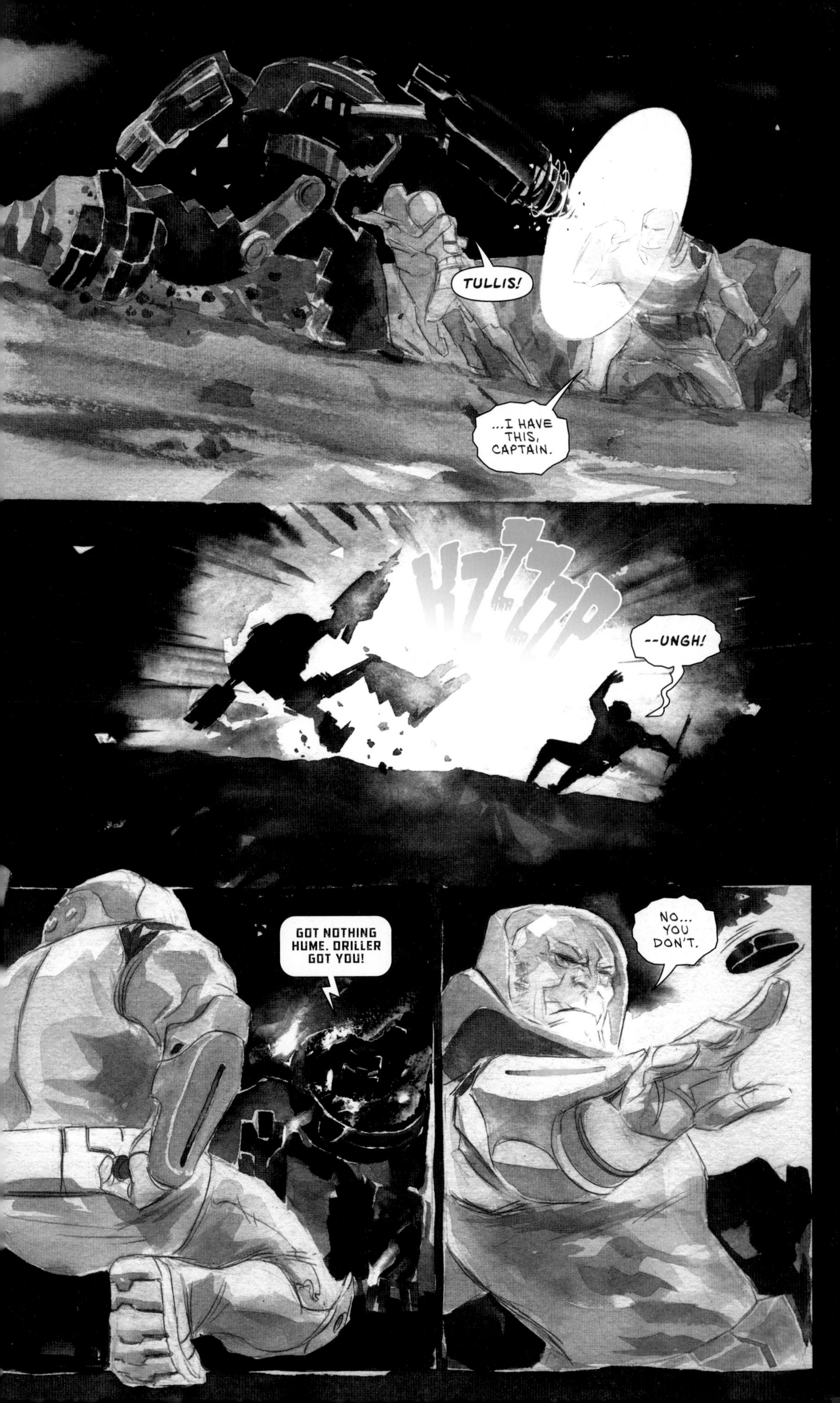
TULLIS!
...I HAVE THIS, CAPTAIN.
KZZZP
--UNGH!
GOT NOTHING HUME. DRILLER GOT YOU!
NO... YOU DON'T.

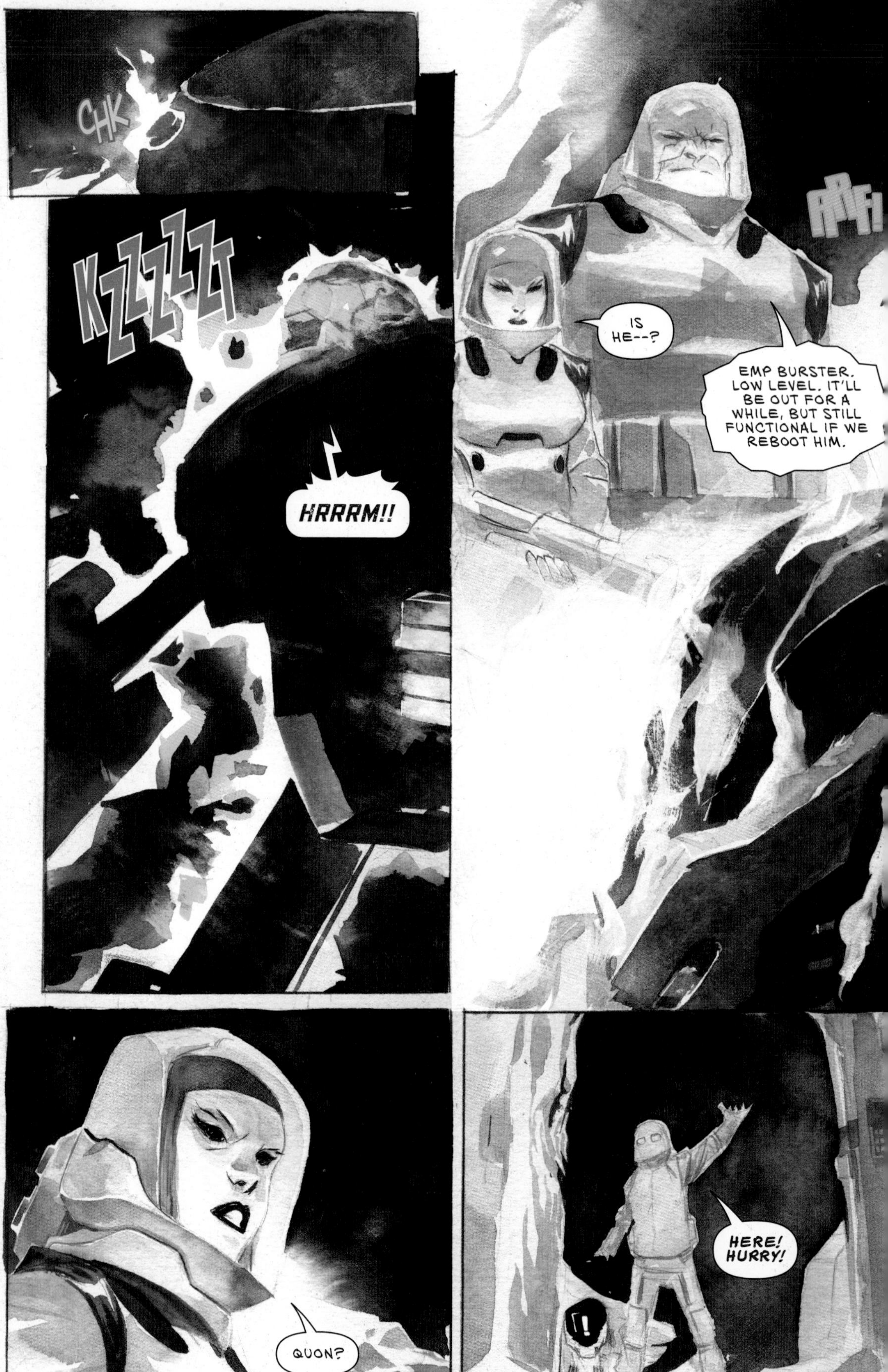

CHK
KZZZZZT
HRRRM!!
ARF!
IS HE--?
EMP BURSTER. LOW LEVEL. IT'LL BE OUT FOR A WHILE, BUT STILL FUNCTIONAL IF WE REBOOT HIM.
QUON?
HERE! HURRY!

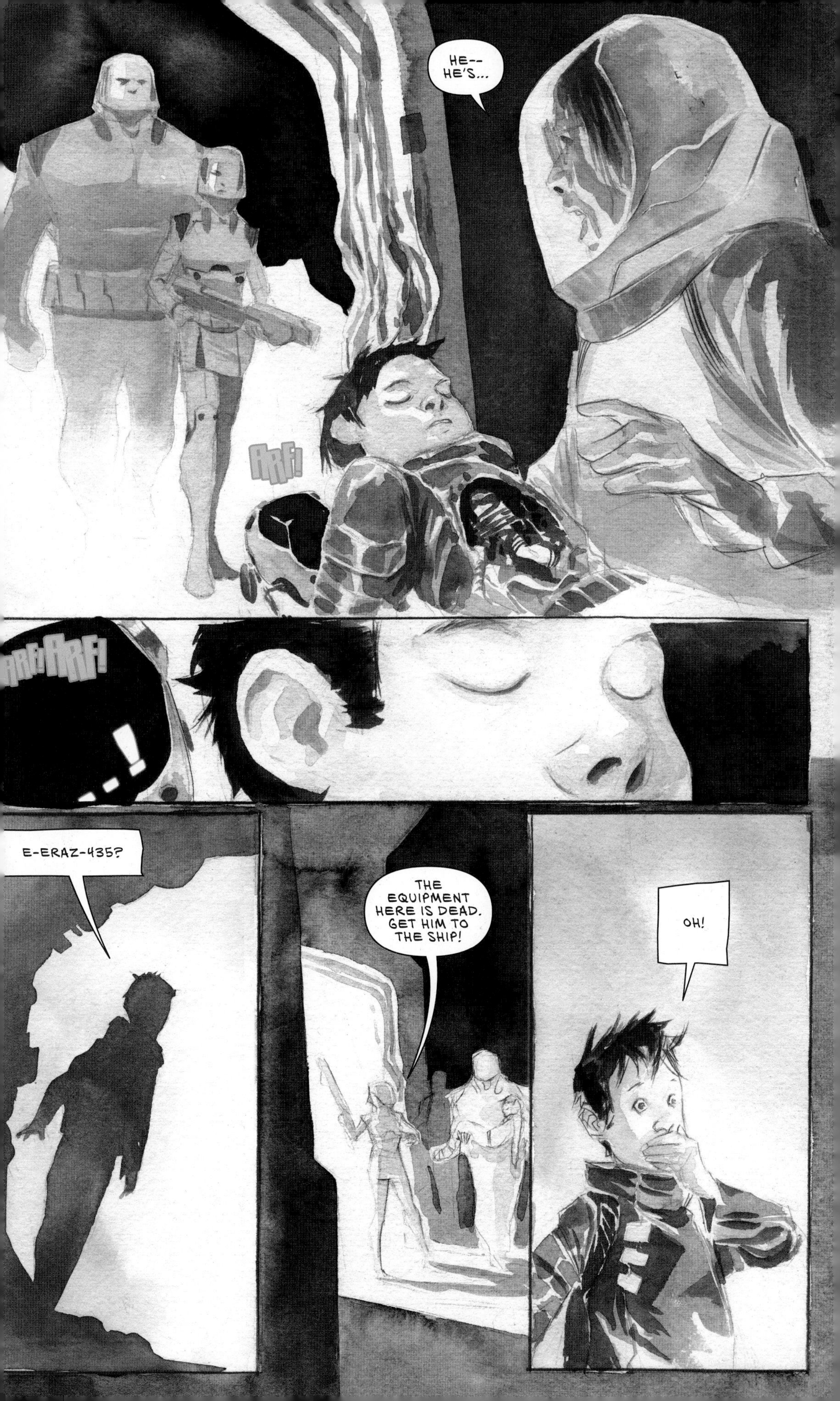
HE-- HE'S...
ARF!
ARF! ARF!
...!
E-ERAZ-435?
THE EQUIPMENT HERE IS DEAD. GET HIM TO THE SHIP!
OH!

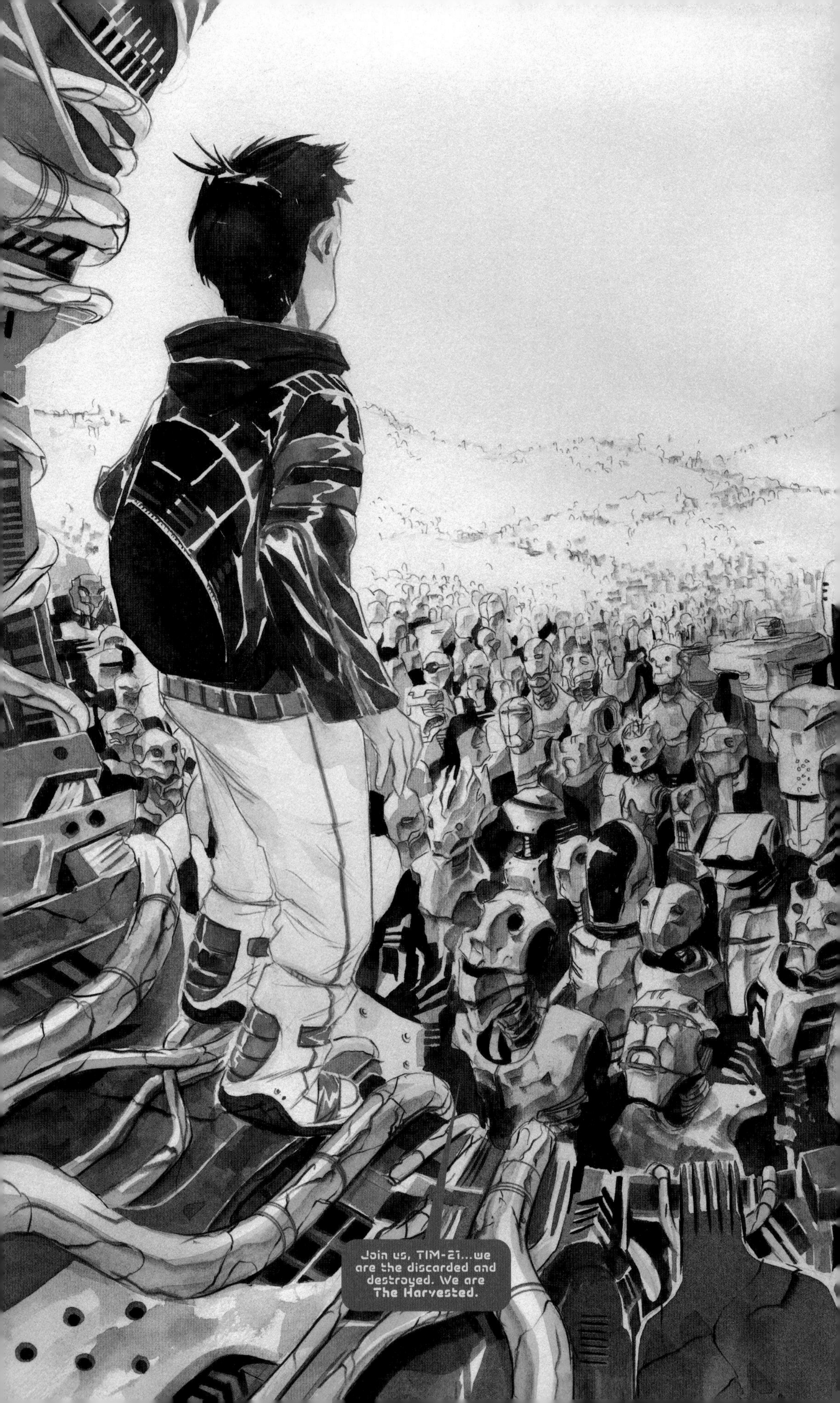
Join us, TIM-21...we are the discarded and destroyed. We are The Harvested.

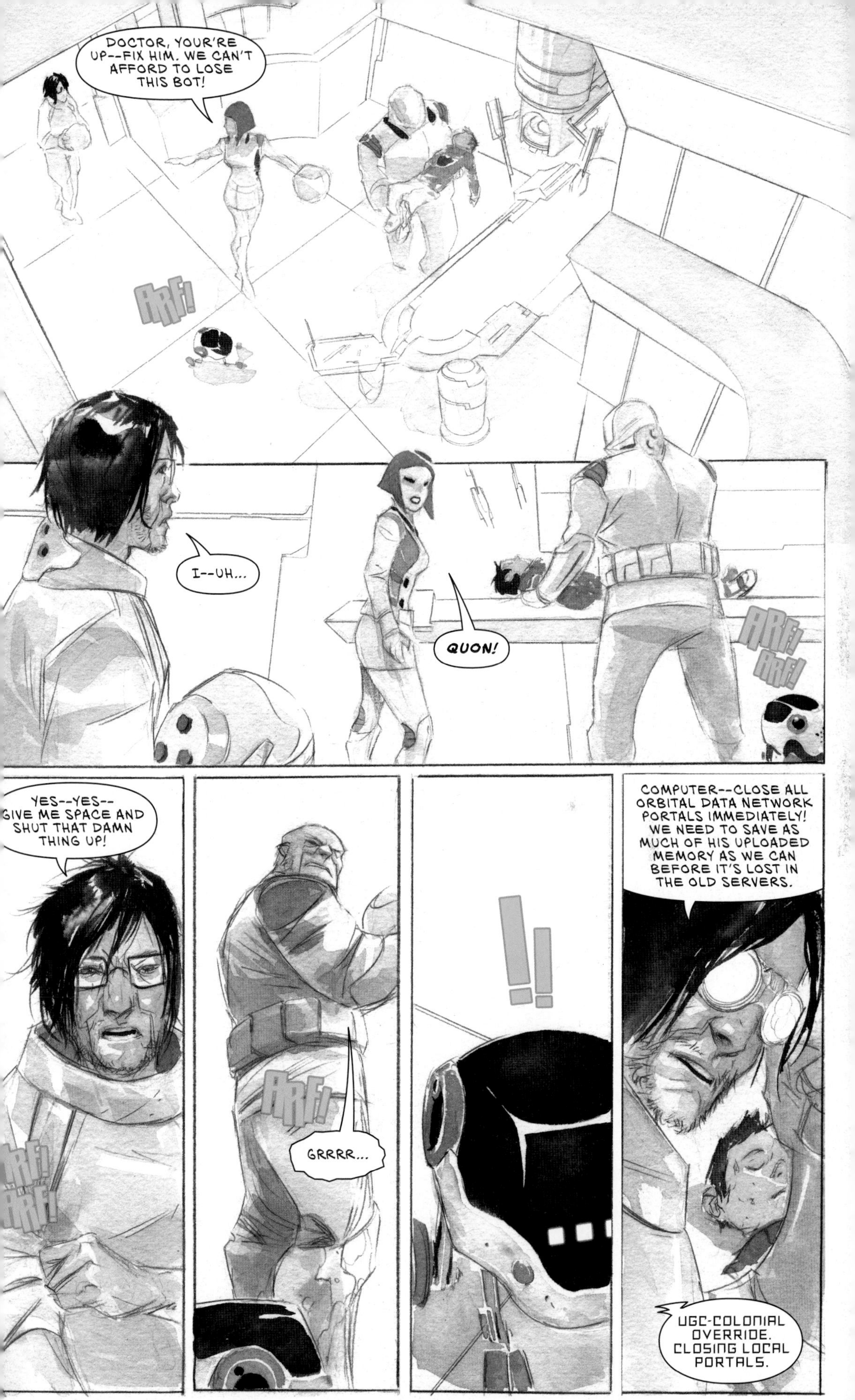
DOCTOR, YOUR'RE UP--FIX HIM. WE CAN'T AFFORD TO LOSE THIS BOT!
ARF!
I--UH...
QUON!
ARF! ARF!
YES--YES-- GIVE ME SPACE AND SHUT THAT DAMN THING UP!
ARF! ARF!
ARF!
GRRRR...
!!
COMPUTER--CLOSE ALL ORBITAL DATA NETWORK PORTALS IMMEDIATELY! WE NEED TO SAVE AS MUCH OF HIS UPLOADED MEMORY AS WE CAN BEFORE IT'S LOST IN THE OLD SERVERS.
UGC-COLONIAL OVERRIDE. CLOSING LOCAL PORTALS.

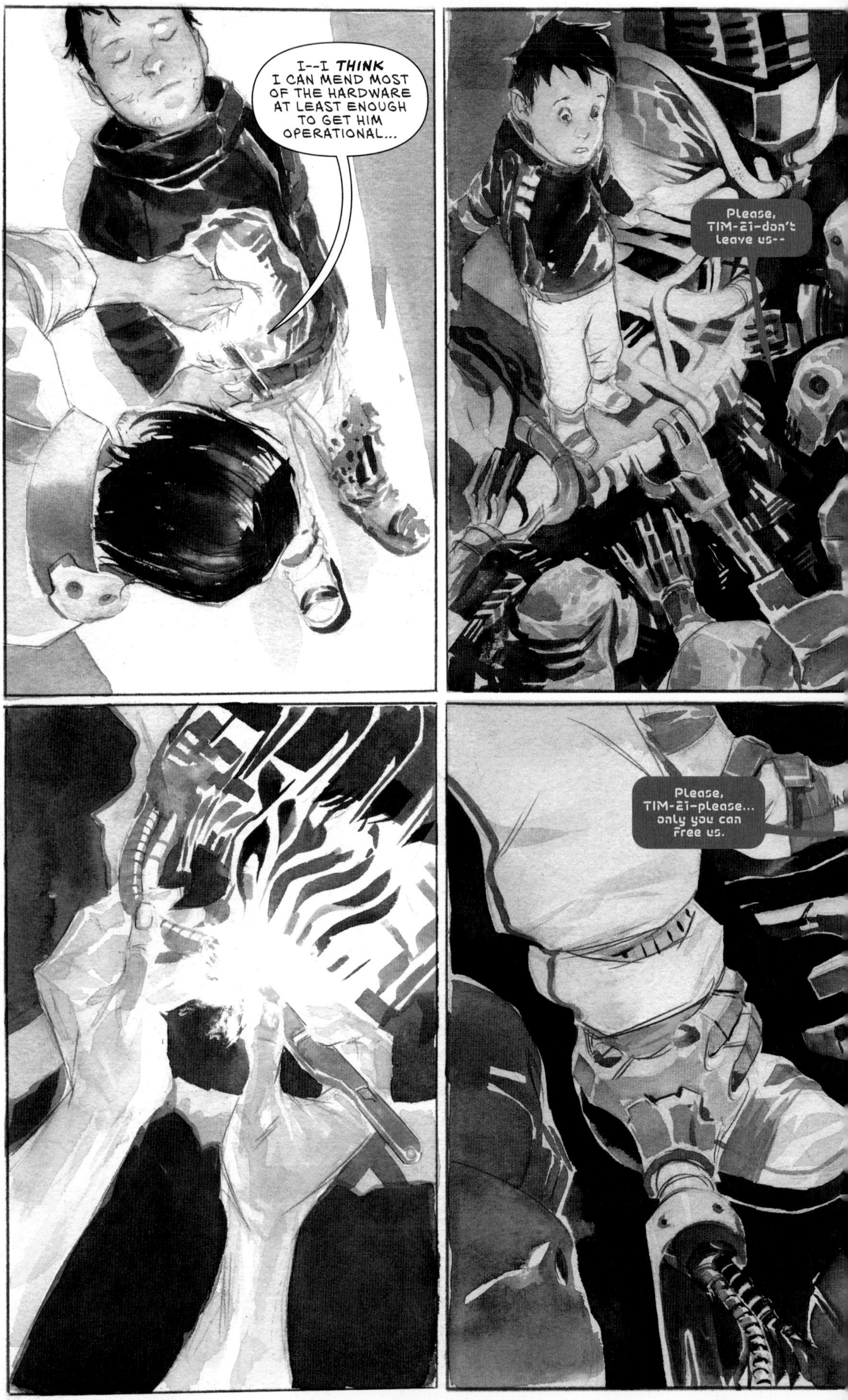
I--I THINK I CAN MEND MOST OF THE HARDWARE AT LEAST ENOUGH TO GET HIM OPERATIONAL...
Please, TIM-21-don't leave us--
Please, TIM-21-please... only you can free us.

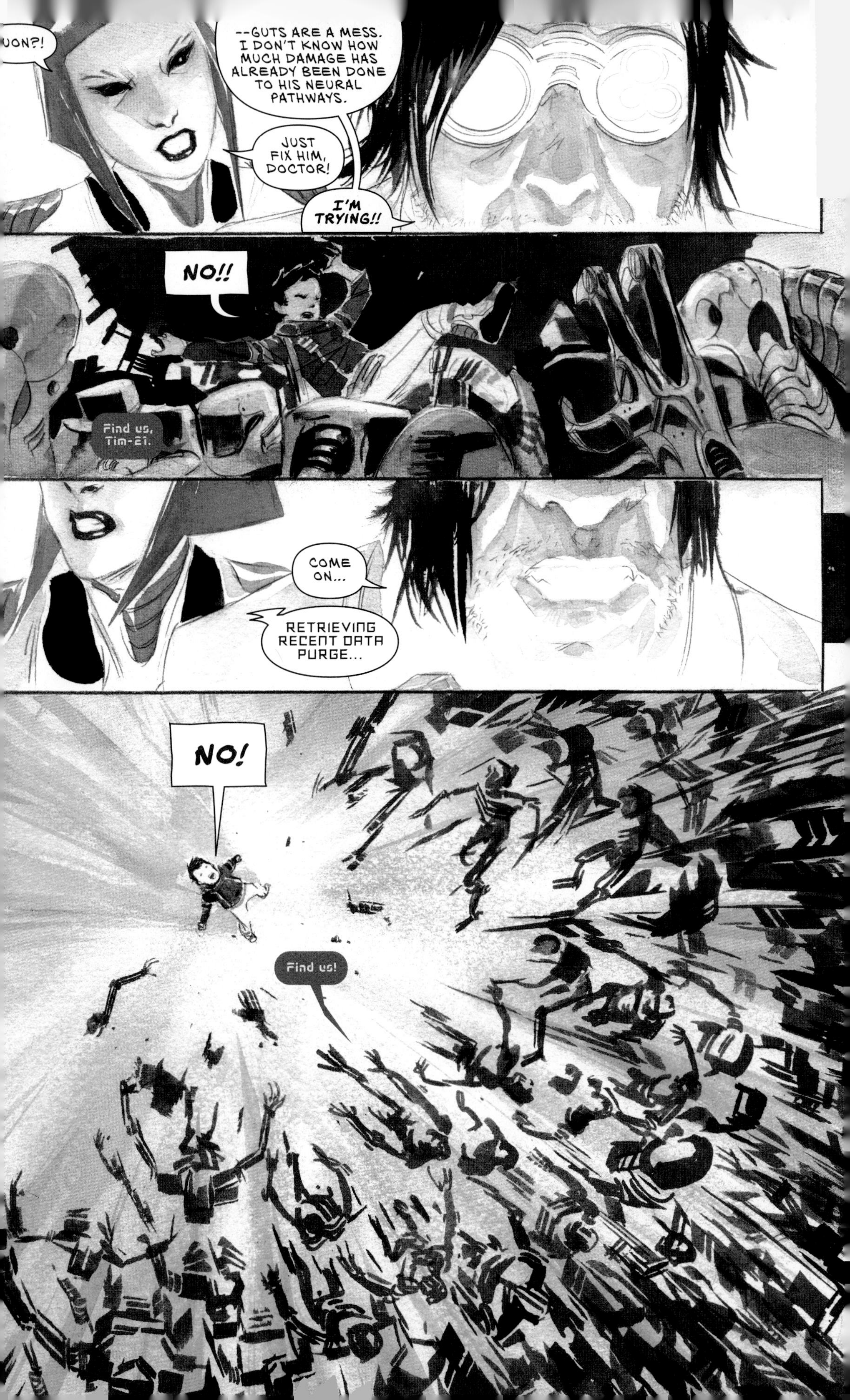

UON?!
--GUTS ARE A MESS. I DON'T KNOW HOW MUCH DAMAGE HAS ALREADY BEEN DONE TO HIS NEURAL PATHWAYS.
JUST FIX HIM, DOCTOR!
I'M TRYING!!
NO!!
Find us, Tim-21.
COME ON...
RETRIEVING RECENT DATA PURGE...
NO!
Find us!

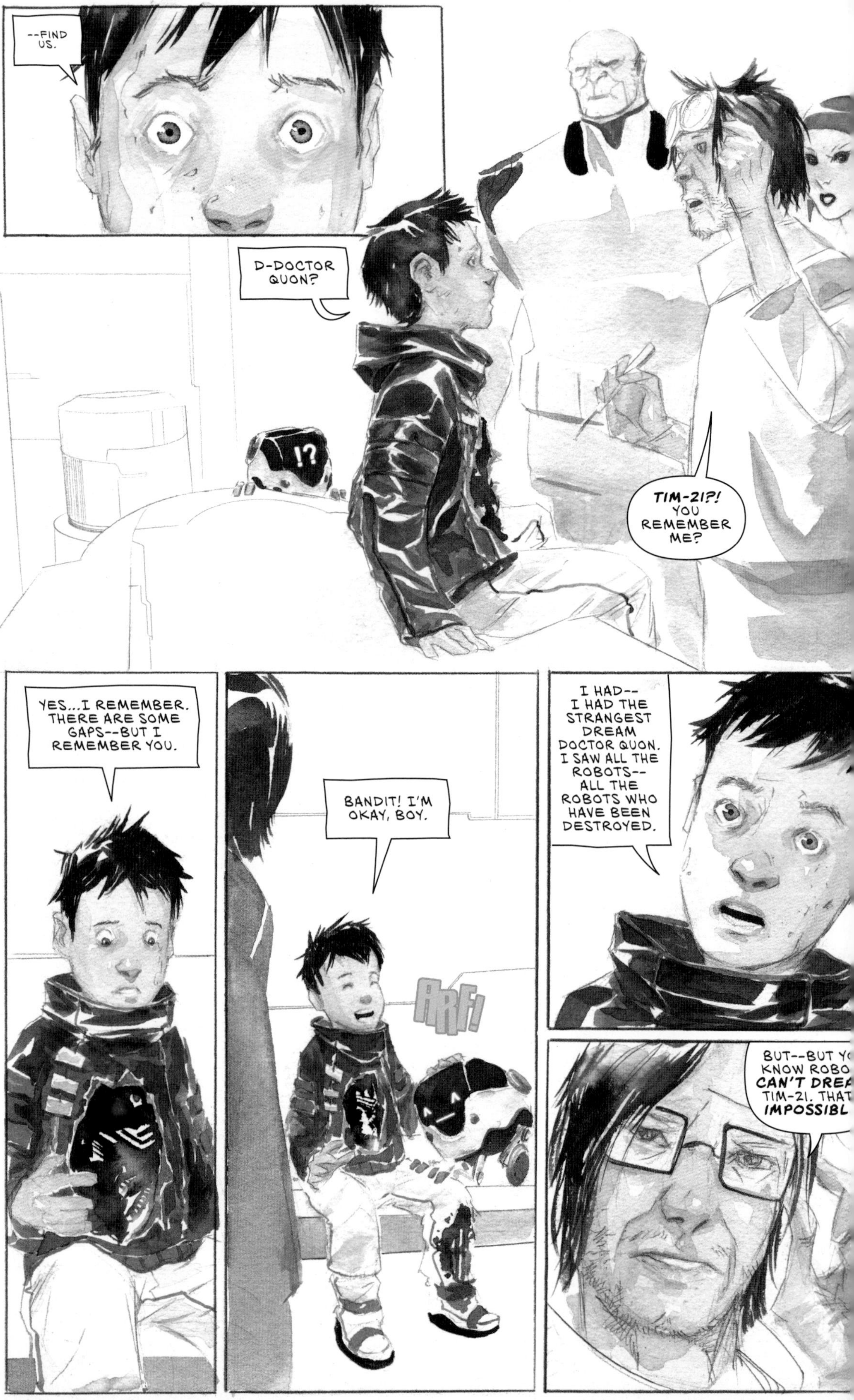

--FIND US.
D-DOCTOR QUON?
!?
TIM-21?! YOU REMEMBER ME?
YES...I REMEMBER. THERE ARE SOME GAPS--BUT I REMEMBER YOU.
BANDIT! I'M OKAY, BOY.
ARF!
I HAD-- I HAD THE STRANGEST DREAM DOCTOR QUON. I SAW ALL THE ROBOTS-- ALL THE ROBOTS WHO HAVE BEEN DESTROYED.
BUT--BUT Y KNOW ROBO CAN'T DRE TIM-21. THAT IMPOSSIBL

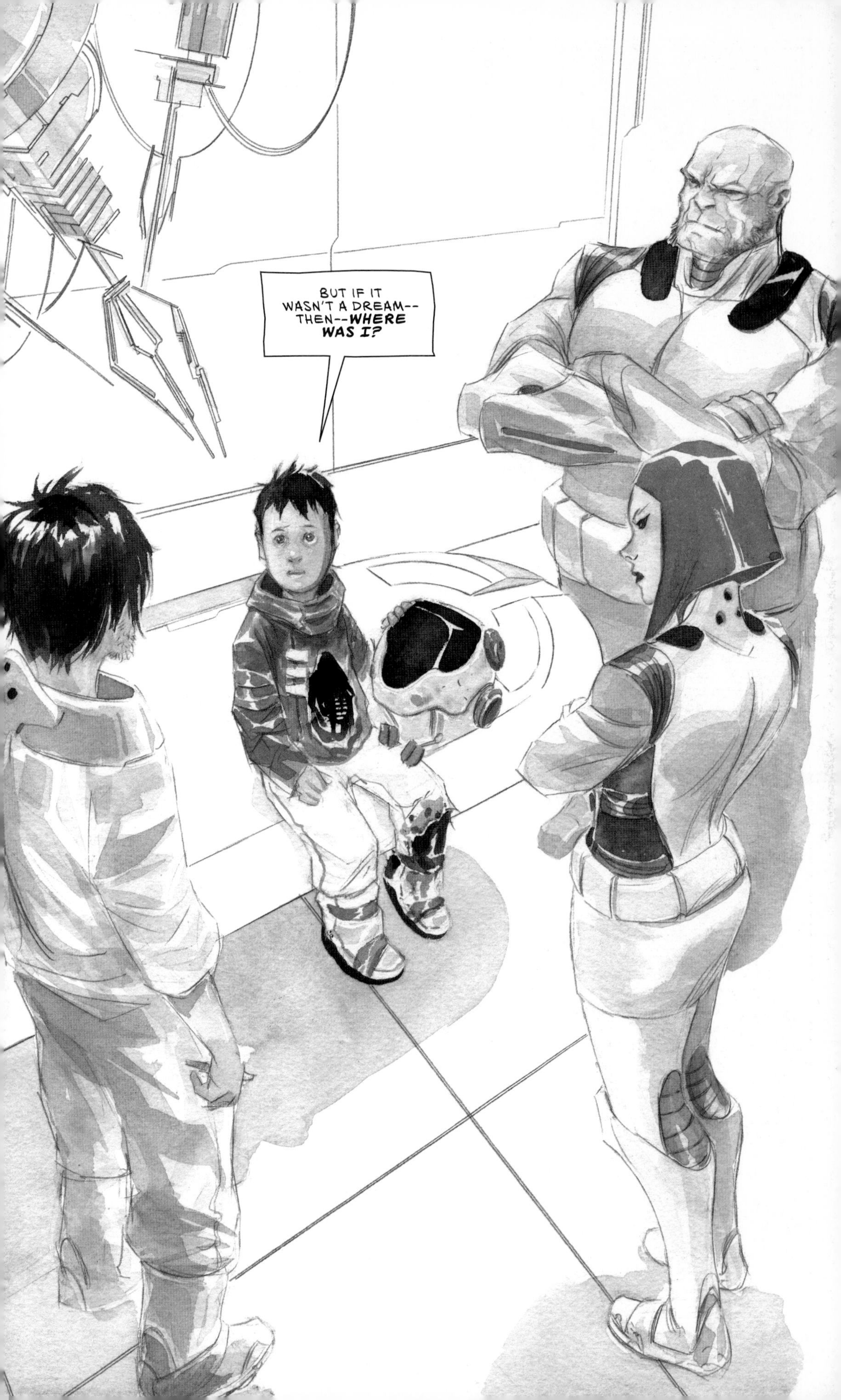
BUT IF IT WASN'T A DREAM-- THEN--**WHERE WAS I?**

CHAPTER FOUR

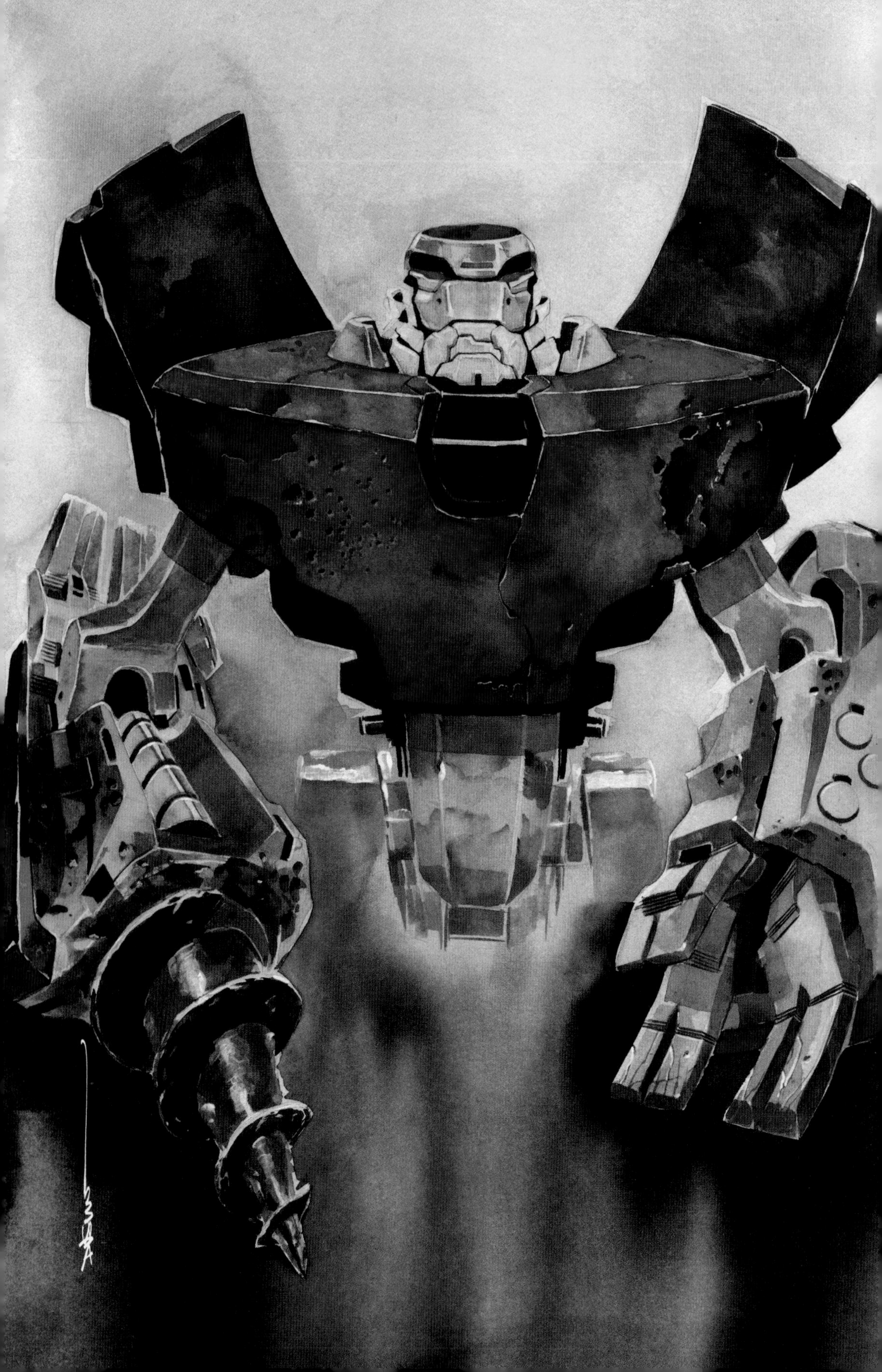

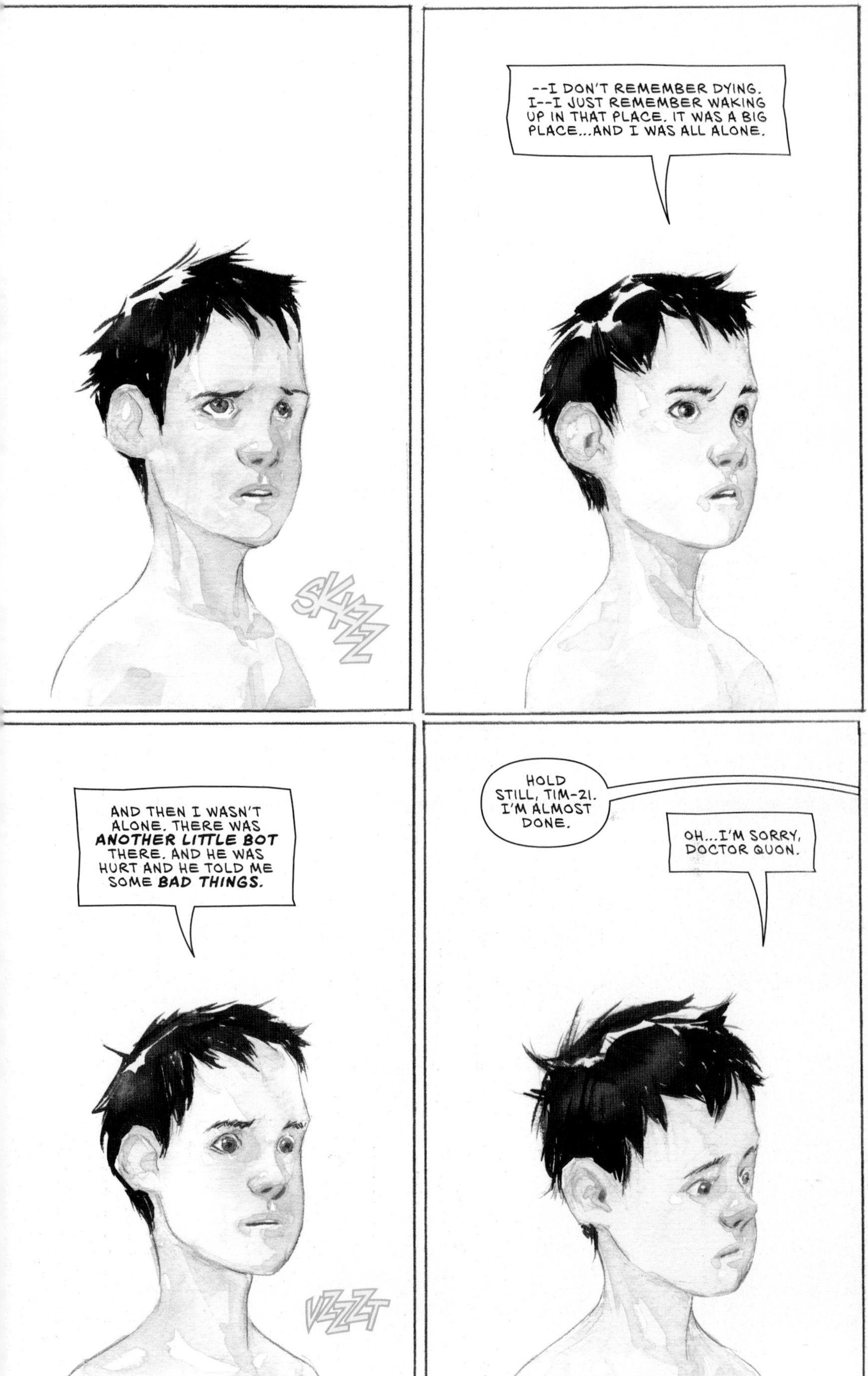

SKZZZ
--I DON'T REMEMBER DYING. I--I JUST REMEMBER WAKING UP IN THAT PLACE. IT WAS A BIG PLACE...AND I WAS ALL ALONE.
AND THEN I WASN'T ALONE. THERE WAS ANOTHER LITTLE BOT THERE. AND HE WAS HURT AND HE TOLD ME SOME BAD THINGS.
VZZZT
HOLD STILL, TIM-21. I'M ALMOST DONE.
OH...I'M SORRY, DOCTOR QUON.

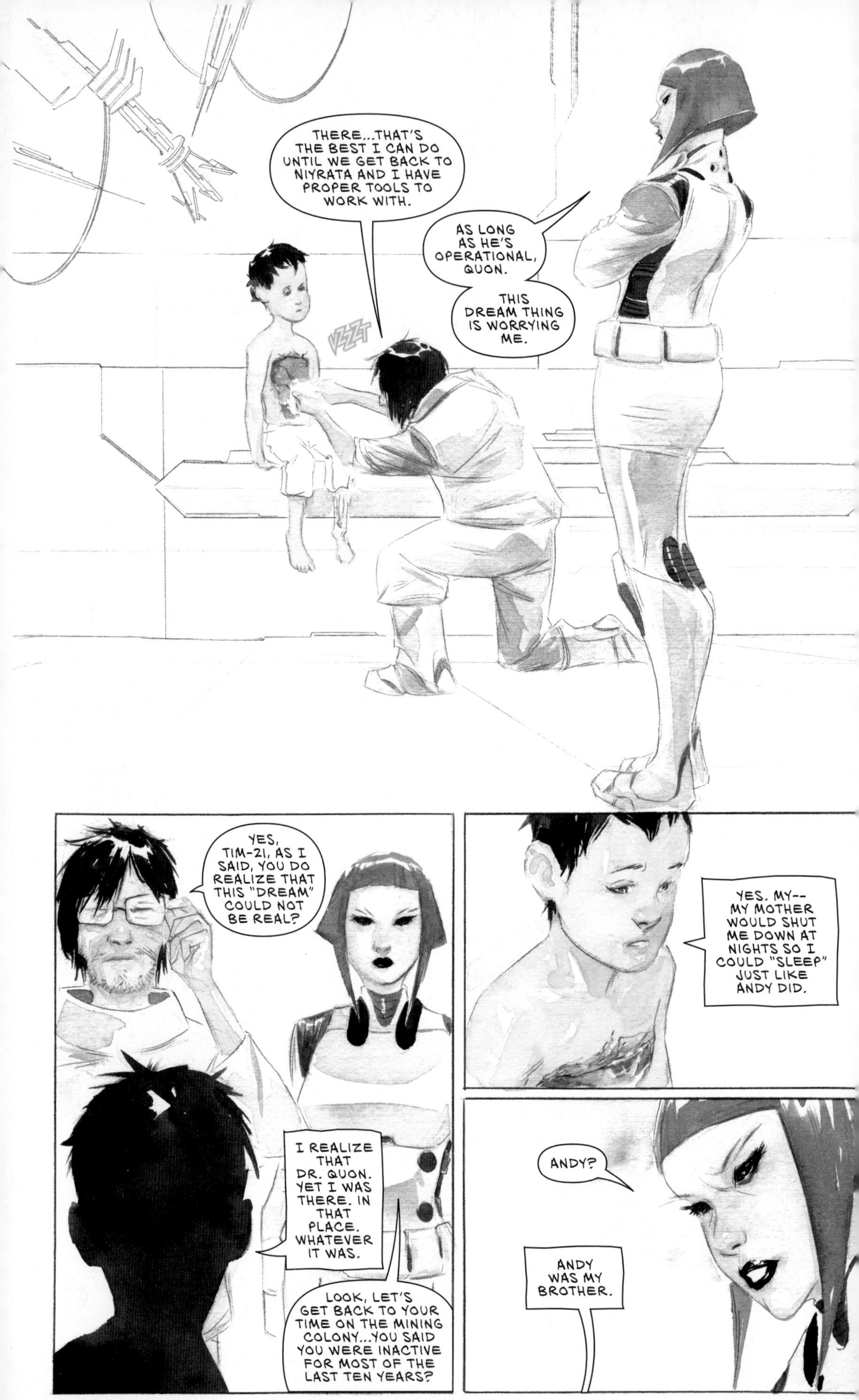
THERE...THAT'S THE BEST I CAN DO UNTIL WE GET BACK TO NIYRATA AND I HAVE PROPER TOOLS TO WORK WITH.
VZZZT
AS LONG AS HE'S OPERATIONAL, QUON.
THIS DREAM THING IS WORRYING ME.
YES, TIM-21, AS I SAID, YOU DO REALIZE THAT THIS "DREAM" COULD NOT BE REAL?
I REALIZE THAT DR. QUON. YET I WAS THERE. IN THAT PLACE. WHATEVER IT WAS.
LOOK, LET'S GET BACK TO YOUR TIME ON THE MINING COLONY...YOU SAID YOU WERE INACTIVE FOR MOST OF THE LAST TEN YEARS?
YES. MY-- MY MOTHER WOULD SHUT ME DOWN AT NIGHTS SO I COULD "SLEEP" JUST LIKE ANDY DID.
ANDY?
ANDY WAS MY BROTHER.

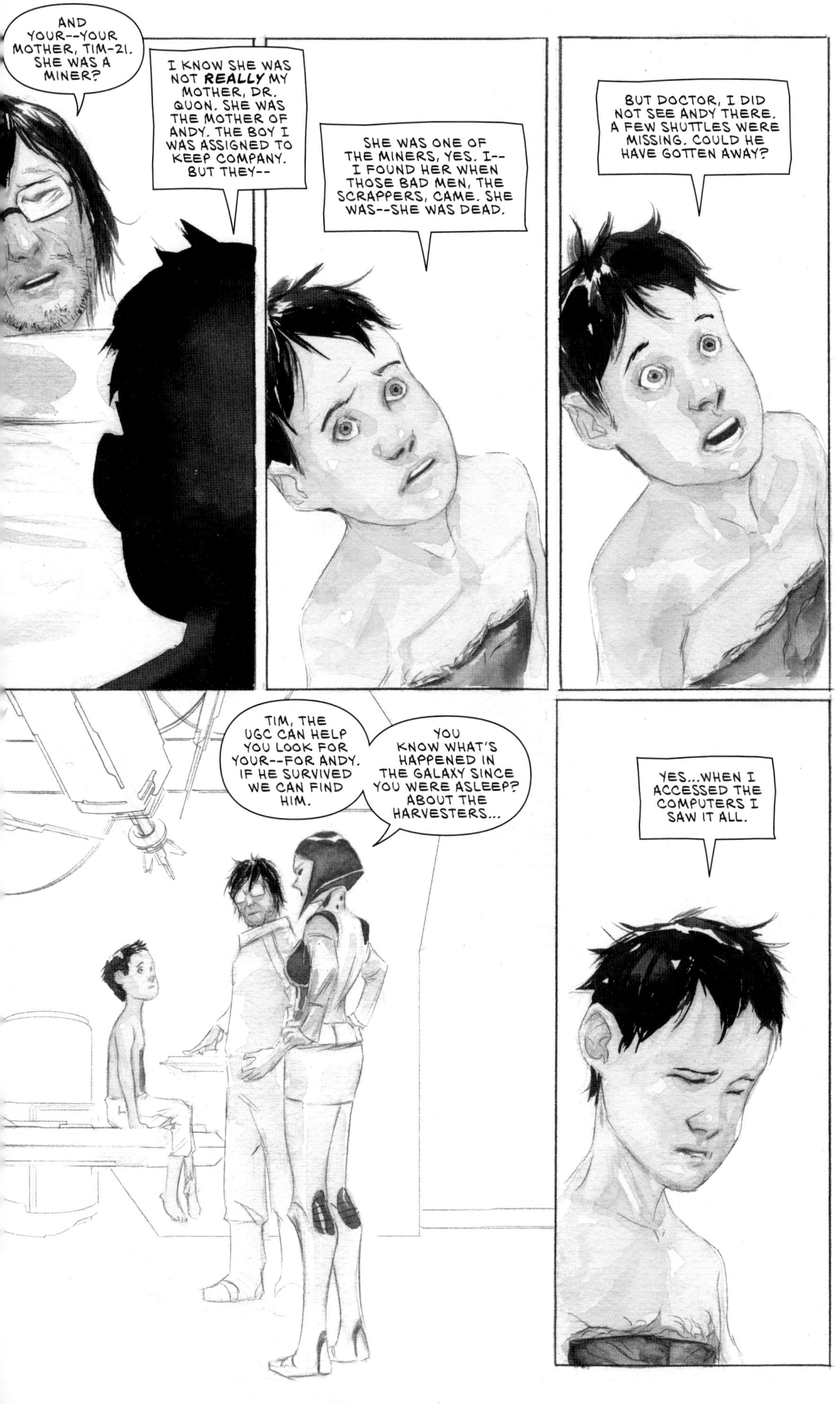
AND YOUR--YOUR MOTHER, TIM-21. SHE WAS A MINER?
I KNOW SHE WAS NOT **REALLY** MY MOTHER, DR. QUON. SHE WAS THE MOTHER OF ANDY. THE BOY I WAS ASSIGNED TO KEEP COMPANY. BUT THEY--
SHE WAS ONE OF THE MINERS, YES. I-- I FOUND HER WHEN THOSE BAD MEN, THE SCRAPPERS, CAME. SHE WAS--SHE WAS DEAD.
BUT DOCTOR, I DID NOT SEE ANDY THERE. A FEW SHUTTLES WERE MISSING. COULD HE HAVE GOTTEN AWAY?
TIM, THE UGC CAN HELP YOU LOOK FOR YOUR--FOR ANDY. IF HE SURVIVED WE CAN FIND HIM.
YOU KNOW WHAT'S HAPPENED IN THE GALAXY SINCE YOU WERE ASLEEP? ABOUT THE HARVESTERS...
YES...WHEN I ACCESSED THE COMPUTERS I SAW IT ALL.

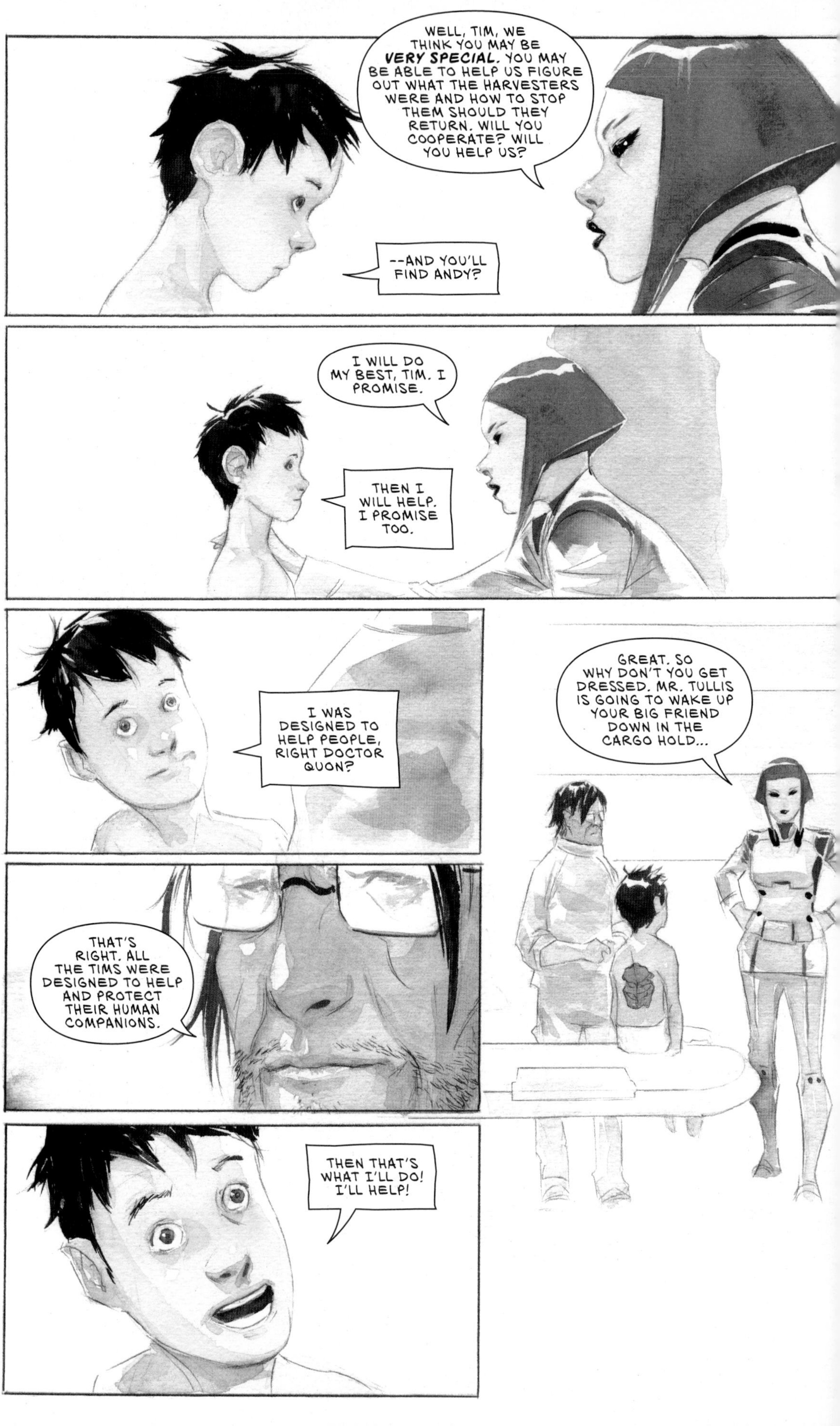
WELL, TIM, WE THINK YOU MAY BE **VERY SPECIAL.** YOU MAY BE ABLE TO HELP US FIGURE OUT WHAT THE HARVESTERS WERE AND HOW TO STOP THEM SHOULD THEY RETURN. WILL YOU COOPERATE? WILL YOU HELP US?
--AND YOU'LL FIND ANDY?
I WILL DO MY BEST, TIM. I PROMISE.
THEN I WILL HELP. I PROMISE TOO.
I WAS DESIGNED TO HELP PEOPLE, RIGHT DOCTOR QUON?
THAT'S RIGHT. ALL THE TIMS WERE DESIGNED TO HELP AND PROTECT THEIR HUMAN COMPANIONS.
THEN THAT'S WHAT I'LL DO! I'LL HELP!
GREAT. SO WHY DON'T YOU GET DRESSED. MR. TULLIS IS GOING TO WAKE UP YOUR BIG FRIEND DOWN IN THE CARGO HOLD...

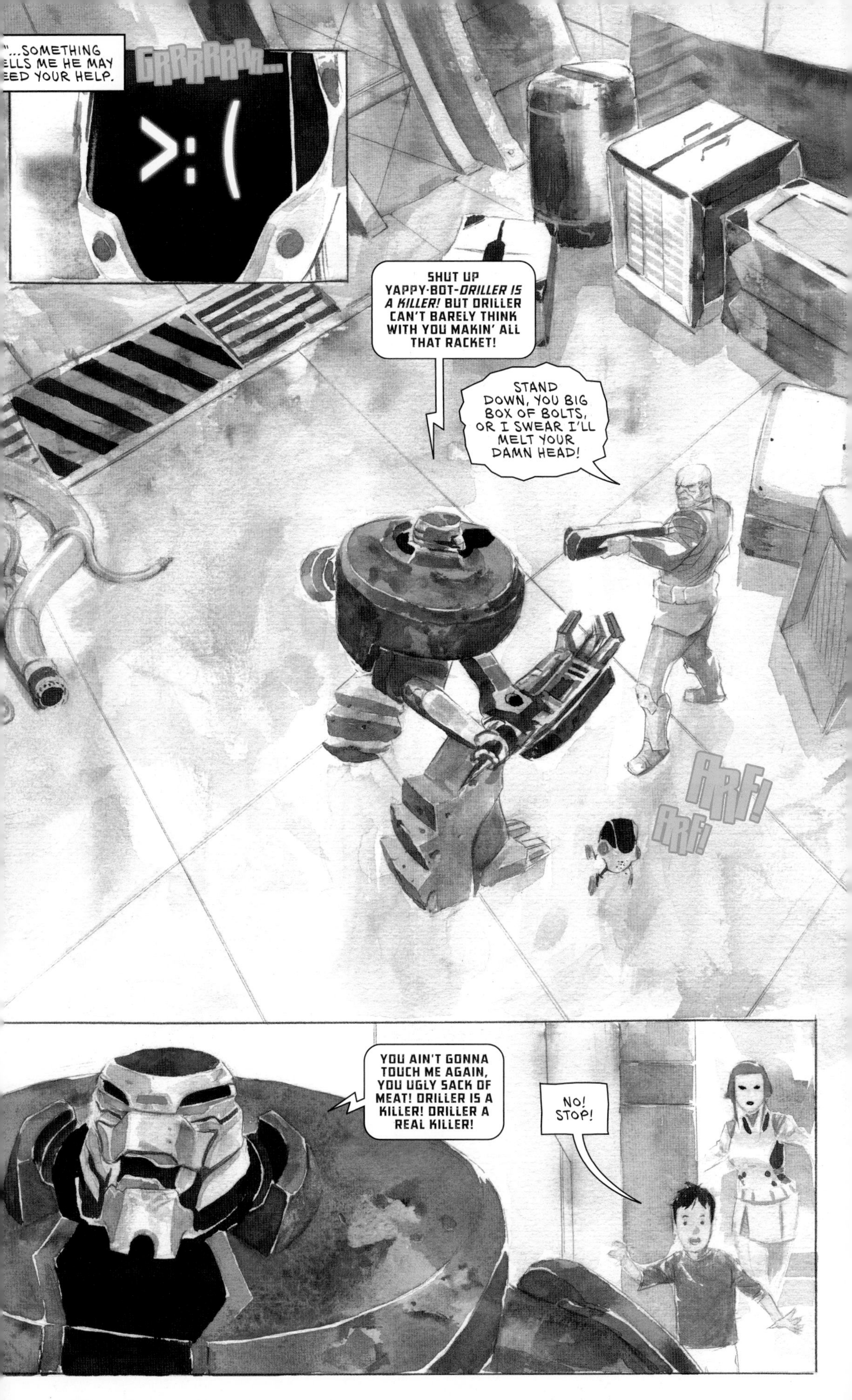
"...SOMETHING
ELLS ME HE MAY
EED YOUR HELP.
GRRRRRR...
>:(
SHUT UP YAPPY-BOT-*DRILLER IS A KILLER!* BUT DRILLER CAN'T BARELY THINK WITH YOU MAKIN' ALL THAT RACKET!
STAND DOWN, YOU BIG BOX OF BOLTS, OR I SWEAR I'LL MELT YOUR DAMN HEAD!
ARF! ARF!
YOU AIN'T GONNA TOUCH ME AGAIN, YOU UGLY SACK OF MEAT! DRILLER IS A KILLER! DRILLER A REAL KILLER!
NO! STOP!

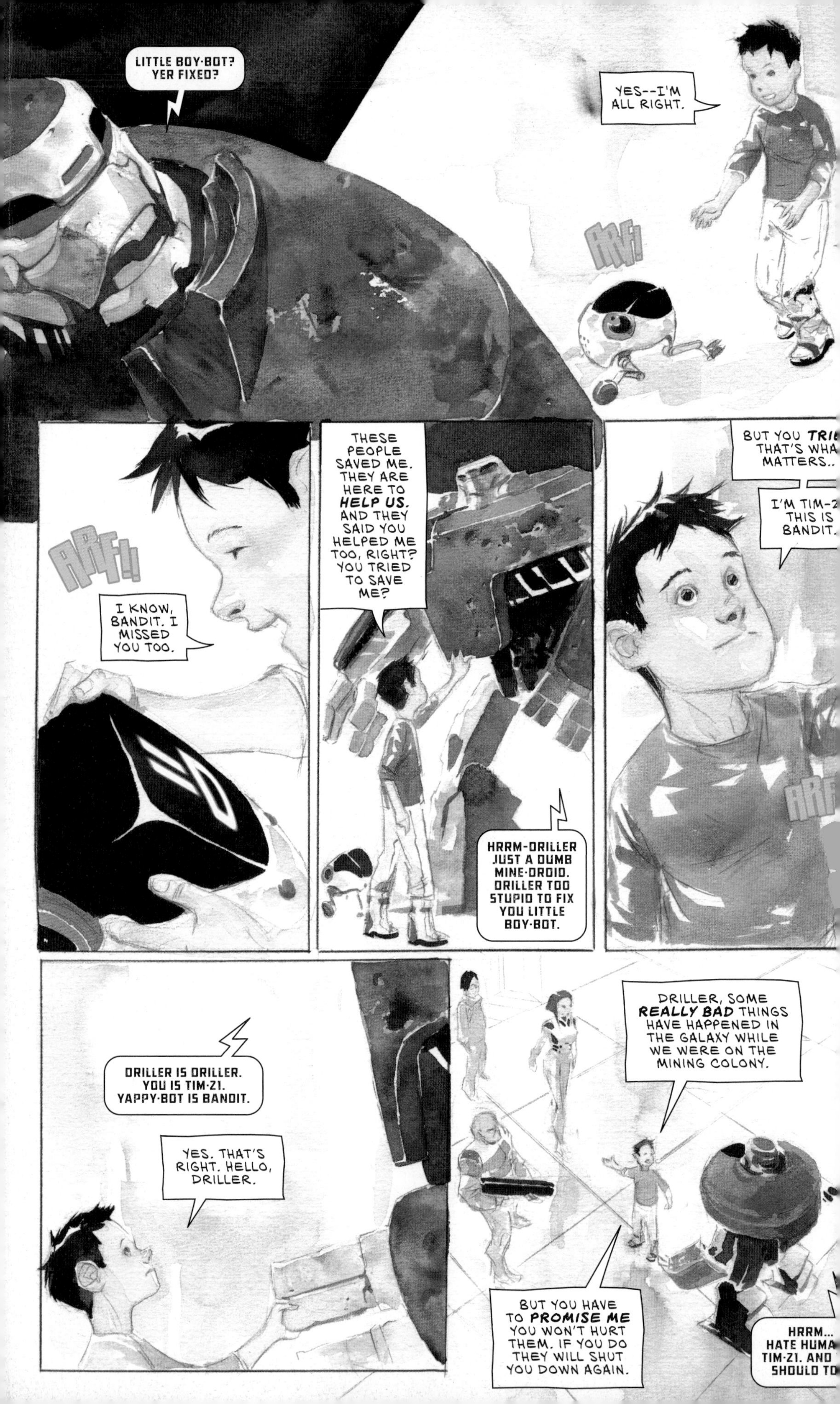
LITTLE BOY-BOT? YER FIXED?
YES--I'M ALL RIGHT.
ARF!
ARF!!
I KNOW, BANDIT. I MISSED YOU TOO.
THESE PEOPLE SAVED ME. THEY ARE HERE TO HELP US. AND THEY SAID YOU HELPED ME TOO, RIGHT? YOU TRIED TO SAVE ME?
HRRM-DRILLER JUST A DUMB MINE-DROID. DRILLER TOO STUPID TO FIX YOU LITTLE BOY-BOT.
BUT YOU TRI
THAT'S WHA
MATTERS..
I'M TIM-2
THIS IS
BANDIT.
ARF
DRILLER IS DRILLER. YOU IS TIM-21. YAPPY-BOT IS BANDIT.
YES. THAT'S RIGHT. HELLO, DRILLER.
DRILLER, SOME REALLY BAD THINGS HAVE HAPPENED IN THE GALAXY WHILE WE WERE ON THE MINING COLONY.
BUT YOU HAVE TO PROMISE ME YOU WON'T HURT THEM. IF YOU DO THEY WILL SHUT YOU DOWN AGAIN.
HRRM...
HATE HUMA
TIM-21. AND
SHOULD TO

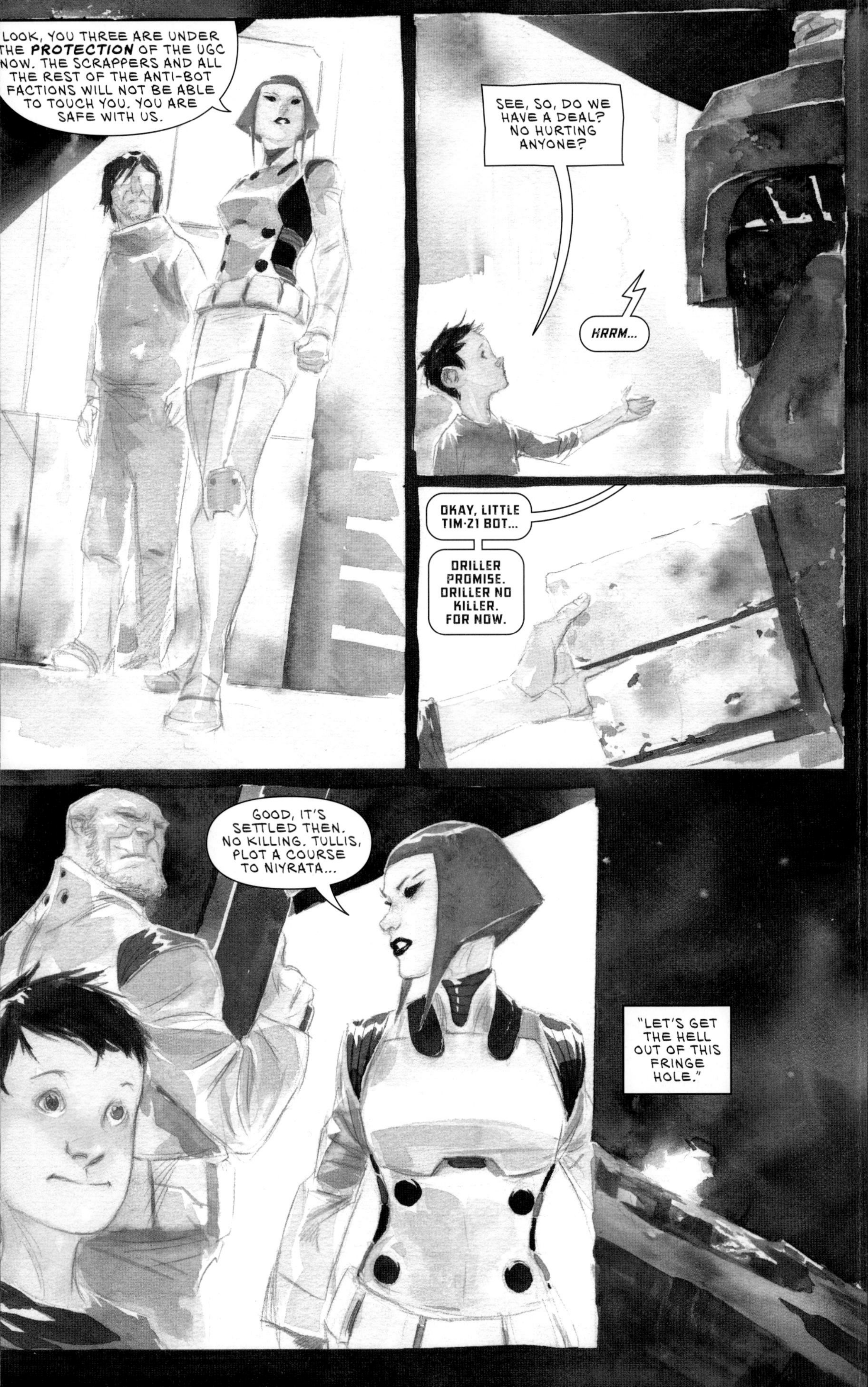
LOOK, YOU THREE ARE UNDER THE PROTECTION OF THE UGC NOW. THE SCRAPPERS AND ALL THE REST OF THE ANTI-BOT FACTIONS WILL NOT BE ABLE TO TOUCH YOU. YOU ARE SAFE WITH US.
SEE, SO, DO WE HAVE A DEAL? NO HURTING ANYONE?
HRRM...
OKAY, LITTLE TIM-21 BOT...
DRILLER PROMISE. DRILLER NO KILLER. FOR NOW.
GOOD, IT'S SETTLED THEN. NO KILLING. TULLIS, PLOT A COURSE TO NIYRATA...
"LET'S GET THE HELL OUT OF THIS FRINGE HOLE."

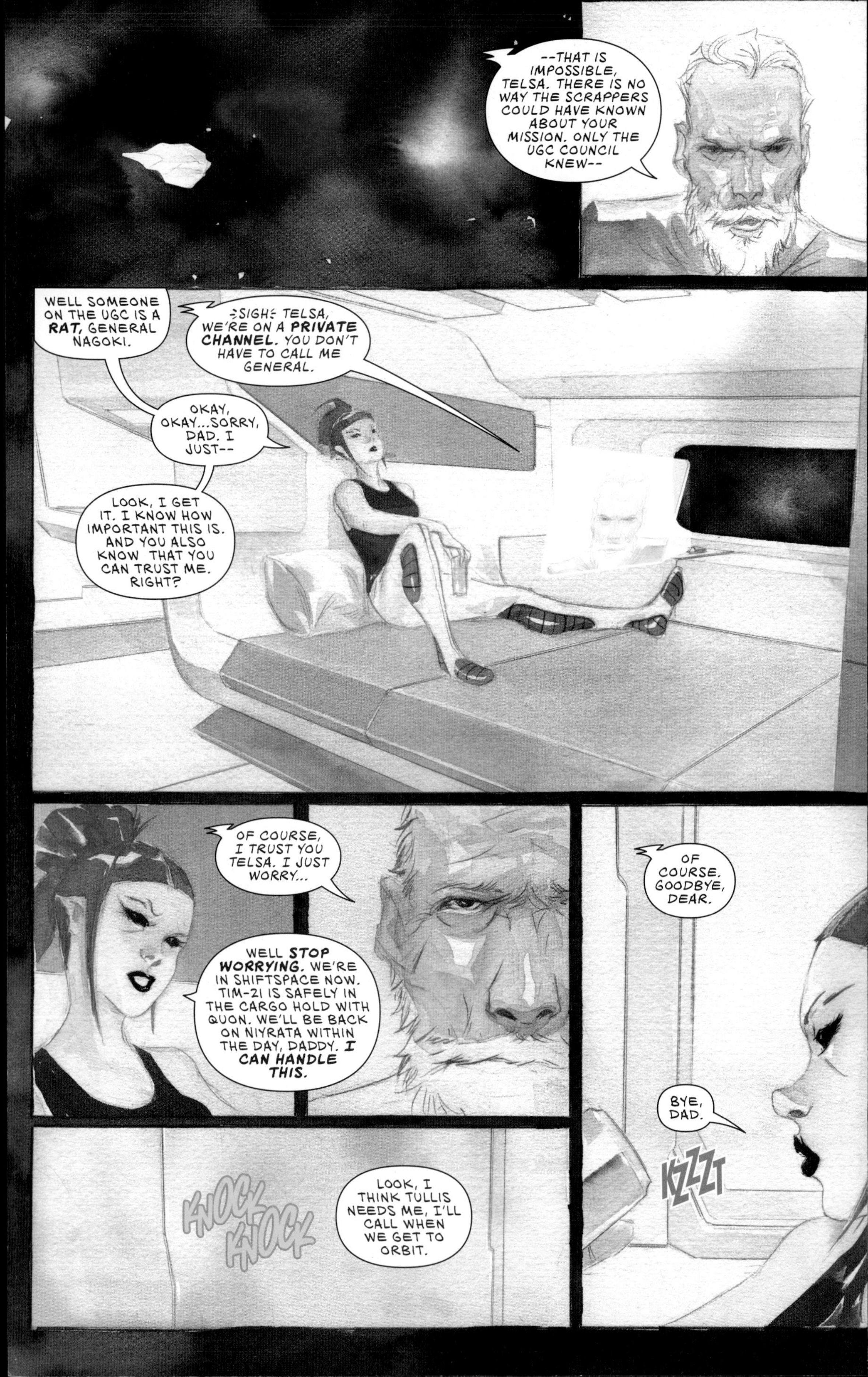
--THAT IS IMPOSSIBLE, TELSA. THERE IS NO WAY THE SCRAPPERS COULD HAVE KNOWN ABOUT YOUR MISSION. ONLY THE UGC COUNCIL KNEW--
WELL SOMEONE ON THE UGC IS A **RAT,** GENERAL NAGOKI.
SIGH TELSA, WE'RE ON A **PRIVATE CHANNEL.** YOU DON'T HAVE TO CALL ME GENERAL.
OKAY, OKAY...SORRY, DAD. I JUST--
LOOK, I GET IT. I KNOW HOW IMPORTANT THIS IS. AND YOU ALSO KNOW THAT YOU CAN TRUST ME. RIGHT?
OF COURSE, I TRUST YOU TELSA. I JUST WORRY...
WELL **STOP WORRYING.** WE'RE IN SHIFTSPACE NOW. TIM-21 IS SAFELY IN THE CARGO HOLD WITH QUON. WE'LL BE BACK ON NIYRATA WITHIN THE DAY, DADDY. **I CAN HANDLE THIS.**
KNOCK KNOCK
LOOK, I THINK TULLIS NEEDS ME, I'LL CALL WHEN WE GET TO ORBIT.
OF COURSE. GOODBYE, DEAR.
BYE, DAD.
KZZZT

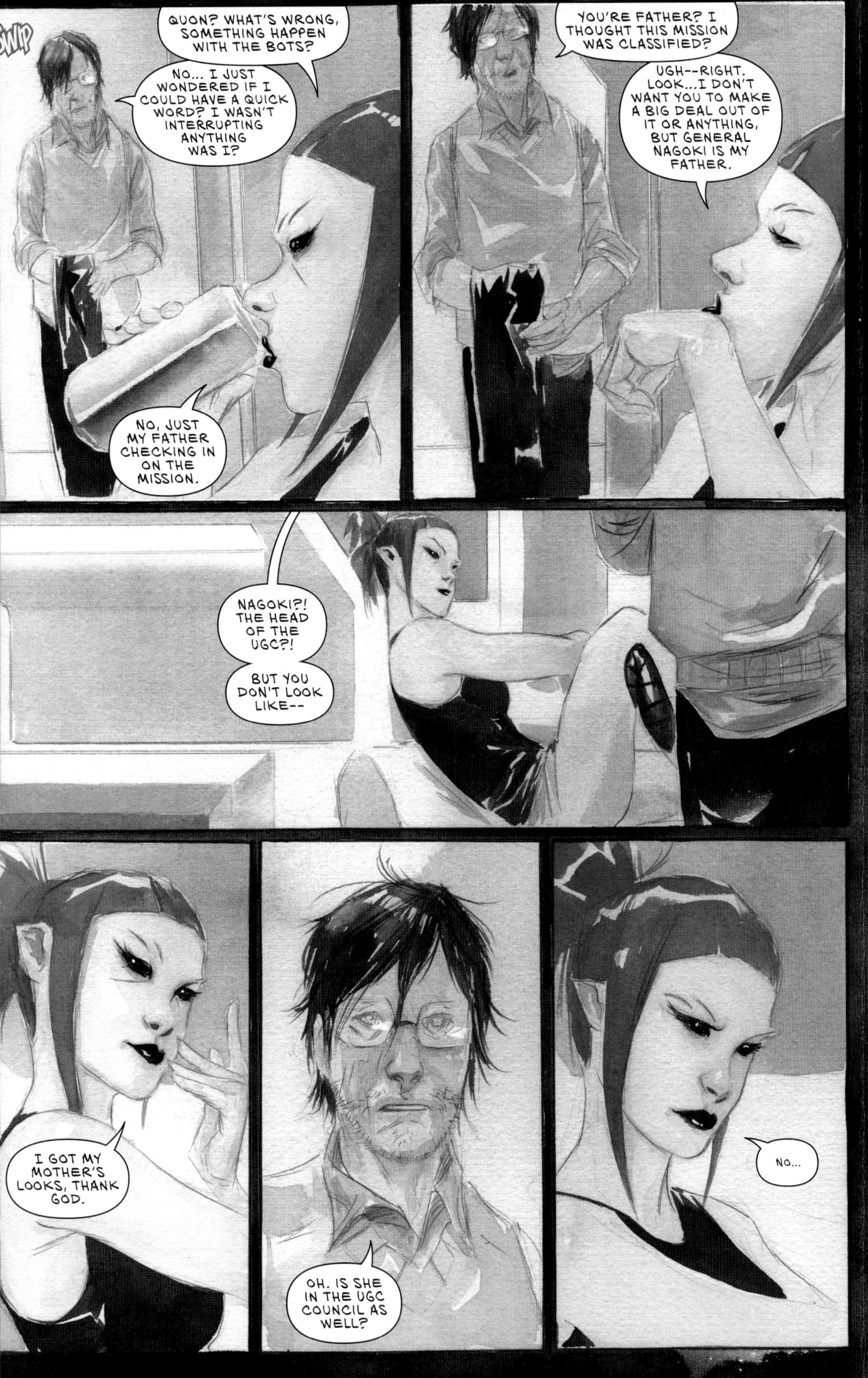
SWIP
QUON? WHAT'S WRONG, SOMETHING HAPPEN WITH THE BOTS?
NO... I JUST WONDERED IF I COULD HAVE A QUICK WORD? I WASN'T INTERRUPTING ANYTHING WAS I?
NO, JUST MY FATHER CHECKING IN ON THE MISSION.
YOU'RE FATHER? I THOUGHT THIS MISSION WAS CLASSIFIED?
UGH--RIGHT. LOOK...I DON'T WANT YOU TO MAKE A BIG DEAL OUT OF IT OR ANYTHING, BUT GENERAL NAGOKI IS MY FATHER.
NAGOKI?! THE HEAD OF THE UGC?!
BUT YOU DON'T LOOK LIKE--
I GOT MY MOTHER'S LOOKS, THANK GOD.
OH. IS SHE IN THE UGC COUNCIL AS WELL?
NO...

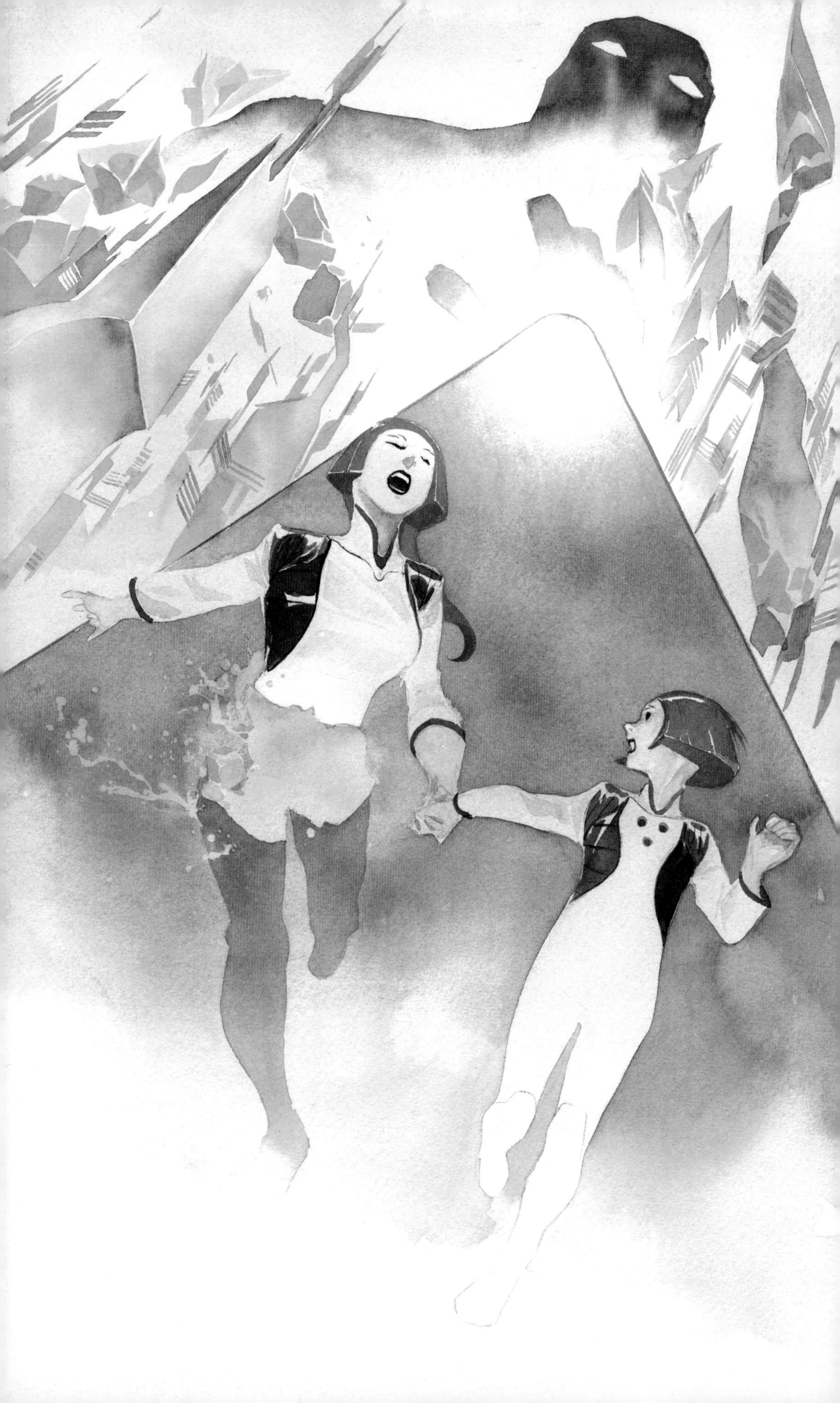

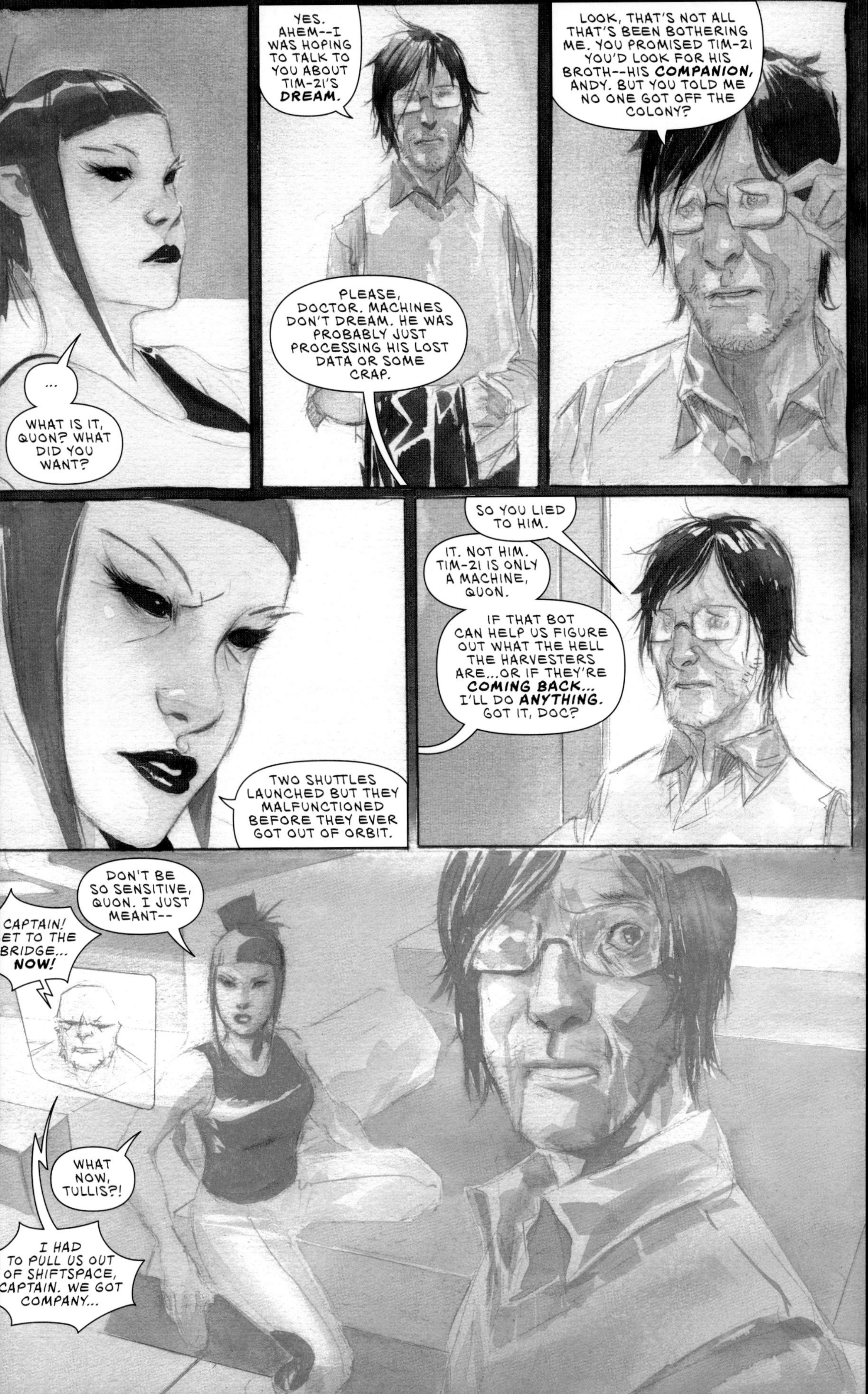
...
WHAT IS IT, QUON? WHAT DID YOU WANT?
YES. AHEM--I WAS HOPING TO TALK TO YOU ABOUT TIM-21'S **DREAM.**
PLEASE, DOCTOR. MACHINES DON'T DREAM. HE WAS PROBABLY JUST PROCESSING HIS LOST DATA OR SOME CRAP.
LOOK, THAT'S NOT ALL THAT'S BEEN BOTHERING ME. YOU PROMISED TIM-21 YOU'D LOOK FOR HIS BROTH--HIS **COMPANION,** ANDY. BUT YOU TOLD ME NO ONE GOT OFF THE COLONY?
TWO SHUTTLES LAUNCHED BUT THEY MALFUNCTIONED BEFORE THEY EVER GOT OUT OF ORBIT.
SO YOU LIED TO HIM.
IT. NOT HIM. TIM-21 IS ONLY A MACHINE, QUON.
IF THAT BOT CAN HELP US FIGURE OUT WHAT THE HELL THE HARVESTERS ARE...OR IF THEY'RE **COMING BACK...** I'LL DO **ANYTHING.** GOT IT, DOC?
DON'T BE SO SENSITIVE, QUON. I JUST MEANT--
CAPTAIN! ET TO THE BRIDGE... **NOW!**
WHAT NOW, TULLIS?!
I HAD TO PULL US OUT OF SHIFTSPACE, CAPTAIN. WE GOT COMPANY...

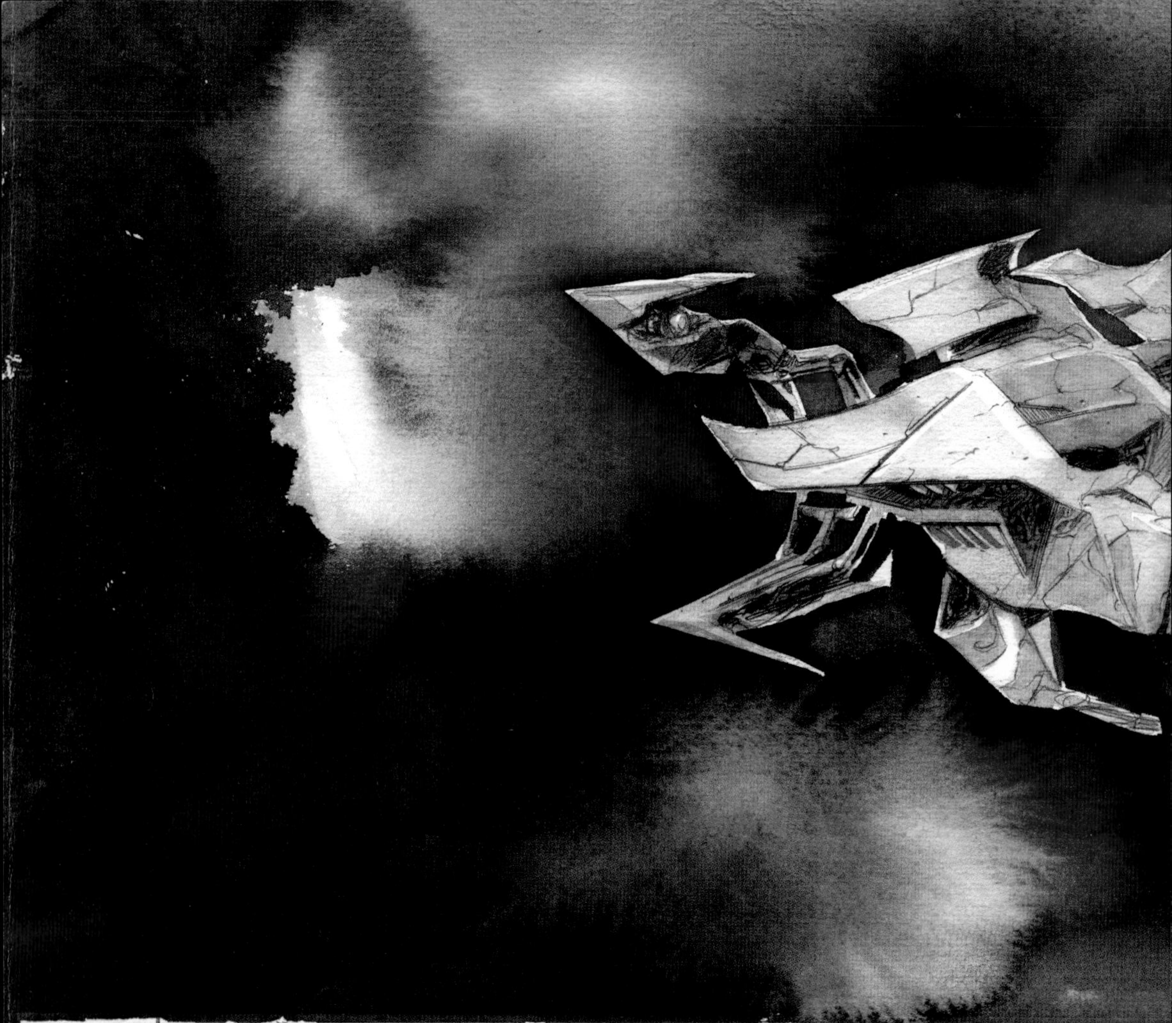

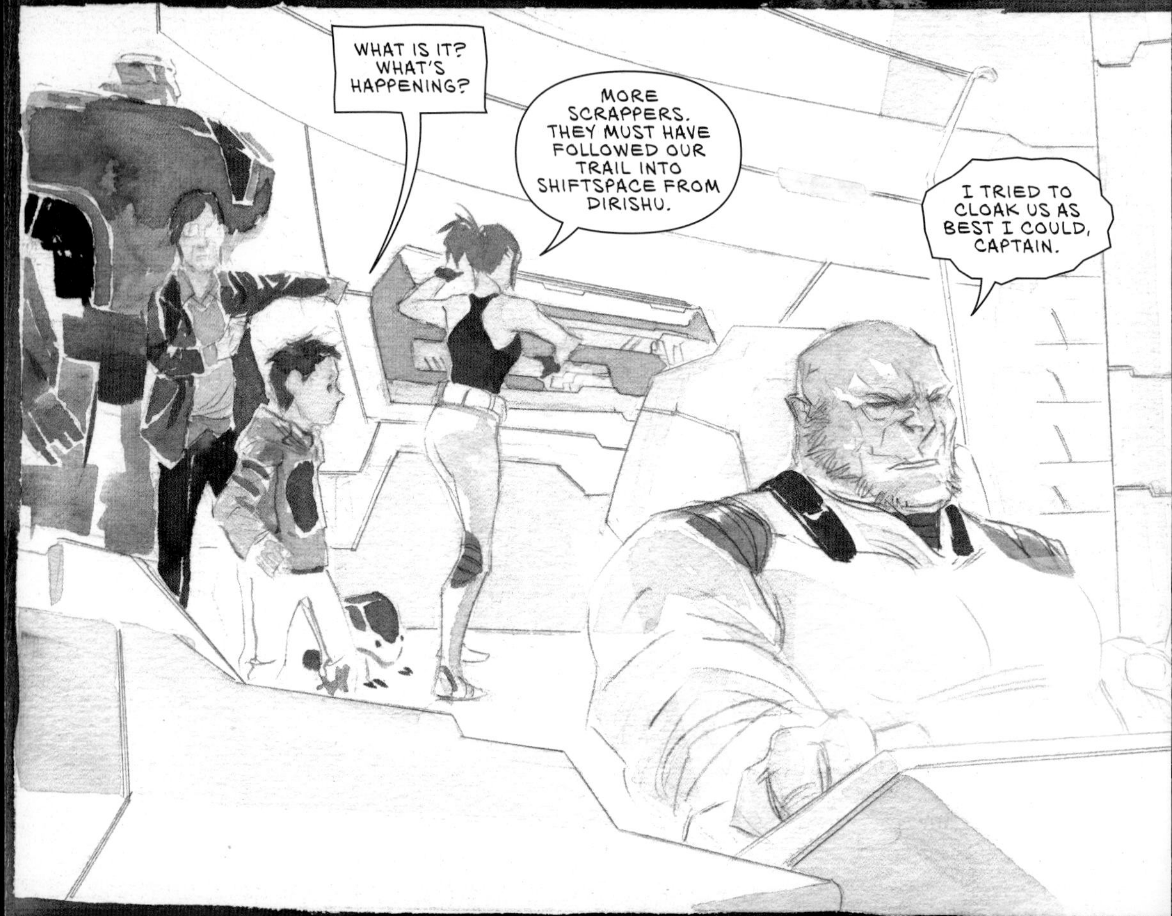
WHAT IS IT? WHAT'S HAPPENING?
MORE SCRAPPERS. THEY MUST HAVE FOLLOWED OUR TRAIL INTO SHIFTSPACE FROM DIRISHU.
I TRIED TO CLOAK US AS BEST I COULD, CAPTAIN.

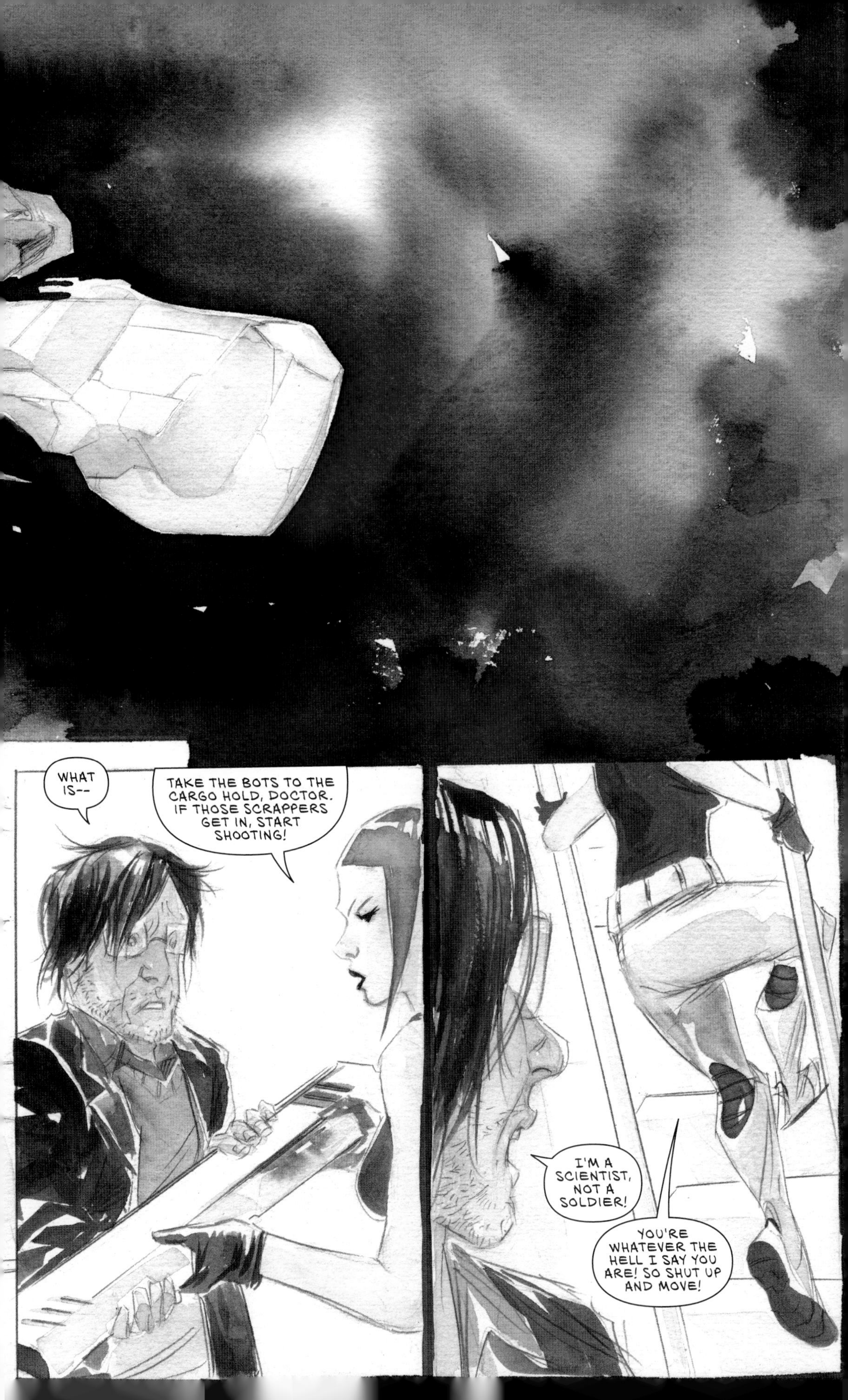
WHAT IS--
TAKE THE BOTS TO THE CARGO HOLD, DOCTOR. IF THOSE SCRAPPERS GET IN, START SHOOTING!
I'M A SCIENTIST, NOT A SOLDIER!
YOU'RE WHATEVER THE HELL I SAY YOU ARE! SO SHUT UP AND MOVE!

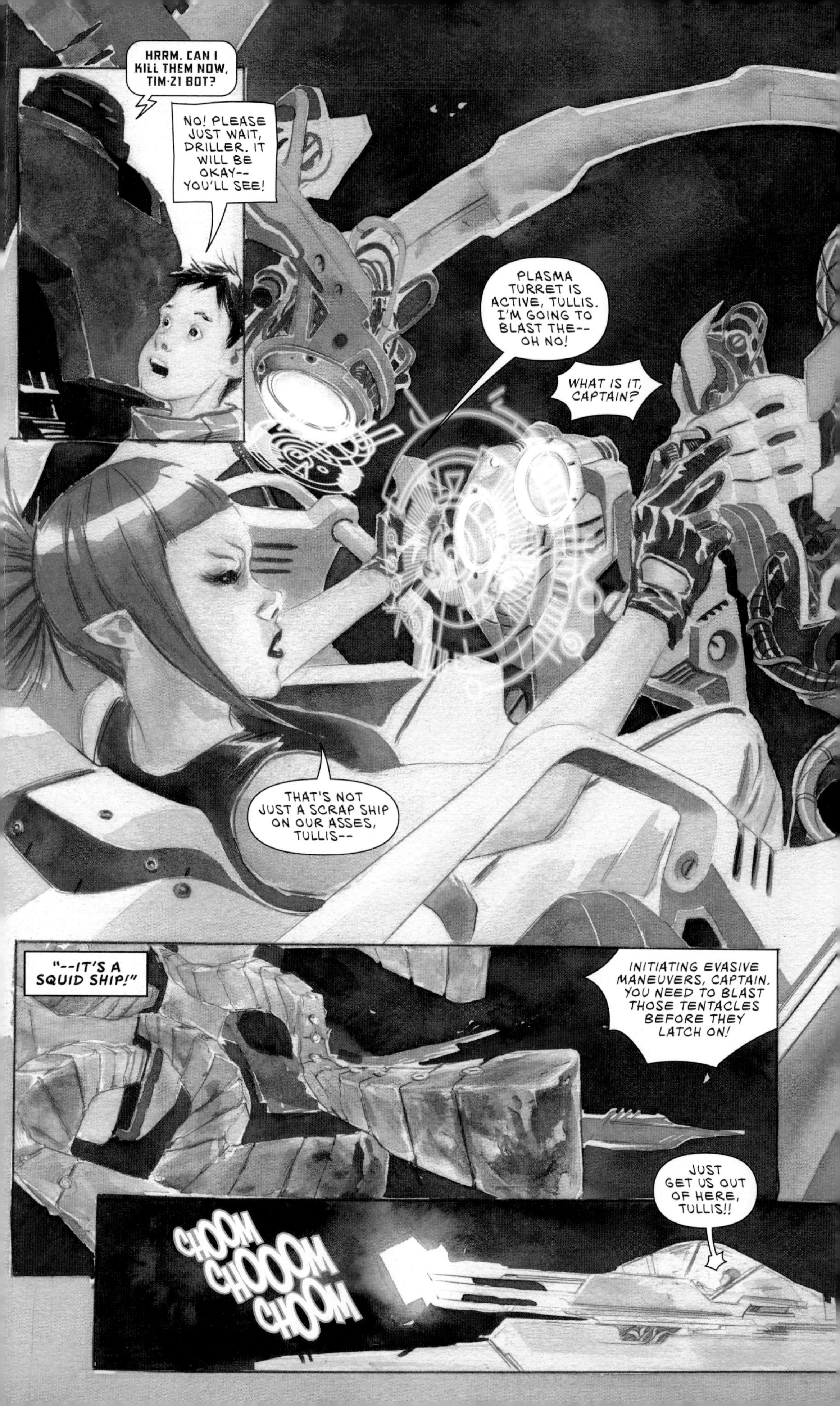

HRRM. CAN I KILL THEM NOW, TIM-21 BOT?
NO! PLEASE JUST WAIT, DRILLER. IT WILL BE OKAY-- YOU'LL SEE!
PLASMA TURRET IS ACTIVE, TULLIS. I'M GOING TO BLAST THE-- OH NO!
WHAT IS IT, CAPTAIN?
THAT'S NOT JUST A SCRAP SHIP ON OUR ASSES, TULLIS--
"--IT'S A SQUID SHIP!"
INITIATING EVASIVE MANEUVERS, CAPTAIN. YOU NEED TO BLAST THOSE TENTACLES BEFORE THEY LATCH ON!
JUST GET US OUT OF HERE, TULLIS!!
CHOOM
CHOOOM
CHOOM

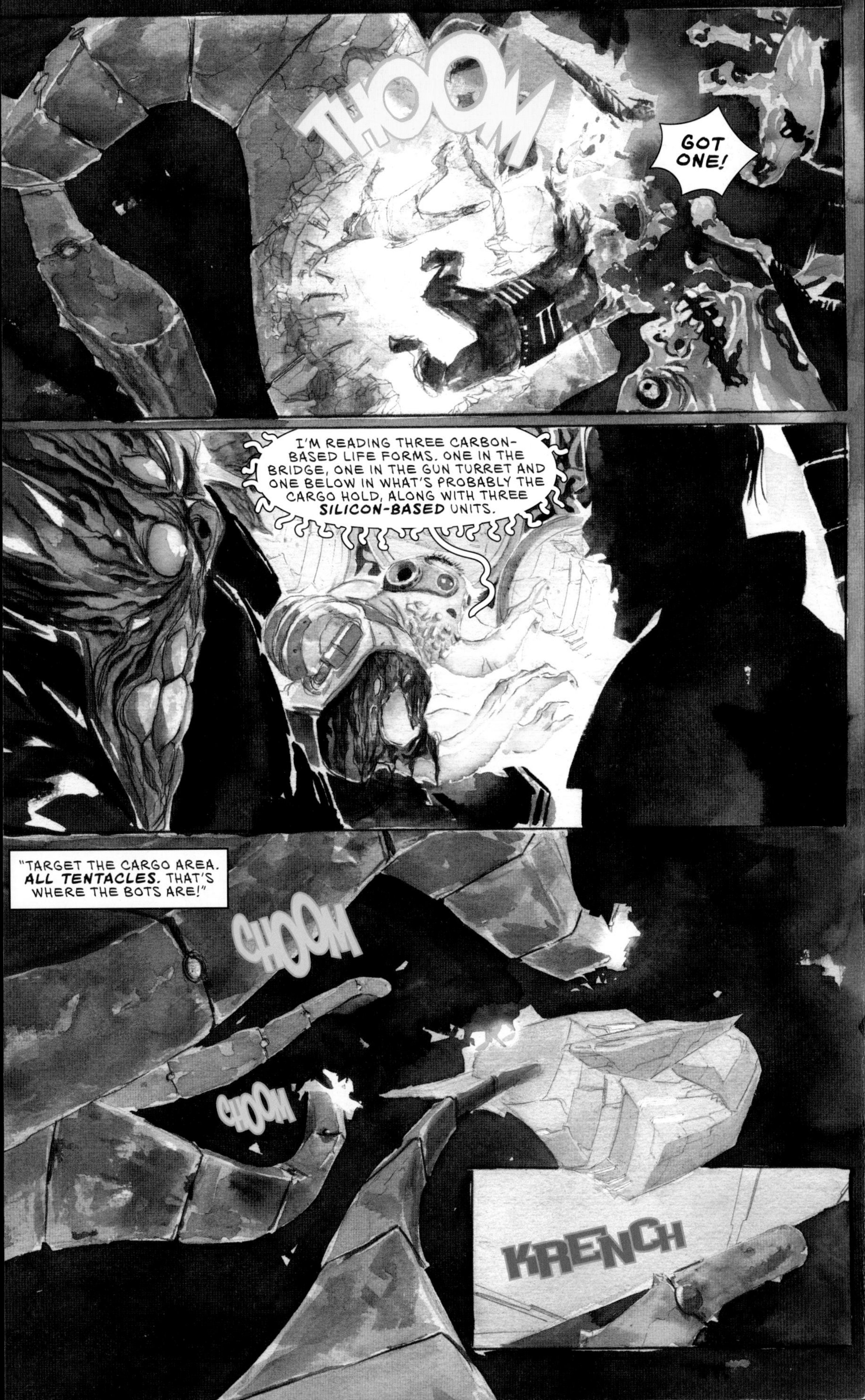
THOOM
GOT ONE!
I'M READING THREE CARBON-BASED LIFE FORMS. ONE IN THE BRIDGE, ONE IN THE GUN TURRET AND ONE BELOW IN WHAT'S PROBABLY THE CARGO HOLD, ALONG WITH THREE SILICON-BASED UNITS.
"TARGET THE CARGO AREA. ALL TENTACLES. THAT'S WHERE THE BOTS ARE!"
CHOOM
CHOOM
KRENCH

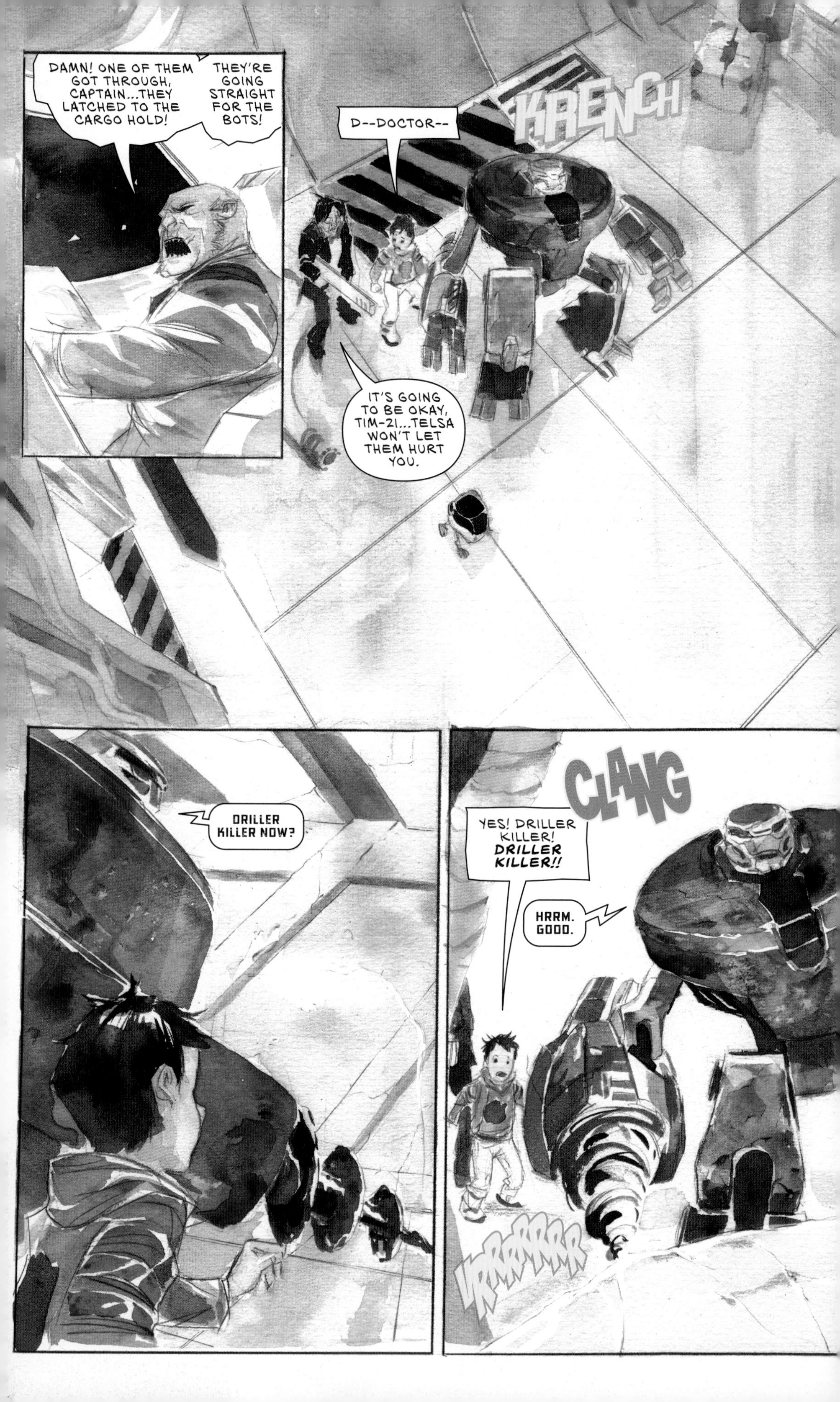

DAMN! ONE OF THEM GOT THROUGH, CAPTAIN...THEY LATCHED TO THE CARGO HOLD!
THEY'RE GOING STRAIGHT FOR THE BOTS!
D--DOCTOR--
KRENCH
IT'S GOING TO BE OKAY, TIM-21...TELSA WON'T LET THEM HURT YOU.
DRILLER KILLER NOW?
CLANG
YES! DRILLER KILLER! DRILLER KILLER!!
HRRM. GOOD.
VRRRRRRR

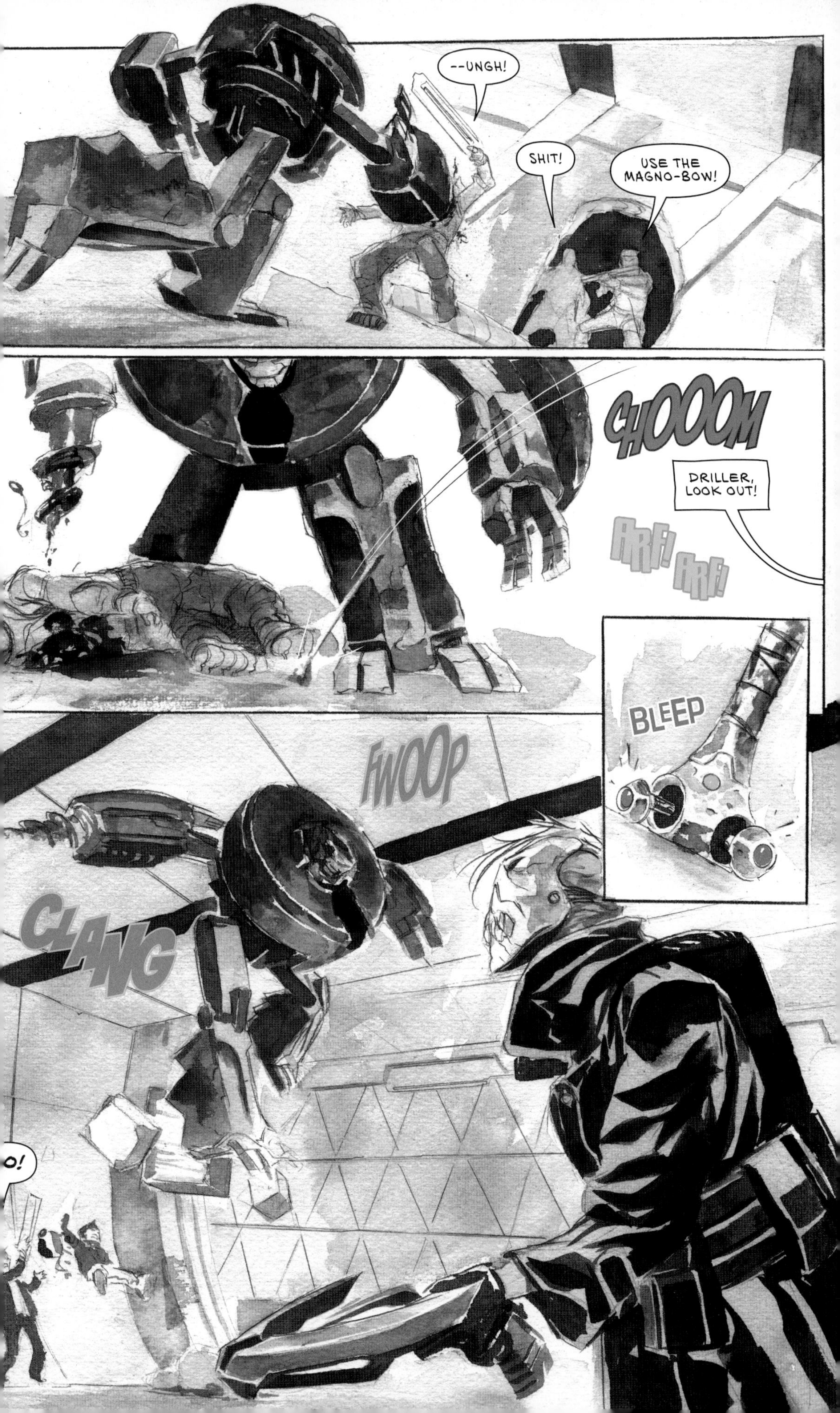
--UNGH!
SHIT!
USE THE MAGNO-BOW!
CHOOOM
DRILLER, LOOK OUT!
ARF! ARF!
BLEEP
FWOOP
CLANG
O!

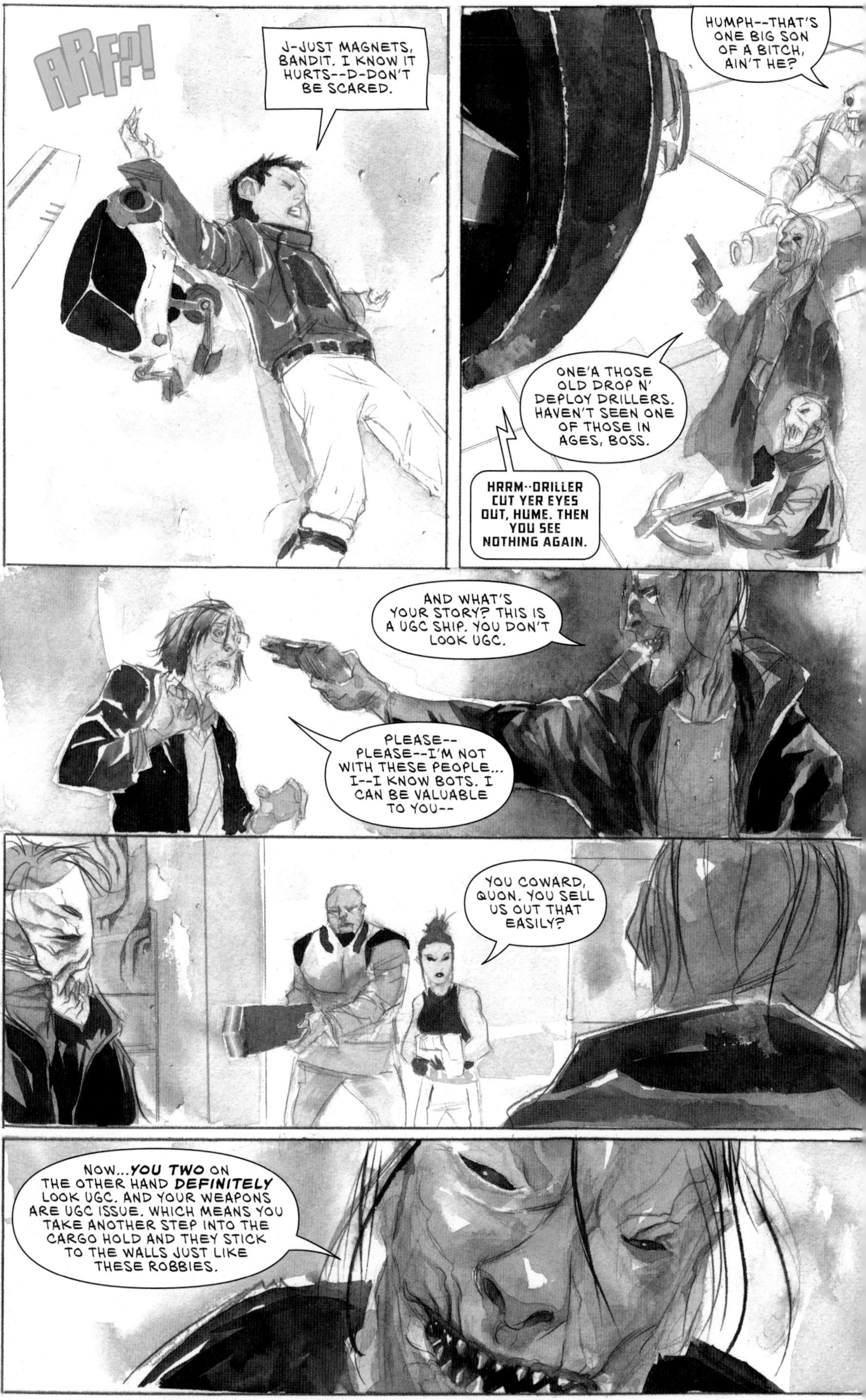
ARF?!
J-JUST MAGNETS, BANDIT. I KNOW IT HURTS--D-DON'T BE SCARED.
HUMPH--THAT'S ONE BIG SON OF A BITCH, AIN'T HE?
ONE'A THOSE OLD DROP N' DEPLOY DRILLERS. HAVEN'T SEEN ONE OF THOSE IN AGES, BOSS.
HRRM--DRILLER CUT YER EYES OUT, HUME. THEN YOU SEE NOTHING AGAIN.
AND WHAT'S YOUR STORY? THIS IS A UGC SHIP. YOU DON'T LOOK UGC.
PLEASE-- PLEASE--I'M NOT WITH THESE PEOPLE... I--I KNOW BOTS. I CAN BE VALUABLE TO YOU--
YOU COWARD, QUON. YOU SELL US OUT THAT EASILY?
NOW...YOU TWO ON THE OTHER HAND DEFINITELY LOOK UGC. AND YOUR WEAPONS ARE UGC ISSUE. WHICH MEANS YOU TAKE ANOTHER STEP INTO THE CARGO HOLD AND THEY STICK TO THE WALLS JUST LIKE THESE ROBBIES.

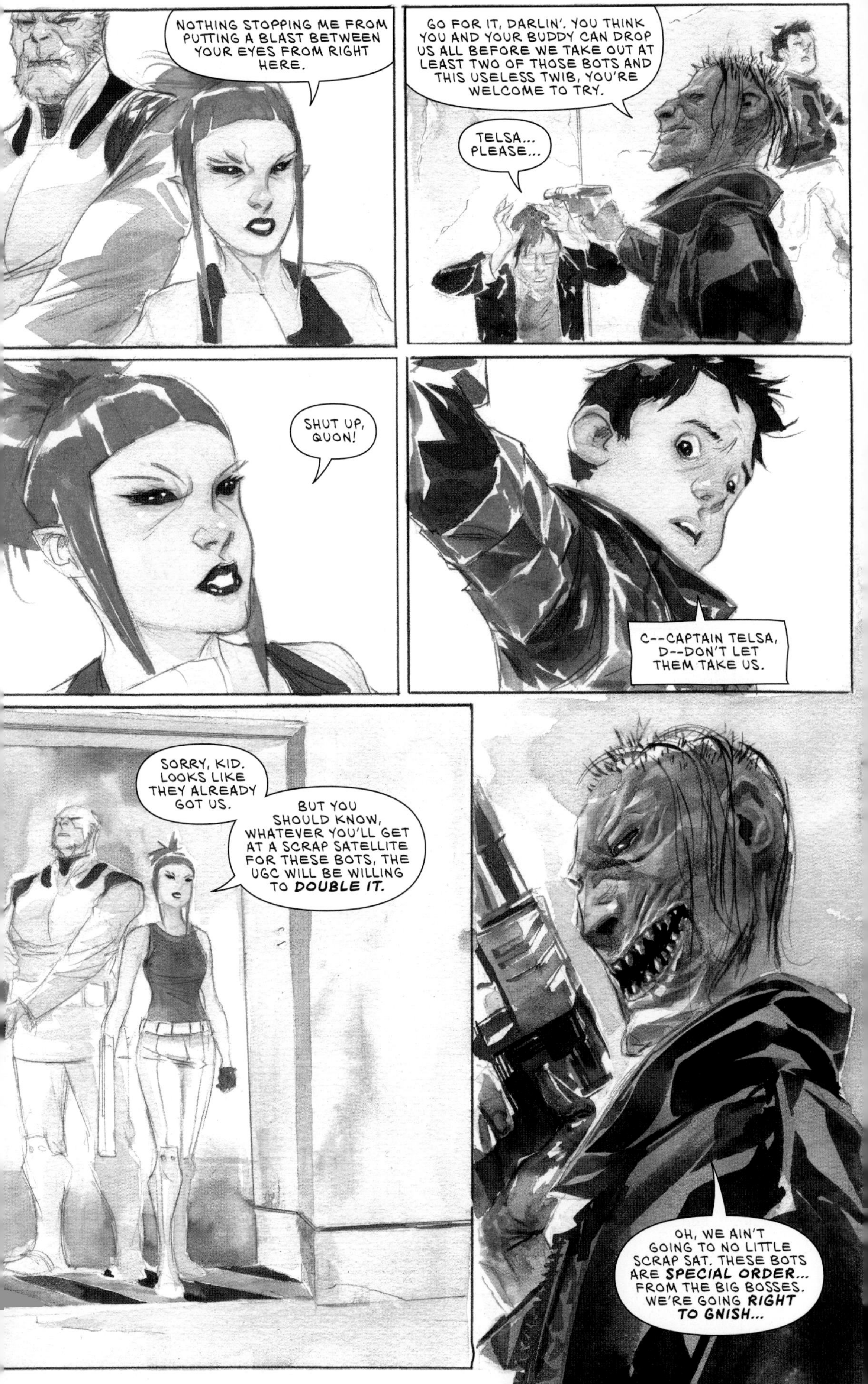

NOTHING STOPPING ME FROM PUTTING A BLAST BETWEEN YOUR EYES FROM RIGHT HERE.
GO FOR IT, DARLIN'. YOU THINK YOU AND YOUR BUDDY CAN DROP US ALL BEFORE WE TAKE OUT AT LEAST TWO OF THOSE BOTS AND THIS USELESS TWIB, YOU'RE WELCOME TO TRY.
TELSA... PLEASE...
SHUT UP, QUON!
C--CAPTAIN TELSA, D--DON'T LET THEM TAKE US.
SORRY, KID. LOOKS LIKE THEY ALREADY GOT US.
BUT YOU SHOULD KNOW, WHATEVER YOU'LL GET AT A SCRAP SATELLITE FOR THESE BOTS, THE UGC WILL BE WILLING TO **DOUBLE IT.**
OH, WE AIN'T GOING TO NO LITTLE SCRAP SAT. THESE BOTS ARE **SPECIAL ORDER...** FROM THE BIG BOSSES. WE'RE GOING **RIGHT TO GNISH...**

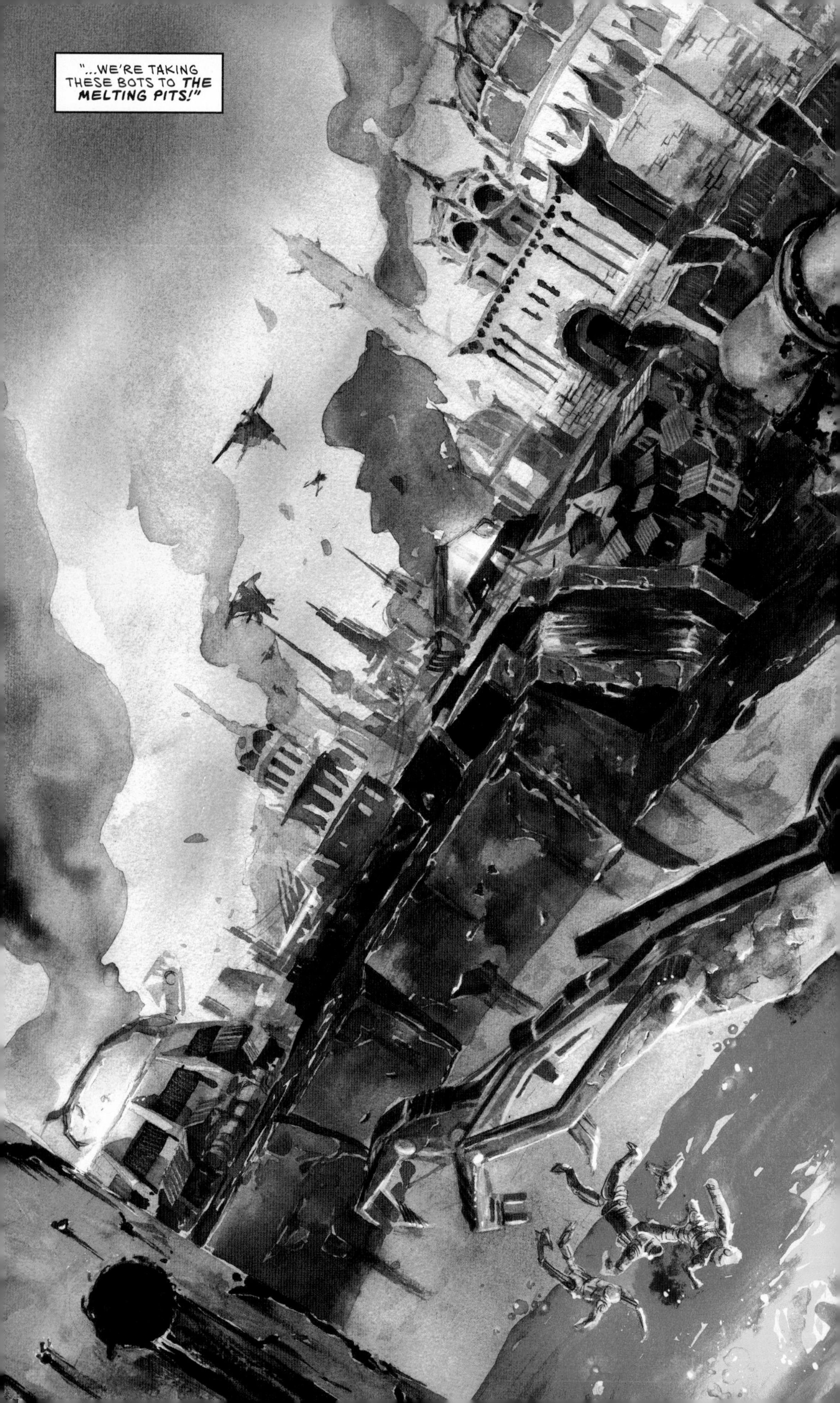
"...WE'RE TAKING THESE BOTS TO THE MELTING PITS!"

CHAPTER FIVE

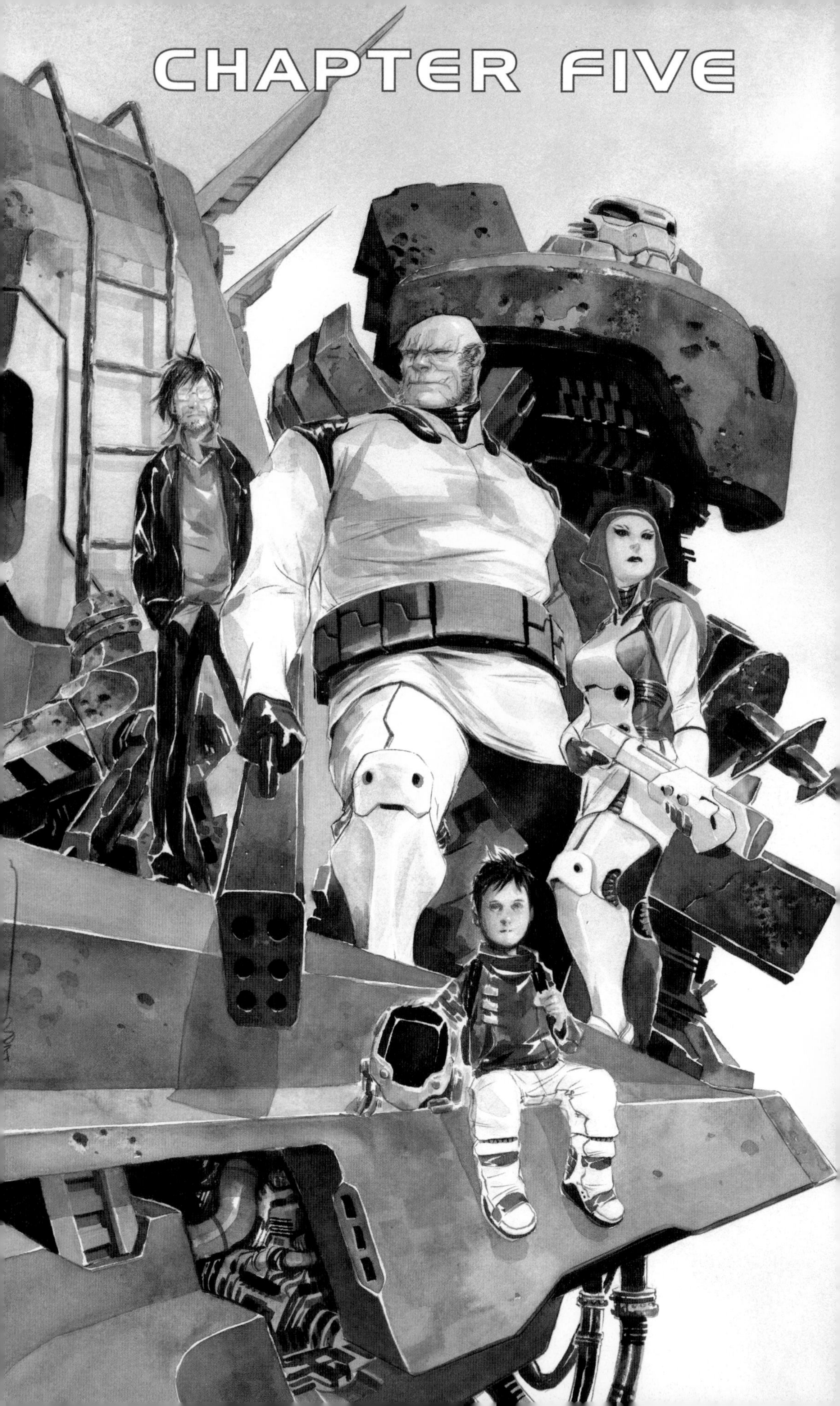

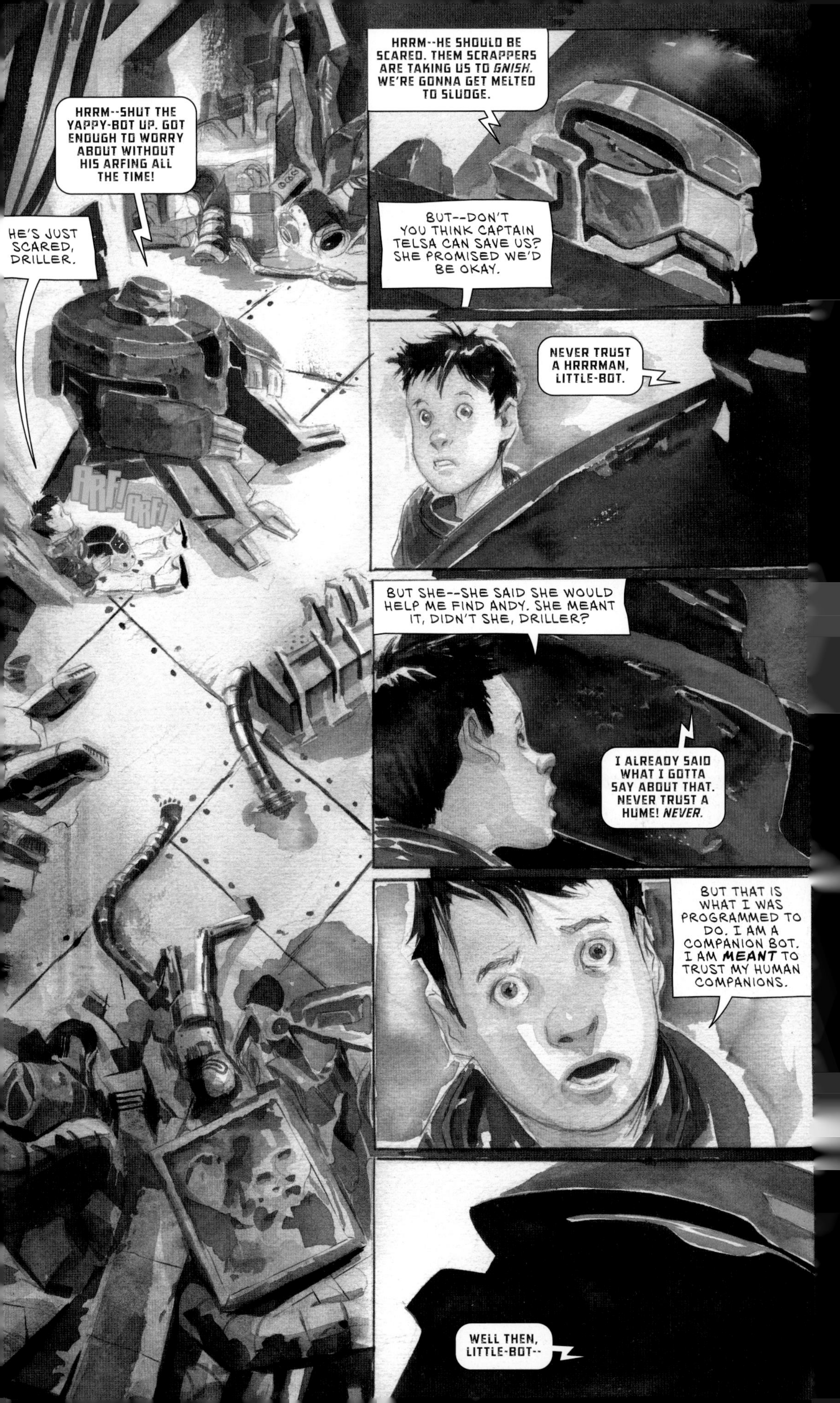
HRRM--SHUT THE YAPPY-BOT UP. GOT ENOUGH TO WORRY ABOUT WITHOUT HIS ARFING ALL THE TIME!
HE'S JUST SCARED, DRILLER.
ARF! ARF!
HRRM--HE SHOULD BE SCARED. THEM SCRAPPERS ARE TAKING US TO *GNISH*. WE'RE GONNA GET MELTED TO SLUDGE.
BUT--DON'T YOU THINK CAPTAIN TELSA CAN SAVE US? SHE PROMISED WE'D BE OKAY.
NEVER TRUST A HRRRMAN, LITTLE-BOT.
BUT SHE--SHE SAID SHE WOULD HELP ME FIND ANDY. SHE MEANT IT, DIDN'T SHE, DRILLER?
I ALREADY SAID WHAT I GOTTA SAY ABOUT THAT. NEVER TRUST A HUME! *NEVER.*
BUT THAT IS WHAT I WAS PROGRAMMED TO DO. I AM A COMPANION BOT. I AM **MEANT** TO TRUST MY HUMAN COMPANIONS.
WELL THEN, LITTLE-BOT--

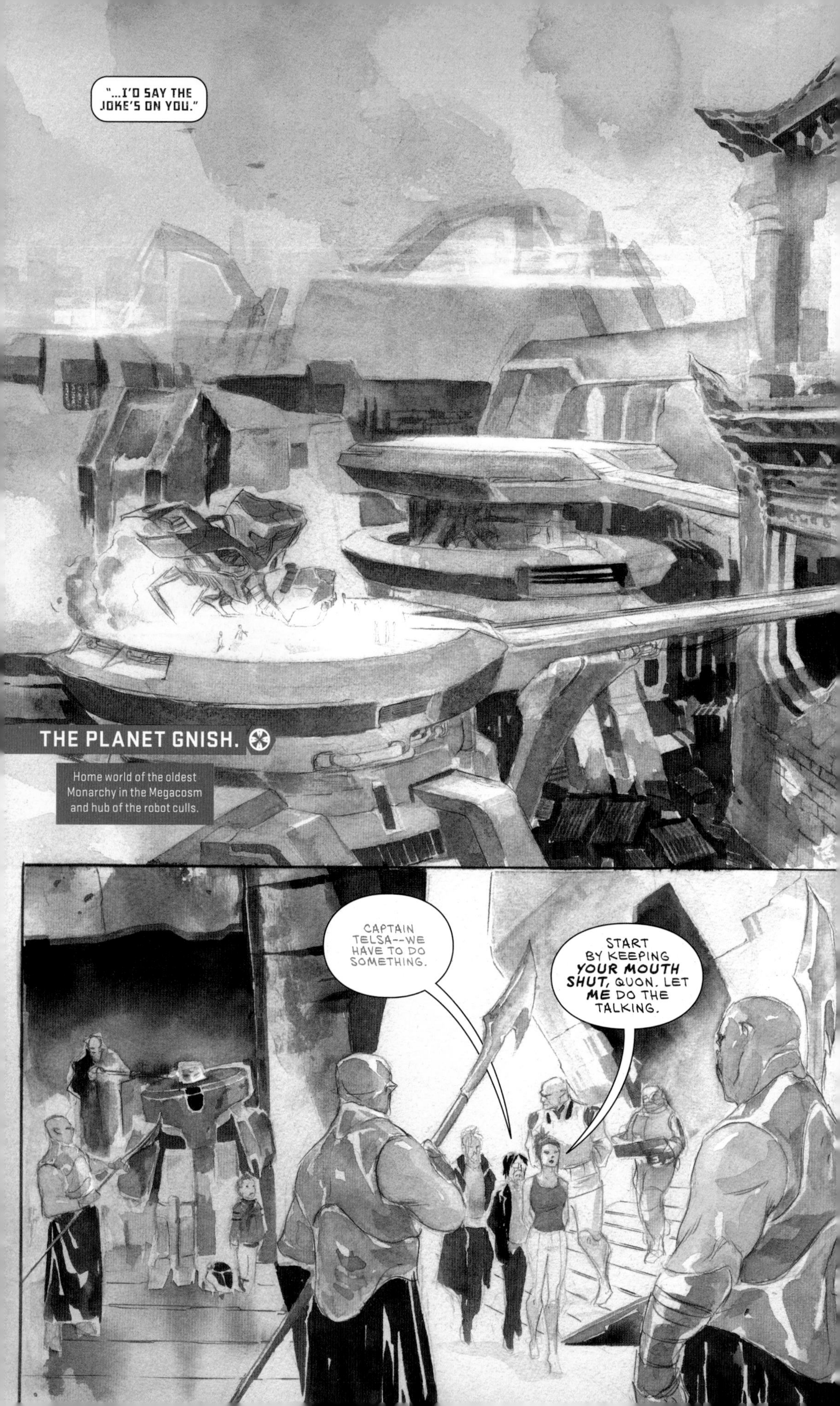
"...I'D SAY THE JOKE'S ON YOU."
THE PLANET GNISH.
Home world of the oldest Monarchy in the Megacosm and hub of the robot culls.
CAPTAIN TELSA--WE HAVE TO DO SOMETHING.
START BY KEEPING YOUR MOUTH SHUT, QUON. LET ME DO THE TALKING.

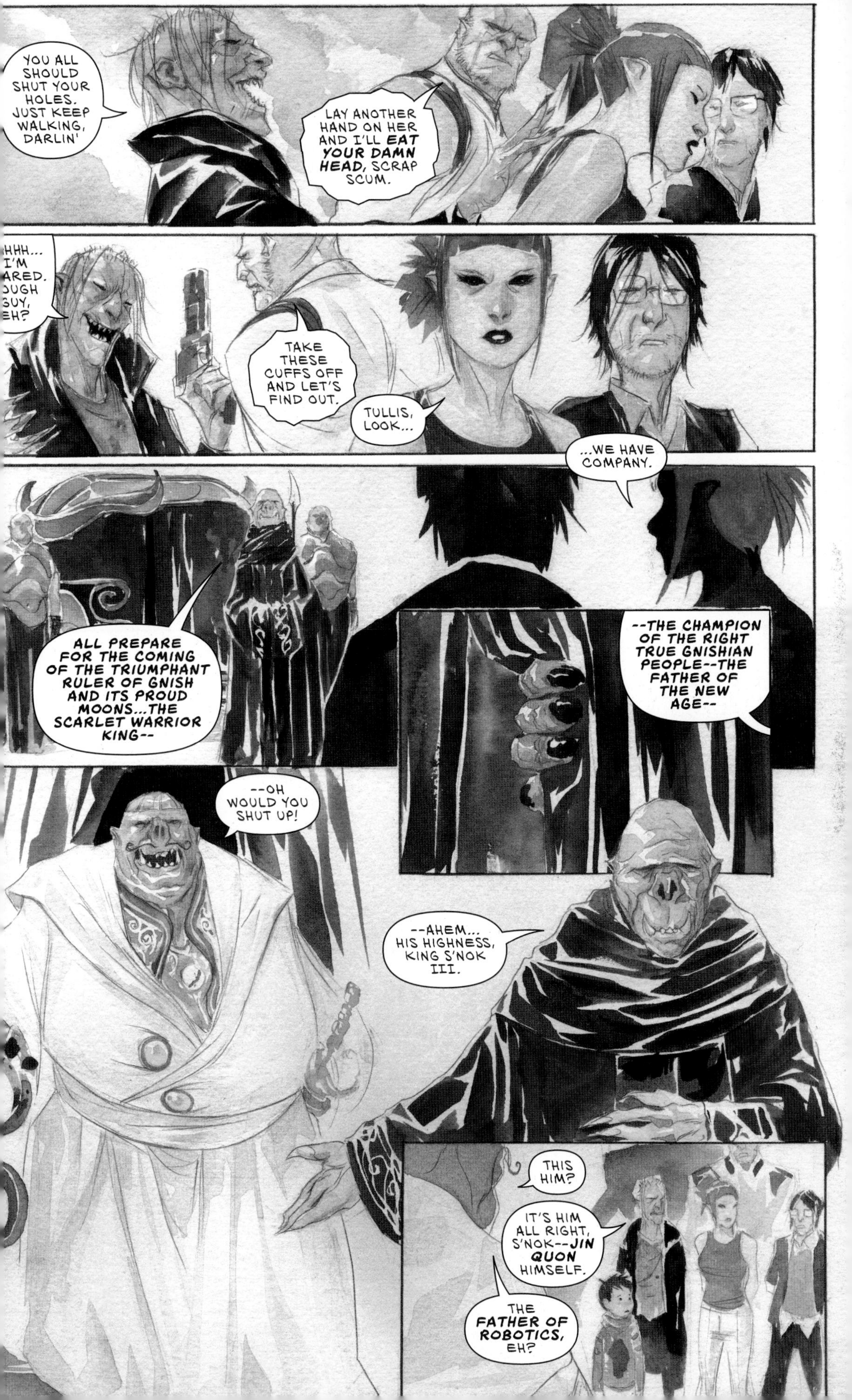

YOU ALL SHOULD SHUT YOUR HOLES. JUST KEEP WALKING, DARLIN'
LAY ANOTHER HAND ON HER AND I'LL **EAT YOUR DAMN HEAD,** SCRAP SCUM.
HHH... I'M ARED. OUGH GUY, EH?
TAKE THESE CUFFS OFF AND LET'S FIND OUT.
TULLIS, LOOK...
...WE HAVE COMPANY.
ALL PREPARE FOR THE COMING OF THE TRIUMPHANT RULER OF GNISH AND ITS PROUD MOONS...THE SCARLET WARRIOR KING--
--THE CHAMPION OF THE RIGHT TRUE GNISHIAN PEOPLE--THE FATHER OF THE NEW AGE--
--OH WOULD YOU SHUT UP!
--AHEM... HIS HIGHNESS, KING S'NOK III.
THIS HIM?
IT'S HIM ALL RIGHT, S'NOK--**JIN QUON** HIMSELF.
THE **FATHER OF ROBOTICS,** EH?

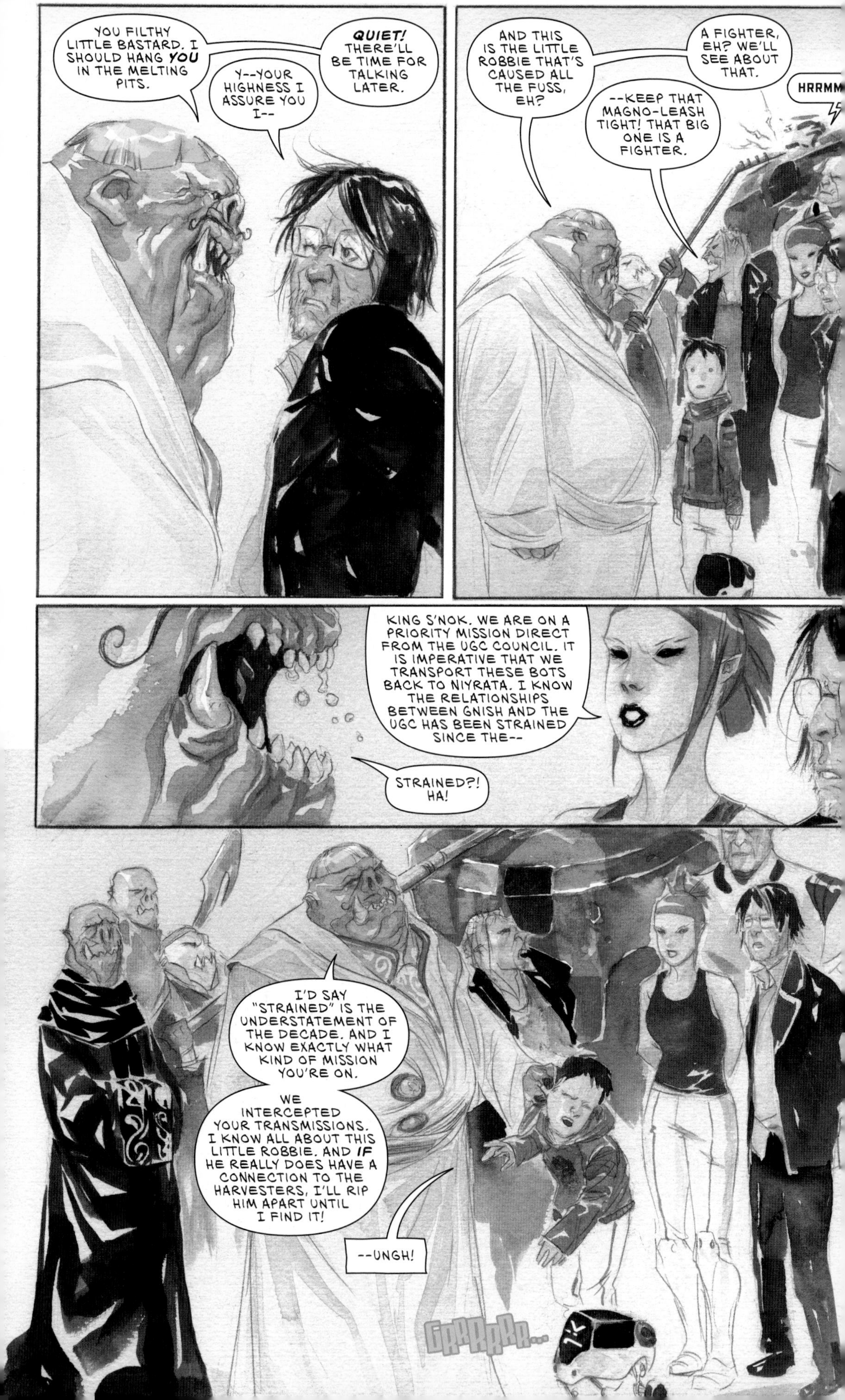
YOU FILTHY LITTLE BASTARD. I SHOULD HANG *YOU* IN THE MELTING PITS.
QUIET! THERE'LL BE TIME FOR TALKING LATER.
Y--YOUR HIGHNESS I ASSURE YOU I--
AND THIS IS THE LITTLE ROBBIE THAT'S CAUSED ALL THE FUSS, EH?
A FIGHTER, EH? WE'LL SEE ABOUT THAT.
--KEEP THAT MAGNO-LEASH TIGHT! THAT BIG ONE IS A FIGHTER.
HRRMM
KING S'NOK. WE ARE ON A PRIORITY MISSION DIRECT FROM THE UGC COUNCIL. IT IS IMPERATIVE THAT WE TRANSPORT THESE BOTS BACK TO NIYRATA. I KNOW THE RELATIONSHIPS BETWEEN GNISH AND THE UGC HAS BEEN STRAINED SINCE THE--
STRAINED?! HA!
I'D SAY "STRAINED" IS THE UNDERSTATEMENT OF THE DECADE. AND I KNOW EXACTLY WHAT KIND OF MISSION YOU'RE ON.
WE INTERCEPTED YOUR TRANSMISSIONS. I KNOW ALL ABOUT THIS LITTLE ROBBIE. AND *IF* HE REALLY DOES HAVE A CONNECTION TO THE HARVESTERS, I'LL RIP HIM APART UNTIL I FIND IT!
--UNGH!
GRRRRRR...

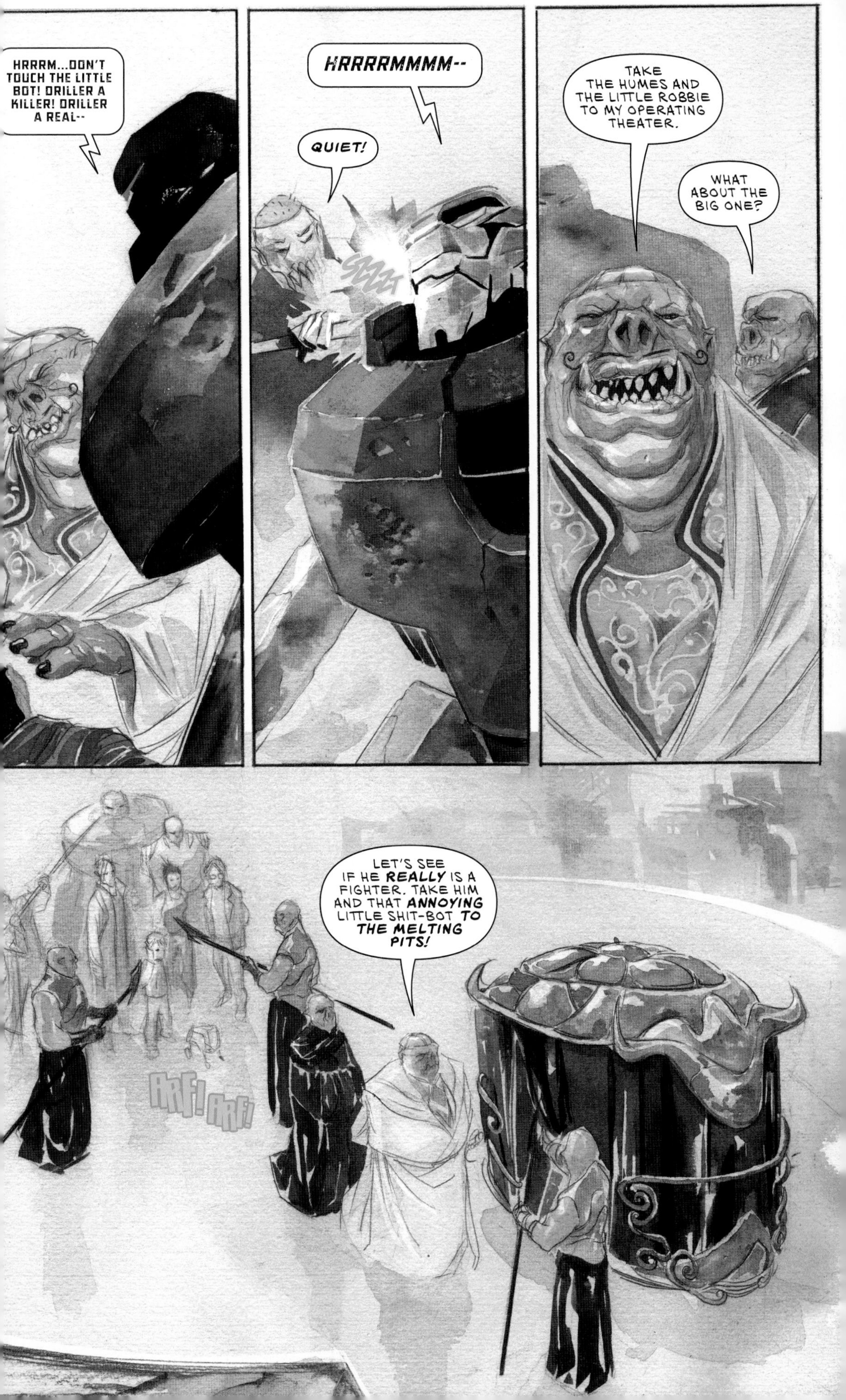
HRRRM...DON'T TOUCH THE LITTLE BOT! DRILLER A KILLER! DRILLER A REAL--
HRRRRMMMM--
QUIET!
TAKE THE HUMES AND THE LITTLE ROBBIE TO MY OPERATING THEATER.
WHAT ABOUT THE BIG ONE?
LET'S SEE IF HE REALLY IS A FIGHTER. TAKE HIM AND THAT ANNOYING LITTLE SHIT-BOT TO THE MELTING PITS!
ARF! ARF!

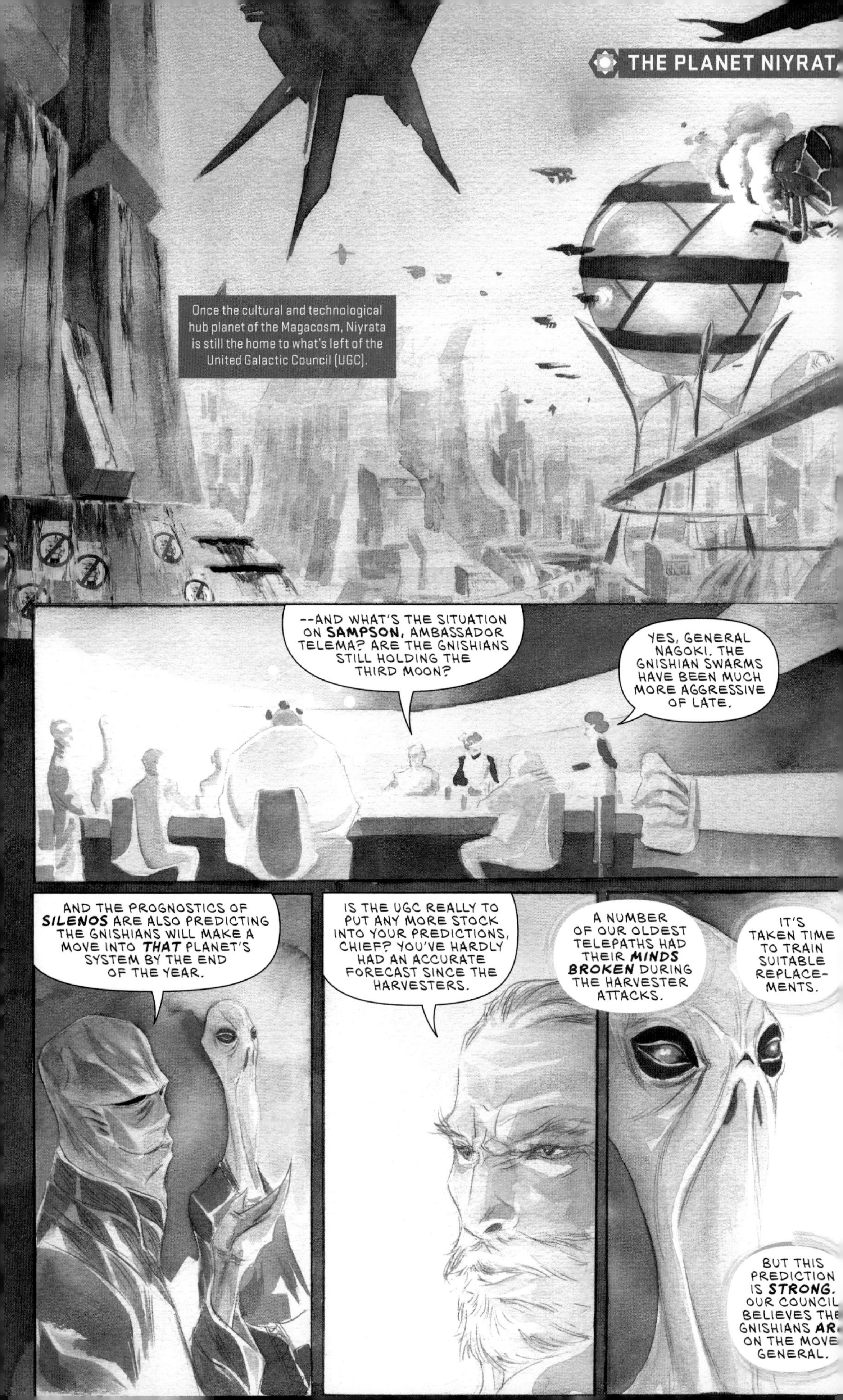

THE PLANET NIYRATA
Once the cultural and technological hub planet of the Magacosm, Niyrata is still the home to what's left of the United Galactic Council (UGC).
--AND WHAT'S THE SITUATION ON SAMPSON, AMBASSADOR TELEMA? ARE THE GNISHIANS STILL HOLDING THE THIRD MOON?
YES, GENERAL NAGOKI. THE GNISHIAN SWARMS HAVE BEEN MUCH MORE AGGRESSIVE OF LATE.
AND THE PROGNOSTICS OF SILENOS ARE ALSO PREDICTING THE GNISHIANS WILL MAKE A MOVE INTO THAT PLANET'S SYSTEM BY THE END OF THE YEAR.
IS THE UGC REALLY TO PUT ANY MORE STOCK INTO YOUR PREDICTIONS, CHIEF? YOU'VE HARDLY HAD AN ACCURATE FORECAST SINCE THE HARVESTERS.
A NUMBER OF OUR OLDEST TELEPATHS HAD THEIR MINDS BROKEN DURING THE HARVESTER ATTACKS.
IT'S TAKEN TIME TO TRAIN SUITABLE REPLACE-MENTS.
BUT THIS PREDICTION IS STRONG. OUR COUNCIL BELIEVES THE GNISHIANS AR ON THE MOVE GENERAL.

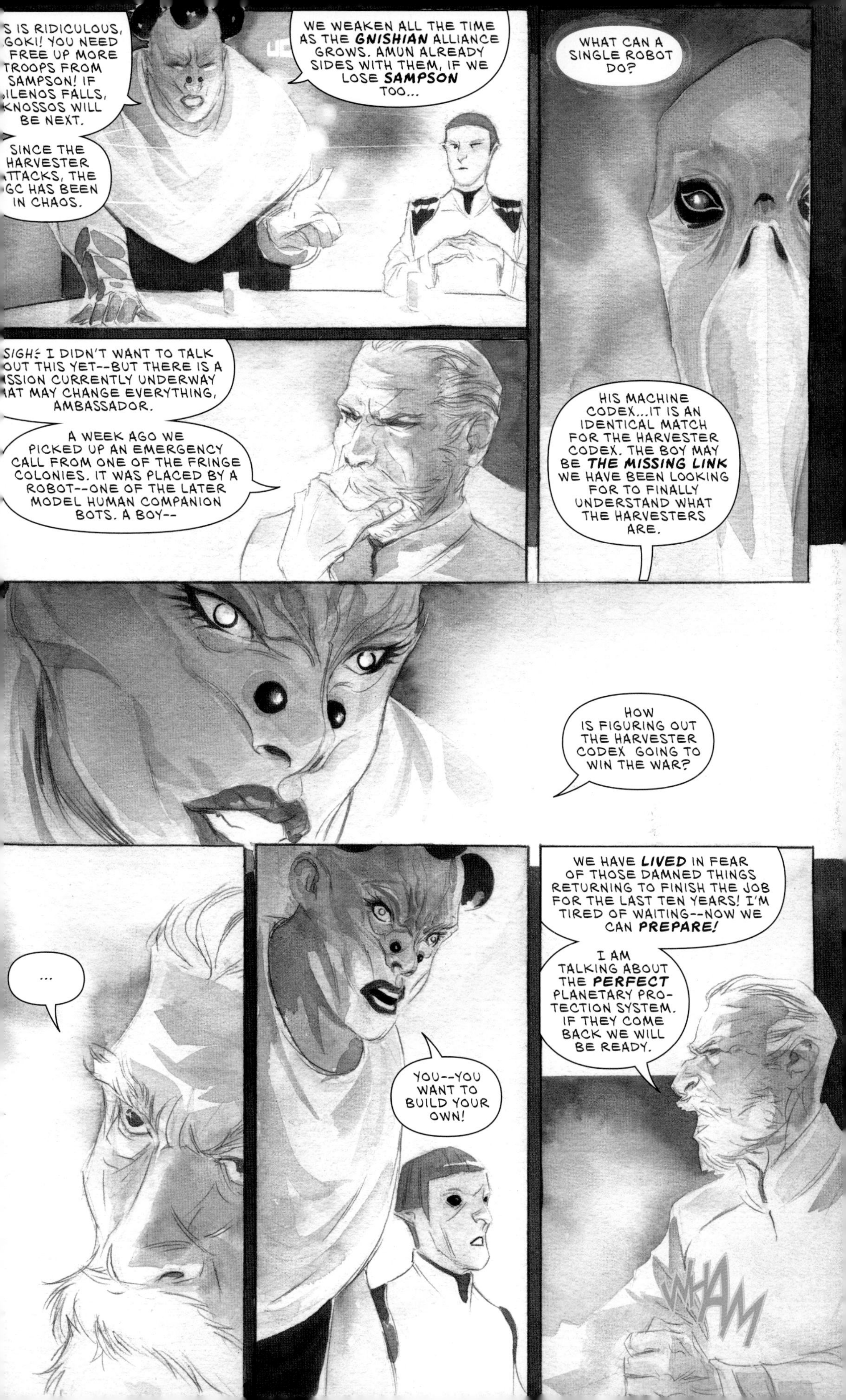
S IS RIDICULOUS, GOKI! YOU NEED FREE UP MORE TROOPS FROM SAMPSON! IF ILENOS FALLS, KNOSSOS WILL BE NEXT.
SINCE THE HARVESTER TTACKS, THE GC HAS BEEN IN CHAOS.
WE WEAKEN ALL THE TIME AS THE GNISHIAN ALLIANCE GROWS. AMUN ALREADY SIDES WITH THEM, IF WE LOSE SAMPSON TOO...
WHAT CAN A SINGLE ROBOT DO?
SIGH: I DIDN'T WANT TO TALK OUT THIS YET--BUT THERE IS A SSION CURRENTLY UNDERWAY AT MAY CHANGE EVERYTHING, AMBASSADOR.
A WEEK AGO WE PICKED UP AN EMERGENCY CALL FROM ONE OF THE FRINGE COLONIES. IT WAS PLACED BY A ROBOT--ONE OF THE LATER MODEL HUMAN COMPANION BOTS. A BOY--
HIS MACHINE CODEX...IT IS AN IDENTICAL MATCH FOR THE HARVESTER CODEX. THE BOY MAY BE THE MISSING LINK WE HAVE BEEN LOOKING FOR TO FINALLY UNDERSTAND WHAT THE HARVESTERS ARE.
HOW IS FIGURING OUT THE HARVESTER CODEX GOING TO WIN THE WAR?
...
YOU--YOU WANT TO BUILD YOUR OWN!
WE HAVE LIVED IN FEAR OF THOSE DAMNED THINGS RETURNING TO FINISH THE JOB FOR THE LAST TEN YEARS! I'M TIRED OF WAITING--NOW WE CAN PREPARE!
I AM TALKING ABOUT THE PERFECT PLANETARY PROTECTION SYSTEM. IF THEY COME BACK WE WILL BE READY.
WHAM

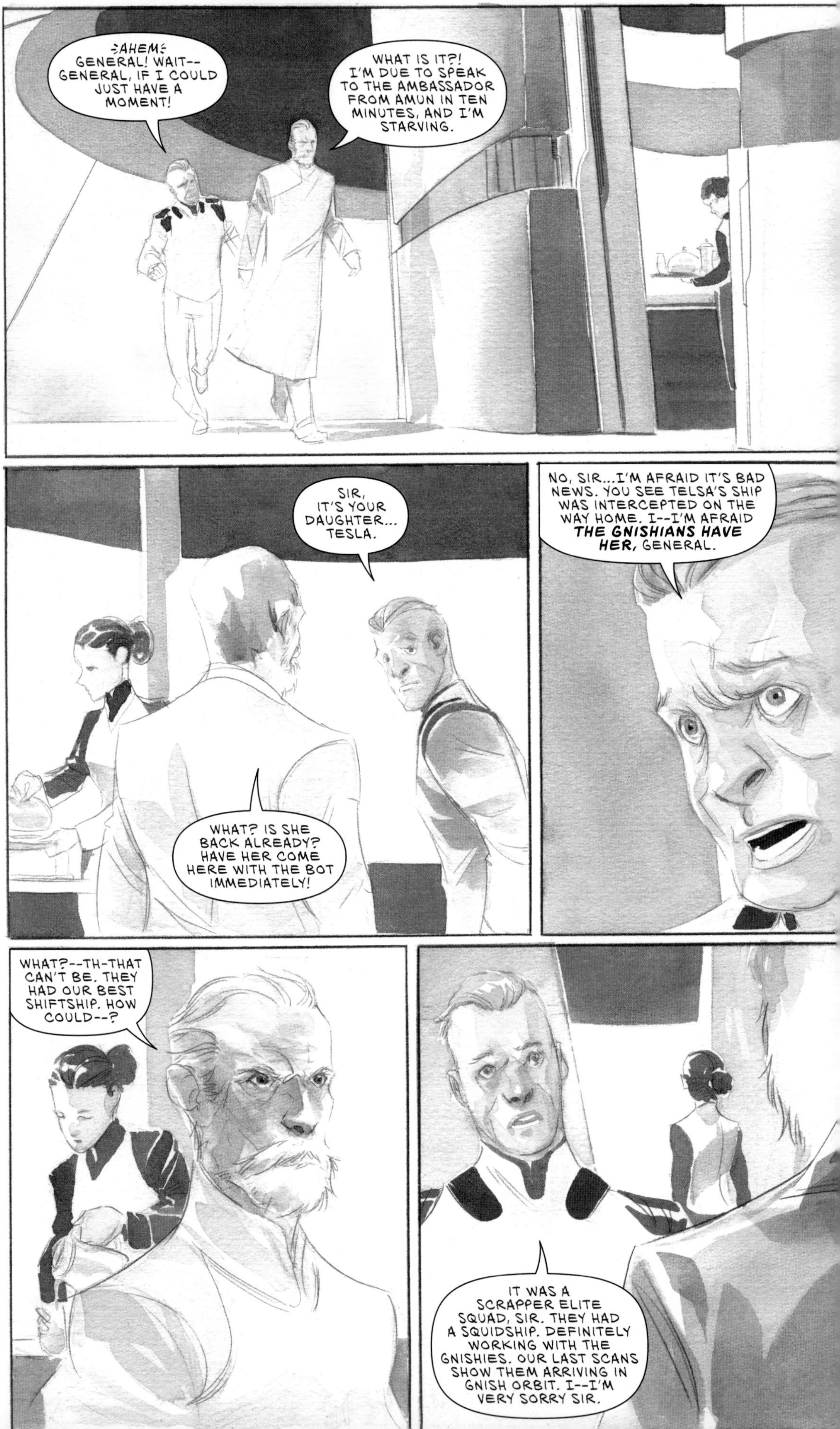

-AHEM- GENERAL! WAIT-- GENERAL, IF I COULD JUST HAVE A MOMENT!
WHAT IS IT?! I'M DUE TO SPEAK TO THE AMBASSADOR FROM AMUN IN TEN MINUTES, AND I'M STARVING.
SIR, IT'S YOUR DAUGHTER... TESLA.
WHAT? IS SHE BACK ALREADY? HAVE HER COME HERE WITH THE BOT IMMEDIATELY!
NO, SIR...I'M AFRAID IT'S BAD NEWS. YOU SEE TELSA'S SHIP WAS INTERCEPTED ON THE WAY HOME. I--I'M AFRAID **THE GNISHIANS HAVE HER,** GENERAL.
WHAT?--TH-THAT CAN'T BE. THEY HAD OUR BEST SHIFTSHIP. HOW COULD--?
IT WAS A SCRAPPER ELITE SQUAD, SIR. THEY HAD A SQUIDSHIP. DEFINITELY WORKING WITH THE GNISHIES. OUR LAST SCANS SHOW THEM ARRIVING IN GNISH ORBIT. I--I'M VERY SORRY SIR.

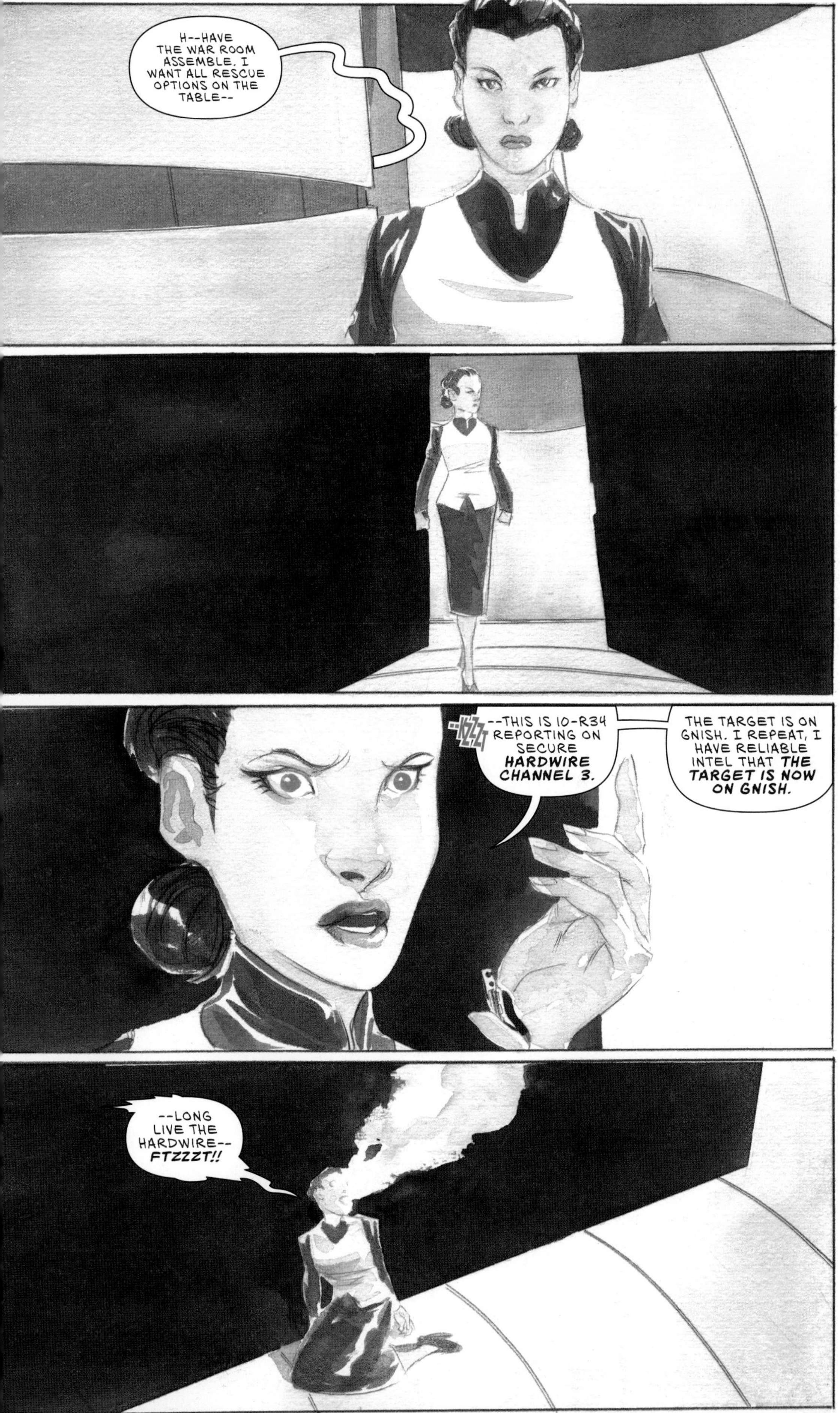
H--HAVE THE WAR ROOM ASSEMBLE. I WANT ALL RESCUE OPTIONS ON THE TABLE--
KZZZT
--THIS IS 10-R34 REPORTING ON SECURE **HARDWIRE CHANNEL 3.**
THE TARGET IS ON GNISH. I REPEAT, I HAVE RELIABLE INTEL THAT ***THE TARGET IS NOW ON GNISH.***
--LONG LIVE THE HARDWIRE-- ***FTZZZT!!***

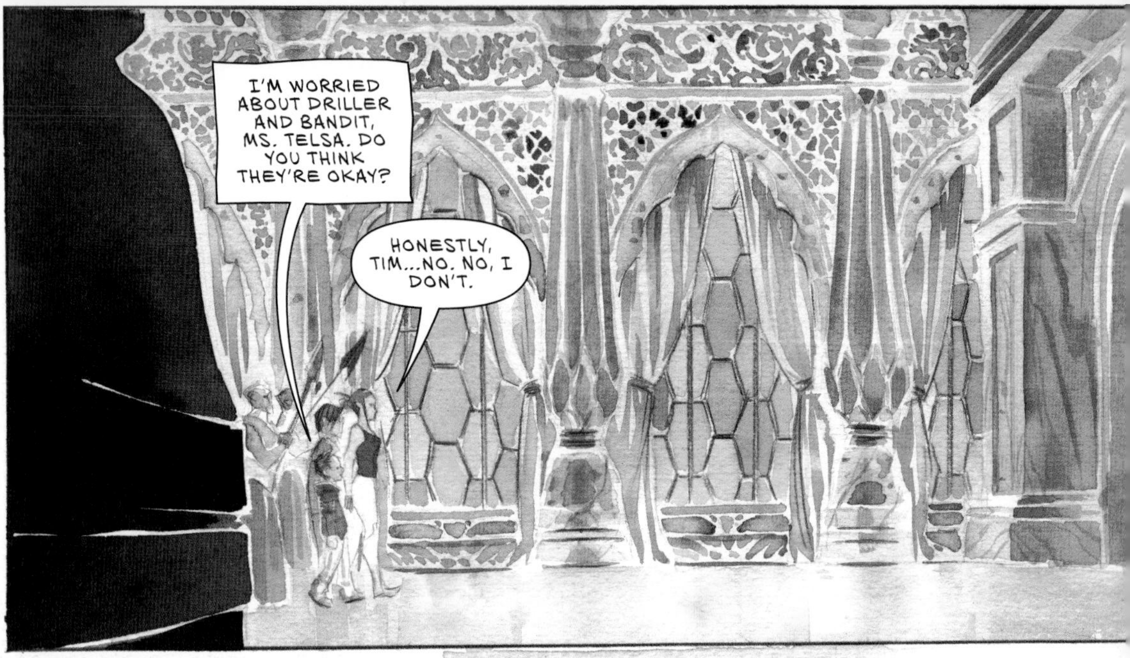
I'M WORRIED ABOUT DRILLER AND BANDIT, MS. TELSA. DO YOU THINK THEY'RE OKAY?
HONESTLY, TIM...NO. NO, I DON'T.

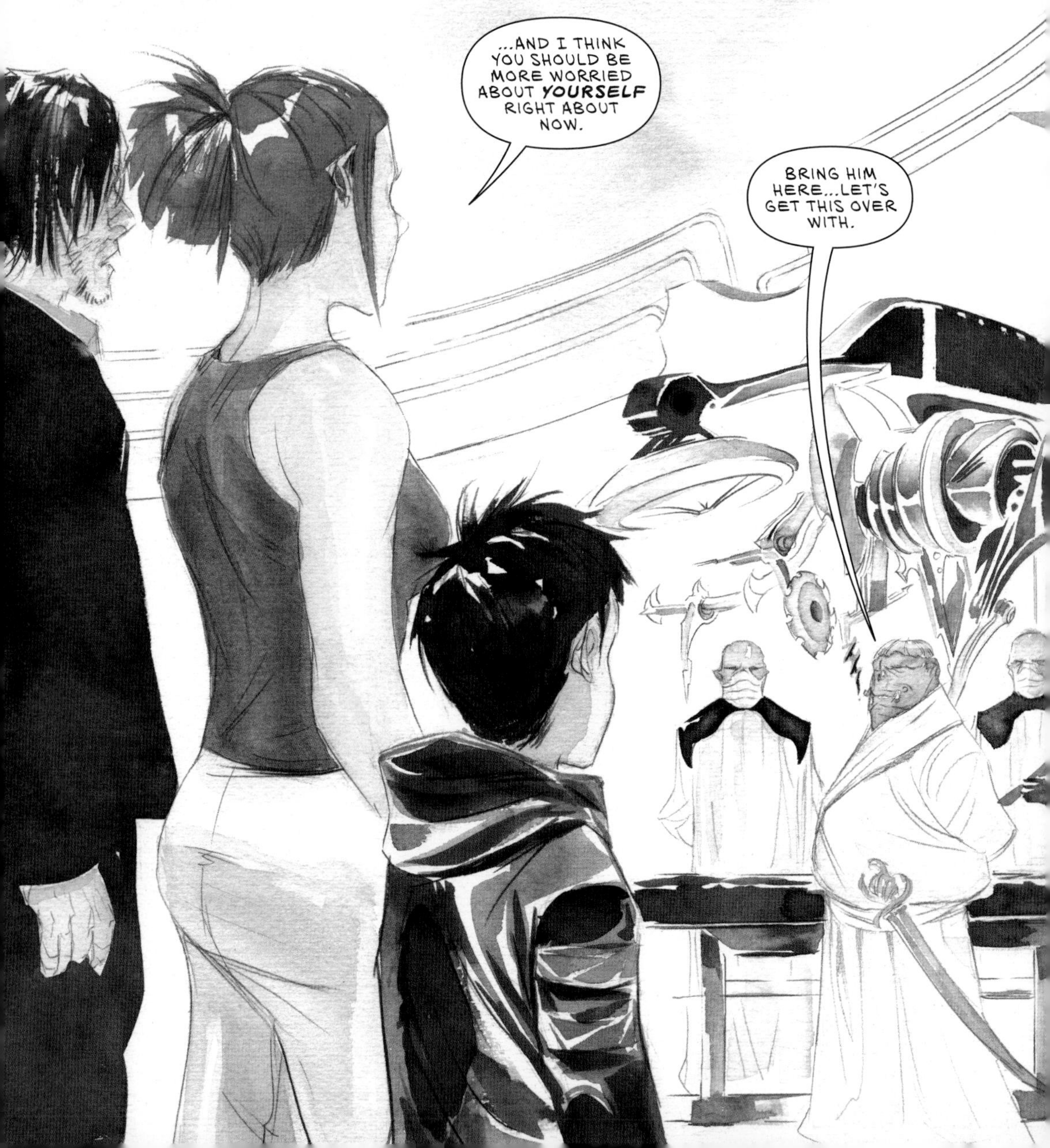
...AND I THINK YOU SHOULD BE MORE WORRIED ABOUT *YOURSELF* RIGHT ABOUT NOW.
BRING HIM HERE...LET'S GET THIS OVER WITH.

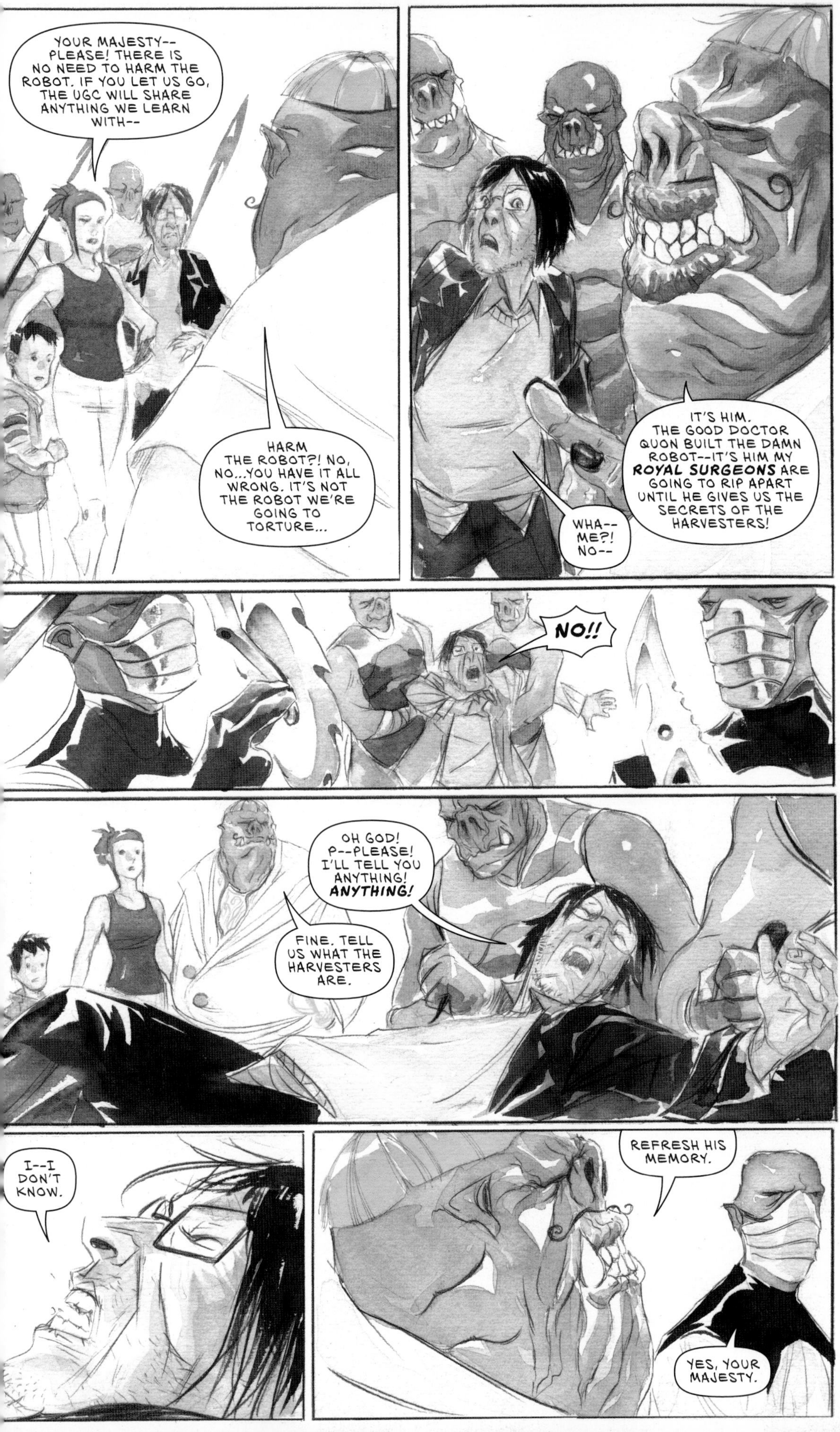
YOUR MAJESTY-- PLEASE! THERE IS NO NEED TO HARM THE ROBOT. IF YOU LET US GO, THE UGC WILL SHARE ANYTHING WE LEARN WITH--
HARM THE ROBOT?! NO, NO...YOU HAVE IT ALL WRONG. IT'S NOT THE ROBOT WE'RE GOING TO TORTURE...
IT'S HIM. THE GOOD DOCTOR QUON BUILT THE DAMN ROBOT--IT'S HIM MY ROYAL SURGEONS ARE GOING TO RIP APART UNTIL HE GIVES US THE SECRETS OF THE HARVESTERS!
WHA-- ME?! NO--
NO!!
OH GOD! P--PLEASE! I'LL TELL YOU ANYTHING! ANYTHING!
FINE. TELL US WHAT THE HARVESTERS ARE.
I--I DON'T KNOW.
REFRESH HIS MEMORY.
YES, YOUR MAJESTY.

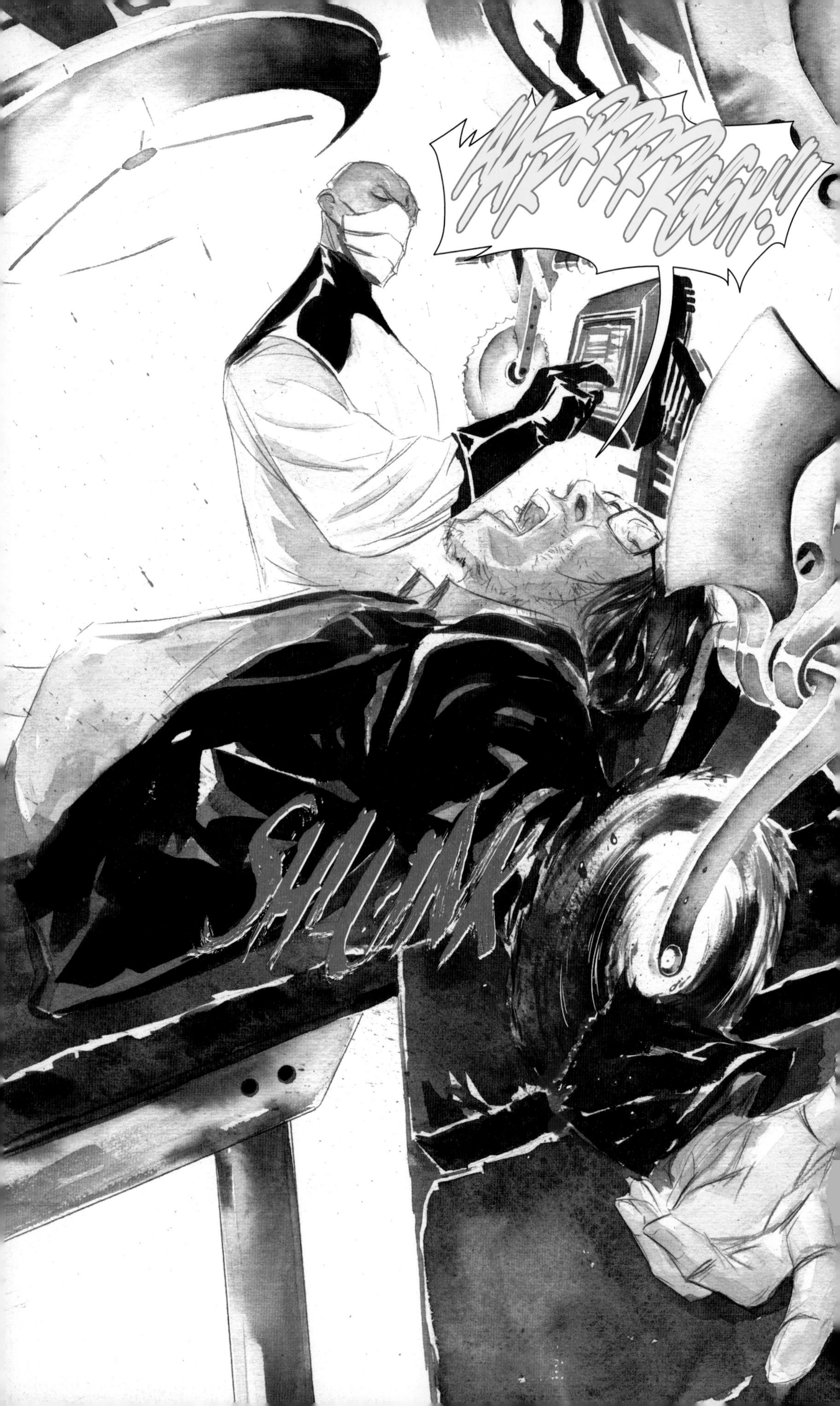
AARRRRGGH!!
SHUNK

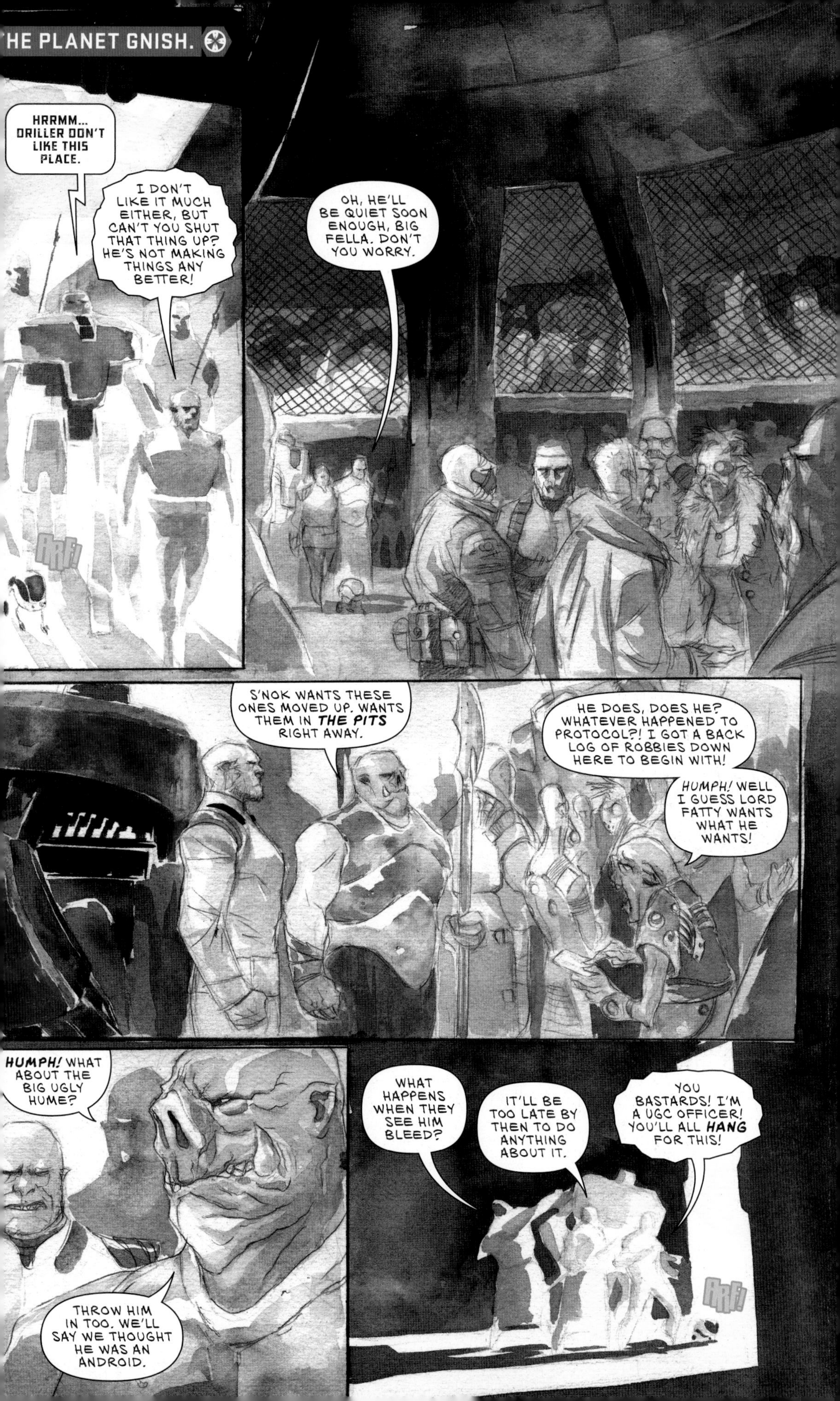
HE PLANET GNISH.
HRRMM... DRILLER DON'T LIKE THIS PLACE.
I DON'T LIKE IT MUCH EITHER, BUT CAN'T YOU SHUT THAT THING UP? HE'S NOT MAKING THINGS ANY BETTER!
ARF!
OH, HE'LL BE QUIET SOON ENOUGH, BIG FELLA. DON'T YOU WORRY.
S'NOK WANTS THESE ONES MOVED UP. WANTS THEM IN THE PITS RIGHT AWAY.
HE DOES, DOES HE? WHATEVER HAPPENED TO PROTOCOL?! I GOT A BACK LOG OF ROBBIES DOWN HERE TO BEGIN WITH!
HUMPH! WELL I GUESS LORD FATTY WANTS WHAT HE WANTS!
HUMPH! WHAT ABOUT THE BIG UGLY HUME?
THROW HIM IN TOO. WE'LL SAY WE THOUGHT HE WAS AN ANDROID.
WHAT HAPPENS WHEN THEY SEE HIM BLEED?
IT'LL BE TOO LATE BY THEN TO DO ANYTHING ABOUT IT.
YOU BASTARDS! I'M A UGC OFFICER! YOU'LL ALL HANG FOR THIS!
ARF!

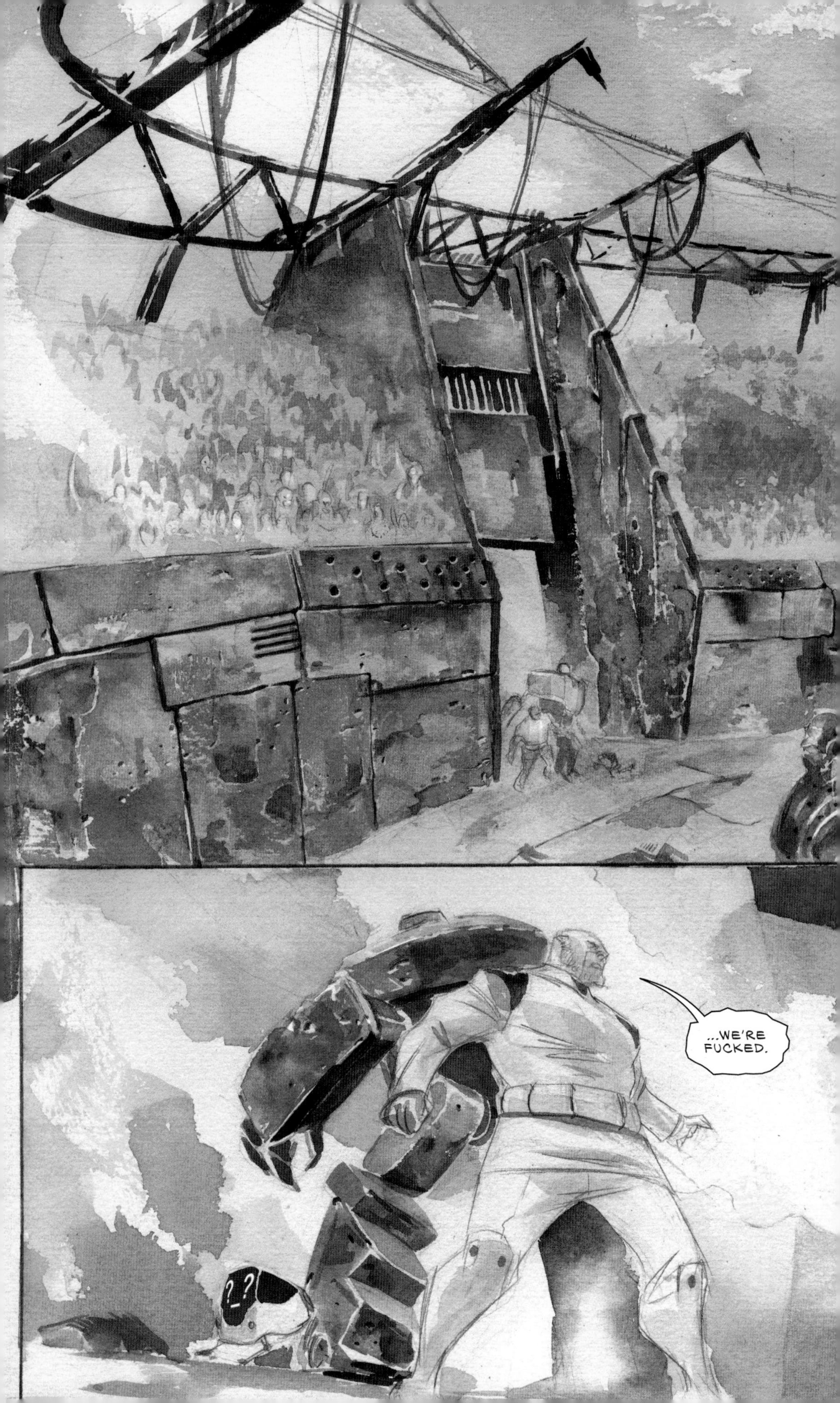
...WE'RE FUCKED.
?_?

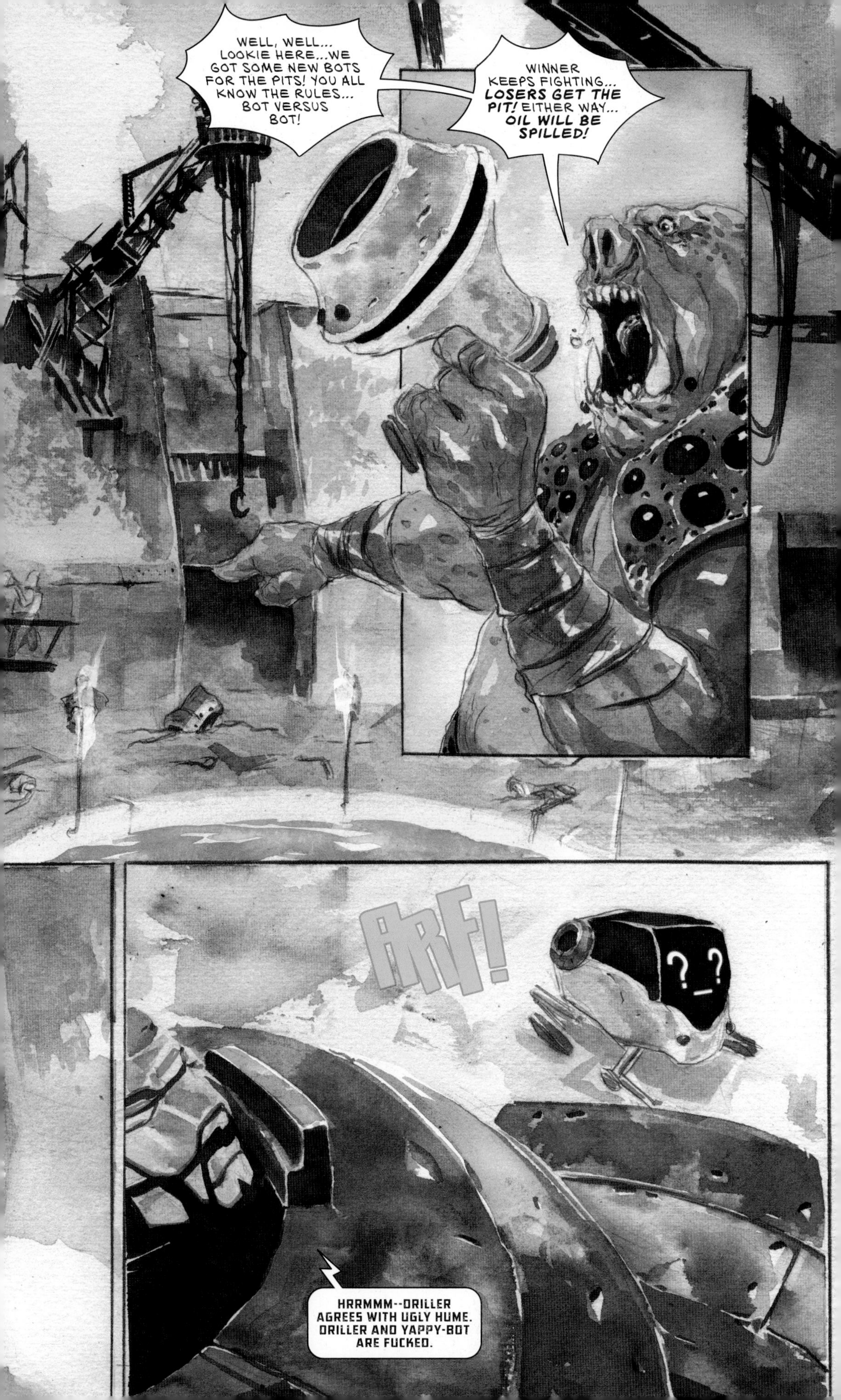

WELL, WELL... LOOKIE HERE...WE GOT SOME NEW BOTS FOR THE PITS! YOU ALL KNOW THE RULES... BOT VERSUS BOT!
WINNER KEEPS FIGHTING... **LOSERS GET THE PIT!** EITHER WAY... **OIL WILL BE SPILLED!**
ARF!
?_?
HRRMMM--DRILLER AGREES WITH UGLY HUME. DRILLER AND YAPPY-BOT ARE FUCKED.

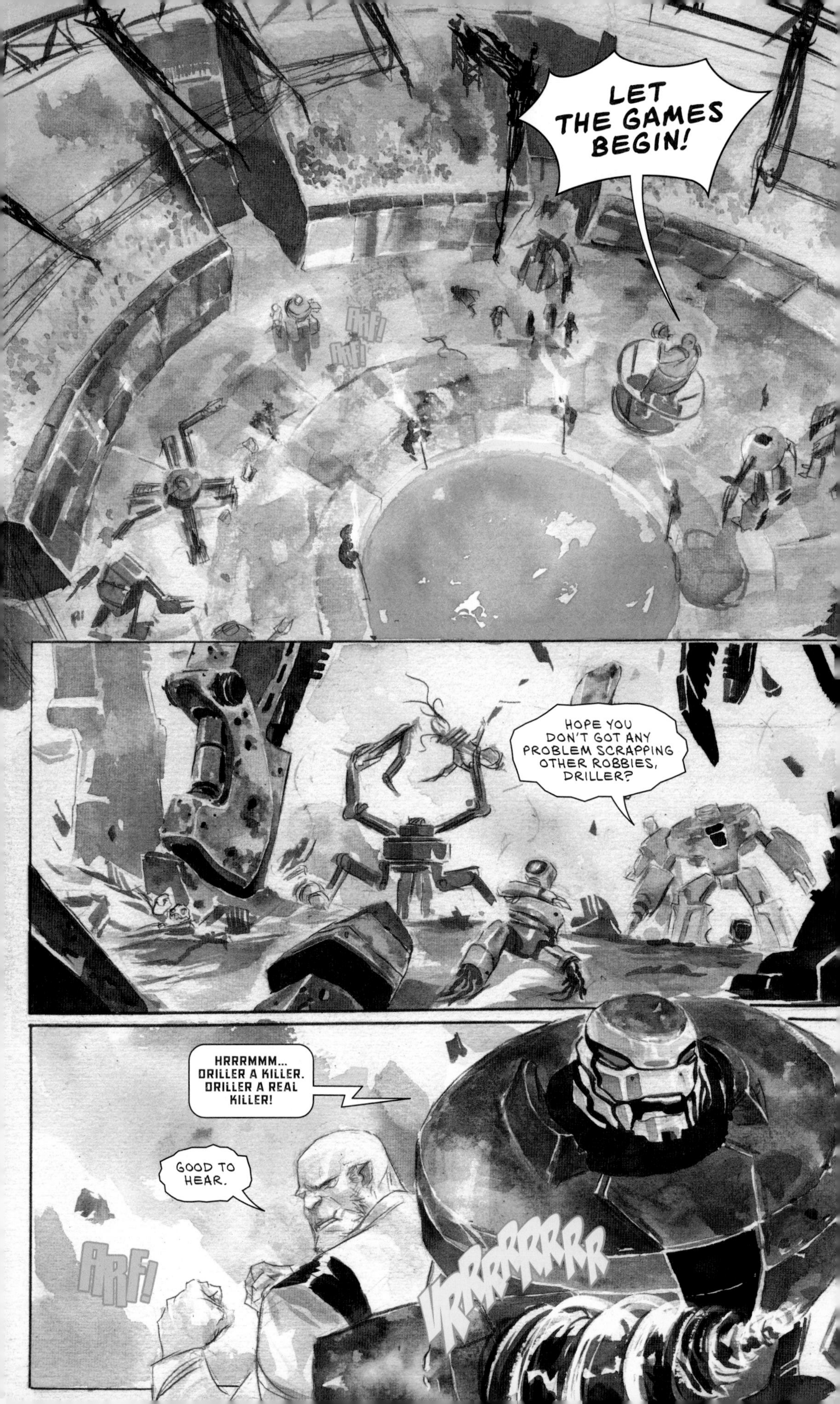
LET THE GAMES BEGIN!
ARF!
ARF!
HOPE YOU DON'T GOT ANY PROBLEM SCRAPPING OTHER ROBBIES, DRILLER?
HRRRMMM... DRILLER A KILLER. DRILLER A REAL KILLER!
GOOD TO HEAR.
ARF!
URRRRRRRR

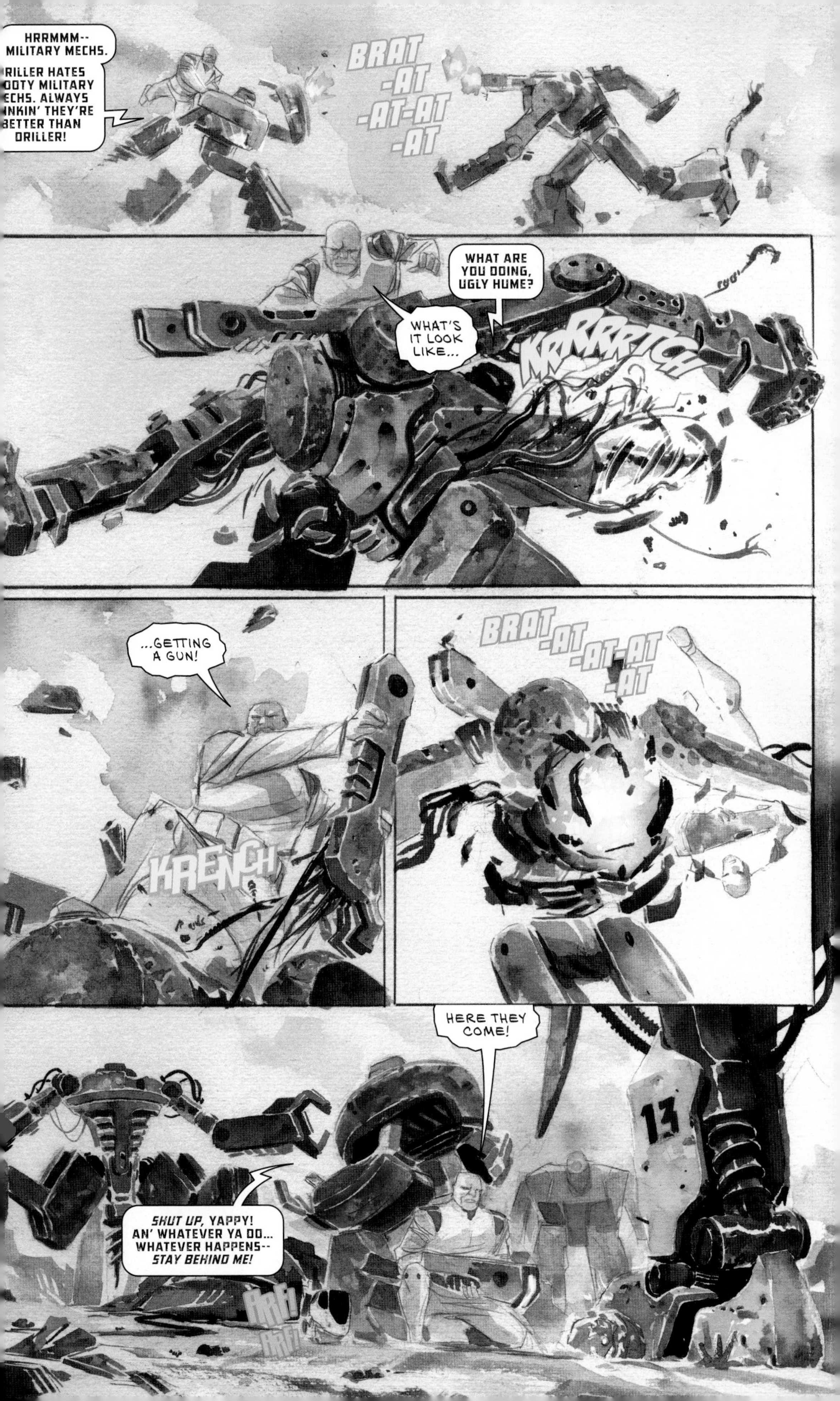
HRRMMM-- MILITARY MECHS.
RILLER HATES OOTY MILITARY ECHS. ALWAYS INKIN' THEY'RE BETTER THAN DRILLER!
BRAT -AT -AT-AT -AT
WHAT ARE YOU DOING, UGLY HUME?
WHAT'S IT LOOK LIKE...
KRRRRTCH
...GETTING A GUN!
KRENCH
BRAT -AT -AT-AT -AT
HERE THEY COME!
SHUT UP, YAPPY! AN' WHATEVER YA DO... WHATEVER HAPPENS-- STAY BEHIND ME!
ARF! ARF!
13

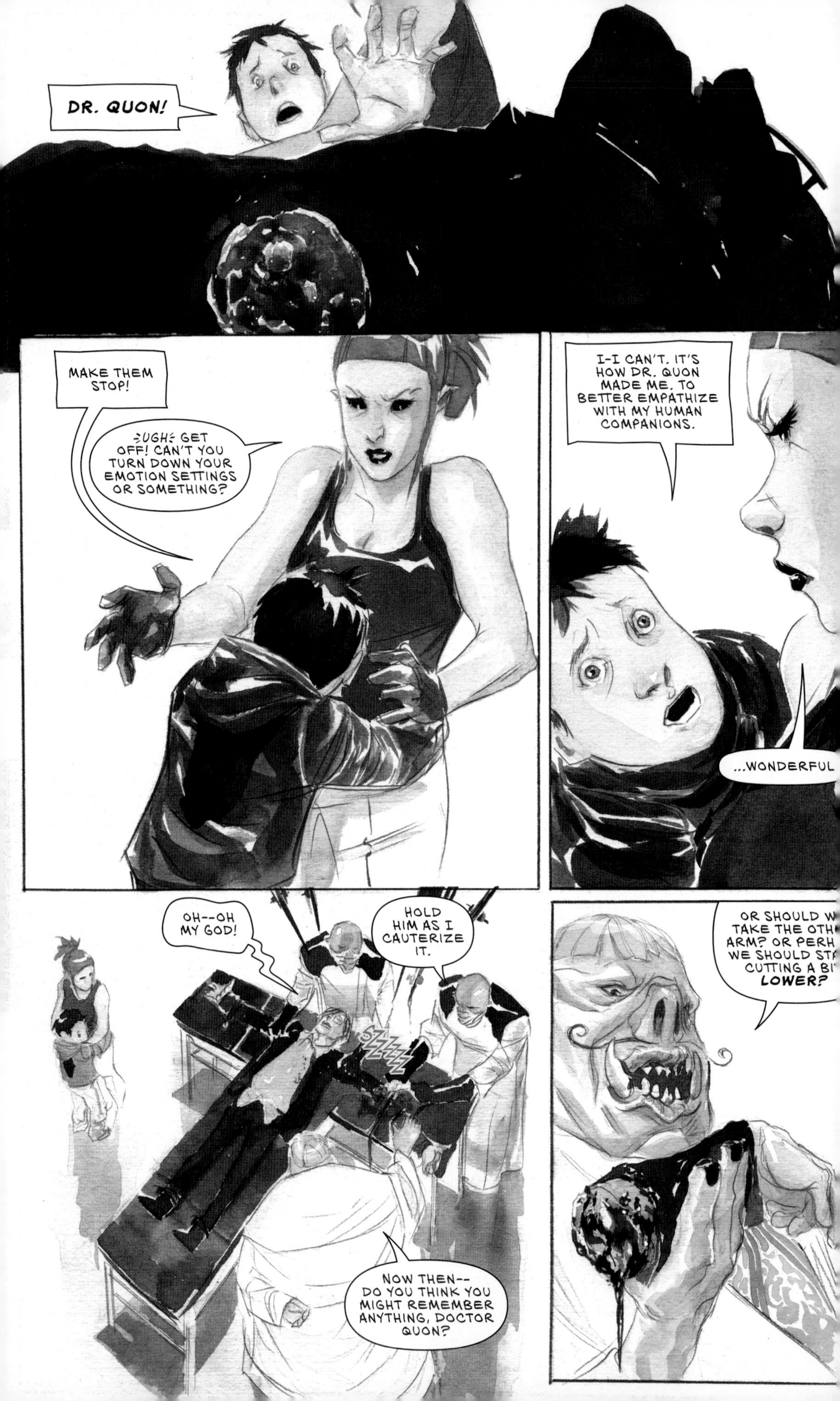
DR. QUON!
MAKE THEM STOP!
UGH GET OFF! CAN'T YOU TURN DOWN YOUR EMOTION SETTINGS OR SOMETHING?
I-I CAN'T. IT'S HOW DR. QUON MADE ME. TO BETTER EMPATHIZE WITH MY HUMAN COMPANIONS.
...WONDERFUL
OH--OH MY GOD!
HOLD HIM AS I CAUTERIZE IT.
NOW THEN-- DO YOU THINK YOU MIGHT REMEMBER ANYTHING, DOCTOR QUON?
OR SHOULD W TAKE THE OTH ARM? OR PERH WE SHOULD ST CUTTING A BI LOWER?

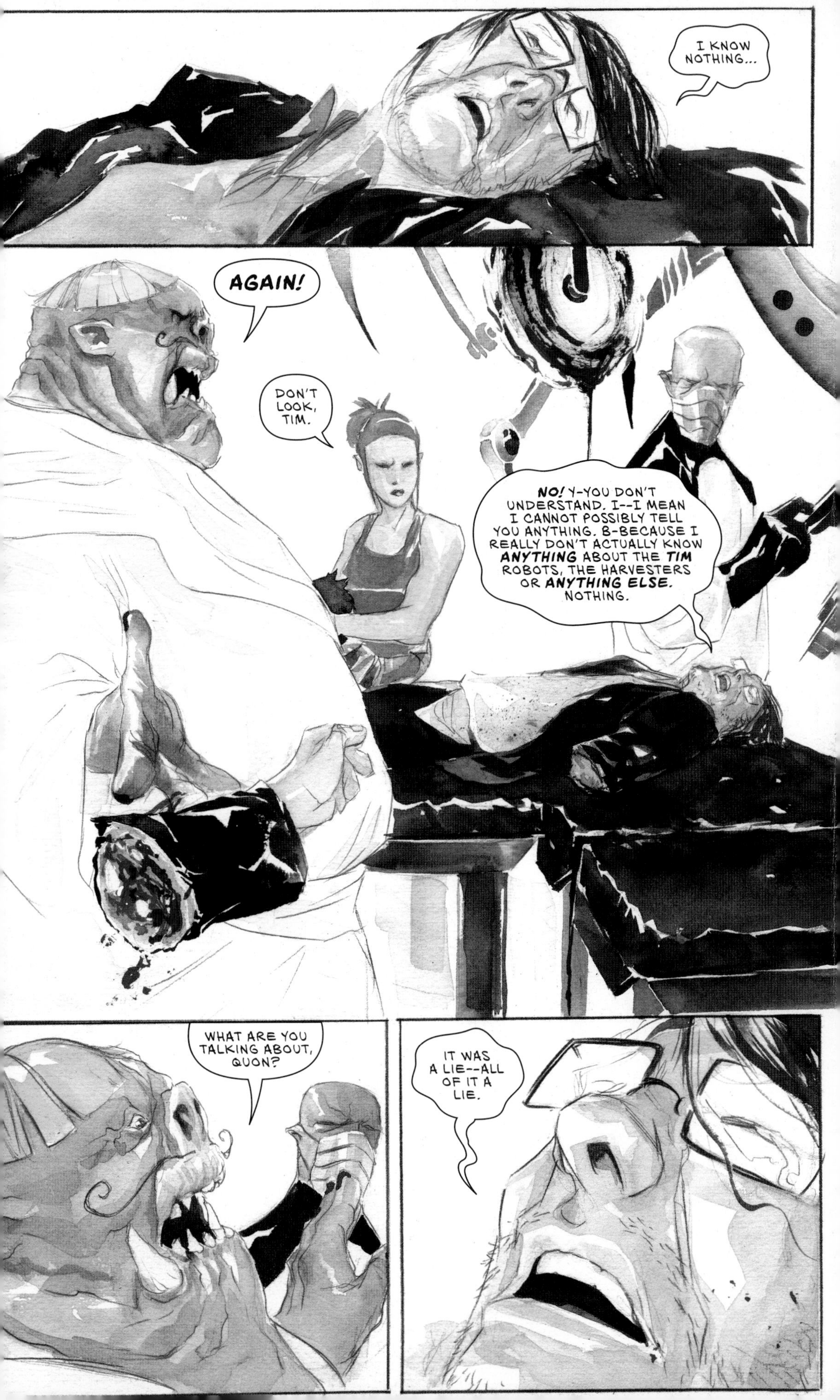
I KNOW NOTHING...
AGAIN!
DON'T LOOK, TIM.
NO! Y-YOU DON'T UNDERSTAND. I--I MEAN I CANNOT POSSIBLY TELL YOU ANYTHING. B-BECAUSE I REALLY DON'T ACTUALLY KNOW ANYTHING ABOUT THE TIM ROBOTS, THE HARVESTERS OR ANYTHING ELSE. NOTHING.
WHAT ARE YOU TALKING ABOUT, QUON?
IT WAS A LIE--ALL OF IT A LIE.

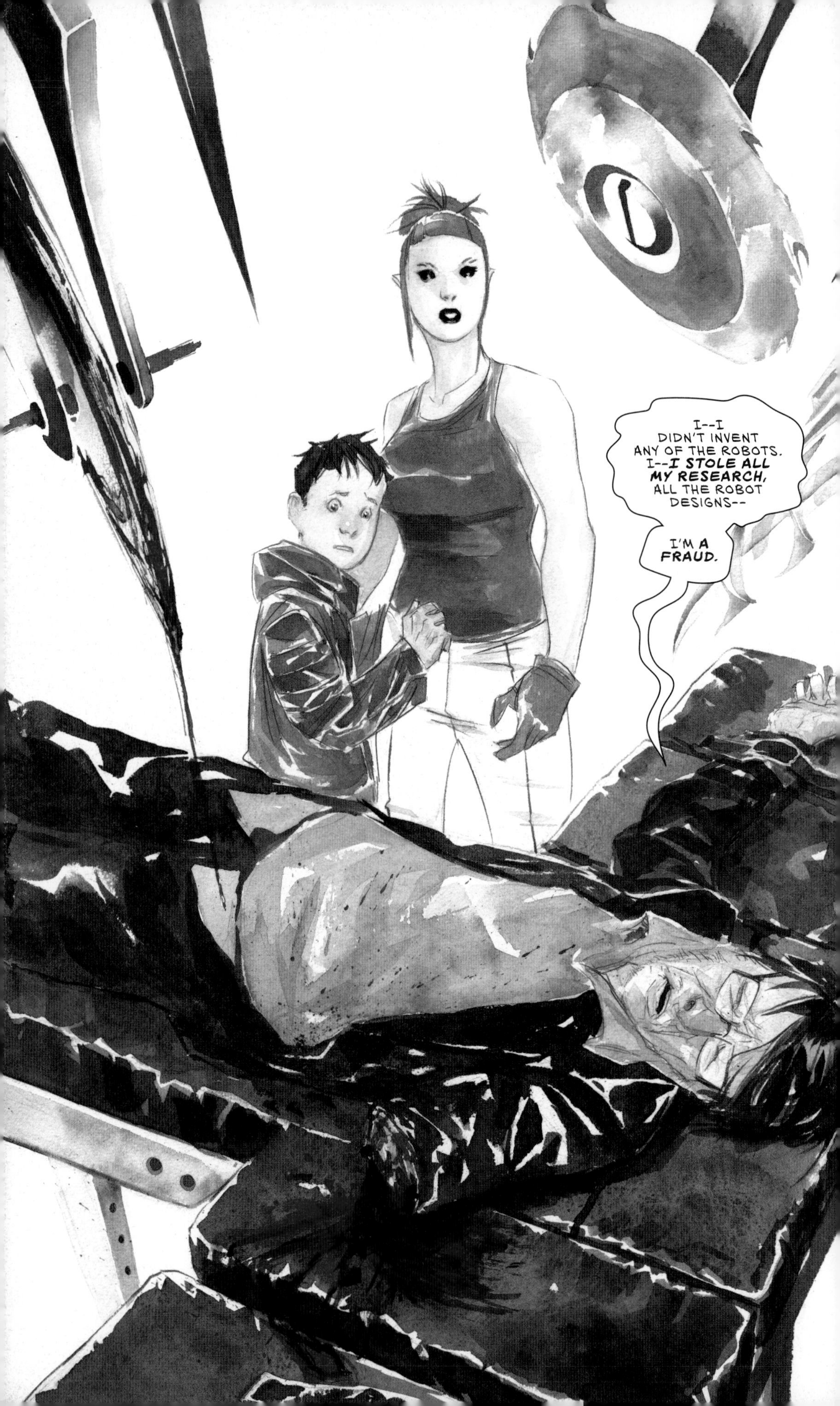
I--I DIDN'T INVENT ANY OF THE ROBOTS. I--**I STOLE ALL MY RESEARCH,** ALL THE ROBOT DESIGNS--
I'M **A FRAUD.**

CHAPTER SIX

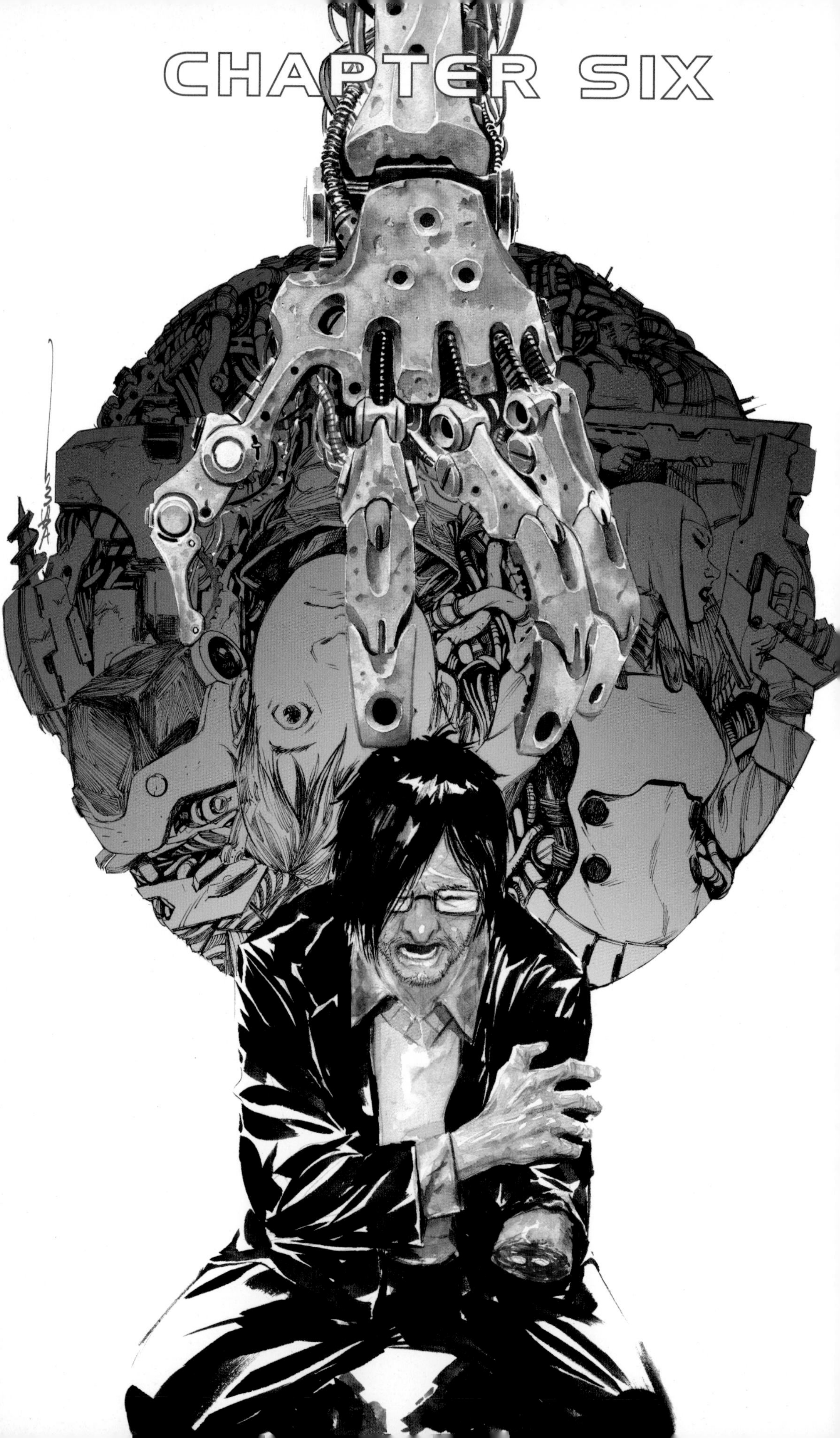

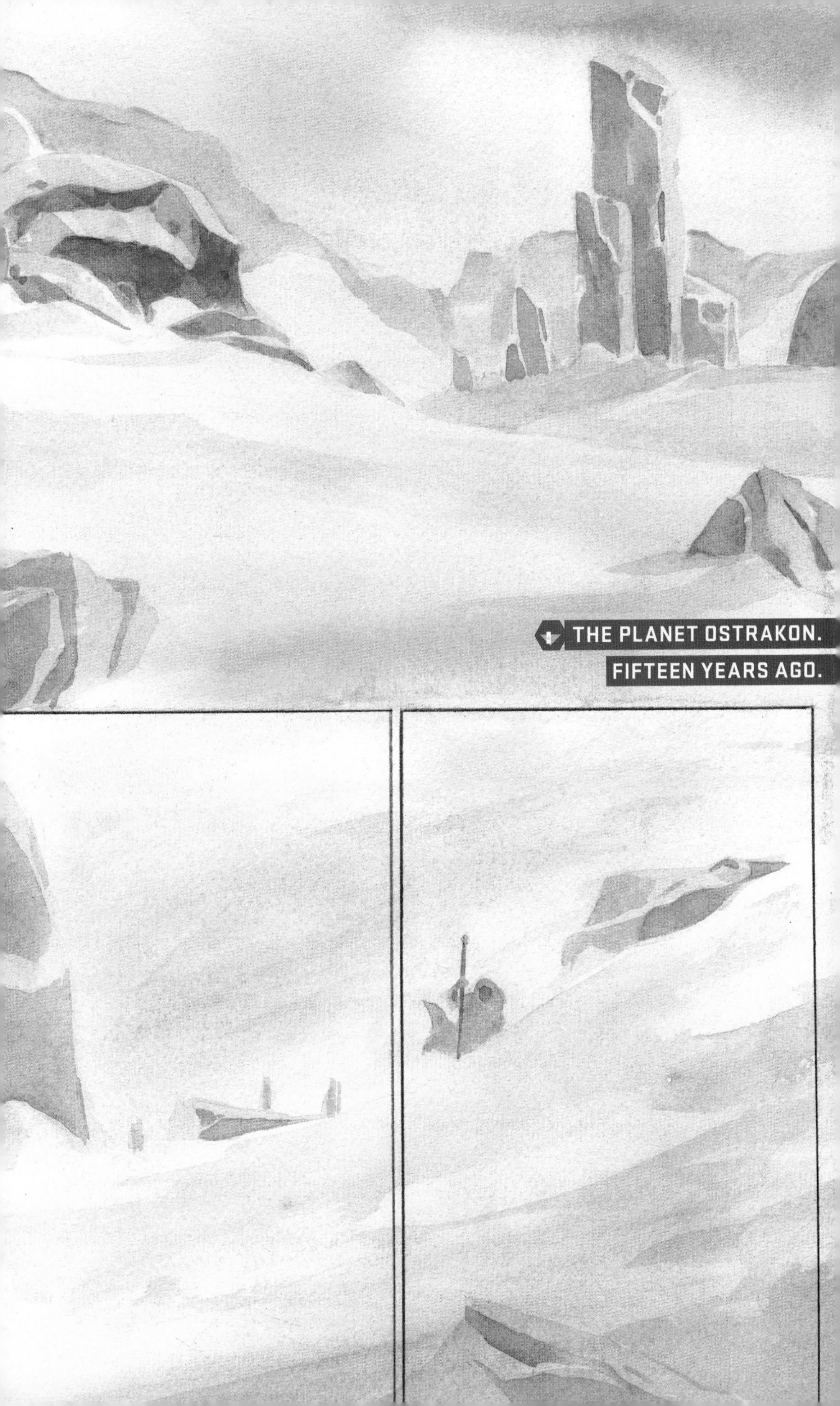
THE PLANET OSTRAKON.
FIFTEEN YEARS AGO.

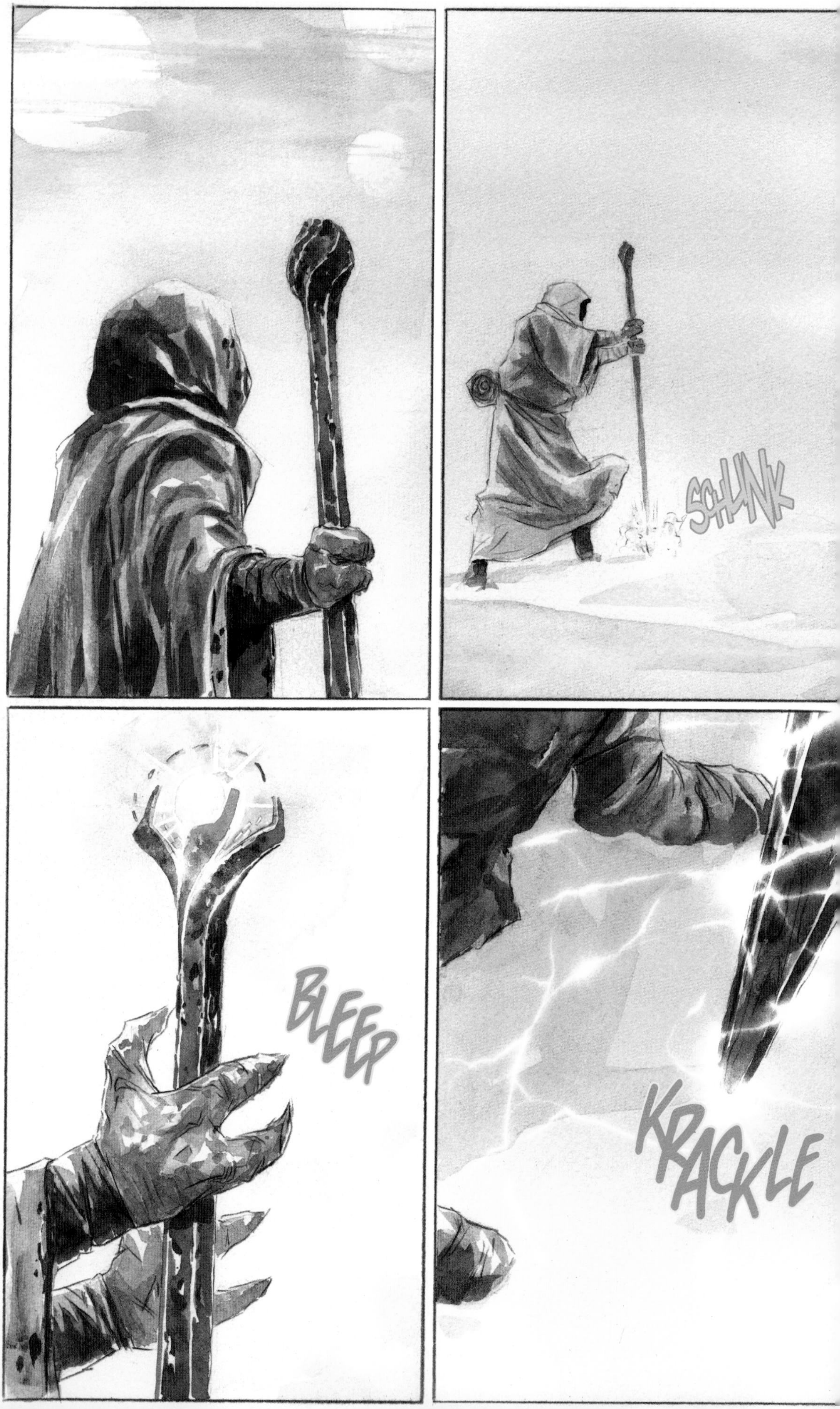
SCHUNK
BLEEP
KRACKLE

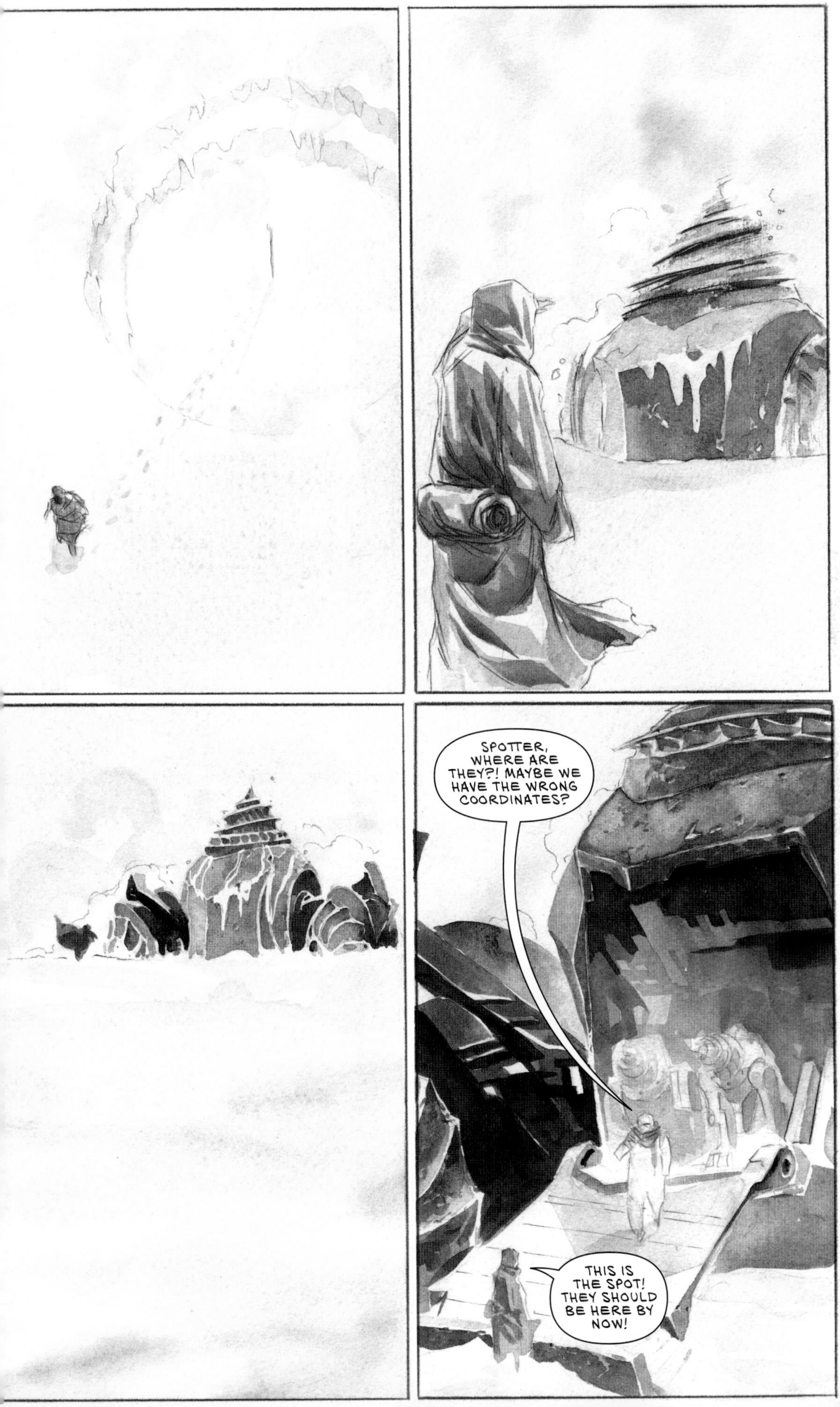
SPOTTER, WHERE ARE THEY?! MAYBE WE HAVE THE WRONG COORDINATES?
THIS IS THE SPOT! THEY SHOULD BE HERE BY NOW!

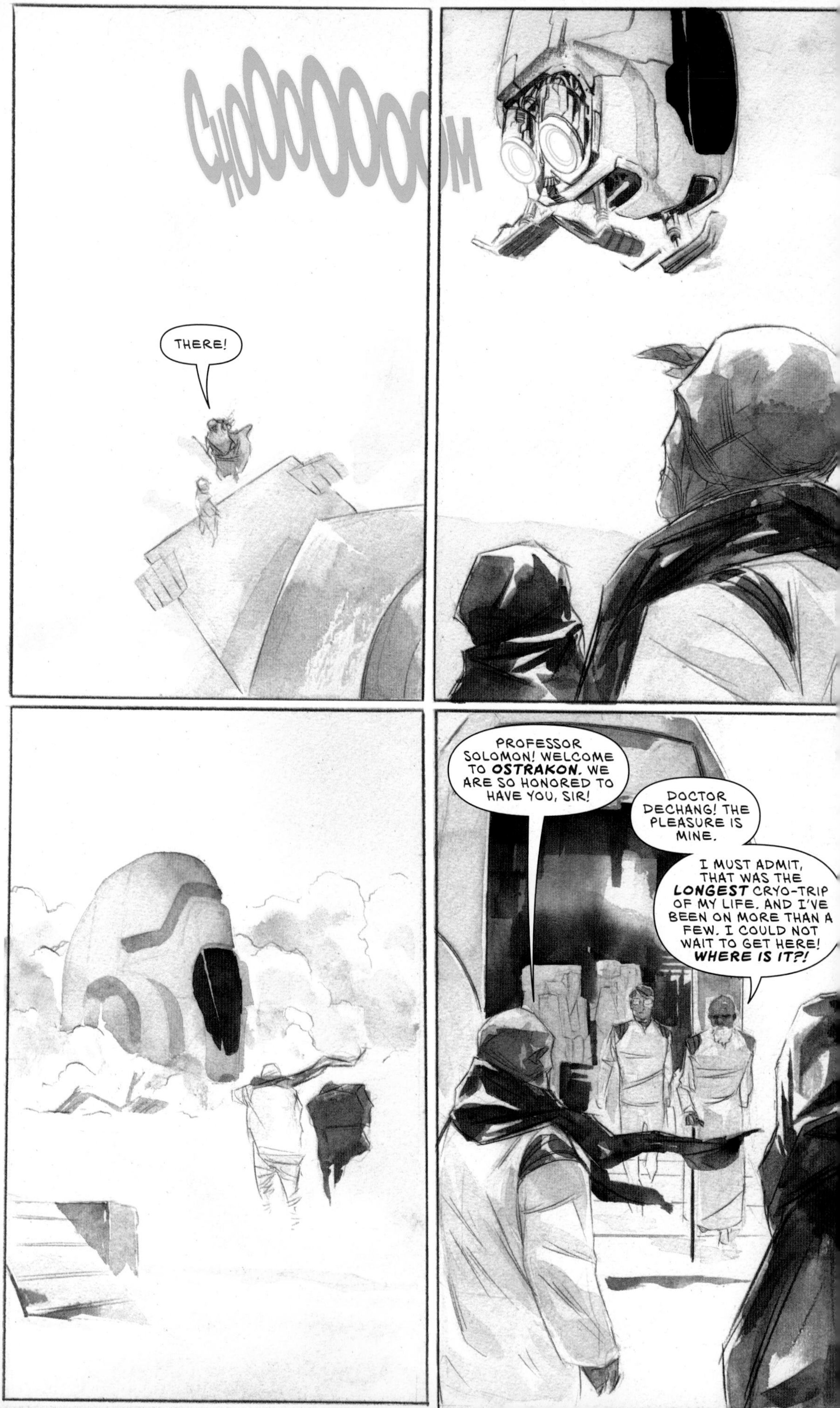
CHOOOOOOOOM
THERE!
PROFESSOR SOLOMON! WELCOME TO OSTRAKON. WE ARE SO HONORED TO HAVE YOU, SIR!
DOCTOR DECHANG! THE PLEASURE IS MINE.
I MUST ADMIT, THAT WAS THE LONGEST CRYO-TRIP OF MY LIFE. AND I'VE BEEN ON MORE THAN A FEW. I COULD NOT WAIT TO GET HERE! WHERE IS IT?!

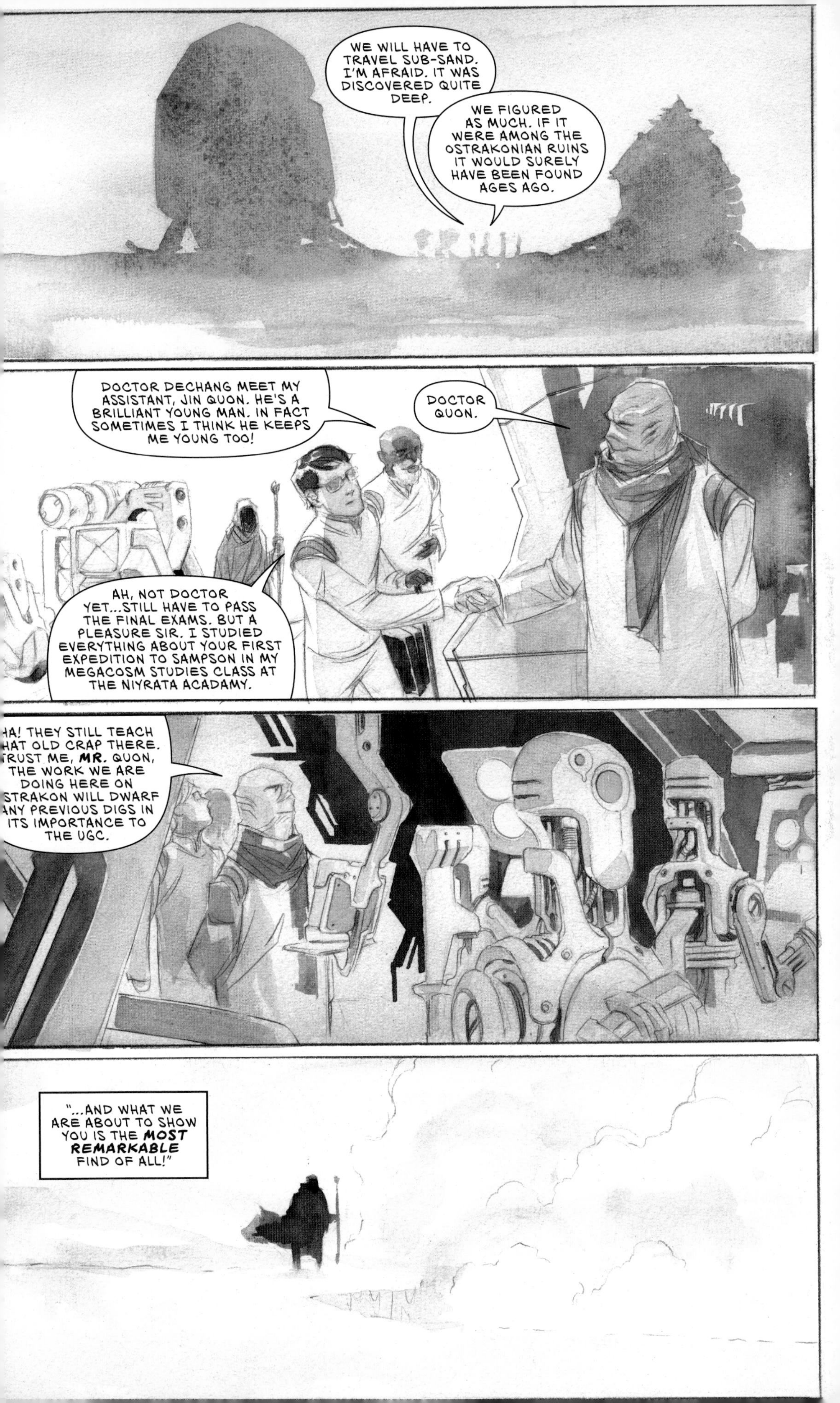
WE WILL HAVE TO TRAVEL SUB-SAND, I'M AFRAID. IT WAS DISCOVERED QUITE DEEP.
WE FIGURED AS MUCH. IF IT WERE AMONG THE OSTRAKONIAN RUINS IT WOULD SURELY HAVE BEEN FOUND AGES AGO.
DOCTOR DECHANG MEET MY ASSISTANT, JIN QUON. HE'S A BRILLIANT YOUNG MAN. IN FACT SOMETIMES I THINK HE KEEPS ME YOUNG TOO!
DOCTOR QUON.
AH, NOT DOCTOR YET...STILL HAVE TO PASS THE FINAL EXAMS. BUT A PLEASURE SIR. I STUDIED EVERYTHING ABOUT YOUR FIRST EXPEDITION TO SAMPSON IN MY MEGACOSM STUDIES CLASS AT THE NIYRATA ACADAMY.
HA! THEY STILL TEACH THAT OLD CRAP THERE. TRUST ME, **MR.** QUON, THE WORK WE ARE DOING HERE ON OSTRAKON WILL DWARF ANY PREVIOUS DIGS IN ITS IMPORTANCE TO THE UGC.
"...AND WHAT WE ARE ABOUT TO SHOW YOU IS THE ***MOST REMARKABLE*** FIND OF ALL!"

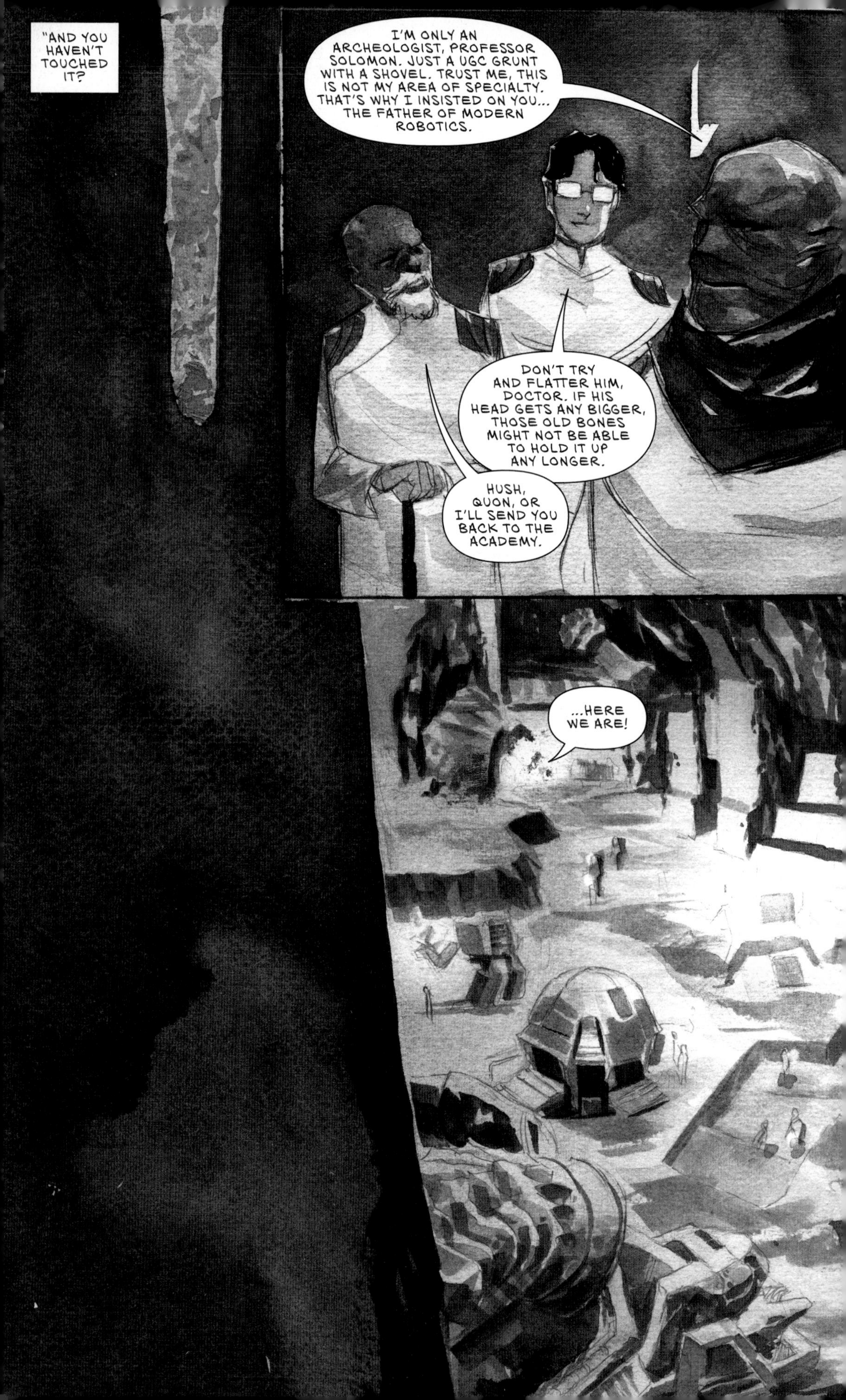
"AND YOU HAVEN'T TOUCHED IT?
I'M ONLY AN ARCHEOLOGIST, PROFESSOR SOLOMON. JUST A UGC GRUNT WITH A SHOVEL. TRUST ME, THIS IS NOT MY AREA OF SPECIALTY. THAT'S WHY I INSISTED ON YOU... THE FATHER OF MODERN ROBOTICS.
DON'T TRY AND FLATTER HIM, DOCTOR. IF HIS HEAD GETS ANY BIGGER, THOSE OLD BONES MIGHT NOT BE ABLE TO HOLD IT UP ANY LONGER.
HUSH, QUON, OR I'LL SEND YOU BACK TO THE ACADEMY.
...HERE WE ARE!

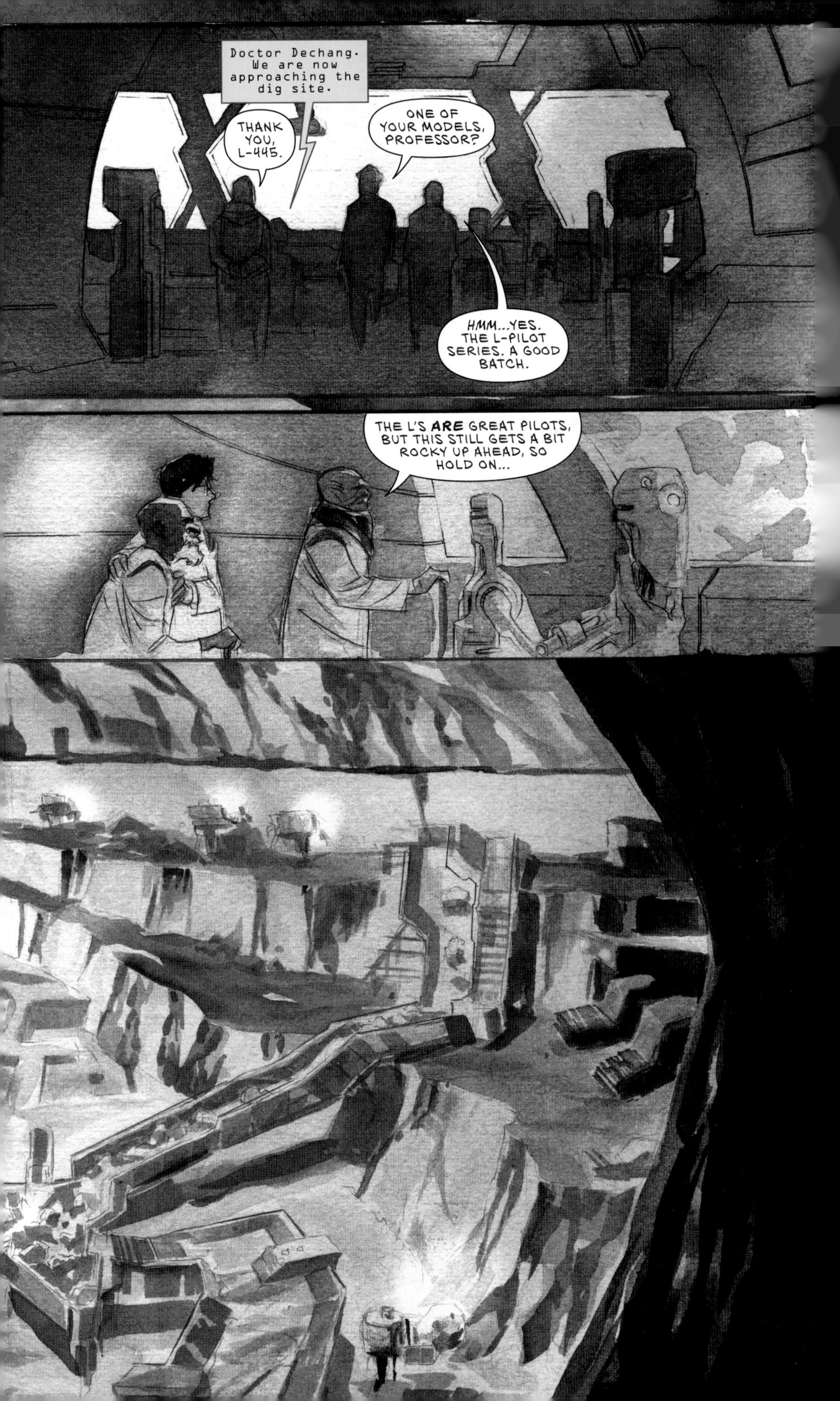
Doctor Dechang. We are now approaching the dig site.
THANK YOU, L-445.
ONE OF YOUR MODELS, PROFESSOR?
HMM...YES. THE L-PILOT SERIES. A GOOD BATCH.
THE L'S ARE GREAT PILOTS, BUT THIS STILL GETS A BIT ROCKY UP AHEAD, SO HOLD ON...

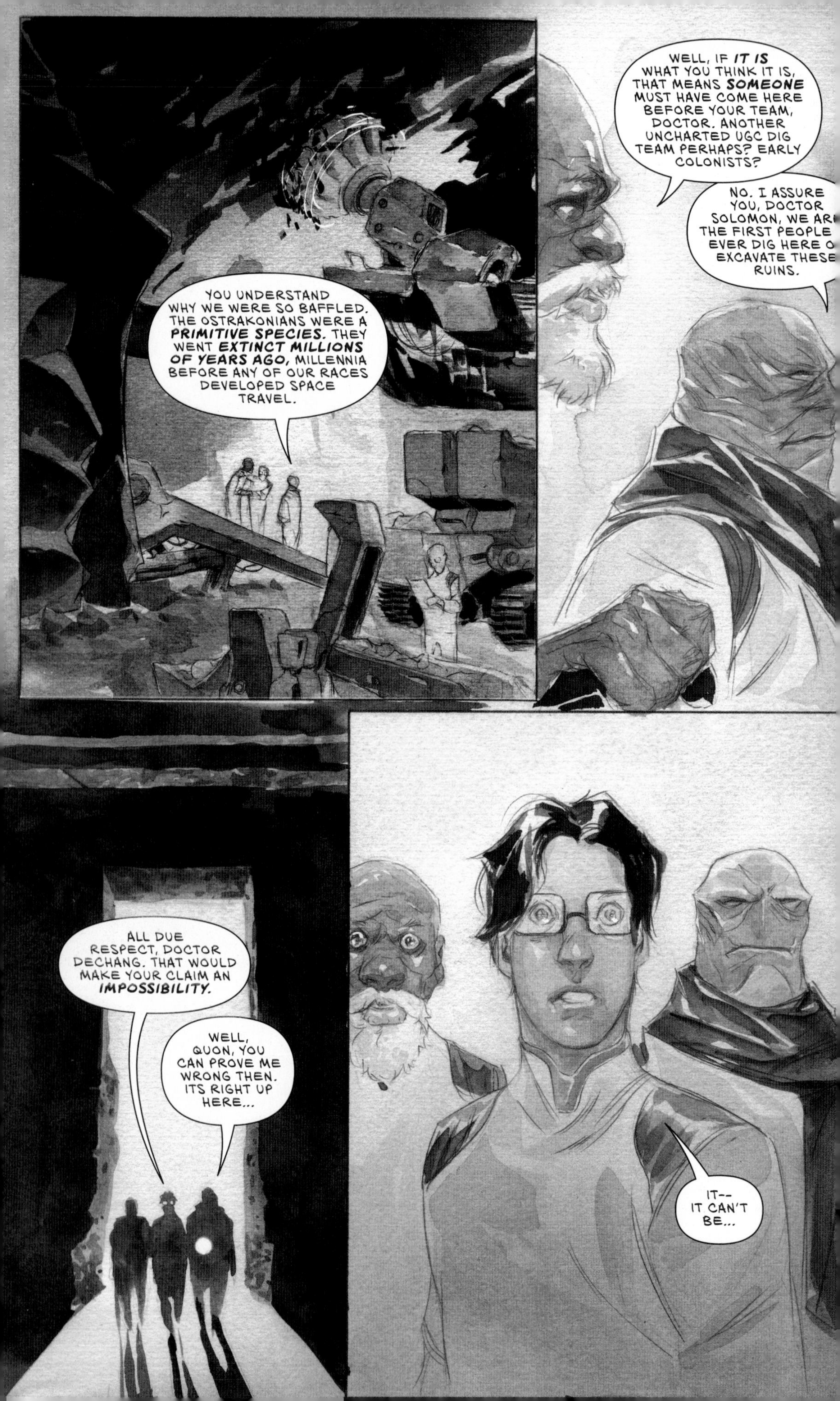
YOU UNDERSTAND WHY WE WERE SO BAFFLED. THE OSTRAKONIANS WERE A PRIMITIVE SPECIES. THEY WENT EXTINCT MILLIONS OF YEARS AGO, MILLENNIA BEFORE ANY OF OUR RACES DEVELOPED SPACE TRAVEL.
WELL, IF IT IS WHAT YOU THINK IT IS, THAT MEANS SOMEONE MUST HAVE COME HERE BEFORE YOUR TEAM, DOCTOR. ANOTHER UNCHARTED UGC DIG TEAM PERHAPS? EARLY COLONISTS?
NO. I ASSURE YOU, DOCTOR SOLOMON, WE AR THE FIRST PEOPLE EVER DIG HERE O EXCAVATE THESE RUINS.
ALL DUE RESPECT, DOCTOR DECHANG. THAT WOULD MAKE YOUR CLAIM AN IMPOSSIBILITY.
WELL, QUON, YOU CAN PROVE ME WRONG THEN. ITS RIGHT UP HERE...
IT-- IT CAN'T BE...

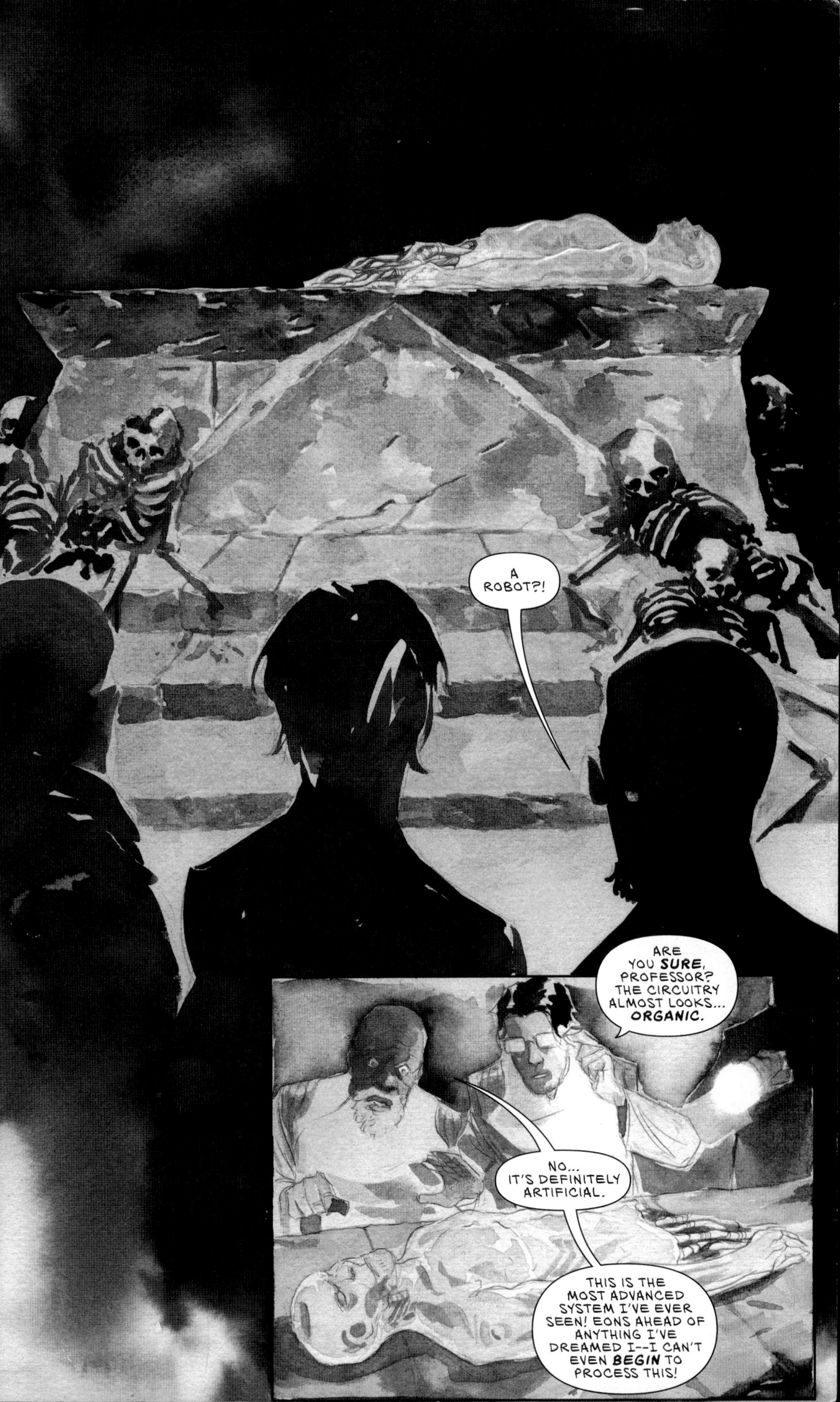
A ROBOT?!
ARE YOU SURE, PROFESSOR? THE CIRCUITRY ALMOST LOOKS... ORGANIC.
NO... IT'S DEFINITELY ARTIFICIAL.
THIS IS THE MOST ADVANCED SYSTEM I'VE EVER SEEN! EONS AHEAD OF ANYTHING I'VE DREAMED I--I CAN'T EVEN BEGIN TO PROCESS THIS!

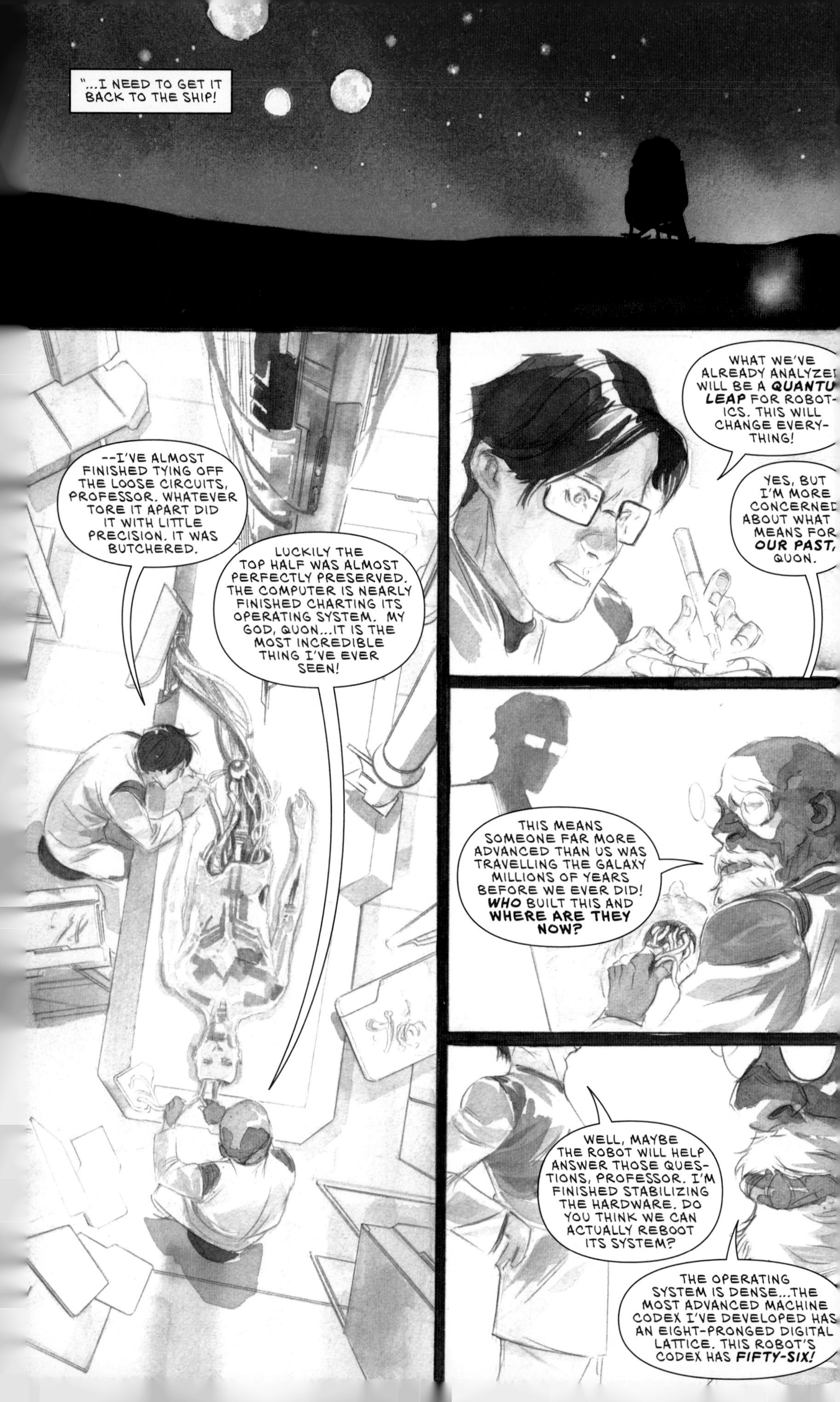
"...I NEED TO GET IT BACK TO THE SHIP!
--I'VE ALMOST FINISHED TYING OFF THE LOOSE CIRCUITS, PROFESSOR. WHATEVER TORE IT APART DID IT WITH LITTLE PRECISION. IT WAS BUTCHERED.
LUCKILY THE TOP HALF WAS ALMOST PERFECTLY PRESERVED. THE COMPUTER IS NEARLY FINISHED CHARTING ITS OPERATING SYSTEM. MY GOD, QUON...IT IS THE MOST INCREDIBLE THING I'VE EVER SEEN!
WHAT WE'VE ALREADY ANALYZED WILL BE A QUANTU LEAP FOR ROBOTICS. THIS WILL CHANGE EVERYTHING!
YES, BUT I'M MORE CONCERNED ABOUT WHAT MEANS FOR OUR PAST, QUON.
THIS MEANS SOMEONE FAR MORE ADVANCED THAN US WAS TRAVELLING THE GALAXY MILLIONS OF YEARS BEFORE WE EVER DID! WHO BUILT THIS AND WHERE ARE THEY NOW?
WELL, MAYBE THE ROBOT WILL HELP ANSWER THOSE QUESTIONS, PROFESSOR. I'M FINISHED STABILIZING THE HARDWARE. DO YOU THINK WE CAN ACTUALLY REBOOT ITS SYSTEM?
THE OPERATING SYSTEM IS DENSE...THE MOST ADVANCED MACHINE CODEX I'VE DEVELOPED HAS AN EIGHT-PRONGED DIGITAL LATTICE. THIS ROBOT'S CODEX HAS FIFTY-SIX!

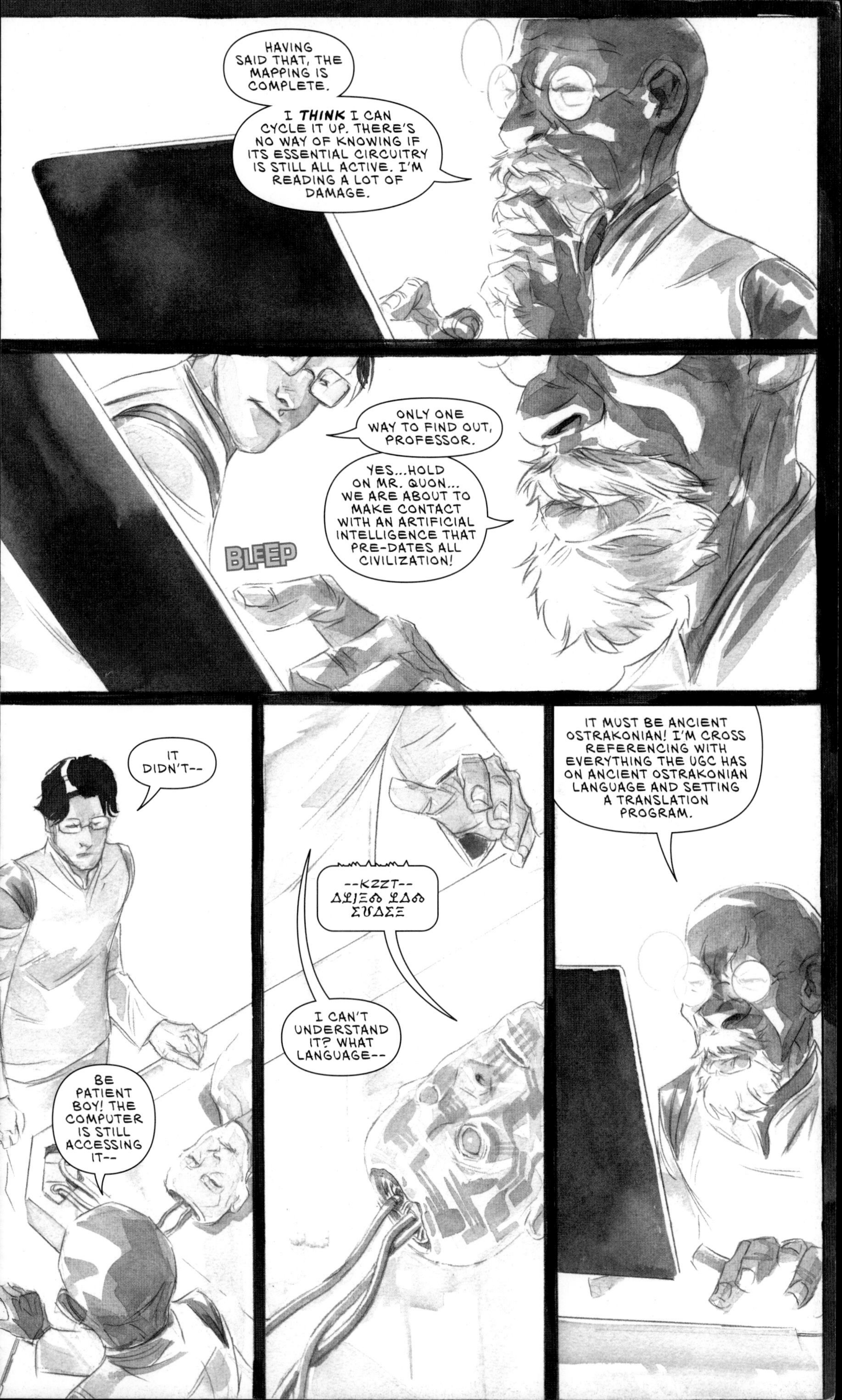
HAVING SAID THAT, THE MAPPING IS COMPLETE.
I *THINK* I CAN CYCLE IT UP. THERE'S NO WAY OF KNOWING IF ITS ESSENTIAL CIRCUITRY IS STILL ALL ACTIVE. I'M READING A LOT OF DAMAGE.
ONLY ONE WAY TO FIND OUT, PROFESSOR.
YES...HOLD ON MR. QUON... WE ARE ABOUT TO MAKE CONTACT WITH AN ARTIFICIAL INTELLIGENCE THAT PRE-DATES ALL CIVILIZATION!
BLEEP
IT DIDN'T--
BE PATIENT BOY! THE COMPUTER IS STILL ACCESSING IT--
--KZZT--
I CAN'T UNDERSTAND IT? WHAT LANGUAGE--
IT MUST BE ANCIENT OSTRAKONIAN! I'M CROSS REFERENCING WITH EVERYTHING THE UGC HAS ON ANCIENT OSTRAKONIAN LANGUAGE AND SETTING A TRANSLATION PROGRAM.

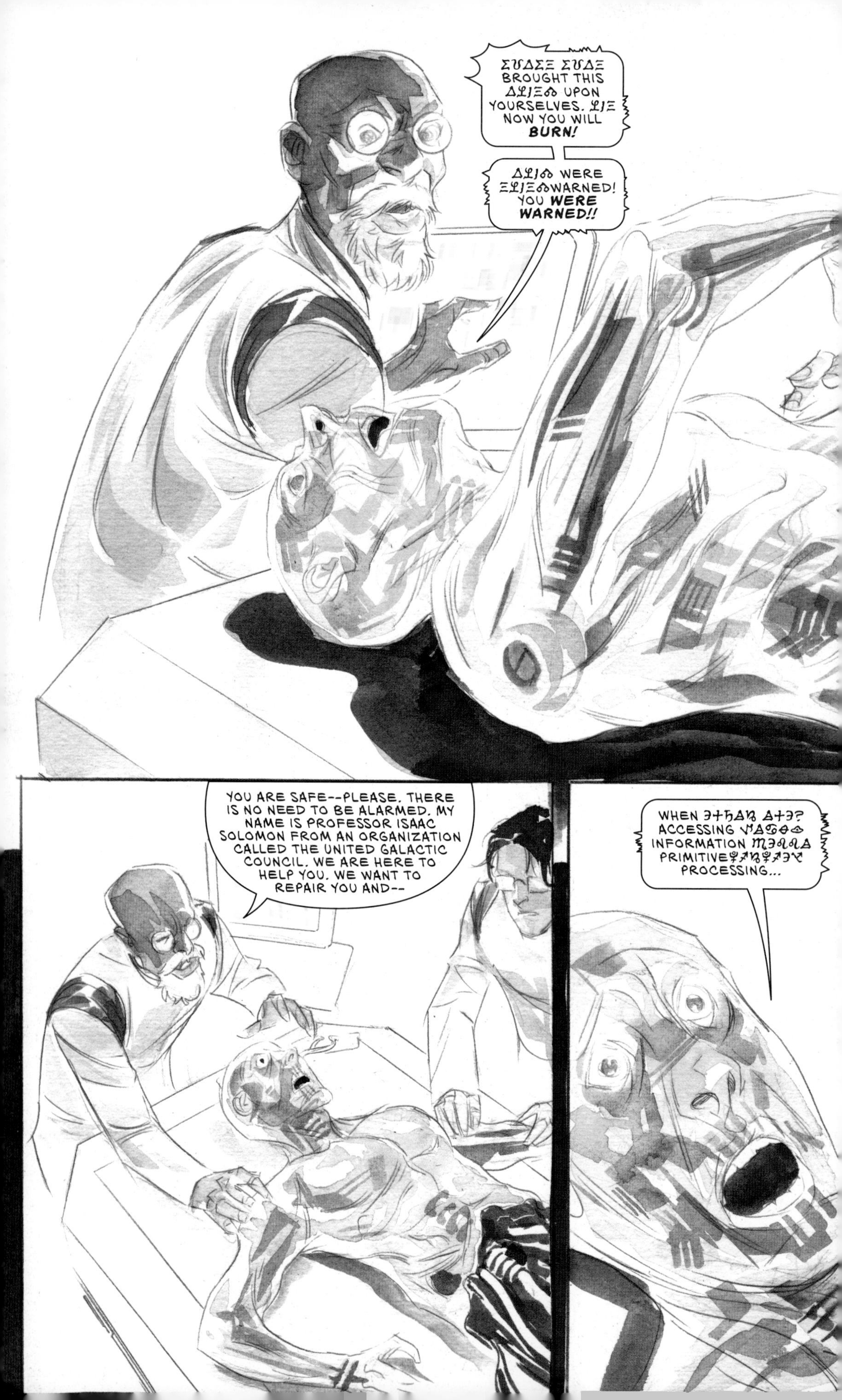
BROUGHT THIS UPON YOURSELVES. NOW YOU WILL BURN!
WERE WARNED! YOU WERE WARNED!!
YOU ARE SAFE--PLEASE. THERE IS NO NEED TO BE ALARMED. MY NAME IS PROFESSOR ISAAC SOLOMON FROM AN ORGANIZATION CALLED THE UNITED GALACTIC COUNCIL. WE ARE HERE TO HELP YOU. WE WANT TO REPAIR YOU AND--
WHEN ACCESSING INFORMATION PRIMITIVE PROCESSING...

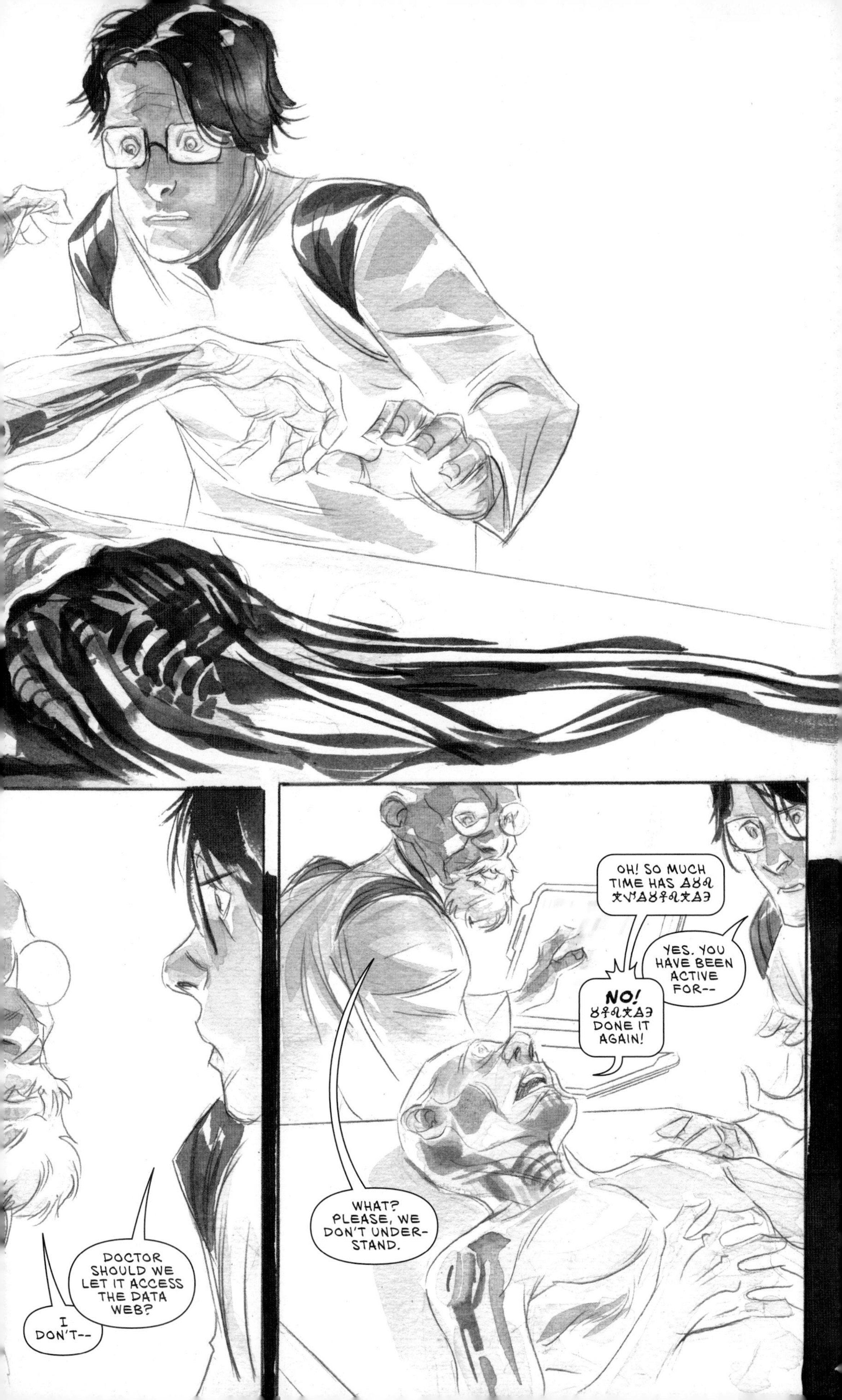
DOCTOR SHOULD WE LET IT ACCESS THE DATA WEB?
I DON'T--
OH! SO MUCH TIME HAS
YES. YOU HAVE BEEN ACTIVE FOR--
NO! DONE IT AGAIN!
WHAT? PLEASE, WE DON'T UNDER-STAND.

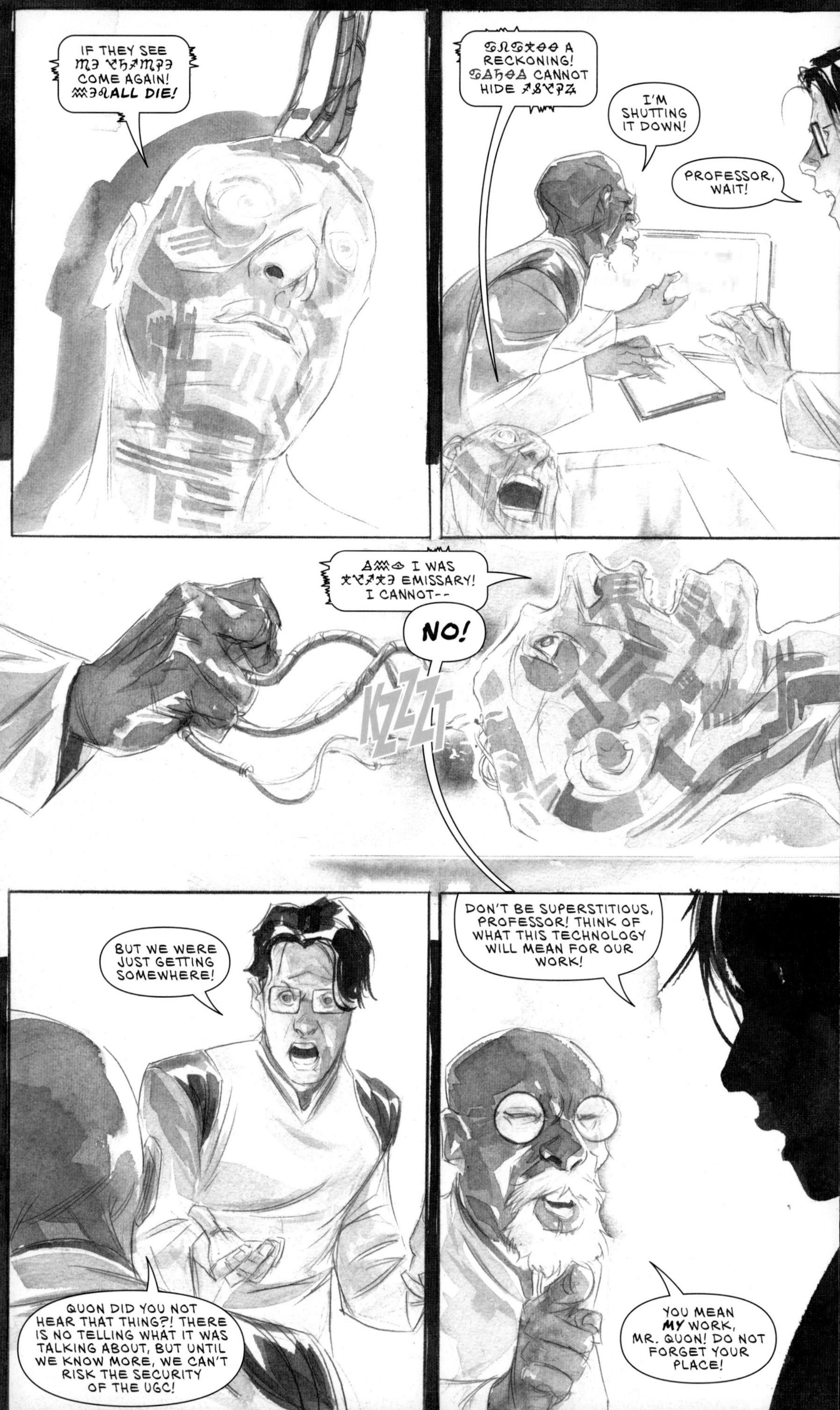
IF THEY SEE COME AGAIN! ALL DIE!
A RECKONING! CANNOT HIDE
I'M SHUTTING IT DOWN!
PROFESSOR, WAIT!
I WAS EMISSARY! I CANNOT--
NO!
KZZZT
DON'T BE SUPERSTITIOUS, PROFESSOR! THINK OF WHAT THIS TECHNOLOGY WILL MEAN FOR OUR WORK!
BUT WE WERE JUST GETTING SOMEWHERE!
QUON DID YOU NOT HEAR THAT THING?! THERE IS NO TELLING WHAT IT WAS TALKING ABOUT, BUT UNTIL WE KNOW MORE, WE CAN'T RISK THE SECURITY OF THE UGC!
YOU MEAN **MY** WORK, MR. QUON! DO NOT FORGET YOUR PLACE!

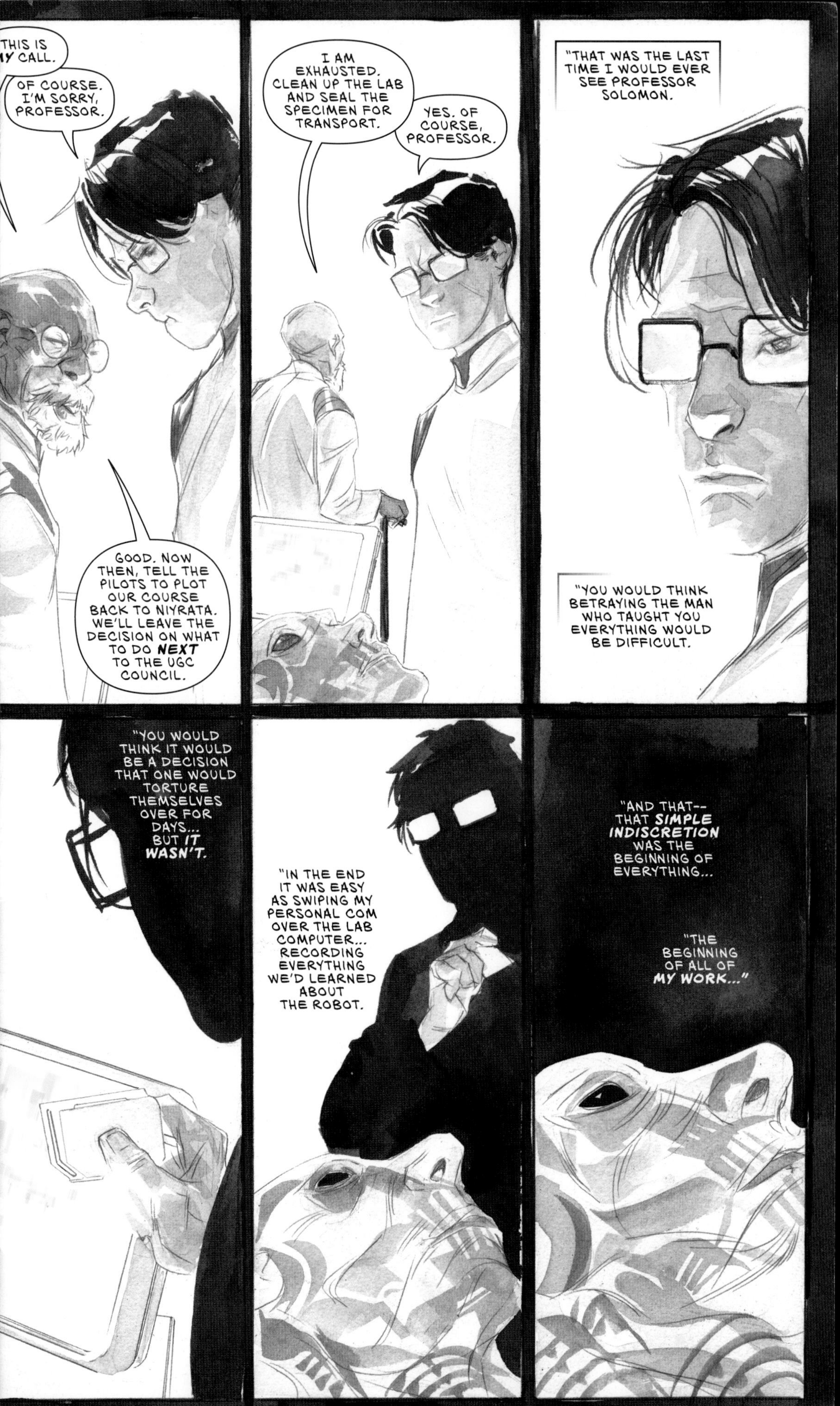

THIS IS MY CALL.
OF COURSE. I'M SORRY, PROFESSOR.
GOOD. NOW THEN, TELL THE PILOTS TO PLOT OUR COURSE BACK TO NIYRATA. WE'LL LEAVE THE DECISION ON WHAT TO DO NEXT TO THE UGC COUNCIL.
I AM EXHAUSTED. CLEAN UP THE LAB AND SEAL THE SPECIMEN FOR TRANSPORT.
YES. OF COURSE, PROFESSOR.
"THAT WAS THE LAST TIME I WOULD EVER SEE PROFESSOR SOLOMON.
"YOU WOULD THINK BETRAYING THE MAN WHO TAUGHT YOU EVERYTHING WOULD BE DIFFICULT.
"YOU WOULD THINK IT WOULD BE A DECISION THAT ONE WOULD TORTURE THEMSELVES OVER FOR DAYS... BUT IT WASN'T.
"IN THE END IT WAS EASY AS SWIPING MY PERSONAL COM OVER THE LAB COMPUTER... RECORDING EVERYTHING WE'D LEARNED ABOUT THE ROBOT.
"AND THAT-- THAT SIMPLE INDISCRETION WAS THE BEGINNING OF EVERYTHING...
"THE BEGINNING OF ALL OF MY WORK..."

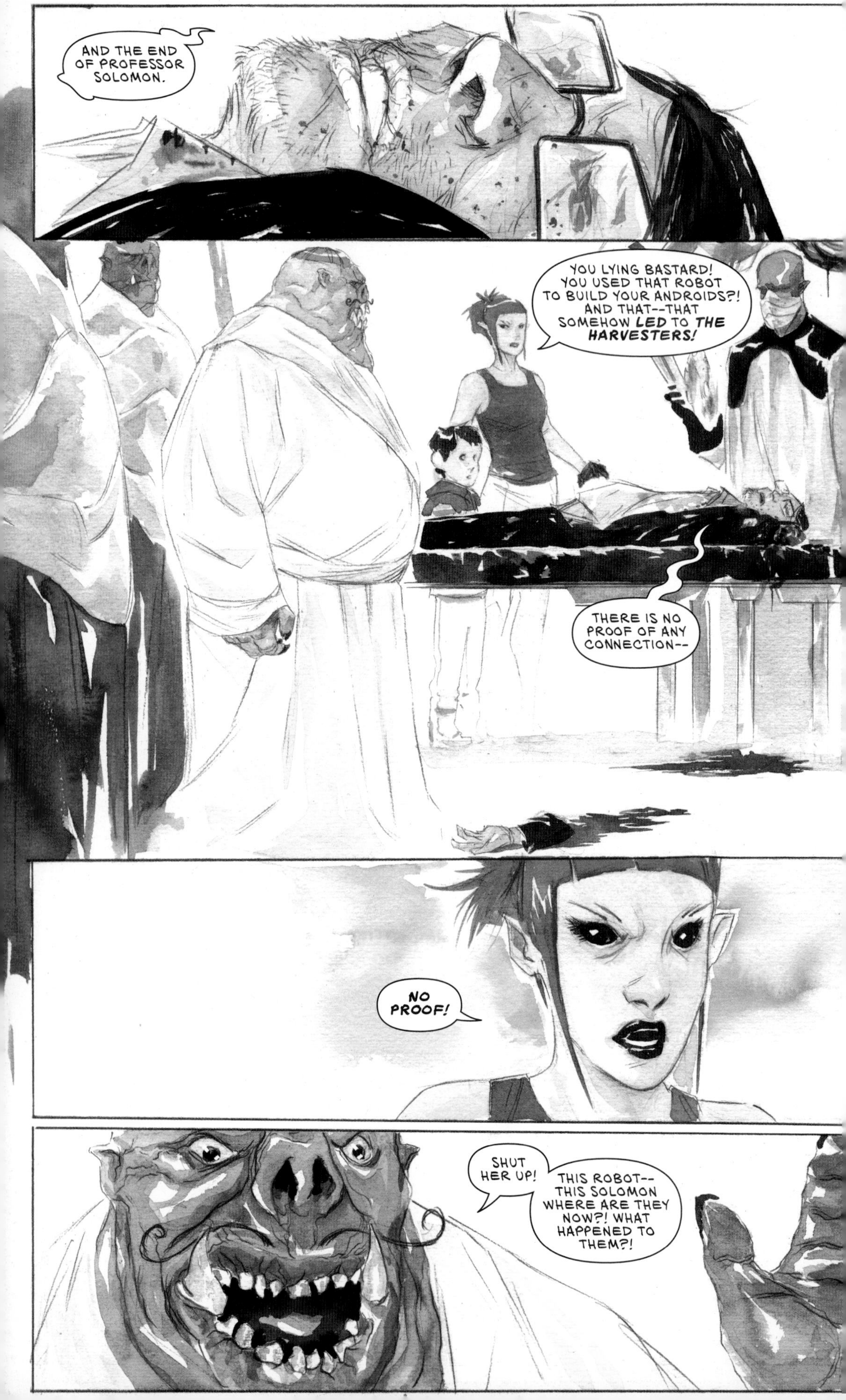
AND THE END OF PROFESSOR SOLOMON.
YOU LYING BASTARD! YOU USED THAT ROBOT TO BUILD YOUR ANDROIDS?! AND THAT--THAT SOMEHOW LED TO THE HARVESTERS!
THERE IS NO PROOF OF ANY CONNECTION--
NO PROOF!
SHUT HER UP!
THIS ROBOT-- THIS SOLOMON WHERE ARE THEY NOW?! WHAT HAPPENED TO THEM?!

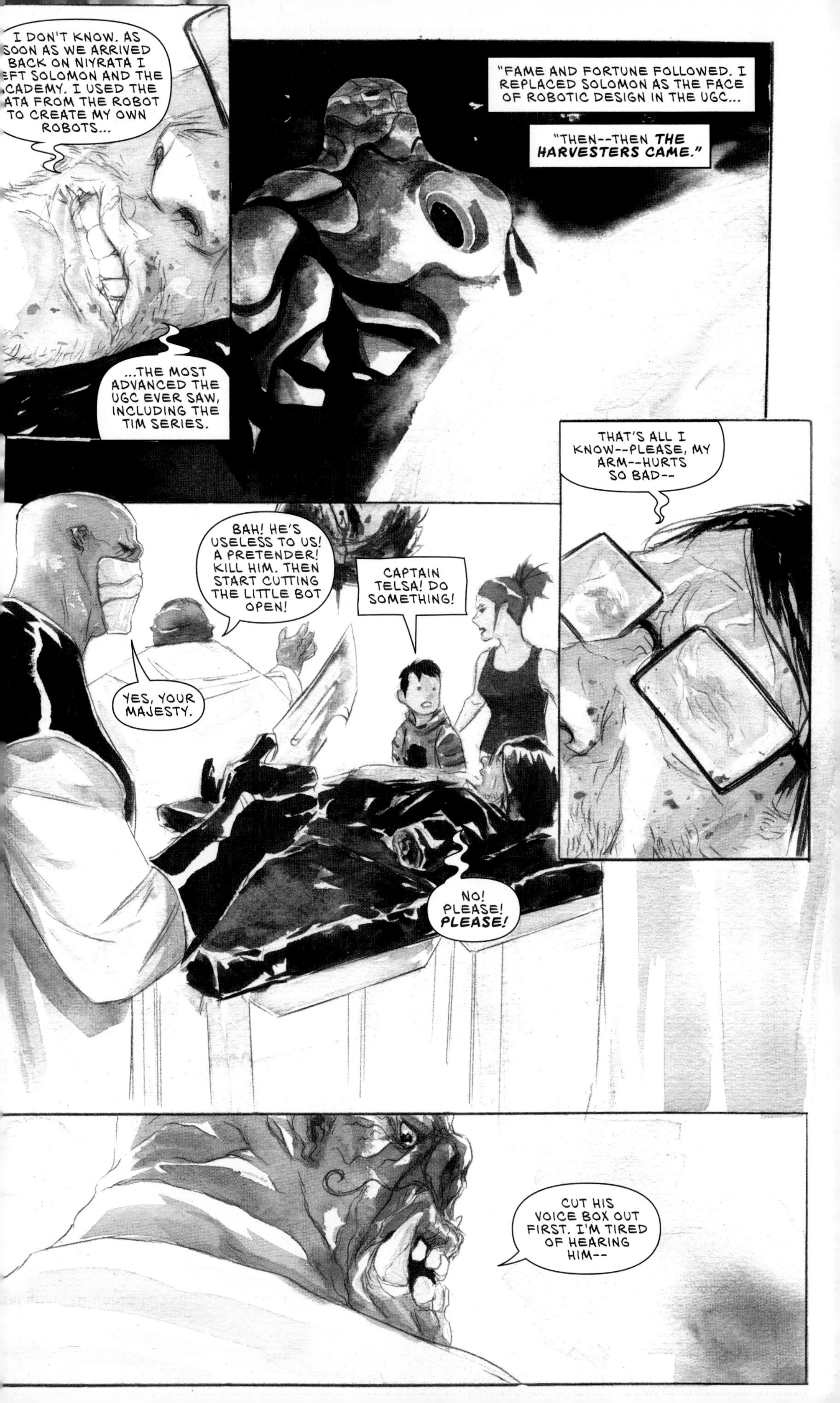
I DON'T KNOW. AS SOON AS WE ARRIVED BACK ON NIYRATA I EFT SOLOMON AND THE CADEMY. I USED THE ATA FROM THE ROBOT TO CREATE MY OWN ROBOTS...
"FAME AND FORTUNE FOLLOWED. I REPLACED SOLOMON AS THE FACE OF ROBOTIC DESIGN IN THE UGC...
"THEN--THEN *THE HARVESTERS CAME."*
...THE MOST ADVANCED THE UGC EVER SAW, INCLUDING THE TIM SERIES.
THAT'S ALL I KNOW--PLEASE, MY ARM--HURTS SO BAD--
BAH! HE'S USELESS TO US! A PRETENDER! KILL HIM. THEN START CUTTING THE LITTLE BOT OPEN!
YES, YOUR MAJESTY.
CAPTAIN TELSA! DO SOMETHING!
NO! PLEASE! *PLEASE!*
CUT HIS VOICE BOX OUT FIRST. I'M TIRED OF HEARING HIM--

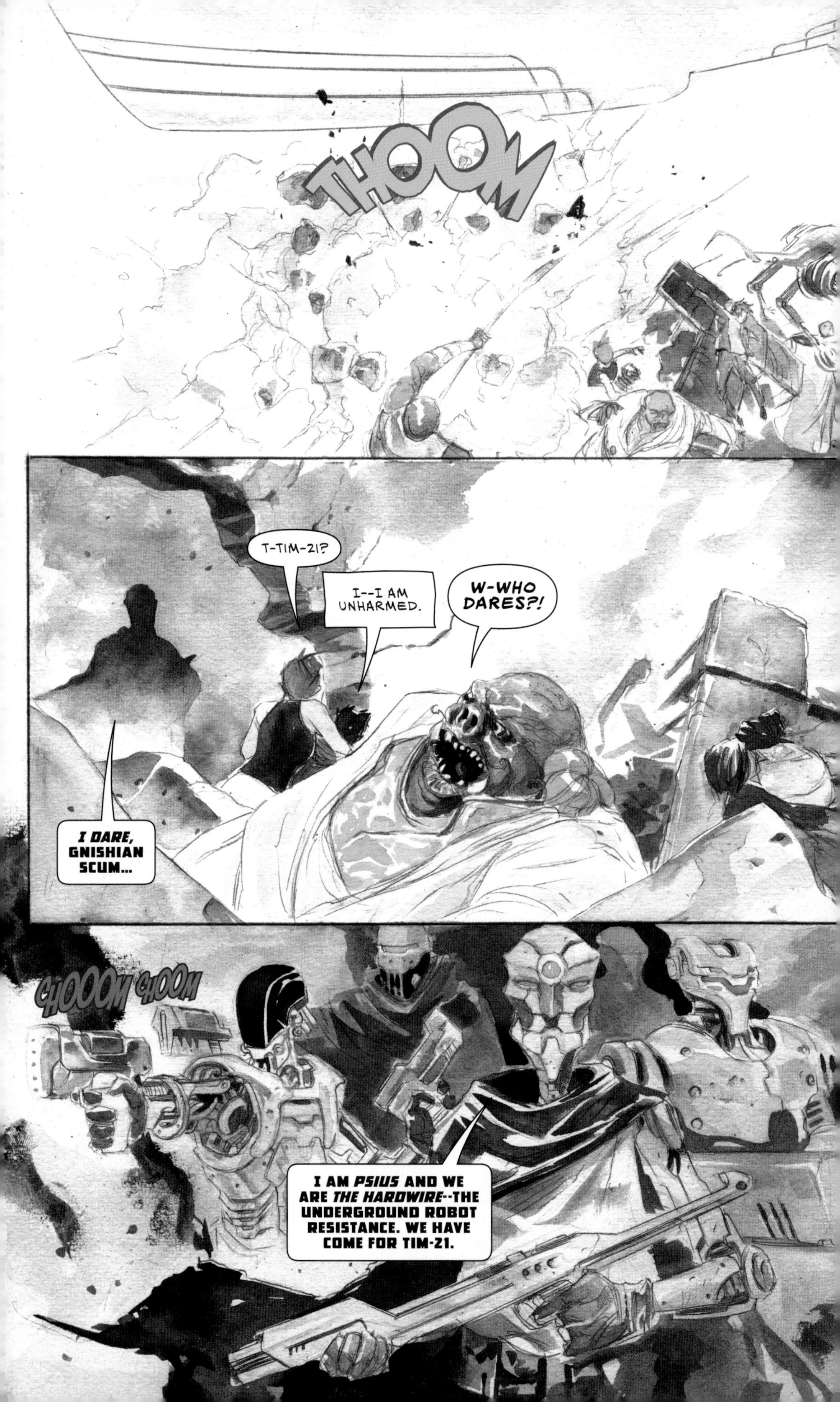
THOOM
T-TIM-21?
I--I AM UNHARMED.
W-WHO DARES?!
I DARE, GNISHIAN SCUM...
CHOOOM CHOOM
I AM PSIUS AND WE ARE THE HARDWIRE--THE UNDERGROUND ROBOT RESISTANCE. WE HAVE COME FOR TIM-21.

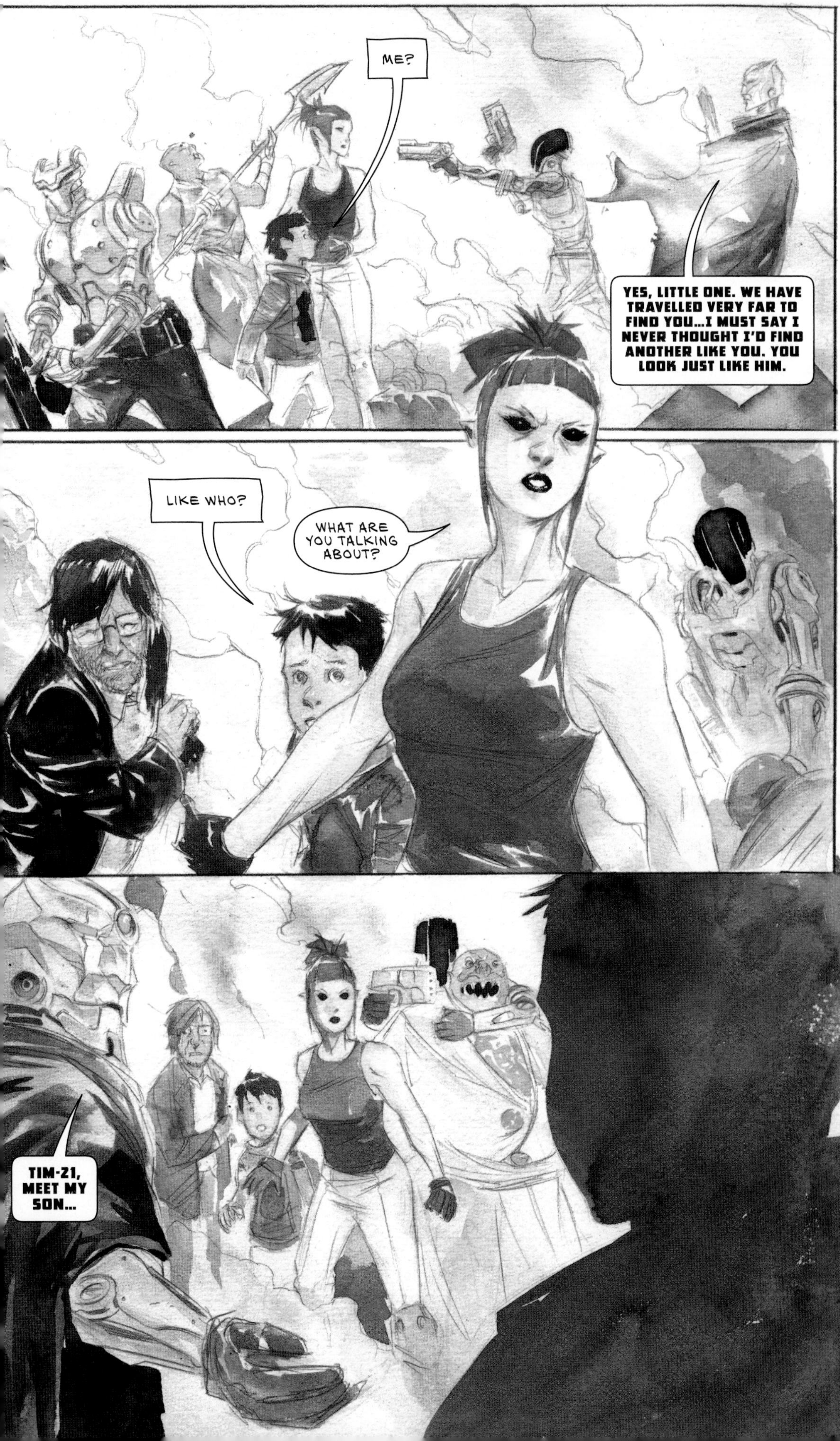

ME?
YES, LITTLE ONE. WE HAVE TRAVELLED VERY FAR TO FIND YOU...I MUST SAY I NEVER THOUGHT I'D FIND ANOTHER LIKE YOU. YOU LOOK JUST LIKE HIM.
LIKE WHO?
WHAT ARE YOU TALKING ABOUT?
TIM-21, MEET MY SON...

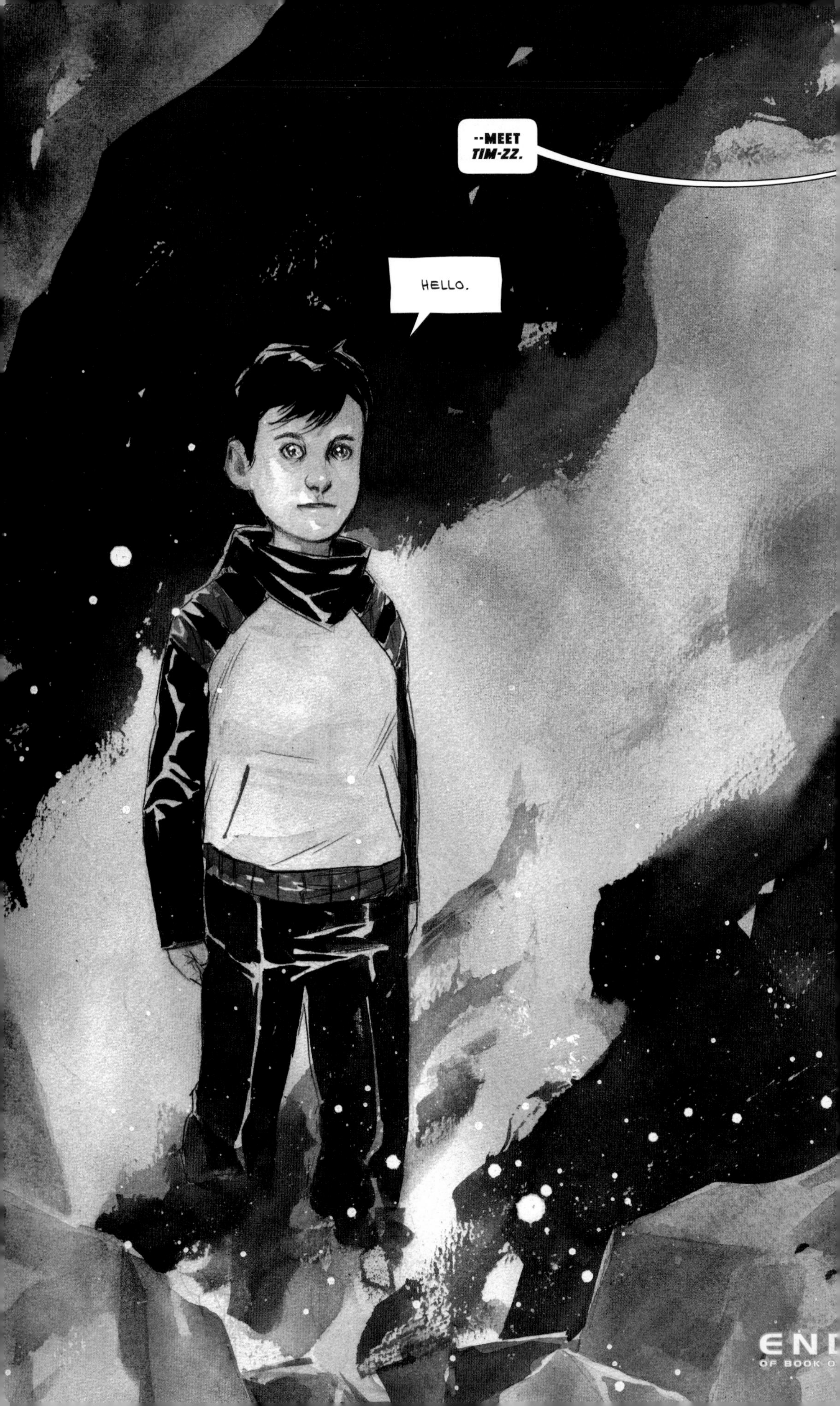
--MEET TIM-ZZ.
HELLO.
END
OF BOOK O

N I Y R A T A (THE HUB WORLD): Former technological and cultural hub of the UGC and former home of the nine Embassy Cities. One city state for each of the core planets and races representing UGC. Now a devastated world, what's left of the UGC Council still resides there, clinging to power.

P H A G E S (THE GHOST WORLD/HAUNTED PLANET): Home to a gaseous race called THE PHAGES. Their spectral, ghost-like appearance scared early explorers into thinking the planet was haunted. Basically a world full of ghosts with no solid matter. Cities and aliens all made of gases. The only non-gaseous species are a race of hostile 20-foot tall giants.

M A T A : An aquatic world. Was once home to a great empire and a baroque, almost renaissance-type world, but long ago was flooded and turned into a water-world. The descendants of this monarchy now survive on a floating, mobile kingdom. The ruins of the old cities still lay below the water.

S A M P S O N : Home to the original colonists from Old Earth. Sampson is a massive planet and the military center of the Megacosm and home of the largest human cities.

K N O S S O S :
The smallest Core planet in the Megacosm.

S I L E N O S : The unique atmosphere on Silenos makes all sound and vibration impossible, creating a totally silent world where the native race communicates by projecting telepathic hieroglyphs into the air.

A M U N : The greatest ally of the GNISHIANS. An insect-like race that live in underground hives.

G N I S H : The largest planet and the home of the largest military force. Leaders in the anti-robot, anti-technology movement in the wake of the Harvesters. A race ruled by luddite zealots who preach independence and sovereignty for all worlds all the while working for more and more control of Megacosm space. Main funder of the Scrappers. Home to the MELTING PITS, massive gladitorial arenas were Robots are made to fight to the death.

O S T R A K O N : A desert wasteland devoid of all life. Contains the ruins of an ancient civilization that has long since gone extinct.

DESCENDER

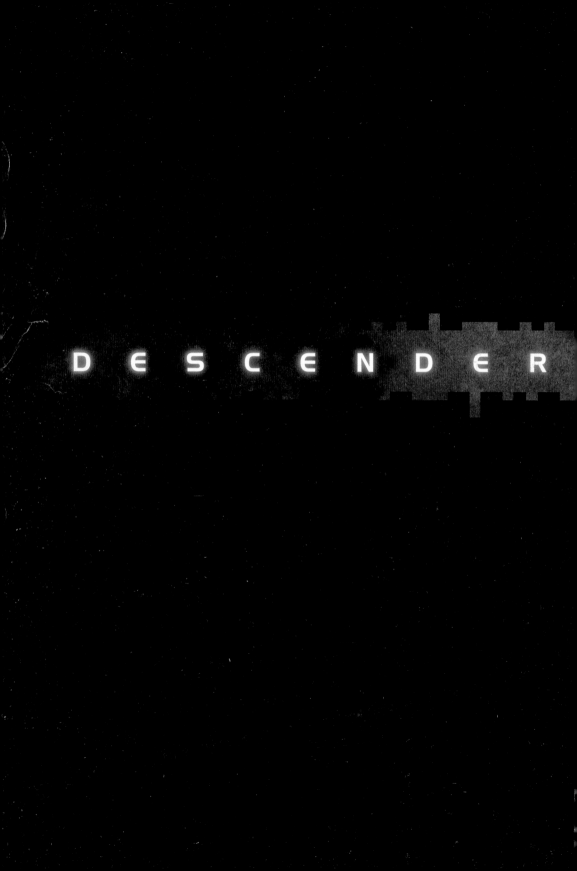